PERSONAL DEMONS

TOR BOOKS BY LISA DESROCHERS

Personal Demons

Lisa Desrochers

PERSONAL DEMONS

TOR®

A TOM DOHERTY ASSOCIATES BOOK

NEW YORK

This is a work of fiction. All of the characters, organizations, and events portrayed in this novel are either products of the author's imagination or are used fictitiously.

PERSONAL DEMONS

Copyright © 2010 by Lisa Desrochers

A Tor® Teen Book
Published by Tom Doherty Associates, LLC
175 Fifth Avenue
New York, NY 10010

www.tor-forge.com

Tor® is a registered trademark of Tom Doherty Associates, LLC.

ISBN 978-0-7653-2808-3

First Edition: September 2010

Printed in the United States of America

0 9 8 7 6 5 4 3 2 1

To Michelle and Nicole,
for inspiring me to be a better person

O human race, born to fly upward, wherefore at a little wind dost thou so fall?

—Dante Alighieri, *Purgatorio*

PERSONAL DEMONS

1

✠

Original Sin

LUC

If there's a Hell on Earth, it's high school. And if there's anyone distinctly qualified to make that statement, it would be me. I draw a deep breath—mostly out of habit since demons don't have to breathe—then look up at the threatening sky, hoping it's a good omen, and pull open the heavy security door. The dingy halls are quiet since the first bell rang almost five minutes ago. It's just me, the metal detector, and a hunched wisp of a security guard in a rumpled blue uniform. He hauls himself out of his cracked plastic chair, looks me over, and scowls.

"You're late. ID," he says in a three-pack-a-day rasp.

I stare him down for a few seconds, sure I could blow him over with a whisper, and I can't suppress a smile when beads of sweat sprout on his pasty forehead. I'm glad to see I've still got the touch even though I'm getting really sick of this job. Five millennia in the same gig will do that to a demon. For this trip, though, the fact that failure will result in dismemberment and the Fiery Pit is all the motivation I need.

"New," I say.

"Put your bag on the table."

I shrug, showing him my hands. No bag.

"Give me your belt. Studs'll set off the detector."

I pull off my belt and toss it at the old man as I walk through the metal detector. He hands it back and hacks, "Go straight to the office."

"No problem," I say, already walking away.

I slide my belt back on and push through the office door. It bangs sharply off the cracked wall and the ancient receptionist looks up, startled. "Can I help you?"

The office is just as drab and poorly lit as the halls except for the brightly colored notices that cover every inch of plaster like psychedelic wallpaper. There's a nameplate declaring the receptionist is Marian Seagrave, and I swear I can hear her joints creak as she pulls herself out of her chair. She's got more wrinkles than a shar-pei and the requisite short, blue, curly hair of all hundred-year-old women. Her round body is clad in the uniform of the ancients: turquoise polyester slacks and a matching floral blouse neatly tucked in.

I meander up to the counter and lean toward her. "Luc Cain. First day," I say, flashing my winning smile—the one that always keeps mortals just a little off balance.

She stares for just a second before finding her voice. "Oh . . . welcome to Haden High, Luc. Let me pull up your schedule."

She bangs on her computer keyboard and the printer buzzes to life. It spits out my schedule—the same schedule I've had for the last hundred years, since the advent of the modern education system. I do my best to feign interest as she hands it to me and says, "Here it is, and your locker number and combination too. You'll need to collect an admit slip from each of your teachers and bring it back here at the end of the day. You've already missed homeroom, so you should go right to your first class. Let's see . . . yes, senior English with Mr. Snyder. Room 616. That's in building six, just out the door to the right."

"Will do," I say, smiling. It won't hurt to stay on administration's good side. You never know when they might be useful.

The bell rings as I make my way out the door into the now bustling halls, and the scents of the sea of teenage humanity hit me in waves. There's the tangy citrus of fear, the bitter garlic of hate, the anise of envy, and ginger—lust. Lots of potential.

I work in Acquisitions, but it isn't usually my job to tag them, just to sow the seeds and start them down the fiery path. I get them going on the little ones. Starter sins, if you will. Not enough to tag their souls for Hell, but enough to send them in our direction eventually. I don't even need to use my power . . . not that I'd feel guilty if I did. Guilt isn't in the demonic repertoire of emotions. It just feels more honest when they come to sin of their own volition. Again, not that I care about being honest. It's just too easy the other way.

In truth, the rules are clear. Unless their souls are tagged, we can't force mortals to do anything out of character or manipulate their actions in any way. For the most part, all I can do with my power is cloud their thoughts, blur the line between right and wrong just a little. Anyone who says the devil made them do it is feeding you a line.

I stroll the hall, taking in the scents of teenage sin, so thick in the air I can taste them. All six of my senses buzz with anticipation. Because this trip is different. I'm here for one soul in particular and, as I make my way toward building 6, a crackle of red-hot energy courses through me—a good sign. I take my time, walking slowly through the throng and scoping out prospects, and am the last to arrive in class, just at the bell.

Room 616 is no brighter than the rest of the school, but at least an attempt has been made at decorating. Prints of Shakespeare's plays—only the tragedies, I notice—grace the walls. The desks are grouped in twos and are nearly full. I walk up the center aisle to Mr. Snyder's desk, holding out my schedule. He turns his slender face toward me, glasses perched just at the tip of his long, straight nose.

"Luc Cain. I need an admit slip . . . or something?" I say.

"Cain . . . Cain . . ." He rakes a hand through his thinning gray hair and scans down his class roster, finding my name. "Here you are." He hands me a yellow admit slip, a composition book, and a copy of *The Grapes of Wrath* and looks at his roster again. "Okay, you'll be seated between Mr. Butler and Miss Cavanaugh." Then he stands, pushing up his glasses and smoothing the unsmoothable creases in his white button-down and khakis. "All right, class," he announces. "We're shifting seats. Everyone from Miss Cavanaugh up will shift one seat to your right. You'll all have a new essay partner for the rest of the semester."

Many of the good little lemmings grumble, but they all do as they're told. I sit in the seat Mr. Snyder motions to, between Mr. Butler—a tall, skinny kid with glasses, bad skin, and obvious self-esteem issues—and Miss Cavanaugh, whose sapphire-blue eyes stare straight into mine. No self-esteem issues there. I feel the play of hot electricity under my skin as I stare back, sizing her up. And her size is definitely petite, with wavy, sandy-blond hair that she's tied in a knot at the base of her neck, fair skin, and fire. A definite prospect. Our desks are grouped together, so it looks like I'll have plenty of opportunity to feel her . . . out.

FRANNIE

Okay, so I'm not generally the swooning type, but Holy Mother of God, I can't believe what just walked into my English class. Tall, dark, and sorta dangerous. Mmm . . . nothing like a little eye candy in the morning to get the day off to a sweet start—and possibly rot my brain. And, *bonus*. Apparently we're gonna be essay partners, 'cause obsessive-compulsive Mr. Snyder is having me move down a seat to make room for him. God forbid we should ever be out of alphabetical order.

My eyes work slowly over his black T-shirt and jeans, not to mention the body underneath—*very nice*—as he saunters over and sits to my left. He folds his tall frame into the attached desk and chair with the grace of a sly black cat, and I swear the temperature in here just shot up ten degrees. The dim classroom lights glint faintly off the three steel bars piercing the outside corner of his right eyebrow as he stares at me through silky black bangs with the blackest eyes I've ever seen.

Mr. Snyder paces the front of the room for a moment, taking silent roll, then says, "Pull out your composition books and *The Grapes of Wrath*. Since Mr. Steinbeck was unable to find a convenient place for a chapter break in the seventy-one pages of chapter twenty-six, you'll recall we arbitrarily imposed one at the end of page 529. Today, we'll be reading the rest of the chapter in class and outlining Steinbeck's major points."

Mystery Boy looks away, finally, and I feel like I've been ransacked—but not in a bad way, if that makes any sense. I feel like he just checked me out from the inside out and maybe kinda liked what he saw.

"Miss Cavanaugh, care to join us?"

Mr. Snyder's voice is like a bucket of cold water to my face—which I probably needed, 'cause things were getting kinda steamy inside. "Um . . . what?"

"Nice write-up in the *Boston Globe* yesterday. I think they captured the essence of your program nicely. I especially liked the picture," he says with a smile. "Will you start the reading off, please? Page 530."

I look around and everyone has their books open, even Mystery Boy. Mine's still in my book bag. So, I'm also not usually the blushing type, but I feel my cheeks burn as I pull it out, flip it open, and start reading. My mouth articulates Steinbeck's description of the preacher Casy's death at the hands of a pick-handle-wielding stranger as his friend, Tom, looks on. But my mind only vaguely registers any of it, 'cause I'm keenly aware of Mystery Boy, sitting only a foot away, staring at me. I stumble on the words when he leans closer and I catch a hint of cinnamon. Mmm . . .

Mr. Snyder comes to my rescue. "Thank you, Miss Cavanaugh." His eyes scan the room.

Pick Mystery Boy.

He smiles at me, then his gaze shifts to Mystery Boy. "Mr. Cain, will you continue please."

Mystery Boy's still looking at me, a wry smile just turning up the corners of his lips. "Certainly," he says, and his voice sounds like warm honey, smooth and sticky-sweet, as he starts reading. But his eyes don't shift from mine to the book right away. "Tom looked down at the preacher. The light crossed the heavy man's legs and the white new pick handle. Tom leaped silently. He wrenched the club free. The first time he knew he had missed and struck a shoulder, but the second time his crushing blow found the head, and as the heavy man sank down, three more blows found his head . . ."

He seems like he's enjoying the gruesome passage. Savoring it, really. Mr. Snyder closes his eyes and looks as though he's meditating. He lets Mystery Boy read through the end of the chapter, which is much longer than anyone else has read all year. I glance around the room and everyone—even tough guy, smart-ass Marshal Johnson—seems hypnotized.

"Would you like me to continue to chapter twenty-seven, Mr. Snyder?" Mystery Boy asks, and Mr. Snyder snaps abruptly out of his trance.

"Oh . . . no. Thank you, Mr. Cain. That will be sufficient. Beautifully done. All right, class, the chapter outline on Mr. Steinbeck's major themes in the second half of chapter twenty-six is to be finished before class tomorrow morning. You have the rest of the period to work."

Mystery Boy turns toward me, closing his book, and I get caught in his eyes for a second. "So, Miss Cavanaugh, do you have a first name?"

"Frannie. You?"

"Luc."

"It's good to meet you. That was a nice little trick."

"What?" His eyes flash as a beautifully wicked grin spreads across his face.

"Reading without looking at the book."

He shifts back in his seat, and his grin falters slightly. "You're mistaken."

"No, actually, I'm not. You didn't even glance at the book till you were on the second sentence, and you were behind turning the pages. Why would you memorize Steinbeck?"

"I haven't." He's such a liar, but before I can call him on it, he changes the subject. "Why a *Globe* article?"

"It's no big deal. Just a thing where we send letters to kids in Pakistan. Kind of like pen pals, I guess. Mostly, it's a way of helping us understand each other . . . you know, our cultures and stuff."

There's a cynical edge to his expression. "Really."

"You want a name?" I shuffle through my bag and come out with a folder. "I have a few more."

"Let me think about it. I'm assuming we're essay partners, whatever that means?"

"Guess so." Despite the freaky reading-without-looking thing, I'm not about to complain. He's definitely a step or twenty up from Aaron Daly, who has taken his bad sinuses across the aisle and is now sniffling all over Jenna Davis's composition book instead of mine. "We're supposed to discuss the reading and come up with a chapter outline with all the major points. Mr. Snyder's big into discussing things," I say, rolling my eyes. That's all for show, though, 'cause I'm seriously into discussing things with Mystery Boy. "So . . . what do you think of Tom's conundrum?"

I write "Frannie and Luke—Chapter 26-2 outline" on the top of an empty page in my composition book.

He raises an eyebrow, slides my pen out from between my fingers, crosses out "Luke," and writes "Luc" above it.

LUC

I watch her write "Frannie and Luke 26-2 outline" in her composition book, and for some reason it really bothers me that she spelled my name wrong. I fix it before answering her. "I think he made some choices that he's now got to pay the consequences for." One of which is eternity burning in the Abyss.

She looks at me, all incredulity. "Just that simple, huh? No extenuating circumstances. No second chances?"

"Nope. Don't believe in second chances." The Underworld's not big on that concept.

She shifts back in her chair and folds her arms across her chest, scrutinizing me. "You've never made a mistake? Done something you were sorry for?"

"Nope."

"Everybody has something they wish they could undo."

I lean toward her and gaze into those sapphire eyes. "What do you wish *you* could undo, Frannie?"

She shudders when I say her name, and I realize I'm being unfair. I pushed a little power at her without really meaning or needing to. But I like the reaction.

When she replies there's more than a hint of pain in her tone, and the faint scent of rose—sadness. I search deep in those eyes to find the root of it. "Lots of things," she says without breaking her gaze.

For some reason, out of the blue, I don't want her to hurt. I feel Hell-bent on making her happy. Just the tiniest push is all it would take . . .

Stop it. Where the Hell did *that* come from? I don't even recognize the sensation that passed with that thought. Demons don't have feelings. Not like *that*, anyway. This isn't a charity mission . . . I'm here for a clear purpose, and Miss Frannie Cavanaugh is showing promise. Lots of promise. As a matter of fact, I'm starting to hope she's The One. And as the bell rings I realize, to my own astonishment, that it's *her* eyes holding *me* locked here instead of the other way around. This is going to be interesting.

She blinks as if startled from a dream and looks down at her empty composition book. "So . . . I guess we didn't get too far."

"I wouldn't say that." I push my book across the desk.

She reads the ten bullet points listed there in block print under the heading "Frannie Cavanaugh and Luc Cain, Steinbeck's Themes—Chapter 26-2" and scowls.

"Oh . . . well, I guess these look okay." Incredulous again. She's fiery for sure. I like a little fire. Makes me feel at home.

"Have you found your locker yet in this rat maze?" she says, throwing her books into her book bag and standing.

"Haven't looked for it." I hold up my only possessions: my composition book and *The Grapes of Wrath*.

"Well, it'll only get worse, so unless you wanna lug all your stuff around with you, I could help you find it."

I pull the slip of paper with the locker number and combo on it out of my back pocket as we walk together to the door. "Number . . . hmm." I smile. The mortal world is so droll sometimes.

"What?"

"666," I say, and she looks at me funny.

"Oh. That's right there." She points across the hall. "Right next to mine."

And even though I know fate is a crock—nothing but an excuse for mortals to make choices they wouldn't otherwise make—this *is* a sign. I look at her more closely. If she's The One, which is starting to look more likely, I need to tag her soul for Hell before some filthy angel beats me to it. Which roughly translates into *now*. Because the fact that she's been so difficult to locate probably means she's being Shielded by them. If they're Shielding her, they're watching her. It won't be long before they know I've found her. I scan the crowded hall. So many prospects, but no angels—so far.

She starts across the hall to her locker and I hang back to admire the view for a few seconds before following her. She *is* petite—maybe five-two. Nearly a foot shorter than my human form. But she's no little girl. There are curves in all the right places.

I laugh at myself. Although lust *is* one of the seven deadly sins, it's not the one that got me where I am and not something I've experienced often in the seven millennia I've existed— though I've used it to my advantage a few thousand times. This *is* going to be fun.

I stride across the hall and catch her just as she reaches her locker. I spin the lock on mine a few times, and it springs open.

"How'd you do that?" she asks, like she could possibly know I used my power.

"What?"

"I had that locker at the beginning of the year and switched 'cause the lock was broken."

"Hmm. They must have fixed it." I'll need to be more careful. This mortal is extraordinarily observant. I slipped up in class by not keeping my eyes on the book—which she'd noticed because her eyes weren't on the book either. And again with the locker, because as I try the real combination, I find she's right: it is indeed broken.

She looks skeptical. "Yeah, I guess, except they never fix anything around here. Welcome to Hades High."

What the Hell? "Excuse me? Hades High?"

"Yeah, get it? Haden High—Hades High. It's just one letter, but it *so* much more accurately describes this hellhole."

"Hmm."

"Well, wouldn't you agree?" She gestures to the cracking plaster, peeling paint, burned-out lightbulbs, gouged gray linoleum, and dented gray metal lockers surrounding us.

"Well, it looks like I've chosen just the place, then." A grin stretches my face. How perfect is it that my target goes to a high school nicknamed Hell? This is too rich.

She looks away and reaches into her locker, but she can't hide the smile playing at the corners of her mouth. "If your 'just the place' is this crappy, washed-up fishing town, then you're more pathetic than I would have guessed."

I laugh—I can't help it—and then shudder when I catch a hint of Frannie's ginger. Mmm . . . pathetic must be her type.

"How come you had to change schools a month before graduation?"

I smile inwardly. "Business."

"Your father's?" she presses.

"In a manner of speaking."

She looks at me and her brow furrows as she tries to figure out what that means. Then she pushes her locker shut with a crash. "So . . . what's your next class?"

I pull my schedule out of my back pocket and shake it open. "Looks like calculus, room 317."

"Oooh, you have Mrs. Felch. Sooo sorry."

"Why? What's the deal with Mrs. Felch?"

Just then the bell rings. She cringes. "First, you get detention if you're not in your seat at the bell—so, sorry—and, second, she bites."

"Mmm. We'll see about that." I kick my locker shut and turn to head to building 3—and don't try to hide the smile that pulls at my lips as her eyes burn a hole through my back the whole way down the hall. A good start.

2

✢

Hell to Pay

FRANNIE

It turns out that I'm a little preoccupied and basically useless in physics lab. Luckily, my lab partner, Carter, is an obsessive science geek who usually wants to do the whole lab himself anyway. So today I put my elbows away and let him have his way with the circuit board. Carter pushes up his glasses and hunches over it like a protective mother while I sit contemplating how it is that Luc shows up out of nowhere and turns me into mush. Which I never am. For any guy.

I follow along with what Carter's doing, 'cause he's not nearly as smart as he thinks he is, and occasionally risk life and limb by sticking my hand in to fix his screwups. But at the end of lab, I look at my write-up and realize I've written "Luc" instead of "ohms" all over it. In pen. This is bad.

Despite my best effort, I catch myself nearly running back to my locker after my double-lab period. But, just as I turn the corner, there's a hand on my shoulder. I spin and find Ryan Keefe, or Reefer to all his friends. He steps up, too close, and stares down at me. Then his lips curl into a lopsided smile and I know what's coming.

"Hey, you," he says, pushing his brown shoulder-length dreads off his face with the heel of his hand.

I slither out from where he's trying to maneuver me against the wall. "Hey, Reef. What's up?"

He props his short, stocky frame against the wall and glances down the hall at his crew, hanging near the cafeteria door. "We want you back," he says with a jut of his chin.

I turn and start walking away, pretending he doesn't still send my pulse racing. "Not gonna happen."

He heads me off with an arm against the wall. "*I* want you back," he says, his voice low.

I hesitate long enough to pull a deep breath before turning back to him. When I do, I try to keep my expression hard, but I feel my heart melt when I look into his big, muddy-brown eyes. "Listen, Ryan. I'm . . . It's not you, really." I cringe at how lame that sounds, but it's true.

He slumps against the wall and looks sick. "Great. The 'it's not you, it's me' speech. Just what every guy wants to hear."

"Sorry, but it is. Me, I mean—not you."

He can't contain his frustration. "Why? Why is it you?"

"I don't know. I guess I'm just not looking for a real relationship."

His smile is dubious. "I'd be okay with that. No strings," he says, like he thinks I'm going to forget he said he loved me.

I smile and shove him, 'cause there's no point in calling him on it. "I'm sure you would."

"Seriously, Frannie. The guys want you back. We can't find anyone nearly as good as you."

"*You* can sing. You don't need me."

"I'm strictly backup caliber. We need a real singer. Female, preferably. You know, for the hotness factor."

I roll my eyes. "Sorry. You should post something. You know, like have an audition. There's gotta be a thousand people right here in this school who can sing better than me."

"We did. Only got Jenna Davis, who sounded like an opera singer, and Cassidy O'Connor, who's hot, but . . ." He cringes.

"I know someone who'd be perfect. She's a friend of my sister's. I'll give her your number."

I start walking again, but his hand against the wall stops my progress. I groan internally and resist the sudden urge to twist him into an arm lock and throw him against the wall.

He leans in, his lips brushing my ear, and I catch the scent of boy musk. He runs his guitar-calloused fingers down my arm, making me shudder. "But I want *you*. I miss you, Frannie."

My heart flutters as I remember how good those lips felt on mine, but I breathe it off. *You don't love me.*

I shrug, duck under his arm, and head down the hall at a jog, only to find my locker surrounded by girls. It's a freakin' who's who of Haden High with Luc right in the middle. There's Stacy Ravenshaw and her cheer-bitches; Cassidy O'Connor, chaste Irish beauty; Valerie Blake, tall, dark, and gorgeous captain of the volleyball team; and Angelique Preston, senior-class goddess—blond, beautiful, and stacked, with the intellectual depth of a mud puddle—front and center.

Suddenly I'm furious. The totally ridiculous and insanely irrational thought—*I saw him first*—shoots through my head. I picture myself pushing and shoving through the fluttering and palpitating crowd to get to him, ripping out handfuls of hair and gouging eyes on the way.

I seriously need to get my shit together. I draw on my judo training to center myself. After a ten-second meditation and a balancing breath, I shoulder my way through the groupies to my locker, where I exchange my books and turn to make my escape . . . just as a hand darts out and burns into my shoulder.

"Hey. What do you have now?" That sticky-sweet, warm honey voice is behind me, so close I can feel its heat.

I turn and smile at Luc as the sharp edge of Angelique's glare nearly cuts me in half.

LUC

She turns and I smell her fury—black pepper—overpowering the ginger lust of the others. Mmm . . . That's a good start. The first step. She smirks at Angelique and says, "History, Mr.—"

"Sanghetti, room 210?" I interrupt.

"You too?"

"Yep." I start to reach out for her arm as she turns up the hall, but I catch myself because I didn't miss the way she flinched back from the heat of my touch when I grabbed her shoulder. I'm literally too hot to handle.

I give Frannie a sidelong glance, and she drops her gaze to the floor.

"So . . . do you have lunch after?" she asks.

"I think so."

"Do you wanna sit with my crew?" She sounds tentative—not her usual confident fire.

"As appealing as that sounds, I have some things I need to take care of. Maybe another day." Truth is, all human food is repulsive, but high school cafeteria food . . . just can't do it.

"Whatever," she says, brushing it off.

I catch a hint of ginger, and everything in me vibrates like a plucked guitar string as a crackle of hot lightning shoots through me. She's The One. I'm sure of it. Her soul is to be tagged, but not collected—which is good, because collection isn't in my job description. She's been tricky, though. The last two demons we sent couldn't find her and are now burning at the bottom of the Fiery Pit. But they were lesser demons—Third Level. So now we've sent in the best, which, of course, would be me. My razor-sharp instincts have gotten me to where I am: First Level, just shy of the council. They've never steered me wrong. And now they've steered me to Haden High, right into the path of one Miss Frannie Cavanaugh.

We walk into history and Frannie sits near the middle of the room. I head up the aisle to Mr. Sanghetti, who is leaning back in his chair, just at the tipping point, with his heels on his desk. I smile as I imagine bumping his chair—just by accident—and sending him over backward.

"Mr. Sanghetti?"

He looks up. "Yes."

I hold out my schedule, and he rolls his eyes, sighs deeply, and makes a huge production of pulling his feet off the desk and dragging his husky, middle-aged frame to a stand. "I suppose you need an admit slip?"

"That's what I've been told."

He rummages in his desk and finally comes out with a crumpled yellow slip of paper, then turns and pulls a textbook from the bookshelf behind his desk.

He looks at my schedule again and writes my book number next to my name on his roster. "Anywhere is fine, Lucifer," he says, handing me the book and gesturing to the room.

"Call me Luc."

"All right then, Luc. Just take any seat," he says with another wave of his hand.

I turn and make my way back to Frannie, taking the desk to her right. As I sit, Mr. Sanghetti starts calling roll.

"Jose Avilla. Jennifer Barton." Hands shoot up in turn. "Zackary Butler. Lucifer Cain."

Her eyes dart to mine and snap wide. I just grin at her.

"Mary Francis Cavanaugh."

I feel my grin widen as Frannie raises her hand. *Mary Francis*. Oh, this is rich.

When Mr. Sanghetti finishes taking roll, he has us turn to page 380 in our text and drones about the fall of Christian Jerusalem during the Crusades.

I just stare at Frannie—excuse me, *Mary Francis*—and chuckle to myself.

And about half the time, Mary Francis is staring right back at me.

Then the lights go down and an image of ancient Jerusalem flashes onto the smartboard.

"What was at the root of the struggle for Jerusalem?" Mr. Sanghetti asks. A few hands go up, and I listen to the answers, remembering how it really happened. Having actually been there makes every history class I've ever taken—all hundred or so—really amusing. It's like that game where someone whispers something in someone's ear to start and it gets passed down the chain until the last person says it out loud and it's nothing like what the first person really said.

FRANNIE

So, I keep looking over at Luc—shoot me, I can't help it—and all through history, he's got this smug little smirk on his face. No idea what that's about, but, now that I think of it, maybe it's good that he blew off lunch. I'm not sure I'm ready to share him with Taylor. She and Riley are always on me about being a charity dater, meaning they think I always choose the needy semi-losers. Riley thinks it's a control thing, and she may be right. I don't do anything I don't want to, and I'm not gonna end up in some relationship where I feel pressured. But there's also the Taylor factor. Since we met in fourth grade our relationship has been a friendly rivalry. Unfortunately for her, I always get the grades. Unfortunately for me, she always gets the guys. All things considered, the needy semi-losers are just a safer choice, mostly 'cause they're not Taylor's type.

But, watching Luc smirk at Mr. Sanghetti, I know two

things for sure: Luc is no needy semi-loser, and Taylor's gonna go after him. So, whatever all of this insanity going on inside of me is, I better get over it.

I'm still staring at him. And, of course, he catches me and locks my gaze with his. When I see that he's not breathing, I realize that I'm not either. I take a deep breath. He seems to notice and breathes deep too. And smiles. And twists my insides into a knot. Ugh!

"Luc, any thoughts?" Mr. Sanghetti is standing right in front of us. How the hell did he get there?

Luc leans back in his chair, lacing his fingers behind his head and straightening his legs out from under his desk, crossing them at the ankles. He stares up at Mr. Sanghetti. "Well, it's really impossible to ferret out a single issue. I suppose it boils down to theology—though the First Crusade didn't even start out as a religious war. I think that Pope Urban was stressing because of the Constantinople crew bailing on him, so he was looking to score some points and bring them back into the fold."

Mr. Sanghetti stands there staring, wide-eyed, for a second, then turns and walks to the front of the room. "Well, I suppose that's one perspective." He turns back to face us. "Not necessarily the *right* perspective . . . but a perspective nonetheless."

Luc leans forward, elbows on his desk, and his eyes flare. Then a calm smile settles over his face. "Well, if you don't want to believe it was just a big power grab, there's also the opinion that a bunch of French nobility were bored stiff and looking for something to do."

And the old "saved by the bell" cliché becomes a reality,

except I'm not sure exactly who was just saved, Luc or Mr. Sanghetti.

I turn to look at Luc. *"Lucifer?"*

"Yes, Mary Francis."

I glower at him. "Your name is *Lucifer*? As in *the devil*?"

And there's that wicked grin again. "In the flesh. It's a common name where I come from."

I pull myself out of my seat. "Where is that?"

His eyes flash, hungry and eager. "Nowhere you've ever been."

I shudder and shake my head. "What some parents do to their kids."

There's an amused gleam in his obsidian eyes as he walks with me to the door. "So let me guess. Mary Francis . . . a good Catholic family with—wait, don't tell me . . . eight kids?"

"Five." I don't like his tone. "Later," I say over my shoulder as I turn toward the cafeteria.

"Later," he says, but I can feel his eyes burn through my back as I walk up the hall.

I'm washed through the door of the cafeteria by the human tide and find Taylor and Riley at our usual table, just inside the door for an easy getaway. The walls, floor, and tabletops in the cafeteria are all puke green so the real puke won't leave stains. Just looking at it always leaves me feeling a little queasy.

Riley's leaning over a book and picking through her salad with a bent fork. Taylor is bouncing in her seat, her spiky yellow-and-pink hair vibrating wildly. Between the bouncing and the lascivious gleam in her eye, I know there's no keeping Luc to myself. She knows.

Despite everything, Taylor has always been exactly what I

needed in a friend. 'Cause, really, we're just alike in all the ways that matter. Neither of us is warm and fuzzy. We both have our boundaries to keep anyone from getting too close. And we've both respected those boundaries from the beginning. I don't know what hers are about, and she's never asked about mine. I've never had to be afraid of Taylor pushing me, trying to get through my defenses. And neither has she.

Riley and all her *feelings*, on the other hand, are dangerous. The first time I ever saw Riley's face, Angelique Preston was grinding a mint chocolate chip ice cream cone into it. It was the summer after seventh grade, and Taylor and I had walked to the ice cream shop, where Angelique had Riley pressed up against the outside of the building. I could tell from the words coming out of Angelique's mouth—something along the lines of "lard ass"—and the wounded and humiliated look in Riley's eyes that this was no harmless prank amongst friends. Without even stopping to think, I yanked Angelique's arm off of Riley and twisted her into a headlock. And, in that instant, all in one fell swoop, I made an accidental friend and a mortal enemy.

Looking at Riley now, she's a mere shadow of her former self. Still curvy, but in a way that turns guy's heads. I would bet money it was in that moment, shoved up against the brick wall of the ice cream shop, dripping mint chocolate chip, that she'd resolved to lose weight.

"Dish!" they both say as I drop my book bag on the floor.

"What?"

Taylor glares at me, which she's very good at. "No holding out, Fee! We know about New Gorgeous Hunk Guy, so dish! Now!"

Great. News travels fast. I go all innocent. "Is he gorgeous? Who said that?"

Taylor's still glaring. "You're such a bitch."

"You say that like it's a bad thing."

"*Spill it!*" Riley screeches, slamming her book down on the table, and everyone in a three-table radius is suddenly staring at us.

"All right. Chill. Let me get lunch," I say looking at the unrecognizable glop on other people's trays as they pass by. "What the hell is that?"

Riley's faces scrunches. "Probably some tofu thing. The district ran out of money again this week."

"Great. Let me get up there before all the salad's gone." I glance to the door, hoping Luc might change his mind, and make my escape as Taylor simmers. I take my time in the line picking all the best pieces out of the wilty scraps of lettuce, spend at least five minutes choosing the biggest brownie, and sip and refill my Coke twice before making my way slowly back to the table. When I get there, I swear there's steam coming out of Taylor's ears.

"Dish, dammit!" she says as I slide into my chair.

"He's just a new guy. Luc." My eyes gravitate to the door, hoping he'll appear there.

"Where'd he come from?"

"No clue."

Taylor's eyes press me. "How'd you meet him?"

"Essay partners, Mr. Snyder."

"Did he ask you out yet?" Riley asks.

I glance at the door again then roll my eyes. "I couldn't even get him to eat lunch with us."

"Hmm . . ." I can see Taylor's gears grinding. "He doesn't really sound like your type."

I just shrug.

Her eyes are eager. "So, maybe you can hook me up with him?"

And there's the knot in the pit of my stomach. "Whatever."

"What about that party Friday? The one at Gallaghers'. You think he'd go if I asked him?"

"You haven't even met him." The acid in my voice startles me. I knew this was coming. Why am I surprised?

Her expression shifts to planning mode. She taps her finger on her chin. "The party's day after tomorrow. If you're not going to ask him, he's mine." She grins at me.

I smile back, as fake and sweet as saccharin. "You know what, Tay? Go to Hell."

LUC

I'm working on those things I need to take care of during lunch, which mostly entail slinking around the parking lots, locker rooms, and loading docks on the prowl for anyone useful. But I've got to say I'm having a harder time focusing than I'd hoped. I'm imagining how a five-two, sandy-blonde would fit just perfectly against my body as I . . .

Okay . . . this is getting ridiculous. *Focus*.

But, for some reason, I find myself meandering past the cafeteria door—not once, or twice, but five times, until I finally give up and go inside. I walk up right behind Frannie, where she's sitting near the door, in time to hear her say, "You know what, Tay? Go to Hell," and I smile, because I think it's cute that she's inviting her friends along.

"Hey," I say. "This seat taken?" My smile pulls into a grin when she nearly jumps out of her skin. Mmm . . . what's that? Grapefruit? Feeling a little afraid, are we? Smart girl. But then I catch a hint of ginger and my grin widens. She wants me. Excellent.

Her friends—a slender blonde with pink highlights, a gleam in her charcoal eyes, and a labret and a shyer-looking brown-haired beauty with intense brown eyes—are both staring at me. I'll work on them later.

"No, I guess." Frannie turns in her seat and her eyes flit to mine. "I thought you had things to do," she says, the disappointment in her voice at odds with the ginger she's giving off.

I scrutinize her as I answer. "Done."

With a flash of her eyes, the blonde stands and presses her hands into the tabletop, enhancing her cleavage as she leans across the table toward me. "Ahemmmm . . . Fee, don't you want to introduce us?" A suggestive half-smile quirks her glossy pink lips, and her eyes never leave mine.

Frannie shifts in her seat, turning away from me so I can't read her face. But I'm sure I catch a hint of anise—licorice—sweet in the air. "Whatever . . . Luc, this is Taylor and Riley."

I nod in their direction. "So why are you sending your friend to Hell? Not that it's a bad thing. Just wondering . . ."

"'Cause that's where she belongs." She glowers across the table at the blonde—Taylor.

"You think?" Riley says with a grin.

"Well, I guess we'll just have to wait and see." I smile encouragingly at Taylor. She might be useful.

Taylor's eyes spark as she says, "So, Luc . . . did you hear about that party at Gallaghers' on Friday?"

And now I understand Frannie's disappointment. Her anise almost knocks me over. Envy. Interesting. I should be able to use that to my advantage.

"Think I heard something about it."

"You going?" Taylor asks.

I give Frannie my best Sensitive Guy Penetrating Gaze. "Depends. Are you?"

She stares for a heartbeat then says, "I guess."

My mouth spreads into a grin. "Then I wouldn't miss it."

I don't miss Taylor's glare or the way Frannie blushes as she turns back toward the table and pulls her hair out of the knot, letting it fall around her shoulders and hide her face. I slip into the chair next to her and pull it up to the table so our shoulders are nearly touching. I'm sure she can feel my heat, but I don't mind getting Frannie all hot and bothered. All in a day's work.

"Will you ladies be needing a ride to this party?"

Frannie looks up, wide-eyed, and shouts, "No!"

Riley and Taylor both laugh, then Riley smiles shyly across the table at me. "What she means is we always go to parties together."

Taylor's eyes are eating me alive. "But we don't always leave together," the blonde says, arching an eyebrow at me and elbowing Riley, who cracks a grin and elbows her back.

"Good to know." I try to catch Frannie's eye, but her face is hidden behind her hair again.

3

✣

Angel Eyes

FRANNIE

The hinges screech as I pull open the door to Riley's rusted hand-me-down Chevy Cutlass and climb in. She just stares at me. "Who are you, and what have you done with Fee?"

"What?"

"You're wearing makeup. What's with that?"

I pick at the stuffing poking out of a tear in the black vinyl seat as she starts down the street. "Dunno. Just felt like it, I guess."

"So, then, nothing to do with Mr. Tall, Dark, and Pierced?"

I ignore the tight knot in my stomach and roll down the window. "You heard Taylor. He's hers. He probably won't show anyway."

"And miss out on all this *hotness*?" she says, touching her finger to my shoulder. "As if! He'll be there." She glances at me again, her expression suddenly serious. "You should go for it, Fee. I can tell you're into him. He could be the one."

The wave of embarrassment takes me by surprise, and words start spilling out of my mouth in a defensive backlash. "Someday you'll stop living in your little fantasy world and get that there's no such thing as 'the one.'"

Instantly, I regret it. I hide my guilt by turning to rest my arm on the window. I prop my chin on my forearm and feel the wind in my face. She drives down the street, adhering to the speed limit and coming to a full stop before turning the corner toward Taylor's.

"I'm sorry, Ry. Don't let my bitchiness get to you. I just don't think I'm meant for all that true love crap . . . I mean . . . sorry . . ." I trail off, lamely.

She sounds like she might cry, so I don't turn to look at her. "You're going to be surprised someday, Fee."

"Whatever," I say as she pulls into Taylor's driveway.

Taylor comes running out and slides into the backseat just as Jackson Harris pulls in behind us. She shoves the back of my head. "Look, Fee. It's your not-so-secret admirer."

I cringe and slide down in the seat. "Great."

Taylor's tone is patronizing. "You should stick with Jackson— a much safer choice."

Taylor's brother, Trevor, bounds down the front stairs and smiles at Riley on his way to Jackson's car. I grin at Riley and flick her thigh as Taylor glares out the window at her brother and mutters, "Jerk."

She's gonna freak when she finds out Riley and Trevor are dating.

"Ready to party?" she yells as Riley follows Jackson out of the driveway.

I slide up and turn to look at her as she undoes the top two buttons on her blouse and pinches her cheeks.

"I guess."

Instantly, her excitement turns to antipathy when she sees my face. "No way!"

"What?"

"You want Luc!"

I try for annoyed. "I think your last remaining brain cell just fizzed out."

"You're so full of shit! Makeup?" She throws her hands up.

Riley smiles into the rearview mirror. "You afraid of the competition, Tay?"

Taylor presses her back into the seat, arms folded tight across her chest and a pout on her lips. "So, what's the deal, Fee? Are you going for it?"

"You need to get over yourself, Tay," I say and turn to stare out the windshield.

We pull up to the party and before we even stop, I'm squinting through the gray dusk, scanning the crowd gathered in Gallaghers' backyard. The Gallaghers have ten kids, one of whom is my sister Kate's boyfriend, Chase. Every high school party since the dawn of time has been in Gallaghers' backyard—probably on account of their dad working nights and their mom being too tired to give a crap what we do.

For a second I'm disappointed, but then sort of relieved, when I realize the face I'm looking for isn't in the crowd.

Truth is, I couldn't answer Taylor's question, 'cause I have no clue what the hell I'm doing. I spent almost an hour getting ready for this party. I even let Kate, our resident style guru, help pick out my outfit and do my makeup. Like it really matters how I look. And I'm nervous as hell, which I never am. Not that I'm overconfident either. I just don't usually give a crap what people think about me.

Taylor grabs my hand. "Come and get a beer with me." She pulls me close as we walk. "He's not here yet," she whispers in my ear.

"Don't care," I say, even though it's a lie.

Her eyes spark. "Good, 'cause I do."

I feel a twinge in my gut, like maybe I swallowed someone's fishhook. *Why does just the thought of him do this to me?* He's dangerous for sure. The kind of guy who could worm his way past a girl's defenses.

We get to the keg, and no-neck football stud Marty Blackstone—who Taylor had her eye on till Luc showed up—makes a big show of flexing his bicep as he pumps the tap.

"Hey, Tay," he says filling a cup, "you guys look parched. Definitely in need of some cool liquid refreshment." He grins and hands her a beer. He hands one to me and Riley too.

Over Riley's shoulder, I see Trevor and his crew piling out of Jackson's car, and all of a sudden I can see what Riley sees in him. He's kinda like my brother, so I never really checked him out like that, but he got cute when I wasn't paying attention. He's got a nice smile and dimples, like Taylor, but other than that, I've always thought of him as short and scrawny. Actually, he's sorta buff, so he must be working out, and he's got this rock-star thing happening with his longish blond hair.

He and Riley keep eyeing each other, and Trevor starts to work his way across the lawn. Jackson follows him, his pale gray eyes glued to me. He sweeps his long brown bangs out of his face for a clearer view, and I look away quickly so he doesn't think I'm checking him out. I'm not. Been there, done that.

At the party last weekend I ended up making out with Jackson in the coat closet. At the time it seemed like a pretty good idea—probably 'cause Reefer was giving me the eye and I was afraid I might cave. But last week at school I found out the problem with hockey jocks. One grope and they think they own you. I still haven't been able to shake him.

"Hey Trevor," Riley says all casual. Her eyes dart to Taylor.

Trevor looks at the ground with a self-conscious smile and a scuff of his toe. "Hey."

"Get lost, Trev," Taylor says, and I watch Riley's face fall.

Trevor recovers fast, though. He loops his arm over Taylor's shoulders. "Yeah, I can see hanging around with me would be kinda embarrassing for you, me being better-looking and all."

I laugh out loud, 'cause it's almost true, then stop abruptly when I feel a hand on my ass. I turn to see all six feet of Jackson standing behind me, grinning.

"Hey, Frannie. How 'bout we pick up where we left off?" he says with an eyebrow wiggle.

The most valuable thing I've learned from judo is control—both physical and emotional—but there's only so much a girl can be expected to take. I press my butt into his hand and smile sweetly just before I grab that hand off my ass, drop into a crouch, and swing him over my shoulder onto the ground in front of me. He hits the dirt hard and lies on his back for a minute, sucking wind. He looks up at me with wide eyes, his mouth fixed in a silent *O*. I bend down with my face over his. "Hey, Jackson. How 'bout we don't?"

Taylor gives me a high five. "Woot! Ninja Chick in action. That was sweet!"

Jackson pulls himself off of the ground, still breathing hard, and Trevor shoves him. "Oh, dude . . . that was pathetic."

Jackson doesn't respond. He just stands there staring at me. I get into fighting stance, thinking this could get ugly, but then he cracks a smile. "Okay, so that's just hot."

Great.

✢

Jackson is hovering. And I'm pretty sure from the way he's looking at me that he's already got me undressed in his pathetic imagination. I've spent the last half hour circling between the group and the bonfire that's just crackling to life, trying to stay out of his reach. I reposition to the outside of the cluster and see Jackson circling the other way to intercept me.

Where is Reefer when I need him?

I kick myself mentally, lean against the porch rail hanging my head in defeat, and wait for the inevitable hand on my ass.

So the voice, smooth as music, scares the snot out of me. "Looks like you could use someone to run interference."

I look up into these incredible sky-blue eyes and, if Heaven had a face, I swear this would be it. His tight white T-shirt shows off his tan and some pretty serious muscle definition. He's leaning on the rail next to me like he's been here all along—like he belongs in this godforsaken place rather than on a beach in San Diego with a surfboard under his arm.

"What?" It's all I can manage.

He smiles and rakes a hand through chin-length platinum waves that seem to change from gold to red and back with the flicker of the flames. "Was I misreading the situation?" he says with a tip of his head toward Jackson.

I roll my eyes. "No, but I can take care of myself, thanks." I push off the rail and head back over to the group.

Angel Boy doesn't follow me. He just leans back and watches as Jackson resumes his stalk. After another lap of the circle I head back to the rail and slouch into it next to Angel Boy. I glare at the ground. "Don't think this means I needed you to rescue me."

He chuckles and I turn my glare on him. "You know what? Just forget it." I push away from the porch rail, but something intense courses through me like a thousand tiny bolts of lightning when his hand touches my shoulder, stopping me dead in my tracks.

"Sorry, I really wasn't laughing at you," he says with a chuckle in his voice. "I was laughing at him." He looks me over and a shiver races down my spine. "He never stood a chance."

"Whatever," I say, leaning back into the rail. Truth is, I came back as much to ogle Angel Boy as I did to get away from Jackson.

"I'm Gabe," he says, turning to face me.

I'm staring at him. Oh, God. *Stop!* I shift my gaze to his chest, which turns out to be no less stareworthy. "Frannie."

He glances at the beer cup in my hand and shrugs away from the rail.

And that's when I hear Taylor's "Oh. My. God." I look over and the whole group is staring at us. Marty has managed to sidle up and slip his arm around Taylor's waist, but she shifts away.

And we're not the only ones to notice Gabe, because I see Angelique and her posse making their way over from the bonfire. She makes a beeline for Gabe as he lifts the lid on the ice chest next to the keg and she leans over it, pretending to inspect the contents of the cooler. What she's *really* doing is pushing her double Ds right up in Gabe's face. I look for Adam Martin—senior-class stud and Angelique's boyfriend—but he's nowhere in sight.

"Something else to drink? Water, soda?" Gabe says, staring at me.

And, mmm . . . those eyes. I feel my heart flutter for an instant, fighting to hold on to its normal rhythm. "I have a beer, thanks," I say, but as I speak, I feel the cup being lifted from my hand.

"And I'll just top it off for you." Luc's hot breath on the back of my neck sends a shiver through me, and my fluttering heart stops. I turn and his face is just an inch from mine. The silk wisps of his tousled mop brush my forehead and I breathe him in: cinnamon . . . mmm.

Taylor's all but losing it. "Holy shit! Where'd you come from?"

Luc straightens up and refills my cup. "I've been around," he says, gesturing to the crowd at the bonfire. But I was just there—and he wasn't.

"Wow . . . okay. This party just got a whole hell of a lot cooler." She looks from Luc to Gabe and back, then eases out of Marty's grasp and meanders over to stand next to Luc. She looks at me with raised eyebrows. "So . . . are we sticking around?"

45

"Uh . . . well . . ." I look to Riley for backup. "I think we're leaving?"

Riley is still staring at Gabe. "Not yet."

Luc hands me my beer and glowers at Gabe, who's moved closer. "Gabriel," he says, his warm-honey voice suddenly cold enough to freeze Hell.

"Hello, Lucifer." And, though his smile doesn't falter, Gabe's musical voice just went flat.

"Wait . . . you *know* each other?" I stand between them, a little wobbly. The air around us seems charged with static electricity, making me tingle all over.

Gabe quirks a crooked smile and eyes Luc. "You could say that."

"Unfortunately," Luc adds. He's sort of smiling, but under that calm demeanor he's anything but calm. Even from a foot away, I can feel the tension in his body, coiled and ready to spring. His jaw clenches and his fists are balled at his side, dying to swing out at something—or someone. As I watch, I swear I see a tiny lick of red lightning flicker over the surface of his hand and disappear between his knuckles.

I just stand here, speechless, my whole body buzzing with the growing electric charge in the air, and try to figure out when I slipped into the Twilight Zone. 'Cause, as my gaze shifts between Luc and Gabe, I know for sure this can't be real. And I start to wonder if maybe Jackson spiked my beer or something.

Angelique, realizing the attention isn't on her, shoots me a glare before peeling off her jeans jacket to reveal a very low-cut tank top. She wedges in front of me, between Luc and Gabe, and I'm actually relieved to be released from whatever that bizarre electric pull was. But immediately, Taylor shoulders her out of the way.

"Where's Adam?" she asks Angelique in a slimy-sweet voice with a matching fake smile.

Angelique grinds her heel into Taylor's foot. "Adam who?"

I start to feel a little dizzy and realize I'm not breathing. I back away from the group, close my eyes, and take a deep breath, trying to collect myself.

"So . . ." Luc's voice, low in my ear, makes me jump. I open my eyes and feel my legs go soft. He quirks half a smile and twists a strand of hair out of my face, looping it behind my ear. "I was hoping you'd let me drive you home."

It's clear from my racing heart that leaving with Luc would be a mistake. I glance at Gabe, who's still staring at me. A hot flush works its way up my neck into my face as I realize staying might be a bigger mistake.

I step up next to Riley. "Are you ready? Let's go." I sound completely desperate, which I guess I am.

She glances over at Trevor and smiles. "Sorry, Fee," she says turning back to me with a shrug.

I feel Luc's heat, too close behind me, but I don't turn to look at him. "I'm ready," he says.

Oh, God. Why can't I breathe?

My eyes slide back to Gabe, which turns out to be a mistake 'cause he's still staring at me, and those blue eyes are doing nothing to help the breathing situation.

I pull my eyes away and spin with my back to both him and Luc—and see Reefer and the band piling out of his black pickup.

Crap.

I turn back to Luc, careful to avoid his eyes. Oxygen deprivation makes thinking a challenge, but I'm able to stammer out, "Um . . . okay. We can go, I guess . . . if you want."

Riley is standing back from the catfight. I raise my voice slightly to be heard over the foray. "Riley." She looks my way. "I'm going with Luc . . .'kay?"

The firelight flickers in her eyes as she smiles knowingly and nods.

I glance once more at Gabe, who holds my eyes with his and shoots me a glowing smile, and then I feel the tips of Luc's fingers scorch through the shirt in the small of my back. I catch his cinnamon as he leans in from behind and whispers, "Let's go."

At his touch, a tingle starts low in my belly and works its way through me, growing in intensity till my whole body is humming—some parts more than others. I let him steer me and my Jell-O legs to his car.

LUC

So, He sent Gabriel. Not an angel—a Dominion. A protector from the Second Sphere. And not just any Dominion, but the left hand of *the* Gabriel. That can only mean one thing: Frannie's soul is worth fighting for.

As we pull away from the party, Frannie checks out the car. "Cool, a Shelby Cobra GT. And in great condition. This is a classic. A '67?"

I can't help smiling. "A '68. You know your Mustangs."

She turns to me and smiles, and I'm suddenly struck with how unbelievably alive she is. Not that all mortals aren't alive by definition, but there are degrees of aliveness. Some people are mostly dead, even when they think they're alive. Frannie's not one of them.

"That was impressive, by the way."

She shoots me a sidelong glance. "What?"

"The flipping the big guy over your head thing."

Her eyes widen. "You saw that?"

"I did. He has to weigh double what you do. Impressive."

She turns away and looks out the window. "Yeah, whatever." But I can tell she's smiling.

"So . . ."

"So, what?"

"Where'd you learn to do that?"

"Judo. Eight years."

"Interesting." I like this girl more every minute. "So . . . where to?"

She turns back to face me with a hint of a smile. "I thought you said you were driving me home." She's starting to relax—moving her shoulders to the beat of the music from the stereo.

"Hmm, did I? Well . . . if that's what you want . . ."

Her eyebrows arch and a shrewd little smile just turns up the corners of her lips. "Did you have something else in mind?"

"We could work on our English outline," I say and almost can't contain the chuckle.

"Really? That's your idea of a hot date?"

"I'm sorry, I wasn't aware we were on a 'hot date.'" And this time I *can't* contain the chuckle when she cringes. "So, how hot would you like it? I'm capable of all levels of hotness, from *Luc*-warm to—and I'm being literal here—hotter than Hell."

I watch her cheeks flush and the car floods with ginger. This is excellent progress.

"Um, well . . . I was thinking more about . . . maybe we could work on that outline . . ." Her voice trails off, and she's as red as the embers of Hell.

"The outline . . . excellent suggestion. Why didn't I think of that?" I turn my most charming smile on her. "Your house or mine?"

Her brow furrows as she contemplates her choices. "Maybe I should just go home," she finally says.

"As you wish."

We ride in silence, but as I take the corner into her neighborhood she blurts, "Do you do coffee hot? There's a Starbucks just around the corner."

The tires squeal as I take the right turn too fast, and I work to hide my grin as she grips her seat to keep from falling on top of me.

✠

"So how do you know that Gabe guy?" she asks over the top of her steaming coffee cup.

"It's a very long story." Seven thousand years long.

"Are you, like, friends or something?"

"Not really. We play for rival teams."

"Like, football?" She looks puzzled, not pegging me for a foot-ball player, I suppose.

I lean forward and gaze into her eyes, brushing my fingers across the back of her hand on the table. I watch as she shudders, and an electric tingle courses through me—excitement? anticipation?—at the rush of her pulse under my fingers. I push with my mind just the tiniest bit. "You know, I'd much rather talk about you. Tell me something I don't know about Mary Francis Cavanaugh."

She swoons a little and stares back for a long moment before saying, "I hate my name," through a haze.

"Then why don't you go by Mary?"

"'Cause that's my sister's name." The fog starts to lift, and she leans onto her elbows on the table, accentuating certain curves and seriously distracting me.

I force myself to breathe deep and look back into her eyes. "Your sister is Mary too?"

"All of them are, but only my oldest sister goes by it."

"How many sisters do you have?"

"Four."

"And all five of you are Mary? That sounds like it'd be confusing."

"That's why we don't all go by it."

"What are the rest of your sisters' names?"

"Well, there's Mary Theresa—she's Mary. And Mary Katherine—Kate. Then me—Mary Francis. Mary Grace—she's just Grace. And Mary Margaret—Maggie."

I bite back the chuckle. This is *sooo* rich. "A good Catholic family," I say, trying to sound sincere.

"I suppose you could say that." Hmm . . . vinegar. Guilt? I'll have to explore that later.

As she sips the last of her coffee, she tips her head back, arching her long, fair neck and pulling her shirt tight across her chest. The wave of desire I feel is almost incapacitating. I close my eyes against it and try to clear my head. *Focus.* When I open them, she's staring at me.

"I probably should be getting home . . ." she says, sounding a little disappointed.

"As you wish," I say, wanting to take her anywhere but home.

FRANNIE

We pull up to my house and Luc kills the engine. The family room light cuts a yellow swath across the front lawn. Dad's waiting up, as usual.

Saving Abel's "Addicted" is blasting out of Luc's stereo, telling me about things happening between the sheets, sending my heart pounding right out of my body and my imagination reeling. I'm no angel; I've been with guys before. Well, not with them like *that*, but almost. Third Base Plus, I call it. But it's always been me keeping score, and none of them have ever wreaked havoc on my imagination the way Luc does. It's like, without ever touching me, he's climbed right into my head and is looking around in there for my dirtiest thoughts and fantasies. And when he finds them, he brings them to life. I'm talking full-color, 3-D sensivision. But what I hate is, I kinda like it. No boy has ever made me feel so totally out of control. It scares the hell out of me—in a giddy-tingly-wild and not-altogether-bad way.

I turn back to find him staring at me, and all of a sudden there's no oxygen in the car. I draw a ragged breath. "So, thanks for the coffee," I say, wanting to bolt out of the car but also wanting to stay all night.

"Was it hot enough for you—coffee hot? Because next time we could try something a little hotter, if you want." Mmm . . . that wicked grin. . . . But I can tell he's trying not to laugh. Is he making fun of me?

"That was . . ." and I don't know how to finish, 'cause what's going on inside is a whole hell of a lot hotter than coffee. It's everything I can do to resist the urge to reach out and touch him. "So, I'll see you Monday." I reach for the door handle with a trembling hand, and suddenly his hand is there, on top of mine.

He leans into me and, with his other hand, he sweeps my hair back from my ear. I feel his lips brush my skin as he whispers, "I'll be waiting."

His hot breath in my ear sends a shiver through me, and I'm mortified when I realize the soft moan I just heard was mine. Embarrassed, I pull at the door handle, but his hot hand is still there, keeping me from opening it.

"What, no goodnight kiss?" he says, and when I turn to look at him, my nose brushes his.

I refuse to give in to the panic bubbling up from my gut—or the part of me that still wants to kiss him. I look him in the eye and work to keep my voice even as I plant my hand on his chest and shove. "Not on the first date."

His expression turns momentarily amused but then softens. "As you wish," he says. His finger scorches a track along the line of my jaw, then he leans back into his seat and smiles. "Pleasant dreams."

I stare at him for a moment more then push open the door and stagger out of the car. He starts the engine as I swing the door shut, but he doesn't pull out. I can feel the weight of his gaze as I stumble up the front walk to the door. And before I close it behind me, I glance back and see the red glow of his eyes in the dashboard lights.

I head quickly up the stairs, and when I get to my room, I hurry to the window and watch Luc's taillights disappear down the street. I stare out the window for a long time at the spot where he dropped me off, feeling my heart pound and that tingle in my belly as I imagine letting him kiss me. I groan quietly to myself, and I walk to the dresser where I pick up my brother's picture. "I'm losing it, Matt," I whisper to him.

Bringing the picture with me, I pull Matt's journal out from under my mattress and open it on my desk. I ease into my chair and read the first lines of my last entry, from Wednesday—the day I met Luc.

So, Matt, you'd have laughed your ass off at me today—drooling over some guy. But there's something about him. I know. Stupid. And not like me. Please strike me with lightning if I turn into some pathetic, weak teenage girl. I so don't believe in all that "love at first sight" crap. I don't believe in love at all, really. But lust . . . is alive and well.

I pull a deep breath, pick up my pen, and flip to the next page.

I struggle with what else to write, 'cause my tangle of emotions is a little confusing and nearly impossible to articulate. But if there's anyone I can tell about how I feel, it's Matt. He was more than just my brother; he was my best friend—the only one who ever really *got* me. I know Matt will keep my secrets. So I tell him everything, no matter how embarrassing. I owe it to him. A little part of mine is the closest thing to a life I can give him.

I start again.

So, Matt. Remember that guy I told you about . . . Luc. I pause, still struggling to frame my thoughts into something coherent that I can put on paper. *I don't know what's wrong with me. Except him. He's wrong. Everything about him is wrong. I can't think or even breathe very well when he's around. But I want him around. I know—I'm losing it. But there's something about him. This weird, dark, magnetic energy, and even though he scares me a little—okay, a lot—it's like I can't stay away.*

I really meant what I said before about the love thing. When Reefer said it he ruined everything. Because love doesn't exist—not really. Grandpa and Grandma are the only ones I've ever seen who were even close. It's dangerous to believe in something that can only hurt you. So I don't.

But Luc . . .

I shudder, looking over the shaky handwriting. I write one more line and close the book.

Just shoot me now.

I haul myself up and get ready for bed. But when I climb in and close my eyes I see platinum curls and shining blue eyes. Suddenly I wish I'd found out more about Gabe. Maybe Riley and Taylor know something. I grab my phone and text Riley. "Did Tay hook up w/Gabe?"

Her reply takes less than a minute. "He left right after u. What happened w/Luc?"

55

"Nothing. Did u find out where Gabe goes 2 skool?"

"No. Why? U want him 2?" I can almost hear her laughing.

"Shut up. Just curious."

I slam down the phone, frustrated, and climb into bed, glad it's the weekend. A few days away from guys will be good, 'cause they're really messing with my mind.

✝

But when Sunday comes, they're still rattling around in there, despite all the judo and meditation to clear my head.

"Hand me the torque wrench, Frannie."

I rifle through Grandpa's tool chest and come out with it. Then I lie on the cement floor of his garage and slide in next to him under his restored '65 Mustang convertible.

The smell of oil and exhaust means Sunday afternoon to me. From the time I could hold a screwdriver without putting my eye out, I've been under a car with my grandpa every Sunday after church. My sisters think I'm weird, but I can't imagine anything better than the feeling of accomplishment when you take something apart and then put it back together with no pieces left over—and it works. Some of my warmest memories are of being on the cold cement floor in this garage.

"It's coming along," I say, looking up at where he's tightening the last clamp on the engine we spent all winter rebuilding.

"Not more than a week or two out. Can ya grab that wrench and hold this bolt while I tighten the clamp?" he says, and his deep sandpaper tone resonates to my bones.

"Sure. You'll let me drive it?"

"You'll be first—after me, course. Reward for all your hard work." He turns and grins. His smiling blue eyes are warm and soft even in the harsh glow of the shop light hanging from the belly of the Mustang.

"Excellent!" I picture myself cruising down the street, top down, music blaring.

He runs his grease-covered hand over his balding head, leaving a large black smudge in the middle of the short gray fringe. "We're almost ready for oil. There's a case in the corner. Can ya pull four quarts?"

"Sure," I say, sliding out from under the car.

"There's a funnel over there too. I'll tell ya when I'm ready."

I grab the oil, bring it back, and twist the oil cap off the engine block. "Grandpa?"

"Yep."

"How did you meet Grandma?"

He laughs—a rich sound that fills the garage and my heart. "At a street race when we were in high school. She was a good girl. Barely been kissed." He chuckles. "But I came along and fixed that."

"When did you know you loved her?"

"The second I saw her."

"How did you know she loved you?"

I can hear the smile in his voice. "She told me . . . and then she showed me, if ya catch my drift."

I try to picture them young, like in some of the pictures I've seen: Grandpa, all strutting around in his jeans with a pack of cigarettes rolled into the sleeve of his T-shirt, and Grandma, the good girl with the mischievous gleam in her eye. And then

I picture my grandma—how I loved to curl up with her on the couch while she read me the classics—and my heart aches. "Do you miss her?"

"Every day."

"Do you believe in Heaven?"

"Yep."

"Do you think Grandma's there?"

"If anyone is, it would be her. I don't think God would hold lovin' me against her."

"Do you think Matt is there too?" I ask past the tight lump in the back of my throat.

"For sure. Sittin' on his grandma's knee."

Even though I know it's all a lie, it still feels good to hear him say it. Like a comfortable old fairy tale. "Thanks, Grandpa."

"I'm ready for that oil. Slow and easy."

"You got it."

4

✠

Heaven Knows

LUC

Monday morning and the hall is crowded with hot, sticky bodies. Mmm . . . just like home. And then I feel it. That itch in my sixth sense. Gabriel.

I swing my locker shut, turn, and there he is, leaning against the wall next to room 616, talking to Frannie. And she's smiling up at him and laughing—and flirting—and blushing.

That bastard's cheating!

Suddenly, I'm flooded with some unrecognizable emotion mixed with rage, and all I want is Gabriel's bloody head in my hands. Except angels don't bleed even when you rip their heads off.

In three long strides I'm across the hall. I realize I'm grimacing and tone it down to my best smirk. "Gabriel."

Frannie looks a little out of it when she turns to me. "Oh . . . Hey Luc."

Gabriel smiles. "Lucifer."

"So nice to see you. What brings you to the humble halls of Hades High?"

"Same as you, dude. A quality education," he smirks.

Frannie's eyes clear a little and shift warily between us. "Play nice." She turns back to Gabriel and touches his arm. "If you need any help writing up that physics lab . . ."

My rage bubbles dangerously close to the surface. I feel my power surge. "You're in *physics* together?" I say, glaring laser beams at Gabriel.

Frannie's beaming at him in a whole different way. "Gabe is my new lab partner."

"Really . . ." I growl through gritted teeth.

He shrugs away from the wall and shifts closer to Frannie. "Just lucky, I guess."

Luck's got nothing to do with it. More like divine intervention.

My appraising eyes shift to Frannie. No real damage done. None that I can't fix anyway. "So, history?" I say.

"Oh, yeah. Let me grab my book." As she moves across the hall, her brow creases. She shakes her head once, pushing off the fog. I turn back to Gabriel as she twists her lock.

"So why did they send you anyway? Seems like overkill. Any run-of-the-mill angel could fail as spectacularly as you're going to."

"We'll see," he says. I don't like the confident smirk on his face. He knows something I don't.

I put on my poker face as I fish for information. "You and I both know you would have tagged her already if you could. What's the hold up? A little too much devil in her?"

He's still smug, but the frustration in his undertone gives him away. I hit a nerve. "You're still the same stupid chump you've always been. All that pride and arrogance that got you here in the first place. I'd think after all these millennia . . . you have no clue why you're here, do you? What the deal is with her?" he asks.

Now *he* hit a nerve. I struggle to keep my composure. He doesn't need to know he's right. "All that matters is Frannie's soul *will* be tagged for Hell—soon."

"Yeah, good luck with that," he jabs. And if I could kill him, I would, but I've tried before and it didn't work out so hot. Turns out the cherub is tougher than he looks.

Then Frannie's back. She brushes against my elbow and a tingle courses through me. "Ready?" she says.

"Yep. Let's go." I place my fingertips in the small of her back and guide her down the hall. He may need to cheat, but I don't. No power, just charm.

FRANNIE

I breathe deep and try to get my head straight. Gabe is kinda dazzling, I guess. I crane my neck and, through the mass of humanity, catch a glimpse of him leaning against the lockers watching me. *God, how anyone can look that good. . . .* I breathe against the flutter in my chest and turn back to Luc, who looks pretty damn good too.

"So, how was calculus?" I ask, ignoring the free-flowing pheromones from all the girls staring at Luc as we weave through the crowded halls. I have to work hard not to turn and gawk at Gabe again. Instead I concentrate on Luc's fingers, burning into my back and making me hot in places I probably shouldn't be.

He quirks an eyebrow. "I think I'm Felch's pet. She likes me."

"Really . . . ? I knew there was something terribly wrong with you." I try to scowl, but the smile I feel creeping across my face ruins the effect. The next thing I feel is Taylor nearly knocking me over as she blows into me from behind.

"Did you see? Gabe's here! Holy God!" she screeches.

I glance at Luc in time to see his eyes flash hot through his genuine scowl.

"Yeah. He's my lab partner in physics." I'm surprised by the possessive edge to my voice. Unfortunately, it doesn't get by either of them. Luc's jaw clenches as Taylor glares.

"He's your *lab partner*?" She shoots a glance at Luc and her voice sours. "The universe is so totally unfair."

I just shrug.

"I'll talk to you at lunch," she says, turning and bounding down the hall.

"Okay . . . so . . . wow," I say.

A spiteful smile flits across Luc's face. "I think you should hook them up."

"Whatever." I step through the door into history, where Mr. Sanghetti looks up and glares his usual dagger at Luc.

Luc looks at me with a wry smile as we take our seats. He

pulls a crumpled wad of paper from his back pocket and tosses it on his desk.

I look at him in disbelief. "That's your report?"

He shoots me a roguish smile and leans back in his chair, lacing his hands behind his head. "Yep."

Feeling all superior, I stick my hand into my book bag to retrieve my report in its shiny plastic cover. But the blood drains from my face when I realize it's not there. In my Luc-and-Gabe-induced haze this morning, I left it sitting on the desk in my room. *Shit!* Mr. Sanghetti never accepts late assignments.

Please give us another day . . . please, please, please . . .

"I know reports are due today," Mr. Sanghetti starts, looking right at me, "but I have a commitment after school and don't want to lug them with me. Hold on to them until tomorrow," he says, and I almost fall out of my chair.

I spend the rest of history trying not to laugh as Luc and Mr. Sanghetti go at it.

"You'll want to study through chapter eighteen for your test Wednesday," Mr. Sanghetti says as the bell rings, glaring right at Luc with a satisfied smirk.

I lean in. "I think Mr. Sanghetti is looking for payback. Good luck on that test," I whisper.

"There's nothing he could ask that I can't answer. Ready for lunch?" He stands and shoots his wad of paper, basketball style, onto the middle of Mr. Sanghetti's desk.

"He's gonna give you a zero, you know."

Luc lifts an eyebrow. "For handing it in early? I'd like to see him try."

"Yeah, well . . . How do you know so much about history anyway?"

"History Channel," he says dismissively.

"You must watch it a lot, 'cause the way you talk, it sounds like you were really there."

There's that grin again. "Does it? Maybe in a past life."

And I start to wonder. 'Cause there's something about Luc . . .

LUC

Frannie and I walk into the cafeteria, and my stomach turns as usual, but this time it's got nothing to do with the food. Gabriel is in *my* seat across from Taylor and Riley. I close my eyes, hoping when I open them he'll be gone—a figment of my imagination. But alas, he's still there, all glowing and larger than life. I think about pushing my power at him—maybe knock the chair out from under him and put him on his ass—but no little nudge is going to touch Gabriel. I feel the electricity crackle over my balled fist, which is starting to glow red, and call back my magic before anyone notices.

Frannie's eyes light up, then she looks at me, shrugs, and strides over to our table, dropping her book bag on the floor and sliding into the seat next to Gabriel. She pulls her chair up next to him—too close.

He shoots me a triumphant glance and moves to put his hand on her back. I'm there in a flash, knocking his hand away. I sit in the chair on her other side, closer than I normally would. I'll have to risk my heat being too much for her. Otherwise, the cheater Gabriel will have her tagged by the end of lunch.

Taylor and Riley are beside themselves. At least they're a bit of a distraction. That will be helpful.

"I'm gonna get lunch. Anyone else hungry?" Frannie says, and I see her foot swing out and kick Taylor in the knee.

"Oh . . . yeah, okay," Taylor says and grabs Riley's arm. The three of them meander toward the lunch line, Taylor looking back over her shoulder the entire way.

I glower at Gabriel. "You need to turn this off. You're going to do some serious damage."

"This is war, Lucifer. All's fair."

"So, your side is resorting to breaking the rules, then? Because it seems so out of character."

"You're going to preach morals to me?" He laughs, one loud sardonic bark. "Oh, this *is* special. Besides, I'm not breaking any rules."

"Maybe not technically . . . I just don't want Frannie to get hurt." Yeah . . . right. That's why I'm trying to drag her into the Abyss for an eternity of pain and torture.

He obviously realizes how absurd that sounds too, because he just stares at me for a long minute before responding. "You know—I believe you. Wow . . ." He continues to stare at me, and I just glare back.

Frannie drops her lunch tray onto the table with the clang of rattling silverware and slides into her seat between me and Gabriel, breaking up our stare down.

"So, are you guys getting caught up?" she says pleasantly, as if it wasn't obvious that Gabriel and I would rip each other's throats out in a second if the opportunity presented itself. "How long did you say it's been since you've seen each other?"

Four centuries. "A while," I say, glaring at Gabriel again.

Riley and Taylor join us with a flourish of tray crashing, eyelash batting, lip licking, and hair flipping.

"So, Gabe," Riley says, shoving Taylor with her shoulder for a better position across from him, "where are you from?"

Gabriel looks at her and smiles. "Heaven," he answers. It's obscene how he glows when he really turns it on. Anybody looking closely enough would see that glow was more than just his sparkling personality.

Taylor elbows Riley and mumbles, "No shit," before beaming at Gabriel and asking, "Heaven, where? Is that in, like, Montana or something?"

Gabriel nods, still smiling. "Something like that."

Taylor and Riley look a little dazed—obviously distraction is the plan since angels can't lie.

"So you went from Heaven straight to Hell," Taylor laughs.

Gabriel's gaze shoots to me. "Hell?" he says, his eyes narrowing.

Taylor leans across the table. "Yeah, *Hades* High . . . get it?"

He shifts in his seat and drapes an arm over the back of Frannie's chair, looking at me with a sardonic half-smile on his face. "So much for home-field advantage."

Frannie shifts closer to him, and I feel my power surge. I breathe it back and lean toward her. "Do you want to get together Sunday? We can work on the next English outline," I say using my most persuasive voice softly in her ear.

"Sorry, I have church and then I go to my grandfather's on Sunday. How about Saturday?"

I should have known, but it still stings. Gabriel is talking to Riley and Taylor, but I see his smile widen, adding to the sting. Cocky bastard.

I pour on the charm—no power, yet. "You can't miss one Sunday?"

She smiles apologetically. "You've never met my parents, but I'm sure you've seen them on TV: the Pope and the Head Nun?"

"That bad, huh?"

"Actually, no. They're really not that bad."

Gabriel's grin widens.

FRANNIE

How to explain my family? It's not that I'm embarrassed by them or anything. I know a lot of seventeen-year-olds who do nothing but bitch about their families. For the most part, mine's okay. Just really religious. But I *am* sort of the black sheep.

"Let's just say I don't always live up to their lofty moral standards."

A grin stretches across Luc's face, and he shoots a glance over my shoulder at Gabe. "I like the sound of that."

Now my face is burning. "It's really not all that interesting. My sisters just do a better job of toeing the line than I do."

His eyebrow shoots up. "Mary, Mary, Mary, and Mary?"

He's such a jerk. "Yeah."

"Are they older or younger?"

"Two older and two younger."

"I haven't seen anyone that looks like you roaming the halls ..."

"My sisters don't go here."

"Really ...?"

So, this is where it gets a little embarrassing. Taylor's grinning at me across the table, and I feel her kick me under it. Bitch.

I stab a cherry tomato with my fork, sending a spurt of tomato juice and seeds into a slimy puddle on the puke-colored table. "I sorta got thrown out of Catholic school."

He laughs right out loud. "Oh ... I *definitely* like the sound of that." His grin is sort of making my heart sputter a little, and his eyes flit to Gabe.

"It's not as bad as it sounds, really," I say defensively. "Just a few little things, but they have this 'zero tolerance' thing over there ..."

Taylor can't contain herself. "She's a conscientious objector."

Luc looks at me. "To the war?"

"To the Catholic religion. She asked too many questions in religion class," Taylor says.

He quirks a brow. "Such as ...?"

I glower at Taylor. "Nothing."

"I would sincerely doubt they throw students out for school for asking 'nothing.'"

"I just had some questions about God."

He leans toward me intently, his elbow resting on his knee, and his eyes smolder. "Do you buy it? The whole God thing?"

I picture Matt in his coffin. Not how he really looked, I'm

sure, 'cause I never saw him. I was too sick to go to the wake or the funeral. The image that haunts me is the one I saw in my head right before he fell. I push back that image, along with the unfathomable grief that's trying to worm its way out of the deep pit I keep it locked in, and try to picture that seven-year-old face now, at seventeen.

"I'm still working some things out." The words squeeze through my tight throat, sounding a little strangled. Really, the only thing I'm working out is how to say the truth out loud. There is no God. There can't be. 'Cause if there was I'd have to hate Him. It's just easier not to believe.

"You believe," Gabe interjects, as if he read my mind.

I glare at him. "You have no idea what I believe."

He picks up my hand and traces his fingertip over my life-line, and a shiver races up my spine. "I've got an idea or two," he says, his blue eyes gazing into mine. And suddenly I'm sure he's seeing right through me—seeing everything. I draw a jagged breath and look away, at Luc.

Concern briefly darkens his face but clears just as quickly. Then he asks, "How about the other side?" with a flash of his eyes and anticipation all over his face. "Do you believe in the devil? Hell?"

I look him dead in the eye. "Yes."

Gabe drops my hand. "Well, that's hardly fair." I hear the smile in his voice, but I don't turn to look, because I'm not going to risk getting caught in those eyes again.

Luc's black eyes flare red heat, and his grin widens as he relaxes back in his chair, draping his arm across the back of mine. "Excellent. So we're on for Saturday? My place?"

Mmm . . . that smile is killing me. But better safe than sorry. "How about my house?"

"With the Pope, the Head Nun, Mary, Mary, Mary, and Mary? Sounds like fun," he says.

I roll my eyes. "Yeah, loads of fun."

5

⚜

Hell-bent

LUC

I sit on the floor in my dark apartment, banging the back of my head against the wall and staring out at the bats flying past my window in the twilight. Pink Floyd's *Wish You Were Here* shakes my bones.

I've never obsessed over a mark before, but all week I've watched her at school with Gabriel and I've felt things I don't even have a name for. All I know is I want him dead. He's got me all jittery, doubting myself, and I'm having to exercise some pretty serious restraint not to climb into my Mustang and charge over to Frannie's house right now.

What would I do when I got there? I know what I'd *want* to do—what I've been thinking about nonstop since the first day we met.

What if Gabriel's there? I flash on him doing to Frannie

what I want to do to Frannie and feel a stab of . . . jealousy? *Really?*

But I know he would never do that, since it would only work to my advantage. He's not here for Frannie's body. He's here for her soul—same as me. What's to stop him from just tagging her soul right now? I could go over . . . just to make sure he's not there . . .

I bang my head into the wall.

And if he *is* there? What then?

I picture myself swooping in like Batman, plucking her half-naked body out of Gabriel's arms just in the nick of time.

So, that's what I want to do? Save her from the nasty angel?

In the silence between songs, I'm startled by the sound of my own sardonic laugh. What is it about that girl? She *is* just a girl. Nothing special. Just a target. *And the object of my fantasies.*

I bang my head harder.

I close my eyes and push her face from my thoughts. I replace it with my boss, Beherit, Grand Duke of Hell and head of Acquisitions. I focus on the thought of what he'll do to me if I fail, hoping fear will take the edge off my obsessive desire.

And it almost works. I feel cold, black dread snake its way through my insides as I picture myself kneeling before Beherit and King Lucifer, awaiting judgment. But the dread shifts to despair that, if my existence ends now, I'll never know what it feels like to touch Frannie, to kiss her, to *be* with her.

I slam my head into the wall.

Suddenly, I need to know why Frannie is so important—what their plans are for her. But I don't know, and I won't. Beherit is paranoid and keeps things close to the vest.

I bang the back of my head against the wall once more to

clear it. *Focus.* Things are going well. The others from Acquisitions weren't able to find her. I did. The rest of my job should be easy, Gabriel or no Gabriel. He's just a minor inconvenience. He seems to be riding her hard with his power, but there's only so far he can take it without working to my advantage. But the image of him . . . with her . . . like *that*, creeps back into my head and I feel my insides twist. I shift the image to *me* . . . with her . . . like that . . . and I feel other things moving inside me.

Tomorrow. I'll have her tomorrow.

I pull my sorry self off the floor and meander into the bathroom, where I stand staring at the shower. How does this thing work anyway? I turn a knob and at first the water spraying from the wall is cool, but then it gets warmer. Wrong one. I turn that one off and turn the other one on full blast. Magicking my clothes away, I step into the ice-cold water.

Focus, Luc.

FRANNIE

"Why doesn't anyone in your family ever talk about your brother?" Taylor dusts off the glass of the picture frame with her sleeve before putting it back on my dresser. It's the one of me in Grandpa's garage, grease smeared on my face, making rabbit ears behind Matt's sandy curls. He's pretending to bang a wrench on my head. We were seven. It was the week before he died.

I press back into my desk chair and swallow the lump forming in the back of my throat, threatening to cut off my airway. "Not much to talk about. It was a long time ago."

"Still," she says, looking back at the picture, "that's gotta be rough."

"It sucks, okay? Can we talk about something else?"

Her eyebrows raise and she holds up her hand. "Sorry."

I breathe deep and drop my head. "Sorry, Tay. But it *does* suck, and there *isn't* much to talk about. It was an accident . . ." As I say it, my throat closes completely. I start to gasp for air, but the stars in front of my eyes get brighter till I'm sure I'm going to pass out.

"Jesus, Fee." Taylor runs to my side.

I grip her shoulder where she kneels next to me. "I'm . . . okay," I gasp.

She springs up. "I'm getting your mom."

"No!" I brace my hands on my knees and work to pull air into my lungs. I shake my head as the stars fade. "I'm okay, really."

"What was that, like asthma or something? How did I not know you have asthma?"

There's a lot you don't know about me.

I glance back at Matt's picture, working to keep the air moving in and out, then look at Taylor and shrug. "Sorry." I turn back to my calculus book on the desk.

Taylor looks at me a moment longer. "You're sure you're okay?"

"Fine."

She sprawls on my bedroom floor, hovering over her calculus book and chewing the eraser off her pencil. "So, how did you manage to get the two hottest guys in the universe as essay and lab partners?"

I don't look up. "Don't know, just karma I guess."

"And now they're falling all over you. I *so* don't get it. It's like you turned into freakin' Paris Hilton."

"Nobody's falling all over me," I scoff, but the truth is she's right. They *are* kinda falling all over me. And the rest of the truth is I kinda like it.

I spread glue on the back of the magazine clipping I just cut out, trying not to gloat, and reach up to stick it on a tangerine patch of wall above my dresser. Taylor gets up and pulls a fistful of Sharpies out of her bag. She walks over to inspect the picture of the Mona Lisa I just stuck to my wall. Shooting a wicked grin at me over her shoulder, she writes, "Mona Lisa," in dark blue ink above it and then scribbles under it, "needs to get laid."

"Your room is almost due for a repaint," she says, looking over my last few years' worth of art as she lowers herself back to the carpet.

Nearly every inch of wall is covered with some random image, from faces to flowers to furniture, most of them sporting some commentary authored by either Taylor or Riley. Every few years we take a trip to the paint counter at the True Value and ask for anything they're throwing away, then we bring it back and take the rollers to my walls. The last batch featured tangerine orange, burgundy, petal pink, taupe, Gumby green, and robin's egg blue, which are now in nearly covered patches all around my room. There has to be at least six layers of paper and paint by now.

I sit back down at my desk under the window and hunch over my calculus book. "I think I might keep it. I'll be leaving for LA in the fall, and I don't want to come home from college to depressing, blank walls."

"I guess. . . . So, are you gonna cut one of those guys loose or what?"

I don't lift my head from my book as I respond drily. "Which one would you like, Tay?"

"Luc."

"What?"

"You asked me which one I wanted. Luc."

I breathe back the flare of jealousy. I knew this was coming. "So what happened to Marty?"

"He's cute and all, but if it's between him and Luc . . . no contest."

"Really . . . why?"

"I don't know. I guess it's the mystery. And the piercings," she says, flicking the ring through the corner of her lip. "And he seems kinda dangerous, which I like. It's sorta like anything could happen when you're with him."

"I guess."

"But for some unknown reason, I think he's really into you." She shakes her head with a smile, then her hand dips into her book bag on the bed and comes out with a two-inch foil square pinched between her index and middle fingers. "Do you even know what to do with him?" With a flick of her wrist, the condom Frisbees across the room, hitting me in the shoulder and falling to the floor at my feet.

I know *exactly* what to do with him. I've been practicing in my dreams. "Whatever," I say, rolling my eyes.

She blows out a sigh. "I think you'd have an easier time shaking Gabe."

My door swings open, and Mom is standing there with

two glasses of milk, like we're still eight years old. "Who is Gabe?"

Taylor cracks a grin as I palm the condom off of the floor and into my book bag. "Just a guy at school," I say as I straighten up in my chair.

Mom smiles. "You should bring him by. I'd love to meet him."

I feel the heat rise in my face and hope I'm not as red as I think I am. "He's really just a friend, Mom."

"I love to meet your friends," she says, handing us the milk and smoothing her skirt.

"I've got a different friend coming over to study tomorrow."

"Oh? What's her name?"

"Him. His name is Luc." I ignore Taylor's grin.

"Well, good. I'll look forward to meeting him." She smiles at Taylor. "I've got chocolate chip cookies in the oven. Save some milk and I'll bring some up in a few minutes."

"Thanks," I say as she turns and leaves, closing the door behind her and leaving the faint scent of jasmine in her wake.

Taylor smirks. "Maybe you should bring Gabe home too. Let your mom help you decide. She'd pick Gabe for sure. He's got a more wholesome feel."

"Leaving Luc for you. How convenient."

The truth is Gabe *does* have a more wholesome feel, but that doesn't keep my dreams about him from ending up in the same place my dreams about Luc do. I feel my cheeks flush just thinking about it.

The tingle that courses through me is followed by a dizzying sense of déjà vu. We've had conversations like this before, and

I could always count on Taylor to scoop the guy. It hits me like a bolt of lightning why I've always kept her close. She's been my safety net. She's always got the guy 'cause I've *let* her—I've wanted her to. Only one guy has ever gotten through that net and turned out to be a little dangerous . . . to my heart, that is. Ryan.

I don't know what's different, but I don't want her to scoop the guy this time. Either of them.

She flops back on the bed and blows out a sigh. "So you *are* gonna keep them both," she says, like she read my mind.

"Maybe." Another thrill courses through me at my revelation. I want them and I'm not giving in to Taylor this time. I mask the smile I can't stop as a yawn.

She lifts her head and glares at me. "Yeah, whatever. Just keep that condom handy."

The smell wafting in under my door makes my mouth water a full minute before Mom shows up with a plate full of hot, gooey cookies. Taylor and I scarf them down and chug the milk. When we're finished with our calculus we head downstairs.

"Mom! I'm walking Taylor home," I holler on our way out the door.

She sticks her head through the kitchen door. "Okay. Come right back."

We step out into the cool night, and Taylor loops her arm around my neck. "So, I heard Reefer tell Trevor you're coming back to Roadkill."

I roll my eyes. "Don't believe everything you hear."

Her lips pull into a mischievous smile. "Reefer's your smart choice, you know—a geek of the Guitar Hero variety. He wants you back 'cause he knows he could never do better than you."

"Thanks, Tay."

"I meant that in a good way," she laughs. "But, seriously, he'll never blow you off. You should think about it."

I glare at her. "Not gonna happen. Anyway, I'm leaving for college in September, so there's not much point—in going back to the band, I mean."

"So, you're sure about UCLA? 'Cause you could still go to State with Riley and me. It's not too late to change your mind, you know," she says.

I look down the street toward Taylor's. There are no street-lights along this stretch of Amistad Road, so it's illuminated only by post lanterns in front yards and the silver light of the half-moon. "UCLA has the best international relations pro-gram in the country. I was really lucky to get in. Plus, the full academic scholarship made it kinda hard to say no."

"I don't know why you think it's your job to save the world."

"If we don't save ourselves, who's going to? Plus, you know I can't stay here."

She looks hurt. "Why? What's so bad about here?"

I hook my arm around her waist as we cross the street and step up onto the sidewalk. The neighborhood is quiet except for the Coopers' cocker spaniel, Crash, who's sticking her nose through a knothole in the fence and having a conniption as we walk by their house.

"Nothing, except if I go to State, my parents will expect me to live at home. Plus, Mary and Kate are there. You know me. I just really need to do something different." We slide past house after house, all the same from the outside, and all quiet tonight.

"You're not the LA type, Fee. They'll eat you alive. Actually,

I'm the LA type," she says, running her hand through her pink spikes.

"You should come with me. How cool would that be? Tay and Fee, tearing up LA."

"Yeah," she says dejectedly, and then I feel bad, 'cause for Tay, it was State or nothing. Her dad's been out of work for over a year. "I'm not even sure about State. If I can't swing a few more scholarships, it ain't gonna happen."

"Well, maybe you can come visit, like, for spring break."

"Yeah, maybe." She sighs deeply and hikes up her book bag with a jerk of her shoulder. Her body tenses under my arm. "They're foreclosing on our house."

"*What?*"

"We have to move."

"What are you talking about?"

"We're looking for an apartment." She quickly wipes away the tear leaking from the corner of her eye as we turn the corner onto her street.

"Oh, man." My stomach's in my throat and I squeeze her. "Tay . . . I don't know what to say."

"Nothing to say . . . except which of those guys you're gonna pick," she says with a weak smile.

"Jesus, Tay. Bigger things to worry about, don't you think?"

"Maybe, but I want to worry about this. So which one?"

"Shut up."

"When you give me a name. Luc or Gabe," she says, turning up her driveway and towing me along by the neck.

"You're ridiculous."

"Name." She squeezes the back of my neck.

"Stop it!"

"Name." Now she's shaking me.

"Fine! Luc." I'm not totally sure if I said that 'cause I meant it or 'cause Taylor said she wanted him.

"Damn, you're harsh! I couldn't even get the sympathy vote," she says, but she surprises me by pulling me into a hug. Her lips hint at a smile as she pushes open her front door. "Text me after Luc leaves tomorrow." She lifts an eyebrow. "I want details," she says with her lascivious smile. She steps in, and I hear her father yelling in the background before she closes the door behind her.

I stand on Taylor's front steps in the moonlight for a long minute, staring up at the constellations swirling above my head. Other than Crash barking down the street, the neighborhood is eerily quiet tonight.

There has to be something I can do to help Taylor. I feel sick as I think about her family getting kicked out of their house. She's lived here all her life. Maybe the church can help. They've gotta be good for something. I'll talk to Dad.

I turn to step off the porch just as the front door flies open and Trevor darts out, slamming into me and sending me flailing down the porch stairs.

"Jesus, Frannie," he says through his surprise, grabbing my arm to steady me.

I brush him off. "Where's the fire?"

"Sorry," he says and starts to back down the driveway. I follow. "You okay?"

He glances warily at the house and spins, walking quickly toward the street. "Yeah. Just needed to get out of there. Thinking about heading over to Riley's," he says, and a wistful smile barely quirks his lips.

"So, when are you guys gonna tell Tay?"

His wistful expression becomes anxious and his eyes shoot to mine. "Don't even think about it."

"I'm not gonna say anything. But you should. And you better not be screwing with Riley."

He stops walking and looks me in the eye. "I'm not," he says as his eyes soften. Then he grins and starts walking again. "But speaking of screwing with people, what's with you and Jackson? He does nothing but drool over you all day. It's totally pathetic."

"I'm not screwing with him. I tell him every chance I get to leave me the hell alone."

"Mixed signals," he says.

"What part of 'get lost' is confusing him?"

"The making-out-in-the-closet part." He grins and nudges my shoulder.

I cringe. "Everybody makes mistakes. Help me out?"

"I'll think about it." He shoots me a sidelong glance. "Does Reefer even have a shot at getting back with you?"

I smile despite myself. "Tragically, no."

"Figured. He's still crazy in love with you, you know."

And that's the problem. He thinks he loves me. I shrug. "He'll wake up one day and realize he was temporarily insane."

"You're busting hearts all over the place," he says with a smile and a wave over his shoulder as he turns to cross the street toward Riley's.

I dig my hands deep into my pockets against the chill that's creeping into the night air and watch my feet shuffle down the sidewalk toward the corner, smiling to myself. Maybe Riley's finally found The One. Too bad she won't live long enough to enjoy it, 'cause Taylor's gonna kill them both.

As I meander down the dimly lit street, I think about why it was Luc's name I blurted under pressure. Gabe is gorgeous for sure, and just thinking about him makes me tingle in places I'll never admit to. He's every girl's dream . . . God knows he's been in plenty of mine. He's also clearly the safer choice, 'cause Luc seems more like he could be every girl's nightmare. Aside from that body—my dreams about which embarrass even me—and that face, there's his dark energy. It scares the hell out of me but also speaks to me like some shadowy siren song that holds me and won't let me go. A girl could lose control with him—which I don't do. Ever.

So maybe that's why I jump when I turn the corner and see the black Shelby Cobra parked across the street and a few doors up from my house. I drift down the street and cross over, wanting to keep walking—to reach that Mustang and take a look inside.

It can't be him, I tell myself. What would he be doing here? I'm obsessed. This is bad. And probably the reason that, when I'm sane, I date guys like Tony Riggins and his graphing calculator. It's hard to obsess over a graphing calculator.

But it's easy to obsess over an insanely gorgeous guy with mysterious eyes. Which is why I'm standing in the middle of my front yard staring at that car. I shake my head, breathe deep, and cut a swath through the damp grass to my front door. But I hesitate there.

I force myself to open the door and slip inside before I do something really stupid.

LUC

Taylor. Taylor's here—not Gabriel. Satan save me, I'm getting paranoid.

Focus, Luc.

I shake my head to clear it and start to reach for the key. But suddenly, before I can turn it, I'm being yanked through space in a dizzying rush. I swallow back the bile rising with the dread from the pit of my stomach and close my eyes against the vertigo. There are only two in the infernal realm who could summon me like this.

Let it be Beherit.

But when my feet land hard on smooth stone and I open my eyes, my panic kicks up a notch. It's not my boss, as I'd hoped. I'm in the castle Pandemonium. In front of me is King Lucifer's intricately carved black obsidian throne, perched high on its dais in the middle of the cavernous, domed room.

It's empty.

I look around for any sign of Him, but the multitude of floating candles reflecting off the smooth, black obsidian walls reveal no one. I'm alone. I stand perfectly still and let the strong smell of brimstone calm me. But when I hear His low whispered hiss in my ear, I jump anyway.

"You've found her." It's not a question.

Reflexively, I turn to look behind me. Not there. But then I feel Him—His stare. I turn to face Him as He hovers high above me, near the domed ceiling. I'm careful not to look directly at Him, but I can see His immense black bat's wings beating in slow rhythm as He lowers Himself to the ground. I drop to my knee, head bowed.

The polished obsidian floor reflects back His image: immense with steaming, black, leathery skin that seems to absorb all the light and radiate it back out of His sharp, angular face through glowing green cat's eyes. His twisted bloodred horns are encircled within a spiked golden coronet. When His clawed feet touch down, He folds His wings and stalks slowly and silently toward me, like a panther approaching its prey.

"Yes, my liege," I reply.

"And you're certain this is the one we seek?" His hiss sends ice up my spine despite Hell's two-thousand-degree heat.

It's only at this second, confronted with the question, that I realize I have nothing to offer as evidence that Frannie is The One. I've always relied heavily on instinct, and my instincts have never steered me wrong. Now would not be a good time to question them.

"Yes, my liege." I stifle the sudden urge to ask why He wants her so badly.

As He passes within a few feet of me, I feel the crackle of electricity—His power—pass between us like a thousand tiny lightning bolts. My own energy surges.

"Rise," He commands, and I'm helpless not to. I watch as He ascends the many stairs to the high throne and throws Himself into it, morphing from His natural form to His human shell— very Zeus-like: long white hair and beard; strong, angular face; and long, flowing red robes cloaking a powerful build. But the glowing green cat's eyes don't change. I feel them as they study me.

"How long?" He barks deeply from on high, his voice changing with his form.

"Not long, my liege." No need to share that Gabriel is running interference and possibly stretching my timeline a bit.

"Excellent." He's silent for a moment, and I'm hoping to be dismissed, but I feel a growing sense of unease as His eyes bore through the top of my bowed head. "Lucifer . . ." He says pensively, "I think you've been underappreciated. Beherit is loathe to give credit where credit is due, but I believe you've been a valuable asset in Acquisitions."

As He pauses again, I find myself becoming even more uncomfortable, unsure where He's going with this. Finally, He stands theatrically and makes His way back down the stairs, long red robes flowing behind—all for show, since He could phase down in a heartbeat if He so chose—until He's standing in front of me. Evil radiates off of Him in waves, saturating my mind with dark ideas and clouding my ability to think for myself.

"Look at me, Lucifer."

Even if I wanted to, I could not disobey. I raise my head and look Him in His deep green eyes, bracing myself against the sudden rush of power as He scrutinizes me. A heinous grin stretches across His face as His energy courses through me.

"Yes. Just as I thought." He turns His back.

My legs go soft, and I feel myself sway nearly to the point of falling as He releases me.

"I'm in need of some new blood on my council, Lucifer. Does

that appeal to you—a post on my council? Maybe head of Acquisitions?"

It's work to keep my face placid—expressionless—as I process that. My boss's job. It's what I wanted—what *every* creature of pride wants. So, why is it terror I feel at the prospect of being on the council—under His constant scrutiny? *No!*

"Yes, my liege."

"It will be your reward, then, when you bring her to me." He paces a wide circle and stops behind me. Suddenly, He sounds weary. "Do you have any idea how tiresome it is to always be second?"

There is no answer to that, and He's not expecting one. I stand motionless as stone and wait for Him to come to the point.

"Since the Beginning, the Creator has had all the power." All my hair stands on end as His power surges and His voice crescendos up to its usual boom. He continues His circle and stands in front of me. Rage etches deep creases between His full, white brows. "It's my turn. This is my chance. I *will* be out from under Him—finally. We won't have to abide by His rules any longer. *I will finally have my rightful place!*" The floor shakes with the boom of His voice, and one of the many white marble gargoyles surrounding the dais topples.

It would be useless—and dangerous—to point out that He agreed to the Almighty's rules in the Beginning for a reason. When they were both still sane, He and the Almighty recognized the need for balance in the universe. Without the lure of Heaven and the threat of Hell, humanity would sink to the pits of depravity, where it would destroy itself, rendering both

Heaven and Hell pointless. Unfortunately, King Lucifer's sanity has been questionable for as long as I've existed.

His green eyes darken to black and, in His rage, His true form dances dangerously close to the surface, shimmering and peeking through His human shell like a mirage. He paces another circle. "Tag her as quickly as possible. The *others*," He chews out the word like a piece of grizzle, "will be coming for her too. I need her, Lucifer. Don't disappoint me."

The others *have already come—in the form of Gabriel.*

He turns in a flourish of robes, and the roller-coaster rush hits me again as I'm dismissed.

I'm suddenly back in my car, waiting for the vertigo to clear. When I remember where I am, I turn and watch the light flick on in the right, second-story window of Frannie's house. I'm still watching as she pushes the curtain aside and peers out into the night, toward me. She drops the curtain and retreats into her room.

When I have my head, I turn the key and drive out of Frannie's neighborhood, secure in the knowledge that she'll belong to Hell, and soon. I won't fail. I wonder idly what my boss could have done to piss the king off so thoroughly that he's being replaced, but I shake my head—not my concern at the moment. One thing at a time. And right now, Frannie is Thing One.

Tomorrow.

6

✝

A Snowball's Chance in Hell

LUC

After my . . . encounter with my king last night, I've had a hard time waiting until two o'clock for my study date with Frannie. I'm electric, my whole body buzzing with anticipation. Because today it's going to happen: I'm going to tag her.

My palms are sweaty as I pull into her driveway. I steam in my natural form, but I don't remember ever sweating before. Not sure what that's all about. Regardless, I wipe my palms on my jeans as I make my way up to the front porch and ring the bell. And I'm feeling . . . eager, I guess, because there's more to my buzz than just the thrill of the hunt. I seem to have missed her a little, and I can't wait to see her.

The door finally swings open, and I smile, anticipating Frannie, but instead there's a man. He's shorter than me, with chestnut hair combed neatly back, wearing a blue button-down shirt with a green tie. When he smiles, I can see Frannie in his face. I hold out my hand before I realize I've done it. He takes it and says "Hello—" but then flinches back from my touch, and the rest of the greeting is lost as his hazel eyes narrow and his face pinches.

"Um . . . hi," I finally say, cursing myself for being so careless. Frannie does that to me—clouds my mind. I need to start using my head.

"You must be Luc," he says warily.

"Yes, sir," I say. I push a little power at him, just to smooth things over, but his face remains cautious. No reaction.

I push a little harder.

Nothing.

A mortal immune to my magic? That doesn't happen very often. Not good. I reach out with my essence to try to read him and get . . . nothing. I can't even tell if he's tagged for Heaven.

"I'll tell Frannie you're here." He turns and leaves me standing on the front porch. I step back and seriously consider getting in my car and driving away, but then Frannie appears at the door. Her hair is pulled back in a knot, a few wisps of sandy waves dangling free and framing her face. There's a flush in her cheeks and a sparkle in her eyes. Her faded jeans and black tank top are snug enough to tease me with her curves without being tight. *Unholy Hell, she's beautiful.*

"Hey," she says with a quirk of her eyebrows. "I can't believe Dad left you standing out here."

I can. I went over like a snowball in Hell. "Yeah . . . well. I don't think I made a great first impression," I say in a low voice.

She surprises me by cracking a smile. "Really?" Then she surprises me again by grabbing my hand and pulling me through the door. I reflexively try to pull my hand away, but she doesn't let it go. I'm surprised once more by my own visceral reaction to her hand holding mine.

She tows me into a small family room where a girl is lounging across the couch. She swings around and sits as we walk in, her hazel eyes working their way over my T-shirt and jeans. Another girl, younger, with long, dark hair, is sprawled on the beige shag carpet with her back to us, messing with a Scrabble board on the low wooden coffee table.

I glance around at the comfortable yet nondescript room. There are three overstuffed brown armchairs scattered between the fireplace and the TV, all empty. A large print of da Vinci's *The Last Supper*, framed in gold, takes up most of the wall over the couch. The rest of the walls are covered with dozens of school pictures: smiling little girls everywhere. The caramel-colored curtains on the front window are pulled back, revealing the large oak tree next to the driveway and my car, front and center.

The History Channel is blaring about Caesar from an unwatched TV in the corner. Frannie picks up a remote from the arm of one of the chairs and turns off the TV. The girl on the couch rolls her eyes and says, "Thank God."

"You know what, Kate? If you'd shut up and watch, you might learn something," Frannie says. Her eyes slip to me as she blushes. "Tell Mom we're upstairs studying, okay?"

The girl on the floor turns and looks at us, her sapphire eyes sparking. "So we don't even rate an introduction or anything?"

Frannie rolls her eyes. "Fine . . . Luc, this is Maggie, and that's Kate," she says gesturing from the floor to the couch.

"Hello," I say, turning on the charm. I walk over to the coffee table and bend over the Scrabble board. "I don't think that's a word," I say to Maggie. "But if you do this . . ." I rearrange what's on the board and add two letters from her holder, "it's a twenty-eight pointer."

Maggie beams at me with those sapphire eyes and says, "Thanks," a little breathlessly.

Kate sighs and smiles, pulling her long blond hair back and tying it into a knot behind her neck, just like Frannie does. "Hey."

" 'Kay," Frannie says, "so we'll be upstairs."

We're around the corner and halfway up the stairs when I hear an "Oh my God," and a round of giggles erupt from the family room. Before we make it to Frannie's room, a woman's voice calls urgently up the stairs.

"Frannie?"

"Yeah, Mom," she answers.

I look down the stairs at a petite woman, impeccably dressed in a white blouse and knee-length navy blue skirt, with short, tidy, sandy-blond hair and concerned sapphire-blue eyes. She's nervously wringing her white apron with her hands. Frannie's father is standing next to her, glaring up at me. I try again to get any sense of him, but it's almost as if he's Shielded. *Why would Heaven Shield Frannie's father?*

Frannie's mom takes a step forward and lays a hand on the rail. "Why don't you and your friend study at the kitchen table? I'm done in there and you'd have room to spread out."

Frannie looks at me, her eyes narrowing. "Um, sure. Okay." She shrugs at me and turns to head back down the stairs.

FRANNIE

Picture those old fifties TV shows they always run late at night on Nickelodeon. You know . . . the ones where the moms all stay home and clean the house in sensible high heels and makeup. Like *Leave It to Beaver*. That's my life. The Cleavers got nothing on us.

In the ten years since my brother died, I've never seen my mother upset—about anything. It's like she's completely numb, humming through life pushing a vacuum cleaner. Sometimes it's enough to make me want to do something totally outrageous just to see if I can get a rise out of her. Wake her up. But maybe she doesn't want to wake up. Maybe it's too hard.

The closest I've ever come to seeing her upset was two years ago, on the day the call came from St. Agnes Parochial School that I was being removed for disciplinary reasons. I actually believe her jaw clenched a little, and her blue eyes might even have been a little moist while she listened to Sister Maria explain I was a disruption in religion class. But when she hung up the phone she smoothed her hair—like that minute jaw clench might have displaced one—then her skirt, smiled, and said, "We'll have to get you registered at Haden High School this week."

So this whole "studying at the kitchen table" thing is a little weird. I've had boys in my room to study before and it's never been a problem. Even Reefer. I guess Luc wasn't kidding when he said he didn't make a great first impression.

We spread out at the kitchen table, and Dad meanders by the door, peering in at us. It's totally embarrassing. Why did he pick today to decide to ruin my life? *Go away.*

I thumb through my composition book and open it to a blank page. "What should we focus on for this outline? Maybe the whole thing with Ma and Tom?" I glance up at Luc as Dad walks by again and cringe at the annoyed set to Luc's face.

Go away, Dad.

But, as I stare at Luc, the creases around his eyes smooth and a smile ticks at one side of his mouth. "Sounds good to me." He raises his voice slightly. "Any thoughts, Mr. Cavanaugh?"

Dad slides around the corner with pink cheeks and suspicious eyes. He sort of stares Luc down, something I've never seen him do before, nods at me and leaves.

"What happened?" I whisper.

He just shrugs.

I shake my head and start writing.

I'm surprised when my sister, Grace, shuffles through the kitchen door on her way to the fridge. She rarely ventures out of her and Maggie's room, which is why Maggie's never in it. She pulls a Coke from the fridge, pops the top, and stares at us from under her blond bangs as she sips. It's a little creepy, actually, how Grace can make you feel like she's looking right into you with those pale blue eyes. She's always been like that.

"Is there something you needed, Grace?" I ask pointedly when her staring starts to get weird.

"No." But she doesn't leave. She just sips her Coke and stares.

I try to ignore her, but it's impossible. "You know, we're trying to study . . ."

She leans against the fridge like she's settling in for a while. "Go ahead."

I scowl at her. "It'd be easier if you left."

"Whatever." She shrugs off the fridge and shuffles back out to the family room, eyeing Luc the whole way.

"Sorry about that. She's just a little . . ."

"Intense?" Luc is watching after her with a raised eyebrow.

I smile. "That wasn't the word I was going to use, but yeah."

When we finish I kinda want to invite him up to my room to listen to my new Fray downloads, but I figure that's pushing my luck.

Then again, pushing my luck is what I do best.

We meander toward the door, but I look over my shoulder when we get there and grab Luc's hand. "C'mon," I say and tow him up the stairs.

He looks a little surprised when I pull him through my door and close it.

"So, you have no clue what happened?" I ask, climbing onto my bed. "'Cause I've never seen my parents act like that before."

"No clue."

I tuck my legs under me and lean on my outstretched arm. "Well, that was really weird. They've all turned into aliens."

He scans my room and cracks an amused smile. "Like *Invasion of the Body Snatchers* . . ." His gaze shifts to me as his eyebrow quirks. "Could happen."

He turns back to my walls and takes a lap of my room.

"Interesting wallpaper," he says, slowing to read some of Riley's and Taylor's captions. He gets to the Mona Lisa and lets out a mirthless laugh. "She did—a lot," he mumbles under his breath.

"What?" I ask.

He looks at me for a second. "Nothing."

And then I remember what Taylor wrote on that picture. "Mona Lisa needs to get laid."

His eyes drop to my dresser, and he picks up a picture frame. He looks at the picture for a long time. Running his finger over the glass, he says, "Who is this?"

"Me and my brother." I look out the window into the swirling storm clouds collecting on the horizon.

He sounds surprised. "Your brother?"

"He's dead," I say flatly.

"When?"

I look back at him, and there's sympathy in his eyes I don't deserve. My insides churn and bile burns my tightening throat. I really don't want to have this conversation.

"Ten years ago." I pull my government book out of my book bag.

"I'm so sorry."

I thumb blindly through the book, pretending to be finding my page, and breathe back the threat of tears.

He eases into my desk chair. "Do you want to talk about it?"

God, no. "Not really." I spring off the bed. "So I downloaded some cool stuff," I say, hoping he doesn't notice the thick sound of my voice. I grab my iPod off the dresser and stick it on the speakers. "What do you want to hear?"

"Depends on what you've got."

I breathe deep and feel my chest start to loosen. "The Fray, always," I say and smile up at him, "but also some new Saving Abel and Three Days Grace."

"Put it on shuffle. I like surprises." A playful smile dances across his face, making my heart skip.

I hit the play button, but I so can't pay attention to the music, 'cause Luc pulls himself out of the chair and saunters toward me. I'm not sure what I'm seeing in his eyes—something seductive and oh-so-dangerous. When that wicked smile curls his lips, the tingle low in my belly explodes through my whole body, making me gasp. But just as he reaches me the door swings open.

And Mom is standing there with fire shooting out her eyeballs.

Shit. I let my hair fall across my face, hoping to hide the color in my cheeks, and turn to her. "Hey Mom."

"I need a word, Frannie," she says without actually moving her jaw. "In the hall," she adds when I don't move.

I turn to Luc and widen my eyes in mock horror.

He chokes back a laugh, disguising the bit that escapes as a cough.

I step out into the hall and close the door. "What?"

"I thought we had an understanding."

"What understanding?"

"I don't want him in your room," she says under her breath.

"How about if we keep the door open?" *Please let him stay.*

She looks at me for a long minute. "With the door open," she says glancing at it, "for a little while."

I work to keep the grin from spreading across my face. I've

pushed my luck enough for one day. "Thanks," I say, pushing the door open.

She looks at me a moment longer then glances in at Luc before turning for the stairs.

I step through the door and Luc has my iPod in his hand. "You've got a little of everything in here," he says. "Jimi Hendrix, Mozart, Nickelback."

I pick my fingernail and grunt my affirmation, embarrassed.

He presses it back onto the speakers. "So, since I'm not being dragged out of here by my ear, I take it you were able to negotiate a truce?"

My stomach turns inside out as he moves slowly toward me. "I guess. Door open was my concession," I say with a shake in my voice, gesturing to the hall.

"Hmm . . ." He stops in front of me—too close—and glances out into the hall as my giggling sisters slither past. "Which, it seems, would have the desired effect of limiting our physical contact." He lifts his hand and strokes a finger along the line of my jaw.

Suddenly, my heart is totally erratic. I feel kinda buzzy and numb. "Yeah . . . well . . ." I snatch my government book off the bed. "Did you finish Coach Runyon's homework yet?"

He quirks a smile. "Nope."

I pull my notebook from my book bag and spread out on the floor. He eases in next to me and leans against the bed. And I try to ignore my sisters as they take turns peering in the door at us as we do our homework.

When we're finished I walk with him to his car.

"So, I guess I'll see you Monday."

"Monday," he says sliding into his car and closing the door.

I lean in the open window and the music surprises me. "What are you listening to?"

"Vivaldi."

"Really?"

He grins and leans closer. "I'm full of surprises."

My heart thumps in my chest, and I smile a shaky smile back. "I'm sure."

His eyebrow arches. "Have fun at church tomorrow."

"Yeah."

He starts the engine, but I'm still leaning on his window. And he's staring at me. I lean in more, close enough to feel his heat. He starts to lean toward me, and my heart feels like some wild thing trapped in my chest, struggling to get loose.

Then my front door swings open, and my parents are standing on the porch. I pull a deep breath, will my vital signs out of the critical range, and stand up, blowing out a frustrated sigh.

Luc's lips pull into an amused smile, sending my heart racing again. "See ya," he says and waves. I watch him back out of the driveway and drive slowly down my street till his taillights disappear around the corner. When I turn back to the house, my parents are still standing there.

"Holy God! What was that?" I say, exasperated, storming up the walk.

"Language, Frannie," Mom scolds.

I roll my eyes. "Whatever. So what's the deal?"

Dad looks at me with concerned eyes. "You're not . . ." he starts, but blushes and trails off.

"What?"

Mom takes my hand and leads me into the empty family room. I can hear my sisters scuffle at the top of the stairs, angling for better listening position. "You're not romantically involved with that boy, are you?"

"You mean, are we dating?"

"Yes."

"No. He's my essay partner." And the object of my fantasies.

"We don't think you should spend any more time with him than you have to."

"Why?"

"He just concerns us, Frannie. There's something not right about him."

"Wow. Okay. So is it the piercings?"

"No, just something in his . . . vibe."

"You don't like his *vibe*?"

I hear Kate and Maggie giggle.

"Just trust us, Frannie. Please. I don't think he's the type of person you should be spending time with."

"Who are you and what have you done with my parents?"

She smiles despite herself and then gives me a hug. "We just worry about our girls, that's all."

So, I guess this is how to get a rise out of Mom. But the truth is I shouldn't be surprised, 'cause Luc definitely does have a vibe. And let's just say it's not likely to impress too many teenage girls' parents.

7

✣

Personal Demons

FRANNIE

I haven't been able to think about anything but Luc since he left yesterday afternoon. Or obsess would be a more accurate term, I guess. The look in his eyes . . . no one's ever looked at me that way before. An aching tingle starts low in my belly just thinking about it, and I glance at Mom, in the front of the family van. If she hadn't come in when she did, I'm not sure what would have happened.

I sit in the back of the van and crank my iPod, looking out the window the whole way to church, hoping for a glimpse of a '68 black Shelby Cobra. But instead, the first thing I see when we pull into the church parking lot is Grandpa's midnight blue '65 Mustang, glimmering in the sun, top down and ready to roll.

"No way!" I squeal.

Mom smiles. "Looks like you'll be riding back to Grandpa's in style today."

"I don't get what the big deal is. It's just some crappy old car. Who'd want *that* when they could have a brand-new one?" Grace says with her usual pragmatism.

"Grandpa would, and I would," I say.

She rolls her eyes and shrugs.

✝

Grandpa is nearly bouncing out of the pew the entire mass. To keep myself from bouncing along with him, I watch Grace kneeling with her rosary. She seemed to go the other way when Matt died, turning to God, like He's going to fix anything . . . or change anything. She's always been too trusting. Gullible, really.

Praying doesn't work. I've tried.

I glance back at Grandpa, remembering the last time I actually got down on my knees and prayed. It was three years ago, after I'd woken late on a Saturday with what felt like lightning shooting through my brain. And what I saw behind my eyelids, when I screwed them shut against the pain, was my grandma lying facedown in her garden in a pool of blood. When I called, no one answered. I told Mom we needed to go over to check on her, but she put me off. I couldn't tell her why we needed to go—it was crazy—so I went to my room and prayed.

When Grandpa got home from fishing that day, he'd found her in the garden where she'd fallen from the ladder, with the pruning sheers through her stomach.

That's when I knew for sure there was no God.

At the end of what feels like an endless mass, Grandpa jumps out of his seat. "Ready for a ride?"

"I've been ready for this ride all year."

"Let's go!"

He makes his way out of the church, me following behind. When we get to the car he opens the driver's door and hands me the keys.

"I'm driving? No way!"

He smiles. "You earned it."

I jump into the driver's seat, turn the ignition, and she purrs to life. The Rolling Stones' "Sympathy for the Devil" is blasting from the radio. I crank it even louder. "This is amazing." I smile so hard my cheeks hurt and wrap my hands around the steering wheel.

His blue eyes beam at me. "Let's roll."

I adjust the mirrors and the seat, then shift into first and slowly roll out of the parking lot. Once we're out of the crowd and on the open road he says, "Give her a little gas. Let's see what she can do."

I hit the gas and fly through the gears, feeling the wind through my hair and the cool morning sun on my skin. "She runs perfect!" I yell over the noise of the engine, the radio, and the wind.

I glance at him and can't miss the pride all over his face. "Ya did a great job."

"Grandpa?"

"Yep."

"If the devil had a car, what do you think it would be?"

The mischief in his voice is unmistakable. "A black Shelby Cobra GT500."

My gut jumps a little. "What year?"

"1967."

Close.

We pull into his driveway. "Leave her out," he says. "We'll take her for a ride later."

"So what's our next project? Another Mustang?"

"Probably. Thinkin' about that '67 Shelby. C'mere. I want to show ya something," he says, opening the front door. I savor the sweet smell of pipe smoke as we weave our way between the worn sofa and the walnut coffee table in the small family room to the bedroom in the back. He grabs a wooden picture frame from the dresser and hands it to me. "Did your grandma ever show ya this?"

"No," I say, taking it from his hand. I look at the picture. It's a young couple; him with dark hair and sky-blue eyes, wearing dark jeans and a black T-shirt. His arms are wrapped around a girl in cutoffs and a red halter top, her sandy blond waves blowing in the breeze. And she's sitting on the hood of a black '67 Shelby Cobra GT500.

"That was the day I asked your grandma to marry me—summer after high school."

"Wow. You were young."

"Well, things were different back then, but I still believe when it's right, ya just know it."

I stare at the picture again—Grandpa's arms around Grandma, holding on like his life depended on it. There's a gleam in her sapphire eyes, and a wicked little smile just curls the corners of her lips as she leans back into him. "She looks happy."

A crooked smile blooms on his face. "We *were* happy. I was a hell-raiser back then. Your great-grandpa thought I was the devil. Tried to run me off with a shotgun." He laughs. "Like that woulda worked if I was really the devil."

"How did you change his mind?"

"Not sure I ever really did. But it didn't take him long to figure out that I loved her. And I always tried to be good to her, so after a while I guess he decided there were worse things I could be than the devil."

I take a last look at the picture and put it down on the dresser, tapping the Shelby with my index finger. "I have a . . . friend who drives a '68."

His expression turns serious and his brow creases with concern. "How good of a 'friend' is he?"

As hard as I try, I can't stop the ridiculous grin that pulls at my mouth. "I'm not sure yet."

He must read something in my face. "Frannie . . . ya know teenage guys're only after one thing, right?"

"Grandpa!"

"It's just the way of things. Don't let no guy push ya into doin' . . . ya know . . ."

"I can take care of myself."

His face remains stern, but his eyes soften and a smile creeps into them. "I'm sure ya can. Have your parents met him?"

"Yeah," I say, then hesitate. "He has them pretty freaked out."

His eyes win out and a smile bursts across his face. "Well,

that's what parents are for, I suppose." His brow creases. "But I can't see how anybody who drives a '68 Shelby could be all bad."

"Thanks, Grandpa." I wrap him in a hug. "I love you."

"I love ya too, Frannie."

✤

When Grandpa drops me off I skip into the house and close the front door. I look up and Grace is there, arms crossed, lips pressed into a hard line, staring at me with her intense blue eyes. "Come talk to me," she says without breaking her gaze.

"What now?"

She grabs my arm and pulls me. "Just come upstairs."

I let her drag me upstairs to my room, and she closes the door as I head toward the window.

"I know you don't do your reading," she starts in her no-nonsense tone, "but Peter 5:8 says, 'Be self-controlled and alert. Your enemy the devil prowls around like a roaring lion looking for someone to devour.' Satan influences the weak, Frannie."

I turn away from the window to face her. "What the hell are you talking about?"

She fixes me in a hard stare. "You know exactly *who* I'm talking about."

I start and my gut twists.

"There's something . . . dark about him," she adds.

I glare at her. "You've lost it, Grace. Get out of my room."

She moves to the door and turns back to look at me, her expression dour. "I'll pray for you," she says.

"Get out!" I bark.

She closes the door, and, when I flop back onto my bed, my head hits something hard. I sit up to find a Bible open to the First Letter of Peter. I throw it full force at the door, where it falls to the floor in a heap, then I sit with my face in my hands.

Grace is crazy. *Isn't she?* Or am I? I'm not sure. It's been a long time since I've felt emotions so big and out of control, and I don't like it. I don't know where all these insane emotions are coming from, but I have to figure out a way to make them stop.

I drag myself off the bed and start working my way through the comfort of my judo routine. I've been doing judo since I was nine. I didn't know why I was drawn to it. I just knew it was something I needed to do. What I know now, looking back, is I truly *did* need it, 'cause I was self-destructing, quietly and privately, after Matt died. Judo was like kid anger management— the only thing that touched my rage. It's a funny mix of letting everything out and holding everything in. The ultimate in control over mind and body. It taught me to stay centered within myself and keep everything else out—superficial. If you don't let anything in, then nothing can hurt you. Never again am I going to hurt like I did when Matt left me. I couldn't survive it.

When I'm finished, I sit on my bed, pull out Matt's journal, and start to write. I tell him everything I dare admit to myself, starting with the fact that Luc is somehow getting through my defenses.

8

✝

Hell on Earth

LUC

I stroll up the hall toward my locker with my fingertips perched in the small of Angelique's back. She prattles incoherently about her weekend, seriously challenging my ability to feign interest. But then I glance up and see Frannie standing at her locker, staring at us, and I let the smile spread across my face. I turn and gaze blindly at Angelique, nodding at her inept platitudes.

When we reach my locker, Frannie's gone, but I can feel her tucked inside the door to room 616, watching. And her black pepper and licorice are laced with a healthy dose of garlic—strong and bitter. I breathe it in as it overpowers Angelique's ginger and savor the crackle of hot energy coursing through me.

"What did you do this weekend?" Angelique asks, pulling me from my reverie and trailing a finger down the collar of her low-cut shirt to her substantial cleavage.

I lean against my locker. "Not much. You?"

"It's almost beach weather so we opened up the beach house. You should come down sometime . . ."

"Sounds good," I purr with my wickedest smile.

The sudden, overwhelming burst of envy, rage, and hate emanating from room 616 is so thick in the air I can taste it, arousing all my senses. Arousing *me*. I bask in it and shudder.

Angelique eases in a little closer, pouts her full, red lips, and brushes her fingers down my arm, hesitating at the lower edge of my T-shirt sleeve, over the tail of the black serpent tattooed around my upper arm. "It's not too far from here. Maybe we could drive down there some night . . . like, Friday maybe?"

I smile, almost unable to contain the thrill coursing through me. A thrill that has nothing to do with Angelique. This is perfect. Just what I was going for.

Yes, this is a much better game plan—the indirect approach. Because what I realized after I left Frannie's Saturday, as I sat in the dark, obsessing and banging my head against the wall— all night—was that the direct approach was kicking my ass.

The thing is, to tag Frannie, I need undisputable claim to her soul. Undisputable claim means more than one sin, unless that one sin is beyond big—a mortal sin. Even the seven deadly sins usually aren't enough just once. I need at least a tendency if not a trend. A pattern. And chipping away at it a little at a time isn't working.

Two weeks. How is this taking so long?

I almost had her in her room . . . I was *so* close. The ginger was pouring off her. It wouldn't have even taken much of a push. But at this rate, Gabriel will beat me to the tag for sure.

Because the other side is that Gabriel also needs a trend, and as far as I can see, he's got it. If they want her—and I'm quite sure they do—I don't know why he hasn't claimed her yet.

But he hasn't, so there must be a reason. Which means I still have time.

Don't panic.

This game plan—the indirect approach—*will* work. It has to.

I saunter into class, ready to bask in Frannie's wild emotions, and slide into my seat. "How was your Sunday?"

She turns and smiles at me. "Fine."

And I realize there's nothing to bask in. The anise . . . the pepper . . . they're gone. I try to pick up anything she's giving off. But there's nothing to pick up. I wipe the confusion from my face and ask, "Do anything good?"

"No."

"You okay?"

"Yep," she says, smiling wider.

Mr. Snyder walks over and tosses a pile of paper onto her desk. "Here's your latest batch of letters, Frannie. Translations are stapled on the front, as usual. Do you need help with postage?"

She smiles up at him—never happier. "No, thanks, Mr. Snyder. Collections were good this month. It's covered."

"Mind if I take a look?" I lean in until I'm close enough she must feel me, my heat.

A shudder? Maybe? Or was that just wishful thinking? "Sorry, they're personal letters," she says without turning to look at me.

"No problem. I'll read the write-up in the *Globe*. Pretty clever system, hooking up with a teacher over there."

"It works. And Mr. Snyder does the translation by scanning the letters and running them through a translator. The translation isn't perfect, but it's good enough. He does the same thing with the ones that come back from Pakistan."

Still nothing. I'm sure I didn't imagine it . . . she was furious.

"All right," Mr. Snyder says, wandering the rows. "Pull out *The Grapes of Wrath* and turn to chapter twenty-eight. Who can give me an example of conflict from this chapter?"

I zone out during the class discussion, focusing on Frannie. And when Mr. Snyder calls on her to read I lean in, as close as I can get without touching her, as she holds her book away from me, to her right, and reads aloud for the class. I close my eyes and lose myself in the silk of her voice.

When she finishes, Mr. Snyder paces the front of the room. "You have a few minutes before the bell. Work on your chapter twenty-eight outlines, focusing on conflict."

She turns to me, and I get caught in her eyes for a second. "So . . ." I finally manage.

"So?" she says.

"Are you going to tell me what's wrong?" Maybe I can get an admission.

"Nothing's wrong." She smiles sweetly. "We're supposed to be working on our outline."

"Hmm . . ." I write "Luc and Frannie" in big block letters in my composition book, then "Conflict" in bigger block letters under it.

She just stares at me for a really long time, and I stare right back, without blinking. When the bell rings we're still staring at each other. She turns away and slides her books into her bag.

"What's wrong, Frannie?" Still hoping.

"Nothing," she says and walks past me toward the door. Almost involuntarily, I grab her arm as she passes. I can tell from the look on her face and the sudden shot of grapefruit that my hand is burning her, but I don't let go.

She looks into my eyes and I search hers, feeling suddenly lost.

"What do you want from me?" she says, pulling her arm free.

Your soul. But more. "Just to know what's wrong. Did I do something?"

"No. I'm fine." And she is. If I don't stop this insanity, I'm going to blow any chance I have at any approach—direct or indirect. So I let her go. Concern flits briefly across her face, then she shakes it off and walks across the hall to her locker.

I hang back in the room, trying to collect myself and figure out what just happened. But then I look out into the hall, to where Frannie slams her locker closed with a crash, and I see Gabriel. That bastard's smooth, I'll give him that. He walks right up to her and leans against my locker, shooting me a glance as I stand in the doorway. I can't hear what he says, but I *do* hear her laugh. My gut does this flip-flop and electricity crackles under my skin. I step through the door into the hall, needing to do something but not really sure what that something is—maybe rip Gabriel's wings off and shove them up his . . .

"Guess who!" Out of nowhere, hands are covering my eyes, and the smell of some rank perfume assaults my nostrils.

Angelique.

Great.

I peel her hands off of my face.

"Walk me to class?" she pouts.

Gabriel's eyes shoot to me again, and his smile stretches into a grin as he places his hand on Frannie's back and steers her down the hall to physics. When she leans into him and wraps her arm around his waist, it's everything I can do not to send a blast of Hellfire down the hall into his back.

I push a little power at a pretty redhead a few lockers away who's been watching me. She strides over and shoves Angelique off my arm.

I look apologetically at Angelique. "Sorry, I promised to walk with . . ."

"Cassidy," the redhead finishes for me.

I spin and follow Gabriel and Frannie down the hall with Cassidy stumbling along beside me.

FRANNIE

I made a mistake with Luc, letting him worm under the edges of my defense. But now he's back on the outside where he belongs, with everyone but Grandpa, and all those crazy emotions are stuffed back into the black pit I keep them locked in. Mental judo.

I sit in physics lab with Gabe and focus on the classwork, pushing everything else out of my head. There's something very peaceful about being around him. Pretty soon I feel calm, like we're alone in the room. Maybe even alone in the world.

My mind wanders off into that world—just me and Gabe, left alone to repopulate the planet. Like Adam and Eve. My pulse flies thinking about exactly what that would entail.

"I'd kill to know what you're thinking right now."

I'm so lost in my fantasy that his voice, low in my ear, scares the snot out of me. I pull the knot out of my hair to hide my crimson face and concentrate on the circuit board, because there's no way in hell I'm telling him what I was thinking. "I was just . . . uh . . ."

"Whatever it was looked pretty intense." His chuckle really pisses me off.

"Okay, I'm thinking about becoming a nun." That's the ticket—swear off guys altogether. There's mental discipline for you.

A sarcastic smile paints his face. "Yeah. Right."

A tiny tendril of anger slips free from the black pit deep inside me, and I lash out. "What the hell does that mean? You don't think I'm good enough?" I rein it in and tighten the lid to the black pit.

He smiles. "For what it's worth, you'd be a great nun, but I'm pretty sure that's not your path."

I start to seethe . . . till I realize there was no sarcasm in his voice. I look up. He's smiling, and those eyes are killing me. I work to keep my breathing steady as he lifts his hand, and I find myself leaning toward him, anticipating his touch on my skin. But his hand barely brushes mine on the way to the circuit board, where he pulls loose the switch I just wired in backward and fixes it.

Oh God. What the hell is wrong with me?

I slip out of my seat at the bell and try to ignore my pounding heart when Gabe loops his arm around my shoulders and walks with me back to my locker. I swap my books and look to see if Luc's coming.

Gabe snorts a laugh.

"What?"

He props himself on Luc's locker and brushes a stray wisp of hair out of my eyes with his finger. "What does a guy have to do to get your attention?"

You're doing it.

A deep tingle starts in my belly as the scent of summer snow washes over me. I close my eyes and focus on my heartbeat, breathing deep and working it back down to single time. I'm afraid to look at Gabe, 'cause he always seems to know what I'm thinking, and what I'm imagining right now is way too embarrassing.

He smoothes a hand over my cheek, and for a second I think the fantasy will come true and he'll kiss me. But when I open my eyes, my breath catches. His eyes lock on mine like they're seeing my soul, and it feels more intimate than a kiss. *Much* more intimate. My legs go soft, and I pull my gaze away just in time to see Luc walk up out of the corner of my eye. Suddenly it feels like I've swallowed a bowling ball.

I turn up the hall without a good-bye and bolt for Mr. Sanghetti's room. But just before I reach it, Reefer corners me. He sidles up and leans into the wall with a hand just above my shoulder, trying to seem all casual. But he's not pulling it off. His jaw is clenched tight and his eyes are way too intense.

"Hey, you." It sounds more like an accusation than a greeting.

"Hey." I lean back into the wall and watch the mass of humanity in the hall behind him.

His eyes bore through me, searching, and his strained, fake smile is gone. "So, who's the guy?"

"Which one?" I say, just 'cause I can.

His big brown eyes widen and his face falls. And my heart clenches into a hard knot.

I'm such a jerk. It's so hard to walk this tightrope—especially when I have no idea what I'm feeling. My insides ache, partly from Luc's bowling ball, partly from Gabe's . . . whatever that was, but mostly from the look in Ryan's eyes. He really is a good guy. I don't want to hurt him. How long is it going to take him to figure out he doesn't love me?

"Joking, Reef. There's no 'guy'—at least not how I think you mean it."

His eyes shift to mine again, his eyebrows lifted. "You sure, 'cause I heard you were hanging with some new guy."

I blow out a sigh. "I'm not hanging with anyone."

He hesitates for a second and his eyes drop to the floor before meeting mine again. His gaze turns hopeful. "So . . . you wanna come to band practice—"

"I'm not coming back." I'm immediately sorry for the hard edge to my voice.

He raises a hand. "Let me finish," he says. "That girl, Delanie, called. She's singing with us tonight. Thought you might want to hear, that's all."

But he's lying. I know that's not "all," 'cause I've seen that look in his eyes before. *You don't love me.* I press harder into the wall to make more space between us. "Maybe."

He leans in and his dreads brush my cheek as he whispers. "'Maybe' is something I can live with."

I close my eyes and breath him in, remembering how easy things were with us . . . till he ruined it. My eyes snap open and my breath catches when I find his face just an inch from mine. I turn my head and look over his shoulder—and see Luc eyeing us from the door to Mr. Sanghetti's room, jaw clenched and eyes raging. He turns and skulks through the door.

I splay a hand on Reefer's chest and push him back gently. "It's probably better if I don't come," I say, realizing anything I do, other than act like a total bitch, is going to encourage him. *You don't love me.*

He looks at me with sad eyes as Trevor meanders by and smacks him on the back of the head with a textbook. He winces but holds my gaze a second longer before breaking free and jogging down the hall after Trevor.

I walk into history and slide into the seat next to Luc, letting myself feel exactly nothing, and ignore all his pointed glances as he and Mr. Sanghetti go at it. At the bell I bolt out of class a few steps ahead of Luc, but he catches me in the hall.

"Who was that?" he asks, trailing a step behind me.

"Who?"

"The guy." He steps up beside me and reaches for my elbow, but I yank it away.

"Reefer." I say, my voice neutral.

He stops walking, struggling unsuccessfully to stop the smile pulling at his lips. "Reefer," he repeats.

I take the opening and storm into the cafeteria, leaving Luc standing in the hall. I drop my book bag at our table and shuffle through the lunch line. When I get back to the table, I find the tall, gorgeous, redheaded Cassidy O'Connor shouldering Angelique out of the way to sit next to Luc. I slide into my seat between Luc and Gabe and clamp down on the lid to my black pit as I feel a wisp of jealousy start to slip out.

Gabe smiles at me as I poke at my salad. "So a nun, huh?"

"Yep." Out of the corner of my eye, I see Luc's head snap up.

"Interesting career choice." He shifts so our shoulders are touching and grins over my head at Luc. "What are you doing tonight? We could finish that lab write-up."

I try to pretend his shoulder touching mine isn't causing totally unrelated parts of me to tingle. "Oh . . . sure. I have judo after school, but you could come over for dinner and we can study in my room after," I say. Luc's shoulder bumps mine, and I turn to find him still staring at me. I ignore the head rush I feel when our eyes connect and turn back to Gabe. "So, around six?"

"That works."

I hear Cassidy's chair scrape back and glance over to see her make her way to the lunch line. I turn and smile at Luc, and my hand tightens around the knife on my tray as I mentally weld the lid on my emotions shut.

LUC

My new game plan basically involves the trifecta: lust, envy, and wrath. Which means I still need to make Frannie want me. And to envy those who have me. And hate them, and me too. It's a tricky balance to strike. Especially when Frannie isn't cooperating. I glance toward Cassidy in the lunch line. I'm finding it a little disconcerting that, other than Cassidy's ginger, I'm getting nothing. Frannie is keeping her emotions extraordinarily under wraps. No pepper, no anise, no garlic. Nothing.

Of course, I'm the one that seems to have jealousy issues. I almost blasted Gabriel just now at the lockers. And after her little show with that Reefer guy in the hall, it's occurring to me I may have overestimated my pull on her. Because when I saw her with him, how close she let him. . . . There was something she was giving off then—the faintest wisp of rose. Sadness.

I turn back to the table, hoping her expression will give her away, but her face is calm and flat.

What does a guy have to do to get a rise out of this girl?

Then I remember Frannie's reaction to Taylor that first day. Her envy. I pitch my voice low, conspiratorially—always better for grabbing the attention of those around you. "So, Taylor, how was your weekend?"

She raises an eyebrow suggestively. "Could have been better." The innuendo is unmistakable.

"I was thinking, if you're free, maybe you'd like to go to the movies tonight."

She launches a victorious glance at Frannie. "Absolutely."

Out of the corner of my eye, I'm sure I see Frannie's posture stiffen as she pretends to be engrossed in conversation with Gabriel. For a split second, just the faintest trace of licorice teases me.

Riley glances significantly at Frannie. With a hint of panic, she says, "We should all go. What do you think, Fee?"

Frannie turns toward the table. "Sorry, what?"

"Movies. Tonight. You in?"

"Oh. No, thanks." She reaches for Gabriel's hand on the table and twists her fingers into his. I seethe as I catch a hint of ginger. "We're slammed with physics homework, right, Gabe?"

Gabriel smirks at me. "Slammed."

Riley's mouth drops open and the silent "What the hell are you doing?" in her hard stare at Frannie is clear.

Frannie ignores her and starts up with Gabriel again.

I had wanted Taylor alone . . . but this could work too. "Mmm. Too bad," I say, nodding at Taylor and Riley. "I guess it's just us."

Taylor turns to glare at Riley.

If this doesn't get a rise out of Frannie, nothing will. The greater the intensity of the wrath the better, and what wrath can be more intense than for a best friend or two who have done you wrong? The indirect approach is going to work. I'll wear her down. If I play this right, as a parting gift, I might also score Riley's and Taylor's souls. Bonus.

But then my stomach lurches as the gravity of the game hits me. Gabriel and Frannie will be together tonight. Alone. I'm taking a huge gamble, betting that he doesn't have enough to tag her yet. And the chip I'm betting with is my own survival.

Cassidy's ginger almost chokes me as she drops her tray on the table and slides her chair close to mine. "Do you want to share my brownie, Luc?"

"No thanks," I say, fighting to keep my panic in check. This could be it. Everything is at stake. Because if Gabriel tags Frannie's soul for Heaven, I'm screwed. Reversing a tag is nearly impossible.

This has to work.

9

✞

The Devil's in the Details

FRANNIE

I figured Mom and Dad would like Gabe—the showing up with flowers for Mom thing was a nice touch—but this is embarrassing. Course, after Luc, they would love anyone I brought home.

Mom took one look at Gabe and decided on eating in the dining room with the fancy plates. "Can I get you anything else, Gabe? More meatloaf, potatoes . . ." she preens.

"No, thank you, Mrs. Cavanaugh. Everything is delicious."

"Well, thank you. We love to have Frannie's friends over."

Some of them, anyway.

I look at Kate and swear she's having some kind of seizure. And if Maggie doesn't drool down the front of her shirt, it's gonna be a miracle. Mary, thankfully, is chatting with Gabe like someone with more than one functioning brain cell. At least I have one normal sister. But Grace is the one that's stressing me. She's staring at Gabe in a very un-Grace-like way—completely awestruck. And instead of eating, I think she's praying or something. I'd say she was lusting on him, but in some really scary, deranged, religious way.

I look at Dad, my eyes pleading for him to do something. He's still in his shirt and tie. He believes dinner is a family event, like weddings and funerals, where everyone should be at their best. "Grace, honey. Are you going to eat?" he says, nudging her elbow.

She snaps out of her psycho trance. "Yes, Dad." But she doesn't eat. She just stares at Gabe some more.

How come I never realized my family is insane?

I'm mortified by the time we finish dinner. "Come on, Gabe. We've gotta finish that lab write-up." I grab his arm and drag him out of the kitchen.

He smiles at Mom. "Thank you for dinner, Mrs. Cavanaugh. It was lovely."

Lovely? Who says lovely?

For the rest of the night, while Gabe and I study in my room, I hear Kate and Maggie shuffling back and forth past my door, giggling.

Ugh!

"One second," I say to Gabe and slide out the door, closing it behind me.

"Surprised you have your clothes on," Kate says. "Thought we heard the bed bouncing." Maggie shoots her a lascivious

123

smile 'cause we all know the only one of us with a bouncing bed would be Kate. She and Chase have been sleeping together since their high school graduation last year.

"Guys, please. You're making total fools out of yourselves. Stop."

"Fine. We'll listen from Maggie and Grace's room," Kate says and turns on her heel.

I stand there for a second, realizing it's not just my emotions that went berserk when Luc and Gabe showed up. The whole universe is out of whack. Not only have all my sisters gone insane, but Kate *never* does what anyone asks her to.

I hesitate before pushing the door open, 'cause at the thought of Luc a desperate little knot forms in my stomach.

He's out with Taylor. Right now. And, if I know Taylor—which I do—they're not just talking.

You don't want her.

I feel guilty for thinking it, and I'm not really sure where that thought came from, but as soon as it's out there, I know it's true. I don't want him to want her.

Don't kiss her. Please don't kiss her.

I slip back through my door and press my iPod onto the speakers on my way back to Gabe. Kicking my shoes off, I spread out next to him on the floor and listen to The Fray's "You Found Me" rip God a new one for not being there when everything was falling apart.

Gabe looks up from his book and, for the first time, I see a scowl darken his face. "This song sucks."

I look him in the eye. "It's one of my favorites."

"Why?"

"'Cause it asks some valid questions."

"Such as?"

"Why God just sits around letting shit happen to good people."

Gabe's posture stiffens. "He's doing a little more than just sitting around."

"How would you know?"

"I just know. There are miracles every day."

"Right. Heaven, God . . . it's all a bunch of crap anyway. A bill of goods that organized religion made up to keep themselves in business."

His scowl deepens, "You might be right about organized religion, but you're wrong about God."

"I thought you were smarter than that. You can't possibly believe there's a God. Not with all the really nasty stuff happening out there."

He looks me hard in the eye. "There is a God, Frannie."

"Who just comes along and snatches children from their families," I spit without thinking.

He looks at me and I can't hold his gaze. My eyes drop and watch his hand slide across the top of his physics book. Our fingers weave together. "People die. That's just how it works."

Glancing up at my brother's picture on the dresser, I feel suddenly exhausted. Too tired to fight. A puff of air escapes my throat and a tear courses down my cheek. "You don't think I know that?"

I want to scream. I want to push him away. But I don't have the energy to do anything except lean my forehead on his shoulder and close my eyes.

LUC

This is perfect. Taylor's ginger is nearly choking me. I'd be hard-pressed to think of a single part of my body that she hasn't touched or brushed against. Everything is going just how I intended.

She and Riley eat their pizza, and I fish for information. So far, I've learned Frannie dates around but doesn't sleep around; that she drinks at parties but doesn't smoke; that, despite the whole religion thing, her parents are pretty laid back; and that I'm not her type. This last according to Taylor.

Truthfully, I'm not being a very good listener because I'm a little preoccupied. Unless Gabriel made the same first impression on Frannie's parents that I did—which is unlikely, slimy angel that he is—he's in her room right now. And, even though the bigger threat is that he'll tag her soul, all I can see is him doing to Frannie what I want to do to her. The irony is that if he did what I'm imagining and took her flesh, it would work to my advantage. Lust is lust, no matter who you're lusting with.

But it would also kill me.

There are myriad emotions whirling through me, some I recognize and others I don't. But the one that's winning out, trumping all the others, is jealousy.

I force a smile. "How long have you all known each other?" I ask.

Taylor grins. "Frannie moved in down the street from me the summer before fourth grade. When she crashed her bike into my dad's car, I knew from the word I heard come out of her mouth..." she traces the letters S-H-I-T in pizza grease on the faux marble tabletop, "...that she and I were gonna be best friends. Even though she went to Catholic school up till tenth grade, we've always hung out. Then Riley," she kicks Riley under the table, "moved in during junior high."

"Yeah. And I had real friends before who didn't get me in trouble all the time," Riley sneers.

Taylor cracks a smile. "Hey, no one's ever twisted your arm. You're responsible for your own actions."

"Yeah, right." She looks at me. "Why is it just occurring to me now that I need better friends?"

I shrug. "I'd say you could hang out with me, but I can't guarantee any less trouble."

Taylor looks at me and then glowers at Riley. "Choices, Ry. We all have choices," she says, clearly warning her friend off.

I slide my foot over and press the side of it into Taylor's. "Yes, we do," I say, my words full of innuendo.

A lascivious smile barely curls the corner of her lips, and I'm overwhelmed by her ginger.

Riley glares at Taylor. "So we should all probably be heading home soon..." Riley has vehemently defended Frannie all night, dragging her into the conversation frequently as if to re-mind me of *my* choices. I know *exactly* what my choices are, and right now my choice is to use Taylor to drive Frannie over the edge. But first I have to lose the chaperone.

"No problem. I'll drop you guys back home." But as I say it, I press my foot harder into Taylor's.

She gets my message and plays along. Standing, she slings her purse over her shoulder and feigns a yawn. "Let's go. I'm beat." But that lascivious smile never leaves her lips.

✤

After I drop Riley off, Taylor eases her hand off the armrest between us and onto my thigh, then pulls back abruptly. "Whoa! I knew you were hot, but Jesus!" she says, and I wonder why she thinks *He* has anything to do with it. She leans back onto the armrest. "So there's a place up near this old quarry . . . it's pretty quiet. We could go up there if you want." She eases her hand back onto my leg.

I unwrap a hand from the steering wheel and lay my arm across the back of her seat. This is what I want—need, really. The surest way I can think of to send Frannie into a rage would be to mess around with Taylor. I lean toward her, feeding off her ginger—letting it take control of me. She shifts in her seat, settling into my side, and I pull her to me. She turns her face into my neck and I feel her hot breath as she nips at my earlobe. Her hand explores my chest and starts to move lower.

I suddenly feel sick.

I can't make myself do it. My brimstone heart feels like it weighs a ton in my chest, dragging me down. *What a sorry excuse for a demon I am.* Taylor's serving herself up on a silver platter, and I can't follow through.

I can't have Taylor as an enemy, though, so I shift away, putting my hand back on the steering wheel, and purr with the smallest power push, "As appealing as that sounds, I have some things I need to handle tonight." Like a cocky angel moving in on my territory. "Maybe some other time?"

Her eyes cloud over a little. "Okay, yeah . . . sure."

We pass Frannie's on the way to Taylor's house, and that bastard's shiny white Dodge Charger is still in her driveway. I look at the clock. Eleven. How long could a physics lab write-up possibly take?

I pull into Taylor's driveway. "Thanks, Taylor. This was fun."

She's recovered, though she still seems a little shaky. "It could have been much *more* fun. You don't know what you're missing," she says, a suggestive pout on her red lips.

"Hmm . . . see you tomorrow." I lean back against my door, out of temptation's reach, and smile as she opens the door and steps out.

I watch her go into the house then drive up the street to Frannie's, where I pull over.

As bad of an idea as I know it is, I can't help myself. I slide out of the car and phase into the oak tree next to the driveway, just outside her window. I don't make a sound as I perch on a branch near the house and listen. It's quiet in her room except for music. This is bad.

The urge to phase in there—just pop into her room and interrupt whatever's going on—is overwhelming. And after what feels like a small eternity I can't stand it anymore. I close my eyes and focus. Gabriel will know I'm there, but, if I'm careful, Frannie won't.

Then I do it. I phase into her room.

But as I'm shifting through planes, I feel like the wind is knocked out of me, like a bird smashing into a window, and suddenly I'm back on the tree limb. A little stunned, I try again. Same thing.

What the Hell?

I remember Frannie's father—how he was immune to my magic. It appears that Mr. Cavanaugh is better connected upstairs than the pope. I can visit the papal palace whenever I like, no problem. Frannie's house, on the other hand, is apparently off-limits.

FRANNIE

Gabe is so close. He smells like snow and summer and it tickles my nose. His touch on my hand is cool and soft. It's how I imagine a cloud would feel. I close my eyes as he leans closer and nestles his face into my neck. His cool breath in my ear makes me shudder as he says, "Everything happens for a reason."

I pull my head off him and look up into his eyes, hating myself for crying. "I don't believe you."

He smooths a tear away with his fingertips and gazes down into my eyes. He wraps his hand around the back of my neck, cradling my head, and brings me to his shoulder, burying his face in my hair. I let him hold me for a long time, feeding off his energy. I've never felt anything like it, but it makes me warm all over. If you asked me right now, I'd have to say I believe in love, 'cause that's what this feels like: pure love.

Could I love him? Is it possible?

Finally, I pull myself out of his shirt and scrub the tears and snot off my face with my sleeve. When I look up into his eyes, they're unsure. He starts to lean toward me, and I tip my face up to meet his, but then his eyes widen and he pulls away abruptly.

"I should probably go," he says with a shake in his voice.

My heart pounding, I shake my head a little and try to focus, but I can't stop the aching deep inside. My emotions are totally out of control 'cause, at this moment, I want nothing more than to forget everything and lose myself in him. I would give him anything.

✝

On his way out, my parents gush all over him. Mom is beaming, hearing wedding bells, no doubt. "It was wonderful to have you over, Gabe. I hope you won't be a stranger."

"No chance of that, Mrs. Cavanaugh," he says. His eyes flit to mine, deep and tender.

"Well, good," Dad says. "So we'll see you soon?"

Gabe smiles, blinding me with the glare. "Absolutely," he says as he backs out the door onto the porch.

We meander down my front steps to his car. "So, I guess I'll see you tomorrow. Thanks for . . . everything."

He smiles softly. "Anytime." He links his fingers in mine, and I feel my heart skip a little at his touch.

When we get to his car, he glances back at the house, at my window, and cracks an amused smile. My heart takes off again when he wraps me in a hug and kisses the top of my head. The curve of his body, hard against mine, is almost more than I can handle. My whole body's buzzing and my breathing is a little ragged as I run my hands over his chest then snake them around his waist and pull him closer. I feel his body tense, but he doesn't pull back. All of a sudden I'm wishing we were back upstairs in my room.

I press my face into him, and he holds me for a really long time then kisses the top of my head again. "Lock up after I leave," he says into my hair. "I'll see you tomorrow."

He lets me go and an unexpected wave of despair washes over me, making me want to reach out for him again. But I don't. "Yeah, okay."

He climbs into his car and the engine hums to life. "I'm serious, Frannie. Lock up."

"Whatever." I walk up my front steps and wave over my shoulder. But each step is harder than the last, as if Gabe is the sun and I'm trying to escape his orbit. I fight the urge to run after him as he backs out of the driveway. I keep moving, without looking back, and just as I open the door, I hear rustling in the tree near the driveway. I look up. Nothing. Maybe just a cat.

I glance back at the driveway, and for a split second I'm sure I see a boy my age with blue eyes and sandy-blond curls standing there.

Matt?

I gasp and do a double take, but he's gone . . . if he was ever really there. I tuck quickly inside, my heart hammering in my chest, and lock the door behind me. I run to my room and lock that door too. Once I catch my breath I walk to the window, lift the blind, and peer cautiously out at the driveway. No one there.

I back away toward the bed and reach under the mattress. When I pull Matt's journal out, I notice my hand is trembling.

Get it together.

I feel the familiar tightening in my throat as I write.

So, Matt. I'm pretty sure I'm going crazy because I thought I saw you in the driveway just now. It had to be my imagination, I know. I'm not that far gone. But you looked just how I picture you in my head . . . how I think you'd look now.

I wish I could really talk to you. I have so many questions I need answers to. Gabe insists God is real. Part of me really wants to believe him. If you could just tell me where you are. . . . Is there a Heaven? God? I'm so confused.

Two tears, big and round, hit the paper like raindrops. I drop my pen and bury my face in my hands. I'm unraveling from the inside, going crazy little by little. I'm seeing things that aren't there. And the guilt sits like a stone in the pit of my stomach.

'Cause it should have been me.

I tuck Matt's journal under my mattress and curl up on my bed, staring at the wall and trying to make sense of everything— of *anything*. But the only thing that becomes sharper in my mind is my raging headache, so I put on some music and think of nothing.

10

✦

My Own Personal Hell

FRANNIE

The sight of Gabe, leaning against the building with his hands in his pockets, stops my heart. *God, he's amazing.*

Dad moves slowly with the line of cars and drops me at the curb in front of the school. Gabe pushes away from the wall and saunters over as I climb out of the car.

Dad looks past me at Gabe, beaming. "Good to see you."

Gabe bends down and peers into the car, hands still in pockets. "You too, sir. Thanks again for dinner last night."

"Our pleasure." Dad waves and pulls away, still smiling, and Gabe wraps me in his arms.

"How are you?"

"All right." Other than not being able to breathe, or eat, or think.

He links his fingers in mine and we walk in silence into the building, where he stands, watching me root through my locker. When I glance up at him he smiles and knocks all the air out of me. He's so beautiful. Like my own personal angel.

And I'm such a shit.

"You good?" he says, gesturing to the book in my hand.

No. "Yeah."

He places a hand on my back to walk me across the hall, but instead, I turn and bury myself in his chest, pressing him back into the lockers. This is what I want. *Right?* To hell with Luc. But when I look up into Gabe's eyes, what I see there terrifies me. He's so open and trusting—and I don't deserve anyone's trust.

I ignore Angelique's smirk as Gabe guides me across the hall to English. When he leaves I drop my head onto my desk, feeling the cold, hard surface press into my skin, grounding me.

Gabe and Luc. They couldn't be more different. So how can I want them both? But I do, in completely different ways. And, after last night, Gabe scares me more than Luc. I don't believe in love, but that's what I felt. I felt it coming from him, and I felt it in me.

I pull my head off the desk and examine my shaking hands—and jump when Luc is there, sitting at his desk next to me. Where Gabe is peace and love, Luc is everything else: lust, passion, with this seductive energy that makes me want him in all the wrong ways. And I'm obviously not the only one he has that effect on. I look up to see Angelique hovering in the door, trying and failing to look all casual, like she's just hanging out.

A sly smile slides across his face as he leans toward me onto his elbows and, for a second, rage burns through me, making me want to wipe that smile off his face with my fist. He stares into my eyes. "Sorry. Didn't mean to frighten you."

But you *do* frighten me. Both of you. You scare the hell out of me.

"Just tired," I say, and it's true. I couldn't sleep last night, 'cause every time I closed my eyes it was either Gabe or Luc on the back of my eyelids. And I didn't want to see where those dreams would go. I rub my eyes so he won't look into them anymore.

I spend the rest of English trying to ignore the building static electricity between us as we work on our outline. But I'm having a really hard time focusing. When the bell rings, Luc and I aren't done. And it's due tomorrow.

Luc leans back and laces his hands behind his head. "Do you want to get together after school or take the zero?"

"What do you think?" I say. My tone betrays my frustration. I slide stiffly out of my chair and make my way to the door.

"Okay, your house or mine?" he says, following me.

So the thing is, Mom and Dad love Gabe. They couldn't stop talking about him this morning. They think he, like, walks on water. Luc, on the other hand, not so much. "Yours, I guess."

"Great," he says as we step out into the hall. He sounds pleased with himself. And makes me suddenly furious.

The lid explodes off my emotional black pit, and I feel my mouth start to move without fully connecting to my brain. I struggle to keep up as words come spilling out.

"Is there anyone in this school you're not dating? Other than me, I mean?" I cringe as I realize what I just said. And apparently I said it loud, 'cause everyone in a ten-foot radius turns to look at us.

"Wow . . . well, I really wasn't aware I was dating anyone at the moment."

Liar. My blood pressure shoots up fifty points and, now that the lid is off the pit, I'm helpless to contain my emotions. "Really? Maybe you should tell that to Angelique, or Cassidy, or Taylor, or Riley."

He leans into the doorjamb, all relaxed, and makes me even madder. "To the best of my knowledge, I haven't been on a date with any of them. I went to the movies and for pizza with Riley and Taylor. As I recall, you were invited. The fact that you didn't join us was unfortunate. And I've never been anywhere with Cassidy or Angelique. As a matter of fact, the only date I've been on would be with you."

"We haven't been on a date," I spit. But then I cringe again, remembering coffee after Gallaghers' party. I was the one who called that a "hot date."

He answers as I work to pull myself together. "Oh, my mistake, then. I thought our coffee date counted."

I look down at the chipping black nail polish on my big toenail and pry up a loose piece of gray linoleum with my flip-flop. I feel my rage slip away as quickly as it came, chagrin taking its place. "So, no beach house?"

His voice lowers to nearly a whisper, but I still hear him clearly over the din of the crowded hall. "No beach house."

I look into his eyes and suddenly feel a little dizzy. My thoughts go cloudy, and I have the urge to dive right into those deep, black pools. I want to know what he's thinking. I want to know everything about him. I realize I'm not breathing and look away, drawing a jagged breath.

"So, are we good?" he asks, his voice soft—almost tender.

I just nod, not really sure what just happened, but not trusting myself to open my mouth again.

I spend the rest the morning feeling like a total dork, and I can't even look at Luc. But when we walk into lunch, and I see the expression on Taylor's face—somewhere between embarrassed and excited—my heart sinks. I should have known something happened between her and Luc last night, 'cause she avoided me all morning. As we slide into our regular seats, I look at Riley, who shrugs. Luc and Gabe are glaring at each other. Nothing new there. So, it's just Taylor that's got something going on.

"Let's get lunch," I say, kicking her under the table.

She looks from me to Luc and back and says, "Okay." But she doesn't look like she has much of an appetite. Her skin is pale with a sort of greenish tinge, clashing with her pink hair.

I drag her by the arm up to the lunch line, with Riley following on her other side, and I notice Riley steal a blushing glance at Trevor, sitting with his crew at a table near the vending machines. Jackson Harris does the eyebrow wiggle at me and crosses his arms over his chest, flexing his biceps in some Neanderthal mating gesture. I roll my eyes. Taylor's too distracted to notice any of it.

"So, what the hell is going on, Tay?"

"I don't know. It's all a little fuzzy."

"What's fuzzy?" I say louder, glancing back to watch the estrogen parade making its way past Luc and Gabe at our table.

"I think I made a move on Luc, but I don't really remember for sure."

"How can you not remember if you made a move?"

"Well, I remember the move . . . I think I'm just blocking the whole thing out." In a very un-Taylor-like gesture, she tips her head down, placing her index finger and thumb on her forehead and hiding her face behind her hand. "It was too embarrassing."

"So . . . when you made this move . . . did he move back?"

She peeks between her fingers and glares at me when I try to hand her a tray. "Like I said, it's a little fuzzy, but I'm pretty sure I crashed and burned."

"Oh," I say, trying to sound sympathetic. I look back at Luc and feel a flutter in my chest when I find him staring at me. I look away and grab a bruised apple from the basket near the register. "Well, I told you guys he's only messing with us. You're lucky he shot you down. There was an angel sitting on your shoulder."

She drops her hand and scowls at me. "I don't want any goddamn angels. And why do you care anyway? You had Gabe all to yourself last night. I should be grilling you."

"Nothing happened with Gabe. Nothing's gonna happen with Gabe," I say, seriously pissed that I'm letting them get to me. But it's a lie. Something happened—to me, anyway—and I have to figure out how to make it stop.

We head back to the table, and I throw down my tray with the resounding crash of determination and finality. "We've decided we want our table back. Girls only. You'll both have to find another spot."

Luc's expression is amused; Gabe's a little surprised.

And Taylor's is livid.

139

She glowers at me. "Who made you dominatrix of the lunch table?"

I glare back. "Was I the only one having that conversation a minute ago?"

"If you don't want to sit with them, why don't *you* move?"

"Fine," I spit.

"Fine."

I abandon my lunch tray and storm away from the table I've sat at with my two best friends every school day for two and a half years. Angelique Preston, two tables away, smirks at me as I flounder momentarily before deciding there are no good options and storming out of the cafeteria altogether. I glance through the porthole in the door in time to see Riley start to follow me. But Taylor slides into my seat, between Luc and Gabe and grabs Riley's arm. Riley hesitates and then sits.

And I'm pretty sure I'm going to kill Taylor.

I can't believe she's letting *guys*, no matter how hot, do this to us. I feel sick to my stomach as I scrub an angry tear from my face and head out to the courtyard. I sit on the grass in the cool spring sunshine with my back against the building and close my eyes.

Breathe.

"Hey."

I jump at Reefer's voice. I open my eyes to find him sitting next to me, staring at me with his muddy-brown eyes. The rest of the band is hanging in the alcove near the gym.

"You okay?" he asks.

"Yeah."

He doesn't believe me, but even though I can see the question in his soft, brown eyes, he doesn't push. I know it's selfish, but I need something easy and familiar right now. I lean into him and he loops his arm over my shoulder. We just sit here for a while as he talks about his brother and his dog and how he learned this new guitar riff.

And it occurs to me he hasn't said anything about us. And his hand is staying put on my shoulder. And it's me pressing into him, instead of the other way around.

I pull myself out of him and look up into his face. Something's different.

"So, how are things with the band?" I ask.

He draws a deep breath. "Good. Really good. Delanie's really great. Thanks for hooking us up."

The tone in his voice catches me by surprise, and now it's my turn to question him with my eyes.

He smiles and drops his gaze to his hands.

So, Ryan and Delanie are making their own music.

"That's great, Reef. I'm really glad it worked out." And that's not a lie. I *am* glad Ryan's moved on. But it doesn't stop the pang of sadness—and, if I'm honest, maybe regret—I feel.

He squeezes my shoulder and stands. "So, you're sure you're okay?"

I smile up at him. "I'm good. Thanks."

He holds my eyes for a moment longer then turns to head across the courtyard.

I listen to Ryan and the band jam for a few minutes then pull my latest batch of letters from Pakistan out of my bag and thumb through them. When I look up, Luc is standing there.

"Mind some company?"

I look down at the letters. "Busy."

I'm hoping he'll go away, but instead he slides down the brick wall and sits next to me. "What are those?"

"Letters," I say, finding the one from my pen pal, Ghalib, and placing it on top.

But, as I look it over, eager to get it translated, it feels like a bolt of lightning hits my brain and I'm suddenly sick.

Oh, God!

I know this feeling. It always means something bad. Suddenly, I'm glad I didn't eat any lunch, 'cause my stomach lurches. I roll onto my hands and knees, gagging.

"Frannie!" Luc stoops next to me. "Are you okay?"

I push the vision of Ghalib, lying bloody in a dirt road, out of my head and look at the letter again. Ghalib is dead. I feel like I'm suffocating. "No." I say, my voice thin.

"What is it? What's wrong? Are you sick?"

How can I explain this to him without sounding insane? But when I look at Luc, something whispers up from my subconscious, telling me he'd get it. He's the only one who won't think I've lost it. "I think Ghalib . . ." But I can't bring myself to say it. "Nothing. I'll be okay," I say, the ache in my chest threatening to dissolve into tears.

He picks up the letter and looks it over. His brow creases. "He's fine, Frannie. He's going to Afghanistan to visit relatives and look for a job. Nothing's wrong."

I don't have the energy to question how he read it without a translation. "He's dead."

"How do you know?"

"I saw him."

He looks shocked for just a moment, and I realize I was wrong about him understanding. He thinks I'm nuts. He reaches down and loops his arm around my waist. "Let me take you to the nurse."

"No!" I say, pulling away. "Just give me a minute." I lie back on the grass, still feeling sick. The vision of Ghalib—and others—won't leave. Matt was the first, but there have been so many others since then. I'm always the first person to know when a family friend or an old teacher—anyone I've ever known—is gone. They're the faces that follow the lightning in my head. Always dead.

After a few moments, I make myself get up off the ground, and Luc walks with me to Mr. Snyder's room, where I write a letter to Ghalib. If I knew how to reach him by phone I would, but I already know it's no use. The date on his letter was a week ago. Mr. Snyder looks concerned, but he promises to translate it and send it off tonight.

For the rest of the school day, Luc doesn't leave my side. Normally I would have a problem with the whole protective thing, but having him around seems to be helping, and by the time we climb into his car after school, I'm starting to feel a little better.

11

✢

The Devil Made Me Do It

LUC

I feel electric. Totally wired. I wanted to know why Hell wanted Frannie so much, and now I do. *Sight.*

She climbs into my car, leans on the door, and closes her eyes. I leave her alone for most of the ride, but finally I can't take it anymore. I have to know.

"Frannie?"

"Yeah?"

"What happened in the courtyard earlier—what you saw . . . does that happen a lot?"

Her expression turns hostile. "I'm not crazy," she growls.

"I didn't say you were. I'm just worried." And curious.

She looks out the window. "Not a lot, but some."

"All your life?"

"Just since my . . . since I was seven."

"What do you see? Things that are going to happen?"

She turns to look at me and a tear slips from her wary eye. "Dead people. I see them dead right before they die." Her eyes drop to her hands. "But I've never been able to stop it."

I can see how this would be useful to the Underworld. If we knew they were on their way out . . . if we could tag them before they went to Limbo . . . that might improve our numbers.

I try to keep the excitement out of my expression and my voice. "That's rough. Are you going to be okay?"

"Yeah, I guess," she says as we reach my apartment complex.

Her eyes dart warily around as we pull in to my parking lot. Not what she was expecting, I'm sure. "This is where you live?"

"Yep. Is there a problem?" I say, fighting the chuckle.

"No," she snaps.

I roll into a parking spot near the door of my building, between a rusted blue Impala and a dented black Ford pickup, and I watch out of the corner of my eye as she looks it over.

The gray day accentuates the gray atmosphere surrounding this side of town. The four two-story cement buildings were once white, but now they're a sooty color from decades of dirt, smog, and rust from the gutters. Most of the windows are intact, but here and there cardboard and duct tape substitute for dirty glass. A plastic supermarket bag blows across the barren ground in the subtle spring breeze and catches in the branches of an anemic shrub near the door of my building.

She looks at me and puts up a brave front as she pushes open her door and steps out. "Let's go."

"Your wish, my command," I say as I move toward the building. I hold the door open for her and she tentatively steps through. She follows me up the filthy stairs to the second floor and waits in the poorly lit hall while I dig out my key and slide it into the lock.

"Are your parents at work?" she asks as I step through the door and turn on a light.

"Probably."

She follows me through. "When will they get home?" Do I detect a shake in her voice?

"No clue."

"Well, when do they *usually* get home?"

"No clue," I say again. She just stares at me. "I never knew my parents." No lie. Demons aren't big on the whole nurturing concept.

"Oh. Sorry." Her eyes shift to the gray floor where cheerful yellow linoleum daisies are straining to peek through years of grime. "So, who do you live with, then?"

"No one."

Her eyes snap back to mine. "You live here by yourself?" A shot of grapefruit permeates the air—Frannie's fear. Mmm . . .

"Yep."

Her eyes shoot back to the door, probably planning her escape.

"If you'd rather go to your house, that's fine," I say in my most reassuring voice.

"Um . . ." She's clearly not ready to walk those coals again. "This is fine."

I go to the fridge and open it. "Great. You want a beer?" I

close the door to the empty fridge as two cold beers materialize in my hand.

"Maybe we should get some work done first."

I open both beers and hand one to her. "I work better when I can relax," I say, drawing a long swallow. She looks at the beer in her hand and takes a tentative sip, then looks around.

I'm a demon, not a pig, so I keep the place relatively neat. The kitchen is clean—no dirty dishes or rotting food—mostly because I don't have to eat. But for that same reason, there's no table. Or chairs. The short row of cabinets is painted black, and the walls that were once white are now more gray, with the paint peeling off and plaster showing through in places.

The studio is small and, other than the kitchen in the back left corner and the bathroom next to it—which is also clean because I don't have to do *that* either—there's a king-sized bed with black sheets, a black quilt, and lots of black pillows that takes up most of the room. It has a large, thick, black rug under it.

"That's a big bed," she says staring at the large black mass in the middle of the room. Then her eyes snap to mine and she turns crimson.

"Mmm," I agree, "and comfortable too."

Her eyes drop to the floor then flit back to me before scanning the rest of the room, careful to avoid the bed. She makes a circuit of the studio, stopping to look at the three Doré prints near the kitchen, depicting different stages of Dante's *Inferno*, and a print of William Blake's *The Temptation of Eve*—the high point of King Lucifer's career.

She makes her way past the bathroom, and I don't miss her

stealth glace at me in the full-length mirror on the back of the door. She continues toward the floor-to-ceiling bookshelves across from the bed, pausing to pick up the very old and well-worn volume I left open on the floor: Dante's *Purgatorio*. I'm partial to Dante, having been his muse. She thumbs through it and her eyebrows shoot up. "This is in Spanish."

"Italian," I correct.

"You speak Italian," she says, unconvinced.

"Sì."

"Say something."

"Sii la mia schiava d'amore," I purr.

Her expression is guarded. "What did you say?"

An amused smile pulls at my lips. "*I'll* never tell." Somehow I don't think she'd agree to be my love slave anyway.

She stares at me with wide eyes for a moment, then lays Dante back on the floor. She pulls another volume—Proust—from the shelf and cracks it open. "French?" she says with fiery incredulity.

"Oui."

She scowls. "You're kidding. . . . How many languages do you speak?"

All of them. "A few."

She turns away from me, replacing Proust on the shelf, and meanders past my window, which overlooks the parking lot, glancing out on her way by. When she turns back to the room and realizes how close she is to the bed she pulls up short. She leans against the wall between the stereo cabinet with tower speakers and the long floor-to-ceiling rack with just about every

CD ever made, but her eyes scan the wall behind my wrought-iron headboard. It's covered with a dark floor-to-ceiling mural of home—the lesser inhabited region of the Abyss farthest from the Gates, where the Lake of Fire meets the high stone Walls of Hell.

Finally, the draw of the mural outweighs her fear of the bed, and she walks over and picks a paintbrush up off the stack of painting supplies in the corner. "Who's painting your wall?"

"That would be me."

She spins to look at me. "No way."

I can't help but smile as she turns back to the mural and runs her finger along the contour of a blue flame emanating from the red molten surface of the Lake. "This is really dark . . . scary, but cool. What is it?"

"Hell."

She turns away from the wall and stands there facing me for several heartbeats. "So, where do you want to work?" she finally asks, looking around.

I shoot a glance at the bed and smile.

She shivers, even though it's far from cold in here, and takes a long draught off her beer. She opens her book bag, pulls her composition book out, and sits on the rug next to the bed, taking another sip.

I walk to the stereo, pop in Linkin Park, and turn it up just loud enough to feel the bass in my bones.

"Where's your TV?" she asks.

I sit on the rug next to her. "Don't have one."

"Then how do you watch so much History Channel?"

I really need to be more careful. "I had one. It broke."

"Oh," she says, pulling *The Grapes of Wrath* from her book bag. "So, what do you think Tom should do?"

"Go straight to jail," and then to the Inferno afterward, "do not pass Go, do not collect two hundred dollars."

She nervously drains her beer. I glide up off of the floor and to the fridge, returning in a second with two more. As I pop the top and hand one to her, I "accidentally" brush my fingers along the inside of her wrist. Her eyes widen for an instant and her breath catches. A reaction to the heat of my touch? Or is it more? Ginger . . . mmm.

Yes, this is much better—the direct approach. Because my last game plan—the indirect approach—sucked. I had to fix it, so I pushed just a little power at her after English. And here she is. With me.

Alone.

A rush of hot electricity plays under my skin as I imagine the possibilities.

She looks at me and takes another hit off her beer. "So, why are you so hard on Tom? What did he ever do to you?"

I laugh. If he wasn't fictional we'd probably be pals. "Well, let's see . . . to me, nothing. But to others, stole from them and murdered them. Nothing major, I guess."

She looks at me, all incredulity. "Did you actually read the book? 'Cause he had good reasons for doing what he did." Mmm, how I love that fire.

"Oh, so there are good reasons for murder . . . I didn't know. So sorry."

"Sometimes. Even our judicial system lets people off if there were extenuating circumstances."

"Hmm, yes, our infallible judicial system."

"And the church too. They forgive people who have killed if they had no choice."

"Okay, don't get me started on the church."

"You're the most cynical person I've ever met."

"Just a realist."

"Maybe that was the deal with my parents. Did you pull this shit on them?"

Her words start to slur a little as she gets more and more agitated, and I fight the smile that's threatening to sprout on my lips. "I barely said hello to them."

"'Cause my parents like everyone—even Taylor. I've never seen them act like that before."

Because you've never brought home a demon before. "Don't know what to tell you. People just react to me that way sometimes." I watch her blush. Her reaction to me seems to be quite the opposite, which works for me. And the beer seems to be loosening her up a little.

We sit for a long while, her staring at me and me staring right back. Finally I say, "Your parents like Taylor, huh?"

Her eyelids look heavy. "She cracks them up. They love her pink hair."

I let myself smile now. "So maybe that's my problem. I need pink hair."

She laughs—a deep belly laugh—and it stirs something in me, makes me feel . . . alive. She leans back against the bed, her laugh becoming more of a giggle, and closes her eyes. Drunk on two beers—a lightweight.

"Mmm ... yeah. Except it'd clash with your red eyes," she says, drifting off.

My red eyes? She *is* observant. But the truth is I can't take my eyes off her. Her breathing becomes slower and deeper as she drifts into sleep, and I'm still staring. I feel it again—lust, who is becoming a familiar old friend. But there's more, something else deeper, just on the edge of the lust, that I don't quite recognize.

I could take her now if I wanted to. And part of me is screaming for that—to take her flesh. But another part of me, connected to that foreign feeling, is also screaming. It's screaming for her soul. I could take *that* right now too. And if I did, we would be together—in every way—for all of eternity.

But she hasn't even been tagged yet. She has to earn her place in Hell. And besides, I have no justification for bringing her soul back with me now—except I want her. I know He wants her too, eventually, but my king has plans for her in the meantime.

It couldn't hurt to have a little taste, though, could it? She won't remember it, and she would never even need to know. I sit for several minutes, staring at her and arguing with myself. But, in the end, unhealthy curiosity wins out and I give in. I lean against the bed next to her and close my eyes, collecting myself. I gather my essence and feel it leave my body and enter Frannie through her slightly parted lips.

The first thing that hits me is how comfortable it is. Usually possession feels tight and claustrophobic, but this ... this feels pleasant. No, not pleasant ... *good*. I work my way toward her mind—not to control it, just to take a peek. I want to know Frannie's hopes, fears, deepest desires. But I pull back at the last second because it doesn't feel right. It feels like an invasion of her privacy.

I chuckle to myself. *Like I'm not already doing that.* Isn't possession the ultimate invasion of privacy?

Instead, I seek out her essence—her soul. And when I find it, it takes my breath away. I've never experienced anything close to its beauty: shimmering opalescent white shot through with silver and rich greens and blues, like mother of pearl. So unlike the seedy, dark souls Collections drag back to the Abyss. And it's spicy-sweet, clove and currant on my tongue and in my nose. But there's more . . . a sense of profound hope and . . . something else.

My slick, black obsidian essence swirls and twines with hers, and I'm embarrassed by the thick, oily feel of it compared to the silk of hers. But as we dance, my brimstone heart soars.

I let myself be with her and it feels like I'm welcome here . . . like she wants me. I lose myself in her, exploring as we dance. When she pulls a shuddering breath and moans—in pleasure?— I realize that maybe this is one place we can *truly* be together. I let my essence get closer and blend it with hers. And in that second, as her shimmering white blends with my glossy black, what I feel is . . . *everything.* I feel an overwhelming rush of sensations with no name, at least in the demonic realm. Things I can't identify or describe. I can't even begin to explain the sensation, except that it's something I've never felt before and it's something *real.*

She moans again and whispers, "Luc . . ." It's a sound like music, but also a wake-up call. I need to get out of here before

I get myself into trouble. But it's nearly impossible to make myself leave. Almost against my will, I compel my essence to seep back out between her lips, savoring their caress as I move between them. As I reenter my own human shell, it suddenly feels empty and cold, despite the demonic heat I bring back with me.

I breathe deep, letting the air fill me, pushing out the building turmoil, and fight the overwhelming urge to jump back into her body.

Satan save me . . . what was that?

I pull myself to my feet, force my eyes away from her and walk to the window, where a small black spider is furiously building a web across the upper corner. I watch for a while as she moves quickly and smoothly around the circle of her lair, efficiently and meticulously constructing the perfect trap. Flawless.

I wonder how mine got so big and out of control.

I have no idea what I'm doing. No game plan. The indirect approach doesn't work when all I can do is obsess about being with her, touching her. But I don't have the discipline to handle the direct approach—clearly. I'm out of approaches.

I sit on the floor next to Frannie and just stare for a long minute. Then I find myself leaning toward her. And I just barely brush my lips across hers.

FRANNIE

In my dream, Luc and I are dancing under the stars. We're so close I can feel him everywhere, almost like he's right inside me. And then we're doing more than dancing, and his touch feels like heaven. I hear myself moan as I climb right into him.

Something very soft but very hot brushes across my lips and, as my eyes snap open, I see him just backing off. In some sort of reflexive reaction—or maybe it's the beer—my hand darts up, wraps in the silky black hair on the back of his head, and pulls his face back to mine. He pulls away just the tiniest bit and I almost let go, but then his lips are on mine again, soft and oh-so-hot.

He has to be about a thousand degrees, and it feels like he's burning my hand and my mouth. But at the same time, it feels so good. I lose myself in his touch, and I swear my head and my heart are both about to explode. No other kiss has ever felt like this. It's electric in its intensity, making every nerve ending buzz. His lips part, and I taste his cinnamon, breathe it in, and it feels like it fills me, like part of him is seeping right into my body, making me whole. But I don't close my eyes, and neither does he. As I watch, his eyes soften and the red glow of the fire that's always present behind the black of his irises flares for a second.

When I finally let him go, he pulls back and looks sorta dazed and confused. Which is pretty much how I feel. He stares at me for a long time, and I start to think I really screwed up. But then concern touches his expression, and he asks, "Are you okay, Frannie?" like his kiss could hurt me somehow.

Am I okay? I'm not sure. 'Cause I feel light-headed, and some sensation I can't even put a name to is rolling through me in waves, making me feel a little sick. I'm drained but energized all at the same time. My heart feels like a frog in my chest, and I start to worry that it might never be the same. I stare at him, trying to catch my breath. But what I see in those black pools does nothing to help my breathing. "Uh-huh. What about you?"

The concern doesn't leave his eyes. "Great," he says, but he doesn't sound "great."

I remember Taylor and feel sicker. "So . . . what happened with you and Taylor last night?"

He looks a little surprised. "Nothing. I thought she would have told you that."

"She was a little fuzzy on the details."

He thinks about that for a long second. "Really. Interesting," he says. Then he looks at me for another long second and his jaw clenches. His eyes shift away from mine, and he examines his hands as he asks, "What about you and Gabriel?"

"Nothing." The giddiness I feel at the revelation that Luc cared more than he let on is immediately crushed by the ache in my chest at my own lie. I close my eyes and drop my head back onto the bed.

LUC

It hits me like a lightning bolt out of Heaven—some giddy, wild feeling, dizzying in its intensity, making me want to run. Run from Frannie. Or to her. I don't know which.

And what I felt when she kissed me—I have no clue *what* that was. Some shift in my core. So, what in unholy Hell do I do now?

My job. She needs to be tagged. Which means I should keep

working my way down the lust path, making the whole wrath and envy thing all that much easier . . . right?

"I guess we should get back to work." Or I should, at least. It probably wouldn't be impossible to get her into bed . . . maybe another beer, a little power push . . . just the suggestion.

And then I catch the scent of warm chocolate. What signal is Frannie's psyche giving off now? One I don't recognize.

"Yeah," she says, smiling. She pulls her composition book back into her lap from where it slid onto the rug.

I stare into her eyes, trying to read her. I'm not sure if this is part of my game plan or not. I'm finding it really hard to look anywhere else. And she's staring right back. I start to reach for her again and she looks like she wants me to, but then I pull my hand back as some jab of something hits me. Because I want her in more ways than I can describe—in *every* way. But something's stopping me from just taking her.

There's some deep, throbbing knot in my chest—my heart? *Are you kidding?* Brimstone doesn't throb. I look at her again, smiling at me. She wouldn't be smiling if she knew what I was. I should tell her. That would be the right thing to do.

Oh, for the love of all things unholy. Is that a conscience? What in Hell's name is happening to me? Is this my boss's idea of a joke? No—as sadistic as he is, I'm pretty sure Beherit wouldn't find any humor in this.

Gabriel.

This has to be his fault, somehow. I'm going to track him down, pluck out his angel feathers, and stuff a pillow with them.

I pull a deep breath and try to clear my head. My gaze returns to Frannie just as a wicked little smile turns up the corners of her kissable lips. I don't remember ever wanting anything so much. If I didn't know better, I'd think I was born of covet instead of pride.

"So . . . chapter twenty-eight . . ." I say, looking away and opening my composition book.

12

✦

Just Like Heaven

FRANNIE

Taylor is staring me down across the table. "He *kissed* you?"

A smile pulls at my mouth. It's been a whole day, and my lips are still buzzing.

The waitress shows up with our mu shu pork, lemon chicken, and shrimp fried rice and slams the dishes down on the table. She throws a handful of chopsticks into the middle of the table, says something sharp in Cantonese, and leaves.

Riley looks after her mournfully as she storms away from our table. "Why does she hate us?"

I shrug, then turn my attention back to Taylor. "You're just jealous," I gloat, scooping some rice onto my plate. I tried to bail on girls' night this week on account of hating Taylor's guts right now, but Riley laid on some big guilt thing, and here I am. So I'm taking full advantage to rub Taylor's face in it.

"So, he really did?" Riley says.

My eyes wander out the window past the flashing neon-green OPEN sign to the empty sidewalks and dark windows of the vacant storefronts across the street. For a second, I'm sure I see a black Shelby Cobra drive by in the glow of the neon lights. Wishful thinking, I guess. I smile sweetly at Taylor. "Well, I think *I* may have really been the one doing the kissing. It's all a little fuzzy."

"See! That's what I mean. Stuff gets fuzzy with him. But he said nothing happened with us . . . ?"

"Nothing."

"And you believe him?" Taylor's waving her chopsticks around wildly, spraying lemon sauce all over the table.

"Well, he didn't seem weird about it or anything. He said he was surprised you didn't tell me that."

"So, *I'm* lucky he shot me down," she says, her face reflecting the disdain in her voice, "but it's okay for *you* to kiss him?"

I can't stop the stupid grin that spreads across my face. "Maybe I was wrong," I say, hoping I'm right. Even if I'm not and he blows me off tomorrow, the look on Taylor's face is almost worth it.

She shakes her head. "You kissed him."

"Yep."

"Like making-out kissing, or just one kiss?"

"Just one." One seriously mind-blowing kiss.

Riley's eyes are wide and her smile's triumphant. "Are you guys, like, dating now?"

"I'm not sure . . . maybe."

"How can you not know if you're dating?" Taylor sneers through a mouthful of pork and cabbage.

"The same way you didn't know if you slept with him."

"I knew I didn't *sleep* with him!"

"Whatever. We haven't been on a real date. So technically, I'd have to say we're not."

"I hate you."

"I know," I say, still gloating. Can't help it. It's sort of a rush scooping Taylor for a change.

The tiniest of wry smiles quirks her lips, then she looks away and her eyebrows shoot up in surprise. "So, that's just weird," she says looking past me. "Did you tell him we were gonna be here?"

"Who?" I turn and see Luc standing just inside the door under the MING'S BAMBOO HOUSE—VERY GOOD FOOD sign. He saunters over.

"I don't want to interrupt anything." His warm honey voice melts me. I really want to climb right into him, but I don't want to be a shitty friend—at least not to Riley. I tear my eyes away from him and check in with them.

"Sit," Taylor says, kicking the chair next to me out.

Luc crooks his eyebrow. "Riley . . . ?"

"We've got a ton of extra food. And it's 'very good,' according to them. Eat," she answers, cracking a smile. Maybe she's not too pissed.

Luc folds himself into the chair next to me and slides it in, leaning toward me so his shoulder barely touches mine. "Thanks, but I'm not really hungry."

"Then what are you doing at a Chinese restaurant?" Taylor scoffs.

"I was just walking by and saw you sitting here."

"Whatever." Taylor shoots a vindictive glance my way. "We were just talking about you." And now I know why she was okay with letting him crash girls' night. "Why are you screwing with us?"

I kick her under the table. "Taylor!"

Riley jumps in. "What she means is, you're not just screwing with Frannie, are you?"

I kick Riley under the table. "Riley!"

Luc is trying not to laugh. "No, this is good. Tell me what you think, Riley."

"Well, I think you're into her . . ."

"And you're okay with that?"

"I guess, as long as you're serious. 'Cause Taylor and I are gonna have to kick your ass if you're just messing with her."

My cheeks are on fire. "Riley, I don't need any help kicking asses."

Taylor's face pulls into an evil little smirk. "Yeah, Luc. Did you know? Frannie has a sixth-degree black belt in judo."

He shoots me a grin. "Yeah. I got that when she threw that guy over her head at Gallaghers'."

I plant my elbows on the table and bury my face in my hands. All the things Taylor could say to sabotage me—nine years of ammunition—spin through my head. In my mind, I beg her to back off. *Please, please, please, Taylor, don't wreck this for me.*

But when I feel Luc's hand ease around my waist, my mind goes blank and my heart starts to career to redline.

"So, to answer your question, Riley: I'm serious," he says, and my redlining heart stops.

"I guess you'll be driving her home," Riley says.

"If that's okay with you."

I pull my face out of my hands. "What the hell? I don't get a say?"

Luc lifts an eyebrow and a smile plays around those lips. I shudder, remembering how good they felt moving on mine. "So . . . ?"

I breathe against the flutter in my chest, hating that he knows how much I want him. I open my mouth to say no. "All right . . . I guess."

Riley pushes her chair back and slings her purse over her shoulder, then grabs Taylor, whose expression has softened. "Let's go."

Taylor pulls herself out of her chair and smiles—a genuine smile that I'm not sure I've ever seen on her face before. But after a second, the smile takes on her signature lascivious edge. She rubs her hands together then raises them up near her shoulders, as if surrendering. "I'm out." She cocks half a smile at me and turns for the door. "Don't do anything I wouldn't do."

What the hell? Taylor backing off? I must be dreaming.

"In other words," Riley says, nudging my shoulder, "anything goes." She drops a huge tip onto the table on her way to the door, trying once again to get on our waitress's good side.

I drop my face back into my hands, too embarrassed to look at Luc now that we're alone.

He leans his shoulder into mine. "Hey."

I don't lift my face out of my hands. "Sorry about that," I mumble into my palms.

"I think it's charming that Riley's looking out for you."

My head snaps up and my cheeks burn. "Charming? Try mortifying."

He smiles his wicked smile and nearly stops my heart. And when he leans in to kiss me, I'm pretty sure it does.

I can't stop my hand from reaching for his face. I feel him shiver in answer and he locks gazes with me. "Let's get out of here," he says into my lips.

An achy tingle spreads through me and I smile a shaky smile. "I know just the place."

LUC

This is unlike anything I've ever experienced. And that's saying something. Of course, that probably has more to do with Frannie than anything else. She seems to have that effect on me—makes everything feel new.

"You have to close your eyes," she says. "It's such a rush. You ready?"

"Yep."

In the heavy night air, so full of the scents of the forest, the only sounds are the harmonies of croaking frogs and chirping crickets—and Frannie's laughter, which is like a music all its own.

"Okay," she says softly, leaning in for a kiss. My lips just touch hers when the gleam in her eye turns impish and she lets go of the rope.

I close my eyes as I swing out over the water, feeling the cool wind in my face and through my hair. I feel like I'm floating through the darkness, and she's right, it *is* a rush. Almost the same as being summoned by King Lucifer—the rush of being yanked through time and space. Except without the smell of brimstone and the dread in the pit of my stomach. I feel a tingle course through my entire body. When I glide through the air back to the shore, I step off of the rope swing onto the rocky edge of the quarry next to Frannie. She laughs again. Her face shines in the pale, silver moonlight, and I feel that same tingle.

She smiles up at me. "So . . . ? Pretty cool, huh?" She presses into me and pulls me into a kiss, setting me on fire with the touch of her lips. Mmm . . . clove and currant on my tongue. Her soul right here for the taking.

The sickle moon is low in the sky, creating shimmering shadows through the trees and casting a faint sheen on the water in the dark quarry. But that sheen isn't enough to conceal the thousands of faceted jewels reflecting off the still surface of the water. I've never seen such a clear night with so many stars. The real show, though, is the cosmos shining in Frannie's eyes.

"Okay, my turn," she says, pushing me aside and grabbing the rope. I hold it steady as she steps onto the wooden disc knotted at the bottom.

"Ready?" I ask.

"Go," she laughs and I let go of the rope.

I watch as she swings away from me, a silhouette against the shimmering water. The end of the rope drags over the surface, creating a ripple and setting the reflected stars in motion. Listening to her whoop and the ring of her laughter, I feel my own laughter bubble up from somewhere deep inside me and erupt. It sounds foreign to me. Happy.

But then she screams, "Oh, shit!" There's a splash followed by a larger ripple.

My laughter chokes off. "Frannie!" I yell, diving in after her. As I break the surface and listen for her, I swear I hear a rough and sultry chuckle from the edge of the quarry that fades into the sound of leaves rustling in the breeze. "Frannie!" I yell again. No answer. Fighting panic, I swim to the spot that the rope reaches at full swing and dive under. I draw on my power and my hand illuminates the murky water around me in a red glow as I swim slowly back toward the rocks. Just before I reach the edge, a hand flails up from the dark depths. I reach for it, pulling her to the surface. Frannie comes up coughing and gasping for air.

"Something . . . grabbed . . . me," she gasps, her teeth chattering so hard I can barely understand her.

Relief washes over me as I loop an arm around her and pull her back to the edge of the quarry. I push her in front of me as we scramble up the slippery rocks and out of the icy water.

"Are you okay?"

"Uh-huh. Just . . . freezing," she chatters back, still gasping for air.

I can already see the steam rising off my wet clothes as we stand in the cool night air, so I wrap my body around hers and pull her hair back, wringing it out behind her. I hold her as my body absorbs her violent shivers, and after a few moments I see the steam start to rise off her as well.

"Mmm . . ." she moans. "God, you're so hot."

I smile. God has nothing to do with it.

"It felt like something grabbed my leg," she finally says as her shaking starts to ease.

"Probably got your foot caught on a tree root."

"I guess . . . but it didn't feel like it."

I hold her as her shaking slows, and we start to sway in rhythm to the chirping crickets. As the moon arcs high over the quarry, over us, I'm completely lost in her. Nothing has ever felt so right—but also so wrong. We dance and there's only the music, her and me. No game plan.

FRANNIE

Even though my clothes and hair are mostly dry, I spend the whole ride back to my house trying to figure out how I'm gonna explain showing up with Luc, looking like this, to my parents. When the house comes into view, I still have no clue.

I'm also trying to wrap my mind around Luc—or really, how Luc makes me feel. It's completely different than how I feel with Gabe, but no less scary. Just scary in a completely different way. With Gabe, the feeling is strong and deep. With Luc, it's wild and out of control. I don't trust Luc. How could I? But I also don't want this feeling to stop.

He pulls into my driveway and cuts the engine. I sit, wishing I could just stay right here forever.

"So . . ." he says.

"So . . ." I say back. And then he reaches for me, sweeping back my hair, and leans in to kiss me. I feel myself turn to Jell-O as his lips move on mine. I have to remind myself to breathe. After a really long time, but not nearly long enough, he pulls back.

"I guess I should walk you to the door."

I pull my wild hair behind my neck and tie it in a knot. "Oh . . . that may not be such a great idea."

He smiles. "Like they aren't looking out the window right now. They know you're with me."

I glance at the house and see the curtains sway from where they were just dropped. The front door flies open, and Mom is standing there in her blue June Cleaver dress and heels, arms folded over her chest and eyes wide.

"And she also knows you just kissed me," he says, his smile stretching into that wicked grin.

Crap. Crap. "Crap."

Luc chuckles then slides out of the car and comes around to open my door. Nice touch. He takes my hand and helps me out of the car. He doesn't let go as we move up my front walk; I love the feel of his hand burning into mine. It's everything I can do not to drag him back to his car and tell him to drive me somewhere we can be alone.

"Good evening, Mrs. Cavanaugh."

"Hello," she says curtly—which, for my mother, is like cursing him out. Then her eyes shift to me and, even in the dim porch light, I'm sure I look a disaster. "What happened?" Her eyes dart suspiciously back to Luc.

I bite back the hysterical laughter that threatens as I think about saying, *Luc ravaged me in his backseat.* Which, now that I think of it, was what happened in my dream last night. But instead, I swallow my pride and tell the truth. "I fell in the quarry. Luc saved me." As much as I hate to admit the whole damsel in distress thing, maybe it will earn him a brownie point or two.

"What were you doing out *there*? That quarry is dangerous," she says, outright glowering at Luc now. "You need a warm shower." She pulls me through the door and slams it in Luc's face.

"It was my fault, Mom. Luc jumped in after me. Really."

She drags me up the stairs. "Thank God you're okay. I told you not to spend time with him, Frannie. We thought you were with Taylor and Riley tonight."

"Mom, I don't know what happened to make you like this about him, but he's not a bad person. Really."

"We'll discuss your consequences later," she says, pushing me into the bathroom at the top of the stairs. "Just get cleaned up."

"My consequences? Like, *punishment*?"

She eyes me thoughtfully, like she's just now realizing she should have had the birds and bees talk with me a long time ago. "We'll talk later," she says and closes the door. *Great*.

I wait to hear the creak of the bottom stair before I pull the door open and run down the hall into my room. I rush to the window and throw it open.

Luc's car is in the driveway, door open, but Luc is nowhere.

"Luc!" I say, my voice a harsh whisper.

"Hey." His voice comes from under my window.

I press my face against the screen and look down just as he walks out from under my window, toward the driveway. "Hey. Sorry about that. My mom's just stressin' a little."

"No problem," he says, looking up at me but also into the oak branches just outside my window.

I smile. "You thinking about climbing that tree?"

He glares up into the tree for just a second and then smiles at me. "If I did, would you let me in?"

I feel my cheeks flush. "Not tonight. I think we've given Mom all she can handle for now."

"You're sure?"

No. "Yes."

He looks only a little disappointed when he says, "Okay. Do me a favor, then. Does your window have a latch?"

"Yeah."

"Close it and latch it, okay?"

I crack a grin. "Why? You can't be trusted?"

"No, I can't. But it's not me I'm worried about at the moment. Just do it. Now, okay?" The urgency in his voice scares me a little.

"What's wrong?"

"Nothing. Just do it. Please," he nearly barks.

"If you tell me what's going on."

"Oh, for the sin of Satan . . ." he starts, exasperated, then glares up at me. "Please, Frannie."

I glare back. "Whatever," I say and slam my window shut.

He just stands there for a minute, looking up at me until I realize he's waiting for me to latch it. I do, grudgingly, and he slides into the Mustang. He backs out of the driveway into the road and I watch till his taillights are lost behind the trees. Leave it to him to ruin my perfect night by turning into a jerk.

But just before I drop the curtain, I look out into the dark, at the tree outside my window.

My breath catches as I stumble back from the window.

And I tell myself the pair of red eyes floating in the branches is just a cat.

A second later, the door cracks open and Kate's head pokes through. "You okay?"

"Yeah." But the shake in my voice betrays my unease.

"What happened?"

"When?"

"Just now. You screamed."

"I did?" I say, thinking of those disembodied eyes and shuddering.

She pushes through the door and closes it behind her. "Yeah, you did. So, you're okay?"

"Yeah, sorry. Something surprised me."

"All right." She turns for the door.

"Wait!" I yell, glancing back at the window. I'm a little creeped out, and I don't want her to leave just yet.

"What?" she says, turning back.

And suddenly I feel a little awkward. "So . . . what's up?"

She just stares at me. "Are you sure you're okay? 'Cause you're kind of losing it."

"I'm fine. I just thought we could . . . you know . . . talk, I guess."

She rolls her eyes and turns for the door again, and suddenly I think of something I really *do* want to ask her.

"Kate . . ."

She barely glances over her shoulder as she reaches for the doorknob. "What?"

"When you and Chase . . . you know. When you first . . ."

She spins toward me, annoyed. "What, Frannie?"

"Had sex . . . when you first had sex. How did you know you were ready?"

Her expression softens and she smiles wistfully. "You just know." But then concern brushes her face. "Don't let anyone pressure you, Frannie. If any part of you is saying no, then it's a no."

But what if all the parts of me are saying yes? I think about Luc, and, even though I'm pissed at him, a tingle starts low in my belly. "Thanks, Kate."

She still looks concerned as she turns for the door again. She closes it behind her and I stand staring at the window for a long time. Finally, I pull out Matt's journal. I climb on my bed, trying to sort my thoughts, then start to write.

So, Matt . . . there's stuff going on inside me that I don't even have words for, so sorry. But it's kind of scary, feeling like this. Out of control.

I stare blindly at the wall, my insides churning.

Luc . . . it's like he's some kind of drug. I can't get enough of him. And if this is how drugs make people feel, then I can see why they get addicted.

I feel a thread of fear wrap around my heart, and I lift my head from the journal and rub my eyes, pushing Luc's face out of my mind.

I don't want to need anybody like that. I'm not going to let myself get addicted to Luc.

I close Matt's journal and sit staring at the wall as everything becomes crystal clear in my head. I can want him physically without needing him. It's called lust. No emotional attachment necessary. And that's what this is—just physical. I'm sure of it.

Gabe, though . . .

As my thoughts shift to him, the tingle in my belly turns into an ache in my chest. 'Cause I'm starting to think whatever I'm feeling for him is deeper than lust and a lot more dangerous.

I was wrong before. Luc is definitely the safer choice. I know what I'm getting, and it won't ever turn into something I can't handle.

LUC

Belias. This is bad. Why would Beherit send Belias? Why would he send *anybody*? I haven't been checked up on in four thousand years. There's no doubt that was him outside Frannie's window, though.

I drive slowly and watch to see if he follows. When he doesn't, I realize it's worse than bad. He's not just checking up on me. He's after Frannie. Swallowing my panic, I circle back, coast up within a few houses, and sit for a second, assessing the situation.

Belias is in Collections. Why would Beherit send Collections? Frannie's to be tagged only. Unless things have changed. And if Belias tags her, her soul will be bound to him. She'll be *his.* Something primal flares in me—something deep and territorial. He can't have her. She's *mine.* Suddenly I'm grateful that Mr. Cavanaugh is in tight with the Almighty. If I, a First Level demon, can't phase into the house, neither can Belias.

I step out of the car and phase across the street. How is this going to work? He isn't going to come with me just because I ask. I creep up under the tree, duck behind the trunk, and call out to him with my mind. *Belias!* I know he can hear me, just like I can hear him. Our nefarious psychic connection binds us, whether I like it or not.

The faintest rustling, no more than a squirrel would make moving through the branches, and Belias is standing beside me. His shaggy black hair partially obscures his glowing red eyes, which illuminate a two-foot radius nonetheless, his sharp cheekbones casting shadows across his face. He grins at me. "Lucifer. It's been far too long."

"What are you talking about? I just saw you a few weeks ago."

"Yes, and the boss says you're taking far too long. Those are his exact words."

"It's only been two weeks. I wasn't aware there was a time limit," I lie.

"Well, there is. In case you haven't noticed, Gabriel is here. If you wait too long, it will be too late."

"You can run along and tell Beherit I have things under control, thank you."

"Mmm . . . yes, it looked that way at the quarry. Very sweet, Lucifer. Though how you could be that close and not take her—her flesh, I mean—I'll never understand."

How did I not sense him there? I'm letting myself get too distracted. And, as the weight of his words hits me, I feel a stab of pure rage slice through me like a razor.

It was Belias.

My fists clench by my sides, and I glare death at him. "You

wouldn't have had anything to do with Frannie's little mishap, then? Because drowning her doesn't seem like the most prudent strategy before she's tagged. Frannie's soul in Limbo would not bode well for us."

A malevolent grin stretches across his face and his eyes flare. "But, see, there's the problem, Lucifer. She shouldn't still *be* untagged. You had the perfect opportunity to take her flesh—the first step to claiming her soul. She was serving herself up. Even you couldn't miss her ginger. But you chose to play the gallant suitor instead of getting the job done. You're losing your touch. A fact that hasn't escaped Beherit."

A combination of fear and panic grips me. The last thing I need is for my boss to be taking notice. "I can't just take her, Belias. In case you've forgotten, there are rules." But as I say it, it feels false—I'm making excuses.

His eyes flash red lightning as he grins wider. "The rules are changing."

"Really? I didn't get that memo."

His grin pulls into a grimace. "This one is important, Lucifer. There's no room for mistakes. Don't blow this."

My king's voice echoes in my head. *Don't disappoint me.*

"That's why I'm taking my time. No mistakes. Now run along. I'm sure Avaira is getting cold."

He smirks. "I could finish this job and get back to Hell before Avaira got cold." Creatures of lust are truly disgusting—which is why I won't let this slimy incubus anywhere near Frannie.

"Well, I could leave you to this," I gesture to Frannie's window, "and go keep Avaira warm for you." I'm bluffing, but he glowers at me.

"The boss is impatient. Don't take too long." Then he phases in a puff of brimstone—poof, gone.

I wait for a long while, still tucked behind the tree, deciding what to do. Finally, I move through the shadows to my car and stay the rest of the night there—watching.

13

✝

A Cold Day in Hell

FRANNIE

My heart is pounding as I wait at my locker 'cause, after last night with Luc, I'm not sure what to expect. I stare blindly at my books and shift my weight from foot to foot, failing spectacularly at trying to appear casual. And then I catch the faintest wisp of cinnamon, and I smile just as his hot hand eases around my waist and pulls me to his burning body.

"Hey, gorgeous."

His voice sends a shiver through me despite his heat. I open my mouth to argue about the "gorgeous" thing, but then I'm too busy melting into a puddle on the floor to actually say anything. I turn around in his arms, and he kisses me. And the crowded hall full of sweaty high school students is the only thing keeping me from tearing right into him. But there's nothing I can do about the stupid grin that pulls at my mouth when he takes my hand and leads me across the hall into room 616.

He leans his shoulder into mine as he reads aloud through the end of *The Grapes of Wrath*, and I catch Mr. Snyder's smile as he notices.

"Nicely done, Mr. Cain," he says with a wink. "There will be no final exam for this class, but your wrap-up essays for *The Grapes of Wrath* will be twenty-five percent of your grade for the course. I've put together some questions to help you frame your final thoughts on this book." He drops a stack of papers at the end of each row, and they're passed down. "You want to take your time on the outline—really formulate your thoughts—before starting on the essay. Utilize all your chapter outlines to pull this together. This is Thursday. I'll give you until Monday to put together your outline based on this list of questions. Your essays will be due the following Monday—the last day of class. Take a minute to read through the questions before the bell."

Luc scans the page, then he looks at me with a crooked smile. "I think we're going to need to spend all weekend locked in my apartment working on these."

I lean into his shoulder. "Will I be your prisoner, or am I free to come and go?"

His crooked smile pulls into that wicked grin. "You won't *want* to go anywhere."

And the bell rings, shocking my heart back into rhythm.

But, when we step out into the hall, I'm shocked again. My heart sputters and nearly stops. 'Cause Gabe is leaning against my locker, smiling at me like some kind of angel.

God, he's beautiful.

My feet stutter, and Luc wraps his arm around my waist to steady me. I take a deep breath and force my feet forward.

When Luc sees Gabe, his hand around my waist tightens. "Gabriel."

I can't look Gabe in the eye, but I hear the disappointment in his voice and it nearly rips me in half. "Walk with me to physics?"

I glance at Luc and pull gently away. "Sure."

We weave silently through the crowded hall, and I feel Luc's eyes burning through my back. I keep my eyes fixed firmly on the gray floor tiles as we walk.

Finally, just before we reach our classroom, Gabe stops walking and says, "So, this is what you want? *Who* you want?"

My heart feels ready to explode, 'cause I don't know what I want. "I . . . maybe."

"Maybe," he repeats.

I can feel the weight of his gaze, so I turn to face him. I start to open my mouth, but there aren't words, so I close it again.

He wraps a hand around the back of my neck and leans in. At first, I think he's going to kiss me, and that aching tingle explodes low in my belly as I realize how much I want him to. But his cheek brushes past mine and he whispers, "Tell me what to do to change your mind."

This.

My mind is totally blank, I can't even remember how to form words. A rueful smile curls his lips as he places his hand on my back and guides me into physics without another word.

As we slide onto our stools, Ms. Billings sweeps by and dumps an armful of lab equipment in front of me. I focus on the lab and try to forget everything. But it's impossible to ignore the aching inside, and the way it's really hard to breathe, and how I want to touch Gabe every time he looks at me.

By the end of class, I'm a basket case. I can't even remember what the lab was about. But, as I rush through the halls to my locker, I see Riley and Trevor tucked into the alcove near the janitor's closet sucking face, which improves my mood. I can't help laughing out loud. Taylor's gonna shit a brick.

When I get to my locker, Luc is leaning against it, looking hotter than Hell. He presses me against the lockers and kisses me, then opens my locker and exchanges my books. Did I give him the combination? I don't remember.

"Ready for Sanghetti-fest?"

"Ready." I feel kind of stupid, 'cause now that I'm with him, I can't wipe this ridiculous grin off my face. So I probably look like a total freak the whole time we're walking to building 2, but his hot hand on my back is all I care about.

After class, we start up the hall for lunch, but I grab his arm. "So—let's not go to the cafeteria today," I say, not quite ready to face Gabe with Luc in the same room.

He grins. "Did you have something else in mind?"

"I've got some munchies in my locker. It's a nice day. We could just hang out on the lawn."

He slides his arm around me, and I almost purr right out loud. "Sounds good."

We collect the bootie from my locker, which mostly consists of Red Vines and Oreos, get some sodas out of the machine, and wander out to the courtyard.

That's when I remember that Reefer and the guys hang out here and jam at lunch. He watches us step through the door.

Luc notices and unwraps his arm from my waist. "We can go somewhere else if you want."

I glance back at Reefer and wave. "No. This is fine."

I pick a spot on the other side of the raised flowerbed in the middle of the courtyard and sit with my back up against it. While Luc runs to his car for a blanket, I drop my head back and bask in the warmth of the sun, listening to Reefer and the guys play. I sing along softly and try to clear my head of anything that matters. After forever, when I realize Luc's not back yet, I open my eyes and find him sitting in the grass across from me, smiling.

"You didn't tell me you could sing."

I drop my eyes and feel my cheeks start to burn. "I don't much anymore."

He gets up to spread the blanket on the grass. We settle in, and I lay back and gaze up at the sky. When I lift my head and glance at Luc, he's still staring at me, a faint smile perched on those lips. All of a sudden I want to kiss him.

"I get the feeling there's more to you than meets the eye, Mary Francis Cavanaugh."

I look away and pull a deep breath. "Not really. So, why do you insist on picking on Mr. Sanghetti, anyway?" I say to change the subject, remembering how they bickered all through class—*again*.

"Just doing my job."

"Really?" I break into the Oreos. "And what, exactly, would that be?"

"Driving him to lie, cheat . . . whatever it takes."

"Whatever it takes to do what?"

"Send him to Hell." He gazes into my eyes, waiting for my reaction.

I just smile, 'cause I got that about Luc a long time ago. "Why him? Why not Mr. Snyder or Mrs. Felch?"

"Because they don't annoy me."

"Do I annoy you?"

He grins. "You are *so* under my skin . . . this annoying little itch that just won't stop."

"Well, I'm going to Hell already, so you're too late."

"You think so?" he says through a bigger grin.

I pull my hair out of the knot and swing around to lay with my head on his thigh, like a pillow. "Yep." I unscrew my Oreo and scrape the white stuff out with my teeth. "And you'll be there too. I can tell," I mumble through a mouthful of greasy sugar.

"Most definitely," he says, brushing my hair out of my face with his finger.

When the Oreos are gone, we pull up the blanket and head inside. Taylor attacks us just inside the door.

"We missed you. Private lunch date?" she says with a raised eyebrow.

"Semi-private. Reefer and the band serenaded us."

She laughs. "That's poetic."

Gabe steps up behind her and looks at me, ignoring Luc. "Can we talk?"

Taylor's smile spreads into a grin as Gabe and I step out into the courtyard. He props his back against the wall, all casual, but his face is intense. "Frannie . . ." He blows out a sigh and looks up at the clear blue sky for a minute as my pulse pounds in my ears. Finally, he looks back at me. "I guess I just need you to know that, no matter what happens with him . . . with any of it . . . I'm here for you." His hand cups my face and his thumb traces the lines of my lips, leaving them on fire. "But, please, think about this. Lucifer is . . . dangerous."

I pull away from him. "So are you!"

My mouth drops open. *Did I just say that out loud?*

From the rueful smile on Gabe's face, it's clear I did.

Oh God. What the hell is wrong with me?

"I mean . . ." but my words trail off, 'cause I have no clue what I mean.

I spin and walk back into the building, my face on fire, and find Luc and Taylor both waiting inside the door. Luc glares at Gabe while Taylor raises her eyebrows over questioning eyes.

I storm up the hall to my locker, leaving them all in the dust, and avoid them like a bad rash for the rest of the day. But Luc slides into the seat next to me in last period government class. "You free after school?"

I know I should say no, but I don't, so he walks with me to our lockers after class and I collect my books. We're making our way to the parking lot, and I'm totally conscious of Luc's arm around my waist, not sure if I want it there or not. I finally decide I do, but before we reach the end of the hall, I glance up to see Angelique Preston glaring at me. Her arms are folded across her chest, nearly pushing her boobs right out of her shirt.

I give her my best smirk.

But as we walk by, she eyes Luc like they're sharing a secret.

And all of a sudden, I come crashing back to Earth.

I look at Luc. I know I can't trust him. So why am I trusting him? Even though I only want his body, I'm not thrilled at the prospect of sharing it with Angelique. As we climb into his car I'm starting to wonder if going back to his place to study is such a great idea. I almost suggest that we go to my house instead, but I really don't want to deal with my alien parents.

I stare at him as we pull out of the parking lot, a contented smile just turning up the corners of his mouth. "So, what's going on with us?"

His smile stretches into a grin. "What would you like to be going on with us?"

I'm in no mood for games. "Cut the shit and just answer my question."

LUC

"Wow. Okay . . ." As I think about Frannie's question, I'm not quite sure how to answer. I'm not sure which would scare her more: "I really want to get you into bed" or "I'm trying to tag your soul for Hell." Both true. But, under all of that, there's more—something deeper that pulls at my insides and makes it hard to think anytime I'm with her. Something I can't even begin to define or articulate.

What does she want me to say? I start cautiously and turn away from the road briefly to watch her face. "Well, I'm not quite sure. I like you a lot." Understatement of the millennium. "So, can we just see where it goes?" Like, to Hell, maybe?

She draws a deep breath. "Yeah, I guess that's fair." Then she looks a little unsure and adds, "But I'm kinda curious. Why me?"

"Why you, what?"

"Angelique, Cassidy, Taylor . . . half the girls in this school are throwing themselves at you. Why would you want to go out with me?"

"Let's just say I've been around the block a few times, but I've never met anyone like you, Frannie. You're one of a kind." All true—and you're also my mark.

We climb the stairs to my apartment, and when I push open the door I realize, too late, that I should have been more careful. There's a long, lean, raven-haired beauty with glowing black bedroom eyes and some serious curves sprawled across my bed wearing . . . well . . . not much.

"Avaira," I say through my surprise.

Frannie's eyes scream fury and she throws up her arms. "I knew it," she says, turning to head back down the hall. "You're such an asshole," she adds without turning around. And I catch the black pepper of her rage. Mmm . . .

It's clear that there's a definite glitch in my radar. First Belias at the quarry and now Avaira in my bed. I should have known she was there before I ever opened the door. And it's more than just Frannie distracting me. My psychic connection to the nefarious seems to be seriously waning.

Belias and Avaira—the dynamic duo. All of a sudden this place is crawling with demons. Which means Frannie isn't safe.

I actually let out a laugh when what I just thought registers. Frannie hasn't been safe since I got here.

I slam the door and follow her down the hall. "Frannie, hold up!" But she doesn't even slow down. "It's not what you think. She's my . . . cousin," I yell after her as I jog to catch up.

Nearly to the top of the stairs, she wheels on me as I approach and spits, "You're so full of shit!"

I smile, trying to defuse this a little. "Have I ever lied to you before?"

She glowers at me. "Yes."

Maybe that wasn't the best tactic. "Well . . ." And I start to say that I'm not lying now, but I am, so that would be a lie.

"You know what? You can take your 'cousin' and go straight to Hell," she says, spinning and running down the stairs.

"Where are you going?"

She says nothing—very, very loudly.

"At least let me give you a ride home."

Still nothing.

I follow her down the stairs and through the door to the parking lot, trying not to smile. She has no idea how adorable she is when she's furious. "Fine, I'll walk you home."

She doesn't look at me. "Just leave me the hell alone."

But the thing is, Hell isn't going to leave her alone. That much is clear.

I back off and let her go—sort of. But I'm not going to let her out of my sight. Because where there's Avaira, Belias isn't far. I strain my sixth sense listening for him. Nothing. But he's here, I'm sure of it. Because it's also clear that Avaira was meant as a diversion, or at least a distraction, for me while he went after Frannie. Creatures of lust think everyone is as single-minded as they are.

We're not more than a quarter mile from my apartment, me

hanging way back, when I catch the thread of Belias's thoughts. Anger. I can't tell if he's angry with me for interfering or Avaira for not sidetracking me. Either way, I pick up my pace and close the distance between me and Frannie, my guard up.

But just as I'm about to call her name, a white Charger pulls up at the curb next to her. Apparently, I'm not the only one keeping my eye on Frannie. And for the first time, I'm glad she has an angel for a wingman.

FRANNIE

"Hey," Gabe says as I slide into his car.

"Hey. Thanks," I say, relieved.

"You look like shit."

I glower at him. "Thanks."

"You okay?"

"Just say it."

"What?" he says with a raised eyebrow.

"I told you so. I can tell you're dying to say it. Just do it so I don't have to sit here like a moron waiting for it."

"Okay. I told you so."

"I must be stuck on stupid or something," I say, glancing out the back window at Luc, fading into the distance as we pull away.

He cracks a glowing smile. "You're not. You've seen the light, yeah?"

I try to smile back. "Yeah, I guess."

"You're just in the unique position of needing to be very careful what you wish for."

What? "What?"

He stares out the windshield. "Have you ever noticed that if you really want something, you usually get it?"

"No." I can think of a shitload of things I want that I don't have, starting with my brother back. But for a brief second, I wonder, 'cause I wanted Luc—stupidly—and I got him, sort of. And Taylor. She's never backed off a guy before. But last night...I shake my head. "No," I say again with more conviction.

He shrugs and drops it, reaching across to weave his fingers in mine. I catch that scent again, like snow in summer. "You good to come over for a while?"

"Yeah. We could work on that physics thing."

"Sure," he says, smiling.

Gabe's house isn't too far from mine and looks like all the other houses in our neighborhood: two stories with white siding, black shutters, and a long front porch. His porch has a ginormous potted Christmas cactus in the corner and a swing near the door. His front walk cuts a gray swath through a lush green lawn and is bordered with short, trimmed shrubs. I follow him up the walk and into the house.

We step through the front door into the family room. It runs along the entire front of the house with windows on either side of the door, looking out onto the front porch. The stairs ascend from the right side of the room and on the left is an arched doorway into the kitchen. The walls and carpet are all white, as is the couch along the back wall and the two high-backed chairs under the windows. There's no TV, but there are white stereo speakers on shelves in the corners.

"Are you still moving in?" I ask, scanning the blank walls.

He smiles and shrugs. "This is pretty much it. We don't need much."

"Yeah, but . . ." I trail off, not sure what to say. It seems weird that there are no family pictures or knickknacks. My mom has pictures and other crap scattered everywhere. But as I settle into the couch I realize, despite the austere appearance, it feels warm and welcoming.

"I've got the cure for all ills," Gabe says and disappears into the kitchen. I dig through my book bag and pull out our physics lab manual. A minute later he comes back with a huge bowl of mocha java lava ice cream and two spoons and sits next to me. He punches the button on a white iPod on the white coffee table. As if from everywhere, there's music.

"You okay with sharing?" he says.

"Sure." I grab a spoon and shovel in a mouthful. "This is my favorite."

He cracks another glowing smile and rakes his hand through his hair. "Seems to be doing the trick."

I smile back 'cause he's right. I don't know if it's him or the ice cream, but I couldn't care less if Luc is shagging Mystery Girl right now.

Okay, as I think about that I know it's a lie, but I only want to kill him a little now—and in more humane ways, like with a gun or a knife, and not so much with my bare hands.

We finish the ice cream and I lean back on the couch. I contemplate cracking open my physics manual and try to convince myself that it's a good idea, but it's a tough sell.

Gabe leans into the back of the couch and loops his arm around my shoulders. "You okay?"

"Yeah," I say resting my forehead against his shoulder and wondering how it is that I can still want Luc so much.

Like he read my mind, he puts his cool hand on my cheek and turns my face to look at him. "Just forget him. He's a jerk." He gazes into my eyes the same way Luc does—like he's seeing my soul.

Suddenly I feel some intense rush of emotion and I want to cry. I close my eyes, focus on the music, and push back the tears. But what I see is Luc's face. "He's a jerk," I repeat, my eyes still closed, trying to make myself believe it.

Like the wings of a butterfly, I feel Gabe's lips, soft on my forehead. And before I even know I've done it, my hands are on his face and my lips are on his. I hear his breath catch and he hesitates, but then his arms are around me, crushing me to him, and his lips move on mine. And I taste cool winter sunshine.

In Gabe's kiss, there's peace like I've never known. Peace so profound I can't even remember hate or anger or pain. And love, limitless and unconditional. His kiss deepens, and I want to just live here forever.

But then his hand on my cheek that had been drawing me in is gently pushing me back, and he pulls away. I stare into his unfathomable blue eyes, lost in there, as his thumb traces the lines of my lips. As I become aware of the room again, I wonder how long we've been kissing. It feels like eternity in the blink of an eye. And it's not till he shifts me gently back onto the couch that I realize, in my need to be closer, I've climbed right on top of him.

His eyes finally close, releasing me, and he leans his forehead into mine. "I need to take you home," he says, his voice barely a whisper. When he opens his eyes, I see regret. Without looking at me, he stands and walks to the door.

The peace is gone, as if it never happened, and I feel frustration and anger flood through me. I haul myself off the couch and yank my book bag over my shoulder.

"Am I really that disgusting?"

"No, I am." He turns and walks out the door.

14

✠

The Devil Takes His Due

LUC

After what happened yesterday with Avaira, this has been the most confusing day of my entire pathetic existence. Sitting next to Frannie in English—wanting to say something, to touch her—was torture to rival the flames of the Fiery Pit. The rest of the day she avoided me, and rightly so. But just at the final bell, when she glanced at me . . . the look in her eyes nearly killed me.

Last night was a living Hell. Thinking about her. Needing to see her. I followed Gabriel when he dropped her off at her house and spent all night there, in my car, as usual. It took everything I had not to climb her tree and push through her window. I've been back and forth all day, because I still have no clue what I'm doing. The one thing I *am* sure of is that I need to protect her from Belias—for a lot of reasons.

Who would have ever thought it? Me, the great protector. It's almost laughable.

But I can't let Belias have her. Frannie is my assignment, and, in addition to really *not* wanting to burn in the Fiery Pit, my pride won't let me fail. If she's that important, I want credit for her soul. My bigger reason, though, is that I know how Belias works, and I can't stand the thought of him touching her, of her soul being bound to him—a filthy incubus. A shudder racks me as my mind shows me what I don't want to see—the image of her, with him, like *that*.

No!

It's not going to happen. I'd rather Gabriel won.

Because I love her.

That's got to be what this feeling is—the giddy rush I feel when I look at her, the way all my insides scream when I think about Belias taking her, the insatiable need I have to be with her. *How is that possible?* There's no crying in baseball and no love in Hell. It's just the rules. You could say it's against our religion, more or less. It flies in the face of everything we are.

But it's there, and it's real, and there's nothing I can do about it. Which means I need to protect her from me too. If I take her the way I want to, she'll belong to Hell, but not to *me*. She's got Sight. King Lucifer will use her until her soul is nothing but an empty husk, then slough her off with the rest of the Shades. I've seen it time and time again. She'll be dead in every way: body and soul.

I've never questioned an assignment before. It's not my place. Most mortals deserve what they get. But Frannie's different. I wasn't lying when I told her I'd never met anyone like her. She doesn't deserve that fate.

I watch her bolt out of last-period government, and a big part of me wants to chase her down, wrap my arms around her, and make everything okay. But the truth is that there is no way for me to do that, because *I'm* what's not okay—me and my brethren. So I glue myself to the chair and watch her walk out the door.

Ten minutes later, I'm still sitting at my desk staring at the door when Coach Runyon meanders up next to me, shrugging into his jacket. He rubs his hand across his coarse five o'clock shadow. "Luc, is there something you need? Because I've got to get to baseball practice."

"No," I say, standing up. "Sorry, just thinking."

"Yes, I can see that." His brown eyes spark as his round face pulls into a knowing smile, exposing crooked teeth. He gives me a sage nod, like he gets the whole crazy girl thing. I'm wishing that's all it was, but it's the whole of Hell that has me more worried at the moment.

"Have you played any ball?" he asks as we walk toward the door. "You've got the physique for it. We could use some muscle at the plate."

"Not for years," I say. But as we pass through the door, my aching heart drops into my stomach as my sixth sense sparks. *Belias!* What am I thinking? He's waiting for an opportunity, and I just gave him one. I should have followed Frannie out to the parking lot to be sure she got home okay. Unholy Hell! How could I be so careless?

"Think about it," he shouts after me as I turn and run up the hall to Frannie's locker.

When I get to it she's nowhere in sight. Fighting to keep the panic in check, I slide to a sit on the floor with my hands on my head, back against my locker, and try to think. She's okay. She has to be. I need to find Taylor and Riley.

Springing off the floor, I run through the halls and catch them on their way out to the parking lot. "Hey, have you guys seen Frannie?" I ask, unsuccessful in my attempt to hide my panic.

"You are *so* lucky we don't kick your ass," Taylor growls through her glare.

"Yeah, okay . . . I get it. You can kick my ass later, but I really need to know where Frannie is."

Riley picks up on my distress. "What's wrong?"

"Nothing, really. I just need to talk to her."

"Why?" Her eyes are wary.

"I just need to know she's okay."

Her eyes soften, and she starts to open her mouth to say something, but, before she can, Taylor blurts, "You should have thought of that before you decided to mess around with your 'cousin.'"

"So you really don't know where she is?"

"No clue. Maybe making out with Gabe," Taylor sneers. I look at Riley, whose expression is heartbroken. She shakes her head.

I drop my head into my hand, warding off the storm that's brewing there. "All right. Thanks."

As I jog toward my car, my sixth sense flares. What if Belias got to her? If he has her, with the ten-minute head start I gave him, it's already too late. A groan escapes my throat as I picture what he would be doing to her right now, and I feel that hot throbbing lump in my chest again. *Damn it all!* If that's the fate I left her to, then I'll gladly burn in the Fiery Pit.

Belias doesn't have her. I can't let myself believe he does. I send that message out into the universe as I slide into my car and sit, weighing the possibilities. If she's not with Taylor or Riley and she's not with me, there are only a handful of people that she might be with. I never thought I'd hope Frannie was with Gabriel. But, right now, I'm more than hoping she's with him. I'm praying for it.

I think about phasing to his house, but if I need to grab Frannie, I'll need my car. I race across town, ignoring stop signs and speed limits, and pull by Gabriel's, focusing hard on his house. With his Hell-forsaken celestial field thrown over it, I can't tell if Frannie's in there or not. I loop around the block, then pull over a few houses up the street and phase behind Gabriel's shrubs. I wait, hoping to catch a glimpse of her through the windows.

What if I'm wasting time and she's not here? What if Belias has her—if she's already tagged or worse? Panic takes over, and I throw all caution to the wind. I stride up the stairs two at a time and knock.

FRANNIE

Gabe won't really look at me, which is good, 'cause I can't bring myself to look at him. But I can't stop thinking about how I felt when he kissed me yesterday and how I want to feel like that again.

I sit at his white kitchen table in awkward silence with a mounding bowl of mocha java lava ice cream in front of me. The only reason I'm even here is that I blasted out of school at the bell, avoiding my locker altogether, and he found me tucked behind a pillar near the parking lot hiding from Luc.

"So, you want to work on that physics assignment?" he finally says.

"Yeah, that'd be good, 'cause I forgot my book."

That's actually a little bit of a stretch. I didn't really forget it. More like I abandoned it along with the rest of the contents of my locker.

He pulls his book out of his bag and drops it on the table just as there's a knock at the door. His brow creases as he glides up out of his chair. "Give me a sec," he says, laying his hand on my shoulder, then he disappears through the kitchen door into the family room and out onto the porch, shutting the front door behind him.

I pull Gabe's physics book open and try to find the right page, but I'm having trouble thinking clearly. Just as I pick up my pencil, I hear muffled voices from the porch that I do my best to ignore—till I recognize Luc's raised voice.

"Is she here or not?"

I stand up and move through the family room to the window, mad at myself for caring. I try to make myself sit back down and ignore him. But, of course, that's not gonna happen, 'cause I'm obsessed, and also stupid, and possibly even insane—so I peek out the window at the front porch. Luc is there, looking wild, eyes glowing and teeth bared in a grimace.

"Chill. She's here." Gabe's voice is low, and I have to strain to hear it.

I watch as a huge breath heaves Luc's chest and the panic leaves his face. He hangs his head and says, "She's safe . . . okay."

Gabe grins. "Dude. You know you really blew it this time."

My heart sinks as Luc replies, "Good." He nods to himself, then he looks up at Gabe, relieved. "Will you make sure she gets home okay?"

Gabe scrutinizes Luc's face. "Tell me what's up."

Luc backs away, toward the stairs. "Just be sure she gets safely into her house with the door locked," he says turning toward his car and striding away.

And as he walks toward his car it's all I can do not to run after him. 'Cause I want to kill him. But I also want to kiss him. The thought of not being with him—not touching him again—is going down like a jagged little pill, leaving my insides a raw bleeding mass of frustrated confusion. As hard as it is to admit to myself, what I feel for Luc is more than physical. It's not love, but it's something.

How can I want them both?

I scramble back to the kitchen as the front door swings open. "Who was that?" I ask all innocent, but the shake in my voice gives me away.

Clearly, Gabe's not in a sharing mood. "No one that matters," he says, but his blue eyes are a shade darker than usual, and his brow furrows as he leans against the counter.

"What's wrong?"

He smiles this completely bogus smile, like that's supposed

to convince me. "Nothing for you to worry about. Everything's cool."

I can't stand it. I have to know. "I know that was Luc. What did he want?" I blurt.

He looks up at me with wary eyes. "You, apparently."

I watch my hand fan the pages of Gabe's book. My legs are jittering under the table, dying to spring out of the chair and run after Luc. I work to keep my voice even. "Why?"

"You'd need to ask him," he says with a note of frustration. He blows out a sigh and slides into the seat next to me, drawing my attention. He looks me in the eye. "So . . . about yesterday . . ." he says very softly, bringing up the elephant in the room.

I groan and drop my gaze back to my hands. I have no clue what to say—what I'm feeling.

He's quiet for an awkward minute then says, "I'm really sorry about . . . you know."

Of course he is. Why would he want to be with me?

Do I want to be with him?

"But I need to know if what I felt . . ." He hesitates and I can't breathe. "Was it really me you wanted?"

I feel dazed, like a rabbit in the headlights. There's nothing I can say to make this right. I lift my head and look at him. He just stares at me for another minute, then his gaze drops to the floor.

"So . . . when you kissed me . . ." He lifts his eyes and I divert mine. I push back my chair, needing space, and walk into the family room, where I drop onto the couch.

Gabe steps into the door. "Well, I guess that answers that," he says through a strained smile.

199

"It doesn't answer anything." I bury my face in my hands. "I'm so confused. I can't stop thinking about Luc. But I can't trust him. And you . . ." I don't even know how to finish that thought.

"You're right. You can't trust him." He slides in next to me on the couch and wraps an arm around my shoulders. And from my body's reaction—the way all my insides flip-flop—it's clear I can't be trusted either.

When I look up at Gabe, my breath catches. I can see everything I want in his deep blue eyes.

But I also see him struggling with himself. I reach up and touch his cheek, and he pulls me into his lap. When he kisses me, it's less desperate than last time. Gentle and soft and so tender that it makes me ache all over. I press deeper into him, wanting him closer, and I'm blanketed in his peace and love.

Oh God, do I love him?

I pull him tighter as the tears slip from my eyes, and he doesn't push me off this time. He pulls me closer. Despite the heat pulsing through me, I shiver.

After forever, when I pull back and look at him, I wonder how I could have ever wanted anything else. And I could almost believe in love. 'Cause it's right there, in his face.

He wipes the tears from my cheek with his thumb.

"Sorry," I say, not quite sure what I'm apologizing for this time. Everything, I guess.

He places a finger on my lips. "No. Don't." He pulls me closer and rests his face in my hair. And I realize he's shaking too.

I pull my face out of his shoulder and look at him. "Are we okay?"

He nods and smiles, but his smile is strained and his eyes are full of doubt.

I feel all my insides contract into a hard ball, 'cause I'm being seriously unfair. I'm such a shit. My chin drops to my chest. "I'm so screwed up."

"You can't help the way you feel, Frannie."

"Yes I can." At least I always could.

"No, you can't, but you have to be careful about what you *want*."

Despite his summer snow, my simmering frustration boils over. It's clear in my voice. "You keep saying that. What does that mean?"

"It means you have much more control over your world than you know." His eyes are intense and he's starting to scare me.

I push away from him and haul myself off the couch. "I think you've lost it, Gabe. I've got control over exactly nothing."

"You'll see it—eventually."

"See what?"

"Everything," he says. I feel a shiver race through me.

He stands and folds me into his arms. "Everything's going to be good, Frannie," he finally says.

But he doesn't sound sure of that. Far from it.

LUC

Arrgghhhh!

The most confusing day of my existence is now officially the most Hellish day of my existence. And that's saying something.

I cruise around the neighborhood trying to settle my nerves

and get my head straightened out. I have one priority: my job. The same one I've been doing for the last five thousand years. It's not rocket science or brain surgery—either of which I could handle better than I did Frannie. It's just tagging one little soul for Hell. Child's play. So why can't I do it?

Rhetorical question. It doesn't matter why I can't do it. It just matters that I can't—which is painfully obvious.

Frannie is with Gabriel. She's safe, from Belias and from me.

I crank the stereo and I drive by Gabriel's again, once, twice, three times. I slow down each time, desperate to catch a glimpse of Frannie through the window. I loop around the neighborhood, past Frannie's and Taylor's, over and over, trying to figure out what's happened to me—reliving the last three weeks of my existence.

I'm burning hotter than the Fiery Pit, but, at the same time, drowning in a torrent of emotions that demons don't feel.

How do I make them stop?

I can't breathe. Then I remind myself that I don't have to. But the hole in my chest still hurts.

Focus. What now?

By the tenth loop of the neighborhood I know what's got to happen. As much as it rips me apart to think about it, I need to leave and let Belias handle this. I let myself get too close.

I drive once more past Gabriel's and feel the ache deep in my chest as I turn west, back toward my apartment. When I get there, I phase back to Hell and out of Frannie's life.

✠

I intend to phase inside the high Walls of Hell, bypassing the Gates (a perk of being a First Level demon) because I'm really in no mood to deal with the Gatekeeper. But as my feet contact the ground, I find I'm undeniably *outside* the stone walls and the Gates. Not a good sign. Privileges have been revoked. As I approach the Gates, the Gatekeeper, Minos, scrutinizes me with a single squinty bloodred eye in the middle of his long, narrow serpent's face. He bends his tall, sleek, scale-covered frame to get a closer look.

"Fallen out of favor, have we?" he says with a flash of his fangs and a self-satisfied sneer. His high-pitched voice stings my eardrums, intensifying the building ache in my head.

Too dejected to argue, I lean on the blistered iron Gates for support. "It would appear so."

Maybe he'll refuse admittance. Fine by me. But dark foreboding mingles with anticipation on his face as he steps aside to let me pass. "We've been waiting for you. I'll be by the Pit later to see you off."

"We'll make it a party. You bring the balloons," I say over my shoulder, passing through the Gates without a backward glance.

Once inside, the first thing I notice is that Hell feels hotter than I remember. Which doesn't make sense, because it's only been three weeks since I was here. And, besides, anything hovering a few hundred degrees at either side of Hell's two-thousand-degree mark is going to feel pretty much the same: hot. Maybe there's something to all that global warming hoopla after all, even here at the core.

The second thing I notice is that I seem to have maintained my human form ... which is now sweating. No matter. This body can be dismembered and thrown into the Fiery Pit as easily as my other.

The third thing I notice is the *real* security. Minos is just for show. Other than the occasional interloper, keeping people out of Hell isn't generally an issue. And, really, what could be more fun than an interloper? No, the real security is Rhenorian and his crew, who keep the minions inside. He props his stocky seven-foot frame against the wall, eyeing me intently from just inside the Gates. His red eyes flare out of a golden-brown face, flat and leathery. When I look his way, a menacing grin splits his face, as if daring me to try to run. He glides his forked tongue along an impressive set of fanged teeth and spins a three-pronged ranseur in his hands. That's Hell's version of a machine gun. It's capable of focusing enormous amounts of Hellfire into a single burst—over and over. It can't kill a creature of Hell, because almost nothing can, but it can make you wish it had.

I meander past the Inferno, inside the Gates. Shrieks of agony and pleas for mercy issue from barely discernable shapes writhing within the eternal flames: the souls of the damned. Tending demons cackle with mirth as they poke at the occasional limb or head protruding from the white-hot flames. Just watching makes me feel all warm and fuzzy. I smile to myself as I take in the pungent smell of seared flesh mingled with decay, earth, and brimstone and revel in the sights, sounds, and scents of home. For a moment, I can imagine that I never left. That the last three weeks never happened.

For a moment.

But as I continue to meander south, skirting the Fiery Pit at a distance, my mood turns. The screeches echoing from these high walls are of a different sort altogether. Demons who have stepped out of line or come up short in the eyes of management scream from their depths. And as I pass the Pit on my way to the Lake of Fire, I notice every demon, especially the tenders of the Pit, leer at me. Nothing makes a demon's day like impending death and destruction.

Then I see Marchosias moving stealthily toward me from the Pit, mottled crimson skin shimmering in the flickering vermillion and indigo light. His glowing red eyes burn as he strokes his tail, and his satyr's hooves crunch over the lava rock as he makes his way toward me.

My first instinct is to run—not sure why—but I stand my ground. Marchosias *is* a tender of the Pit, but he can't take me until I'm summoned and sentence is pronounced. Besides, if demons have friends, which is debatable, then Marchosias would be mine. He's currently on canine patrol, apparently, because he's got an immense black Hellhound in tow.

"Thought you could just slide right by without stopping?" he says with a sneer on his flat, pinched face. I take an involuntary step back as he approaches. Few, other than King Lucifer Himself, radiate evil as thoroughly as Marchosias.

"Hoping."

The Hellhound sits at Marchosias's side, nearly as tall as me, and the smell of rotting meat permeates the strong scent of brimstone. "How long have you been here?"

"Not long."

"How did you end up on my list?"

"No clue."

"Hmm . . ." He glances across the Lake of Fire toward Flame

Island and the distant black mass of Pandemonium, its high castle walls and jagged spires towering over all of Hell. "The only reason you've lasted this long is because Beherit is preoccupied trying to save his own skin."

I feel myself shudder, but it would be a mistake to show weakness. "What's up?"

"Just avoid Pandemonium. King Lucifer is meeting with the council, and it's a bloodbath up there." Marchosias's eyes shine with malice, white fangs glimmering through his sinister grin. "Word is, your boss is on the chopping block. Something big's brewing topside, and Beherit's not getting the job done." His grin pulls into a leer. "You wouldn't know anything about that . . . ?"

"No," I lie, because that's what we demons do, but also because I feel sudden and overwhelming despair that this is my existence. This is all there is in my world. Our only source of joy, if demons are even capable of that emotion, is the pain, suffering, death, and destruction of others. "Tell me what you've heard."

"There's a mortal the king wants, and Beherit's crew," he leers at me, "is falling down on the job."

"What's so important about the mortal?"

"Word is this person is exceptionally gifted."

Is Frannie exceptionally gifted? I'm sure there are others that we're after. "Gifted how?"

The pure evil in his grin makes me hope we *are* talking about someone other than Frannie. "Sway," he hisses.

The force of that one word is like a wrecking ball, knocking me senseless. *It can't be Frannie.* Frannie has Sight. I don't even want to think about what would happen to a mortal with the ability to sway others' thoughts and emotions here in the Underworld. There have only been two others, and things didn't end well for the one that belonged to Hell. In a daze, I turn to continue walking, but Marchosias grabs my arm, his claws nearly piercing my human flesh.

"So, I'll be seeing you later." His eyes flare red heat and a mirthless smile quirks his mouth as he flashes his fangs.

"I'm sure. Try not to enjoy yourself too much," I say, walking away.

Finally, my head starts to clear, and I reach my sanctuary: the sliver of Hell from my wall mural. I walk along the cragged banks of the Lake of Fire until I reach the southernmost tip, where the lake meets the Walls of Hell, and the river Styx flows in from the south. Here, the distant shrieks of the damned and the mirthful laughter of the infernal blend and echo off the high walls like a dissonant choir. This is my cathedral.

Sitting on a pitted lava outcropping over the Lake of Fire, I let the music of Hell welcome me home for the last time. I stare out over the lake at the glossy black hulk of Pandemonium, perched above all of Hell on Flame Island. I admire the orange and red roiling molten lake swirling around the large crags of brimstone, pointing like accusing fingers at Heaven. Its accompanying light show—flickering scarlet and indigo with blue and white flame eruptions—is like Hell's fireworks. And as the clouds of sulfuric gas emanating from those eruptions engulf me, I breathe them in, savoring the smell of brimstone as it stings my human nose. It's easy to forget how beautiful home is, at least to us demons.

But then I remember Frannie's soul—how it took my breath away. True beauty. Nothing like any soul I've ever seen in Hell before. Will it still look the same when Belias is through with it?

Pushing that thought away with the ache in my heart, I close my eyes and lay back on the sharp lava rocks. But all I see, feel, taste, smell, as vividly as if Frannie were right here, is her—the essence of the girl who made me question all that I am. If I didn't know better, I'd swear I feel a trickle of moisture evaporate into a puff of steam at the corner of my eye. What I'm sure I *do* feel is my brimstone heart breaking as I lay back and wait for the summons. Because there are no second chances in Hell.

FRANNIE

I stare out the windshield as Gabe drives me home, lost in his thoughts. I lean my head on the window as we drive by Taylor's, and out of nowhere, I feel the lightning strike my brain.

Not again.

And, sure enough, as I groan and close my eyes against the pain, I see Taylor's dad, laid out on his bed . . . not breathing. My head spins. I'm going to be sick.

"Stop the car!" I yell, and I open my eyes to see that he already has. I push the door open and puke on the pavement. When I turn back to Gabe, he's not scared or concerned. He's totally calm. I bolt out of the car and run back to Taylor's, pounding my fists, one on the door and the other on the bell, till the door opens.

Taylor's face twists into a scowl. "Fee . . . what's the deal?"

"Where's your dad?" I pant.

"Sleeping . . . why? What's going on?"

"You need to check on him. Right now!"

"Oh, that's not such a good idea. Seriously, Fee. What's up?"

I push past Taylor and climb the stairs to her parents' room. She catches me halfway up the stairs by the back of my shirt and nearly pulls me over backward, but I hold tight to the rail and continue my forward progress, pulling her behind me.

"You can't go in there, Fee. Stop acting so insane!"

I drag her up the rest of the stairs and push open the bedroom door. And there he is, just like I saw him—except I can see his chest rise and fall. He's just sleeping.

"Oh, God." I turn back to Taylor, who's already pulling me out the door. "Sorry . . . I thought . . ." But as I glance back at him, I see the empty pill bottle on the carpet. I pull against Taylor and take another step into the room. There are three more bottles on the nightstand—all empty.

"Taylor," I say, pulling free of her, "call 9-1-1." I run to the side of the bed. "Mr. Stevens, wake up!" I shake him. "Can you hear me?"

Nothing.

Taylor just stands there. I push past her to the phone on the other nightstand and dial 9-1-1. As I explain the emergency, Gabe steps into the room and puts his arm around Taylor. She barely seems to notice, standing rooted to the floor staring at her dad, her eyes wide.

The ambulance arrives five minute later and, as they load her dad in, she turns to me. She doesn't say anything, but the question is clear in her eyes. It's a question I can't answer. I just shrug. Taylor climbs in with her father, and, as they pull out, sirens blaring, I let loose a flood of unexpected tears. Gabe pulls me to him and walks with me to his car.

"You did a good thing, Frannie." He doesn't question how I knew. He doesn't question anything. He just holds me.

"It's my fault," I manage through the sobs.

He lifts my chin with his finger and looks me in the eye. Then his lips trace a course from my forehead, down my temple, across my cheek and brush across my lips. "You need to stop blaming yourself for every bad thing that happens," he says, his voice low.

I push him away. "I was going to talk to Dad. Have the church help them." But I got so wrapped up in my own drama that I forgot. The wave of guilt crashes over me and I let it. I want to feel like crap. It's the least I deserve.

We pull into my driveway, and Gabe looks around warily, reminding me of Luc doing the same thing the other night. As Gabe steers me up the walk, I slide on my sunglasses so Mom won't see my red-rimmed eyes.

"You going to be okay?" Gabe's voice is soft and sympathetic. It almost makes me cry again. I swallow back the lump in my throat.

"Yeah."

"Okay . . . so you're not going anywhere else?"

"Not that I know of."

"Good. Lock the door behind you." He wraps me in a hug, his eyes still darting around.

"Why does everyone want me to lock everything? What's wrong?"

Pulling away from me, he diverts his eyes, staring at the shrubs next to the front porch. "Nothing, really. Just better safe than sorry these days."

"You're such a bad liar," I say, pushing him further away.

He pulls me back to him, and when he kisses me I press into his hard body. I trail my hands along his chest and down his sides. "Come in with me," I say, suddenly not wanting to be alone.

He blows out a sigh then quirks a lopsided smile. "I'd love to, but I need to have a conversation with Lucifer. Promise me you'll lock the door and stay inside."

"Whatever," I say, feeling disappointed and weary, and wondering if I have the energy to climb the stairs. "Will you come back?"

"When I can." He pulls away and looks me in the eyes. "You're sure you're okay?"

"I will be."

"Get some rest." He leans in and kisses me, then opens the door, pushing me gently through. "I'll be back," he says. He smiles, but his eyes are still dark and darting.

I close the door and call out into the unusually quiet house. No answer. Wow. Since no one's home, I do what Gabe asked and lock the door.

I only make the third stair before my shaky legs won't carry me any further. I turn and sit, hugging my knees to my chest. How could I have forgotten to talk to Dad? The one thing I could do to help Taylor and I blew it. Depression settles over me and I tip to the side, lying across the hardwood stair, and think about what a shitty person I am.

But I stopped it.

That's something, I guess. It's the first time I've seen it and been able to change it. There's a little comfort in the thought.

After forever, I drag myself up the rest of the stairs. When I get to my room I crank my stereo and flop back onto my bed, staring at the ceiling. When I close my eyes, Luc is there. And it's not just the image: I can feel his dark energy, smell his cinnamon. I'm furious with myself when I feel tears seep out of the corners of my eyes. I won't cry—not over him.

I haul myself up, wander to the window, and lift the blind. Gabe is long gone, but I swear I see the sun glinting off the windshield of a 1968 Shelby Cobra GT through the trees.

Luc?

I imagine running out there and throwing myself at him. But then I flash on Mystery Girl lounging across Luc's bed and think about calling the police instead. Report him as a stalker.

I peek again. Still there, parked two doors down on the other side of the street. In front of the Brewsters'. In the same place he was parked the night I walked back from Taylor's. What the hell does he want from me?

With a sudden burst of energy born from rage, I yank my door open and fly down the stairs and out the front door in a flash. The grass is cool under my bare feet as I storm across the lawn. As I cross the street to Luc's car, I hear loud music pounding and shaking the pavement under my feet. The glare of the sun off the window makes it hard to see into the car, but he's there, sitting in the shadows. The music volume lowers as the window rolls down. I lean on my hands on the car door, and I'm just about to lay into him when my breath catches and I pull back.

It's not Luc. But I swear it could be his brother.

"Oh, sorry," I say when I get my bearings. "I thought you were someone else."

The stranger smiles at me, eyes glowing. "I'll be whoever you want me to be," he purrs. His voice is velvet and there's something entrancing about it—about him. His intense black eyes won't release me.

I stare into them as the haunting rhythm of Incubus's "Love Hurts" plays from his stereo, asking if there's a spell that I'm under keeping me from seeing the real thing.

"You look so much like a . . . friend of mine," I say, but my voice sounds to me like an echo from some distant source.

He smiles Luc's wicked smile. "I hope he's a close friend."

I feel my thoughts slip into a black fog. "Um . . . close . . . yeah . . ." And my mind goes totally blank as I walk around the car and open the passenger door.

15

✝

All Hell Breaks Loose

LUC

I grab Frannie's arm just as she slides into Belias's car. His hand
darts out and grasps her other wrist as he jerks the car forward,
pulling Frannie along, then stops.

I'm acutely aware that if Belias and I play this tug-of-war
with Frannie, it will tear her apart—literally. But I'm just as
aware that if I let her go, she's his, and I won't get her back. I let
my power flow, weighing the risks. If I hit Belias with it while
he's holding Frannie it could kill her. And even if it doesn't, any
retaliation would. My only hope is that he gets that Hell loses
either way. Because right now, Frannie is untagged. If she dies
here, at our hands, there's not much question her soul goes the
other direction—which would mean dismemberment and the
Fiery Pit for both of us.

I glance down at the ball of power illuminating my right fist, then look up at him, the threat clear on my face. "Belias, be reasonable. We're on the same side and she's my assignment. Just let me take care of this."

His eyes glow red and the smell of brimstone permeates the warm spring air. "You had your chance. King Lucifer is very disappointed. Told me so Himself when He offered me Beherit's job."

"Yeah? Well, get in line," I say weighing my options. Phasing out of here with Frannie is impossible. Her mortal body wouldn't survive the shift. So there's only one choice.

Everything inside me screams as I force my fingers open and let go of her arm.

Belias's face pulls into a grin that would cause any mortal to wet themselves. "Wise choice," he says, releasing Frannie's wrist and reaching across to pull her door closed.

At that second, I summon my infernal power—more than I ever thought I could handle—and level a blast at Belias. A red streak of lightning-hot Hellfire shoots from my fist, lighting up the car and hitting him square in the face. It knocks him back into the door. Clenching my teeth against the pain of that much energy coursing through my body, I lean in and scoop Frannie out of the seat. As she falls out into my arms, she shakes her head and looks up at me, stunned but okay.

I take off running up the street, Frannie in my arms, but Belias phases in front of us, face dark and smoldering—literally. "Nice trick," he says through gritted teeth, "but you forgot something." He raises his right fist, glowing red and hot, and points it at me. "I can do that too."

I glance down at Frannie, cradled in my arms. "Don't be stupid,

Belias. You'll kill her, which will only earn you a one-way trip to the Fiery Pit. No kudos, no credit, no promotion. They'll be no hiding what happened. King Lucifer will know before you ever report back."

His grin falters slightly as he lowers his fist. But then I catch his glance over my shoulder and draw my power back, throwing a field over Frannie, just as Avaira's blast hits me in the back. And, *fuck*, that hurts!

I stagger but manage to stay upright. Shaking off the pain, I look down at Frannie's face. Her eyelids flutter and her breathing is shallow. Black dread creeps through my chest.

How could I have let this happen?

From my arms under Frannie, I push a little heat. Just enough to make her skin flush and cause her to sweat. Without taking my eyes off Belias, the bigger threat, I say nonchalantly, "Good job. You two really *are* that stupid. I've always suspected that's why you could never make First Level, Belias. Just not smart enough. Take a look at what your girlfriend did." I roll Frannie slightly in my arms so he can see her eyes and the sweat starting to roll off her forehead, as well the steam I'm providing as a prop. "You've killed her. She's toast." And the thing is, I really hope I'm bluffing, but I'm not totally sure, because the scent of clove and currant is unmistakable—her soul on the surface, waiting for an angel to come collect it.

Belias's expression turns to rage, but it's not directed at me. He's looking over my shoulder at Avaira. "Damn it, Avaira. That wasn't the plan!"

"Sorry." I can hear the smirk in her sultry voice. "It was just too easy. I didn't think I hit him that hard."

"You stupid bitch. Now we're all slated for the Pit. What were you thinking?" In his rage, his true form shimmers dangerously close to the surface, peeking through his human shell.

The humor is gone from Avaira's voice, replaced with alarm. "It was an accident. We won't go to the Pit."

Belias sends up a growl and is gone in a puff of brimstone. A second later his Shelby, still idling on the curb, peals out. I turn and Avaira is gone too.

In all my existence, I can't remember ever being so scared. I look down at Frannie and turn off the heat. She looks up at me, her head clearing now that Belias is gone. No angel has shown up to take her yet, so maybe she's okay. I pull her tight to my chest, not sure if it's me or her shaking so hard. I nuzzle my face into her hair and I breathe her in.

"I couldn't let him have you," I mumble without thinking.

She looks up at me, eyes at half-mast. "Couldn't do *what*? What's going on?" Her voice is weak and thick, her words a slur.

How to answer? The truth? Well, I almost let Belias, an incubus, seduce you and suck out your soul.

No.

I force a smile and work to keep my voice even. "You were getting into some stranger's car, Frannie. Didn't your mother ever warn you about strangers?"

Her brow creases as though she's fighting to remember something, but she doesn't respond.

Belias's noisy exit has attracted the attention of some neighbors. Thankfully, it's broad daylight, or Avaira's red blast would have lit up the neighborhood. Nevertheless, I see the blind being lifted in the house across from Frannie's, so I hurry to get her inside. I carry her past my Shelby into her house and up the stairs to her room, where I lay her on the bed and check her over quickly. Still warm, but her breathing and heart rate are better. I hang my head as a huge wave of relief washes over me.

She's okay.

I start to move to the window to check for Belias, but her hand shoots up and grabs mine.

"Hey," I say. "You need to get some rest."

"Stay." Her voice is weak but determined.

She pulls harder on my hand, and I sit on the edge of the bed, raking back the sandy-blond waves stuck to her sweaty forehead with my fingers. "I really think I should go, Frannie. Things won't go well if your parents get home and find me in your bedroom. I'll be right outside. I promise."

Her voice is stronger and her eyes plead with me. "Stay."

I breathe deep, resisting the urge to kiss her. I'm completely unable to say no to her. "As you wish."

I sit on the bed for a long time and watch her breathing become deeper and more regular as she drifts off into sleep. *What the Hell am I doing?* I was able to leave the Abyss because I entered on my own—I hadn't been summoned—but it's only a matter of time. And when the summons comes, it's all over. Do I have days? Hours? Whatever it is, it's not enough. And whatever the outcome, whether I tag her or not, I won't be able to stay with her. My chest throbs at the prospect of leaving Frannie again.

I lean down and kiss her forehead then let go of her hand. Or at least try to. But her eyes snap open and she holds tighter.

"Where do you think you're going?" She's half asleep, but the undertone of panic is undeniable.

There's no fighting it. If she needs me to stay, there's no way I can make myself leave. I smile at her. "Nowhere, if you don't want me to."

At first she smiles back, but then her expression changes. There's confusion in her sapphire eyes and stamped all over her gorgeous face as she remembers that she hates me.

"I can't trust you. You're like this Jekyll-and-Hyde person," she says, still holding tight to my hand.

I just shake my head as my brimstone heart breaks. The game is over and I've clearly lost—in every possible way. Because I love her. But I can't have her.

I stand up, needing to get away from her before I do something to hurt her worse. This time she lets me go. "You're right," I say. "You can't trust me."

FRANNIE

I heave myself up to sit on the edge of the bed, feeling shaky. I watch Luc walk out my door and know I should let him go. But my last shreds of better judgment and common sense give way to this primal need I have to be with him.

"Wait! Don't go."

He turns in the door. "Frannie, you're making a huge mistake. You really need me to leave."

I'm still shaking as tiny scraps of memory tease me. I remember going out to yell at Luc . . . but it wasn't him. After that, it's all a blur. My eyes drop to the comforter and pick at the pilled surface. "Who was that guy?"

He leans on the doorframe, facing me. "His name is Belias. He's dangerous."

"Why was he here? What did he want?"

Luc just stares at me and shakes his head.

"He looks so much like you," I finally say when it's clear he's not going to answer.

"Yes. I suppose that's a product of where we're from. We do tend to look alike."

I lift my gaze and lock it with his. "And where is that, exactly? You always change the subject when I ask."

He looks me in the eye for a long time as he contemplates his answer.

Finally, I roll my eyes. "If you have to think about it this long I know whatever you'll say is bullshit. Just forget it."

He turns to walk out the door again. "Sorry. But you wouldn't believe me if I told you," he says over his shoulder from the hall.

"I wish you'd try me."

He turns back and steps slowly into the door with that same lost look on his face I've seen before. His mouth opens to say something but then closes again. He shakes his head. I stare at him, sure the answers are there, just under the surface, and I could see them if I look hard enough. He opens his mouth again, then his gaze drops to the floor and his shoulders slump as he says, "I really need to go."

My heart pounds. I know I should let it drop, but there's something else I need to know. "What about that girl? The one in your bed? Is she, like, your girlfriend from home?"

He lifts his gaze and watches me cautiously as he answers. "No. Actually, she's Belias's girlfriend, Avaira."

I can't control the jealous edge to my voice. "Hmm. So nice of him to share."

"It's not like that, Frannie," he blurts. "They're here for—" He stops abruptly, his eyes boring into mine. "She's nothing."

He drops his head and shakes it again, and I'm afraid he's going to leave.

I bite back the next remark that pops into my head, which has something to do with Mystery Girl's bra size being larger than her IQ. "So, if it's not like *that*, what *is* it like? She was in your apartment—in your *bed*. Does she have a key?"

He just stares at me forever, eyes storming, then he walks fully into my room and drops into my desk chair, staring at the carpet. "No. She doesn't have a key. No lock would keep her out."

"What does that mean? Is she, like, stalking you or something?"

"In a manner of speaking." He lifts his eyes to mine and, if I didn't know better, I'd say I saw trepidation there. "There are things about me you don't know."

I scoot toward him on the edge of the bed. "I'm sure. So, tell me."

He stares at me for another eternity, then leans his elbows on his knees and laces his fingers into his mop of black hair, staring at the floor again. "I'm not what you think I am."

"I don't think you're anything."

He lifts his head and almost smiles.

I cringe. "I didn't mean that how it sounded. I mean I don't really care what you are, I guess. Or something like that. So what don't I know?"

He stands and takes my hand, pulling me off the bed and into his arms. I want to pull away but don't.

He blows a sigh into my hair and groans.

I lift my face to look at him. "You can tell me."

But instead, he gazes down at me with all kinds of promises in his eyes. Even though I know how stupid it is, and I know beyond a doubt that he's going to hurt me again, I lean in to his kiss.

When I look back into his eyes, they're still storming. "I haven't been completely honest with you," he says. Then he backs away and stares out the window. "Satan save me, I haven't been honest with you at *all*."

"Tell me," I say again, stepping toward him.

He heaves another sigh and sags back into my desk, like holding himself up is suddenly too hard. Then his eyes raise and lock with mine, and he looks sullen but determined. "Belias, Avaira, me . . . ," he says slowly, as if every word hurts him, "we're all from—"

"Frannie?" Mom's voice calls from the bottom of the stairs. It scares the hell out of me. How did I not hear her come in?

I jump and step back from Luc. "Yeah, Mom."

"Is that . . . Luc's car out front?" It's like she has trouble even saying his name.

A nervous grimace dances across Luc's face.

"Yeah, Mom."

Her voice shoots up an octave, and I hear her feet hurry up the stairs. "Is he up there?"

"Yeah," I say, grabbing his hand and pulling him to the door.

She's at the top of the stairs, her eyes wide, when we step into the hall.

"Hey. We were just working on calculus homework," I say, dropping his hand and willing the color out of my cheeks.

"Oh." She's all but glaring at Luc. "Wouldn't you have more room at the kitchen table?"

Just then the back door slams and Grandpa's sandpaper voice bellows through the house. "Hey! Whose Shelby's parked out front?"

My heart soars. "Grandpa!" I squeal just as he appears at the base of the stairs. His blue eyes smile up at us.

"That would be mine," Luc says.

"Restored or original?"

"All original."

Mom steps aside and lets Luc pass by her. He nods and smiles—a soft, reassuring smile—as he passes.

"Who does your maintenance?" Grandpa asks as Luc makes his way down the stairs.

"I do."

"She's a beauty," he says, slapping Luc on the back. "Mind if I take a look under the hood?"

"No problem." Luc shoots a concerned glance back up the stairs and then heads out the front door with Grandpa.

"Why was he here?" Mom hisses. "We were clear. You're not to see him—especially not alone."

"Mom, please. You never said I couldn't see him. I don't know what your deal is with him, but I wish you'd cut him some slack."

"Frannie, we've discussed this. Let me be perfectly clear. You are *not* going to date that boy."

This is unbelievable. "You're being so ridiculous."

And you're also too late.

223

I walk to my window and look out as Luc lifts the hood of the Shelby and he and Grandpa duck under it. What's his deal? *Belias, Avaira, me, we're all from . . . ?* What? What could be that bad? We're all from jail? The loony bin?

What?

Outer space? The future?

I lean my elbows on the windowsill and watch him with Grandpa. Could he say anything that would change how I feel when I'm with him? I don't think so. And, besides, he's not the only one with secrets. God knows I've got some.

Like Gabe. Who I kissed. Who I'd kiss again.

I groan and drop my forehead into my hand. *What the hell am I doing?*

I pull my forehead out of my hand and rest my chin on it. Luc looks up at me from the street, and I buzz all over.

Belias, Avaira, me, we're all from . . .

I know nothing about him or about Gabe. They both came all out of nowhere and totally turned me inside out. Why can't I stop thinking about them?

Belias, Avaira, me, we're all from . . .

I'm not going to sleep well tonight. I can tell already.

LUC

"You're killin' me. This is a classic. How many miles?"

"Only about thirty thousand," I answer.

He leans in to get a better look. "Holy Jesus. This baby's

worth some serious cash. All original—and looks almost new. How long have ya owned her?"

"Bought it new."

He lifts his eyes from the engine block and laughs out loud. "She was built before you were, son."

Oh, yeah. "I meant my grandfather. He bought it in '68."

He nods to the '65 convertible in the driveway. "Frannie could help ya with the maintenance. She's the best vintage Mustang mechanic I know."

I glance up at her window and smile when I see her, elbow propped on the sill and cheek resting in her hand, watching us. My need to be that hand—to touch her face—almost knocks me over. Satan save me, I can't stand being this far from her. I force my eyes away from her, back to her grand-father.

"Really. That's a tidbit that she didn't share."

He looks at me, all humor gone from his face. "I hope that's not all she's not sharin'."

I draw a deep breath and look him in the eye. "Frannie is special. I'm not taking any chances with her." Except almost letting Belias suck out her soul and trying to drag her into the Abyss. But other than that . . .

"She *is* special. Too good for any of you," he says, gesturing vaguely in my direction with an elbow. And he has no idea how accurate he is. "Treat her right." His eyes flit up to her window and back.

"You're right. She's much too good for me. I've tried to tell her that."

He smiles. "But she won't listen. She's a stubborn one. Just like her grandma."

"I won't let anything happen to her," I say.

He stares hard into my eyes. "I'll hold ya to that. And if it does, ya know who I'm comin' after."

"Yes, sir."

Then he takes me completely by surprise. "Do ya love her?"

I just stare at him for a long second. Something sharp twists in my gut, and I look up at Frannie in the window. As hard as I've tried to deny it, or at least convince myself that it didn't matter, I know it as surely as I know I'm going to the Fiery Pit because of it. "Yes, sir."

"Have ya told her?"

"No, sir."

"When were ya plannin' on gettin' around to that?"

"Soon," I say with a smile.

He smiles back. "Good."

16

✣

The Devil You Know

FRANNIE

I can't remember once in my life ever hating that it was the weekend. But this weekend was hell. There were nightmares about alien body snatchers and convicts with hooks for hands. There were dreams about Luc and Gabe that I blush just thinking about. And twice I was sure I saw a black '68 Shelby drive past my house.

Belias, Avaira, me, we're all from . . .

And all day today at school I've felt like I was on some kind of possessed seesaw, up and down with Gabe and Luc. But after last-period government, I waste no time grabbing Luc's arm and dragging him to the parking lot. We climb into his car, and, as soon as the doors are closed, his lips are burning into mine. It feels amazing, so it's really hard to push him away.

"Tell me," I say into his lips.

"What?" he says into mine.

I force myself to push back from him. "What you were going to say Friday—in my room—before my mom showed up."

He reaches for me. "I don't remember."

I push back harder. "Belias, Avaira, me, we're all from . . ." I say to jog his memory.

For a second, his face pinches in a wince. "Later."

"Now."

His eyes grow hard, like black obsidian. "It's nothing."

"It didn't seem like nothing Friday."

He leans back in his seat, closes his eyes, and blows out a sigh. "You really don't want to know."

"Yes, I *really* do."

He pulls his head off the headrest and looks at me with tortured eyes. "I've done some pretty awful things."

I feel my gut knot. "So who hasn't?"

"I mean it, Frannie."

But all I can think is that there's nothing he could have done that's even close to what I have. And suddenly my throat is closing and my chest is tightening. And there's no air in the car. I push the door open and sort of stagger out onto the pavement.

Luc is there in a heartbeat. He pulls me to him, keeping me from falling over. "Frannie, what's wrong?"

Secrets.

I lean into him for a long time, gasping for air, then shove him away. I hate that he's here, seeing this. And I hate more that he thinks I need his help.

"I'm fine," I lie.

I can tell he doesn't believe me, and I don't care. But when he wraps his arms back around me, I let him. He sits me back on the seat of the car as my breathing eases.

"Sorry," I say without looking at him.

"What happened?"

"Nothing." I spin my legs into the car and grab the door handle. "Let's go."

He steps back and I close the door.

He's right. I don't really want to know his secrets. The ones I already have are enough.

✝

Our bodies move together to the pounding rhythm of Depeche Mode's "Personal Jesus." As hard as it is, I push Luc's burning body away from mine and sit up on his big black bed, working to catch my breath. "I don't think Mr. Snyder is gonna accept 'we were too busy messing around' as an excuse for this outline not being done."

Luc grabs my hips and pulls me back down next to him. "We could try 'my dog ate it,'" he says hopefully, wrapping his arms around me again. I glower at him for a second before he groans and says, "How fast can we get this thing done?"

I slide up and prop myself against a stack of pillows on the headboard. "We only have the last few questions. It should go pretty quick."

He gets his composition book off the floor and sits against the headboard next to me, but he's not writing. He's staring at me. "You're going to have to put your shirt on, or I'm not going to be able to concentrate on this," he says after a minute. "That red bra is way too hot. I didn't think the pope let good Catholic girls wear red bras."

"I'm not a good Catholic girl, remember? I got thrown out of Catholic school."

"I remember," he says, and his smile makes my heart skip.

As Depeche Mode urges me to "reach out and touch faith," I trace the coil of the black serpent tattooed around his upper arm and ogle his bare chest.

"Okay, so . . . Steinbeck . . . ," I say to distract myself from that smile—and that body. I draw a deep breath and pull my shirt on over my head. Looking down at Mr. Snyder's handout, I read, "What is he saying about the character of man?"

"That anyone can justify anything, no matter how wrong."

I raise an eyebrow. "Really? 'Cause I didn't get that. I'm thinking his major upshot is that circumstances dictate actions."

"Same thing."

"Not really. Think about it. All through the book, Tom does things . . . makes choices based on what he and his family need at that moment. It's not like he just wakes up one day and says, 'Gee, I think I'll go kill somebody today.'"

"Okay, but then he *does* kill someone and goes on the run, where he's not helping his family because he can't work, and he may end up hurting them if they get caught helping him. So you can't say he only does things for the good of his family. People do things, and they wrap those choices in all kinds of noble garb, but in the end it's all self-serving."

I put the handout down. "Wow . . . so people are all just lying, scheming, self-serving shitbags?"

"Yep, pretty much."

"With no redeeming qualities whatsoever?"

"Sounds about right."

"That's sad," I say, shaking my head.

"Sad, but true."

"Okay, so what about Rose of Sharon at the end? She loses her baby but then breast-feeds a starving man. What's self-serving about that?"

He looks at me for a minute then smiles. "Sorry, you lost me at 'breast,'" he says, glancing at mine.

I elbow him. "You're such a pig."

He grins. "I'm not a pig, I'm a guy—which, now that I think about it, is pretty much the same thing. Point taken."

"I bet your heart is coal. It's no wonder you see the world through Hell's glasses," I say. Opening my composition book, I flip to the page headed "Steinbeck, wrap-up essay outline, Frannie and Luc" and write my last few bullet points. When I'm done I hand it to Luc and watch his face screw into a scowl.

"Well, your glasses are rose-colored, because this list is incredibly naïve."

"Just 'cause I don't choose to believe that everyone's evil doesn't make me naïve."

"Yes it does, but that's all the better for me. So where were we?" he says with a grin. He throws the composition book on the floor and eases my shirt over my head, staring at my red bra.

"I'll show you naïve," I say.

His eyes flash and I swear he stops breathing when I smile my own wicked smile and reach behind my back to unhook my bra, tossing it to the floor on top of my shirt. I roll in next to him on the bed and feel my skin melt into his. Luc kisses my

231

neck and my ear, his hot breath pebbling my skin with goose bumps.

"Mmm, you're beautiful," he whispers in my ear. I shudder as a massive rush rolls through me. So is he.

My whole body is a live wire. I'm absolutely buzzing, every nerve ending on overload. With all the others, there was never any question that I was going to stop. I've never been ready. But none of them have ever made me feel like Luc does. Everything about him is wrong, but nothing has ever felt so right. The way I can't get him out of my head and my heart only feels full when we're together, how he makes everything feel new and exciting, the way I can picture myself with him—telling him everything.

He kisses me deeper as a tear slips from the corner of my eye. I feel like I'm suffocating, but I can't push him away. I want him closer.

LUC

All I can feel is her body next to mine. All there *is* is her body next to mine. The rest of the universe, Heaven and Hell included, has disintegrated into nothingness. By all that is unholy, I'm going to have her for all eternity. I won't stop until she's mine . . . in the Abyss . . . where she doesn't belong . . .

I push the thought away and focus on Frannie. Her eyes are closed and she's pressing into me, kissing me. I feel her hands on me—all over me. "Don't stop," she whispers hot in my ear, but she has no idea what she's asking. Because, despite what she thinks, she *is* naïve. I know what lurks in the hearts of man and in my own brimstone heart.

All I have to do is take her. This is the first step on her path to the Abyss. She wants it; I want it . . . oh, how I want it.

I breathe in her chocolate and ginger—taste the currant and clove of her soul. I feel her hands on me, pulling at my jeans. Her kisses become deeper and more urgent. I can't wait any longer. I need her. Now.

I'm just on the edge of magicking the rest of our clothes away, imagining how her skin will feel against mine, picturing us together, when she pulls back and her eyes pierce mine to my black core. She lifts her hand, tracing my lips with the tip of her trembling finger, and I'm overwhelmed with the scent of warm chocolate.

Chocolate?

Could it be . . . *love*? Does she love me?

As her eyes lock on mine again, it all becomes clear. I'm going to stop, because somewhere along the way I've developed a human conscience, and that conscience is telling me that, no matter how much I want her with me forever, this is wrong. She needs to know what I am, to have a choice. I kiss her again, one last time, as if my life depended on it—which it pretty much does since, if I take this route, my next stop is the bottom of the Fiery Pit.

"We can't do this, Frannie." She looks away as I prop myself on an elbow above her. "Look at me," I say more firmly, "I'm not who you think I am."

And then I do it.

I feel myself cringe against her inevitable reaction as, with my mind, I push aside my human shell and let her see me in all my Hellish glory: dappled copper skin, shaggy black hair dangling in my slanted, bloodred cat's eyes; a straight, red gash of a mouth in my flat face; and the requisite black horns, of course. I can feel the fire under my skin as I start to steam, and I pull away, sure I'll burn her in this form.

I don't know why, but I thought I might not feel as much for her when I shed my human shell. I was wrong. It turns out I feel more—for her and for me, because my love for her triggers disgust and loathing for myself. And the smell of brimstone, usually so pleasing, is making me sick. *I'm* making me sick.

I expect a scream and maybe the rustling of sheets as she backpedals away from me on the bed. I don't hear any of that, but I can smell her fear, sweet orange hanging thick in the air. I'm afraid to even look at her, sure I'll see my own disgust mirrored in her eyes.

But when I *do* look, I can tell she's not seeing me. Not really. Because what I see under a thin veil of shock is curiosity. Her eyes are wide and her breathing fast as she struggles to put words together. "So . . . what . . . I mean . . ."

"I'm a demon, Frannie," I interrupt, the anger in my voice directed inward. "From Hell."

She just stares at me, taking everything in, and myriad thoughts swim in her blue eyes. "From Hell," she repeats, her voice shaking.

"From Hell," I say softer, realizing that I've made a terrible mistake. What was I thinking? That she'd love me anyway? *You're a fool, Luc.*

The bedsprings creak as she hugs a pillow in front of her and sits up. Doubt clouds her eyes and a tear slips over her lashes, coursing a crooked path down her cheek, as she processes what she's seeing. "A demon . . ."

In answer, I groan and drop my face into the pillow. Because I know any minute she'll run. When the horror of the whole thing sinks in—when she figures out why I'm here—she'll run screaming from my apartment, and I can't bear to watch.

But the weight of her silence is crushing me. I roll off the bed and move to the window, staring blindly at the parking lot. She sniffles and I turn to face her. She just stares at me with big, frightened eyes, and I hate that it's me that's scared her. I feel myself being drawn back to the bed to comfort her.

But I can't go back.

I can never go back now that she knows what I am. I've lost her.

Self-loathing overwhelms me, and I start to hope that the invisible fist clenching my heart will snuff out its rhythm and kill me. But instead of directing my fury where it belongs, I hear my voice, low and strangled, lash out at her. "*What the Hell is wrong with you?* You should be terrified! Run!"

For a moment, she looks like she might. And I really want her to. I want her to run hard and fast and never look back.

But, Satan save me, I want her to stay more.

It's a good thing that I don't have to breathe, because I'm fairly certain I wouldn't be able to. I lean back against the wall, slouching down it and staring at the ceiling with my fingers laced over my horns, and wait an eternity for her to do something. Anything.

Finally, unable to help myself, I drop my gaze back to her.

Her face is brooding, her brow creased. Her voice is heavy, pensive. She hugs the pillow tighter. "This can't be real." She rubs her eyes and looks back at me.

I would give anything for it not to be. I hang my head. "It's real."

For a minute she's quiet and I can almost hear her thinking. "I've always known there was something . . . dark . . . and sort of dangerous about you," she says, finally.

I slide up the wall to a stand. "Are you hearing me, Frannie? I'm more than 'sort of dangerous'!"

She flinches a little but doesn't move from the bed. I watch, expecting terror to dawn on her face at any second, but instead, her expression turns furious and black pepper floods the room. "Why didn't you tell me?"

"I'm telling you now."

"I mean before. You let me . . ." she spins off the bed and glares at me, gripping the pillow so tight I'm sure it will rip. "I love you," she spits in accusation.

She said it.

And it's there—warm chocolate underlying the scorch of black pepper in my nostrils. In that instant, all my insides turn to pure energy, and I feel my brimstone heart explode.

But it doesn't matter, because this is the part where she runs.

Her eyes widen as what she just said dawns on her. She slides back onto the bed and sits there, for a long, agonizing minute, staring at me, her jaw slack and disbelief stamped all over her face. "I . . . I didn't . . ." Her eyes drop to the sheets.

There's nothing I can say. I can't reach out to tell her I love her too. So I hang my head and wait for the slam of the door as she bolts.

But the door doesn't slam. Instead, she says, "So, what's the deal? Do you have to go back?"

I look up and a sardonic bark of a laugh leaves my throat. Of all the things she could have asked . . . "Eventually."

She grabs her shirt from the floor, tugging it over her head, then glares at me. "I knew you'd leave."

My lips pinch together in a grimace, and I shake my head. "*That's* what you're worried about? For the sin of Satan, Frannie, I'm a demon. You should be *hoping* I'll leave."

"Fine," she says, shoving her composition book into her book bag. And that's when I notice the shake in her hands. "I'll save you the trouble," she snarls.

She throws her book bag over her shoulder and searches the floor as my insides churn.

"Damn it!" she yells in frustration. "Where are my goddamn flip-flops?"

I bend down and scoop them off the floor, holding them out to her.

She storms over and rips them out of my hand. But then she hesitates, staring at my horns. She starts to lift her hand as her eyes drop to mine, the curiosity back. "Can I . . ." But then she drops her hand and shakes her head, as if trying to clear it.

"What?" I hear the hope in my voice and despise myself even more for it.

"Nothing." She wheels and strides toward the door. But before she reaches it she spins back. She stares hard into my eyes for a long minute then pulls a deep breath. "So, now that I know what you are, am I going to Hell for falling for you anyway?" A shaky smile plays at the corners of her mouth as she wipes a tear off her cheek with the back of her hand.

And, suddenly, warm chocolate overpowers her black pepper. Just for a second, the heart throbbing in my chest doesn't feel like brimstone. I can't believe that she knows what I am—the real me—and she loves me anyway. But then the reality of that sinks in.

"Frannie, no . . . this isn't right," I groan. I let my knees buckle and slide down the wall to sit, my head in my hands. She shouldn't still love me. This can only end badly.

She walks back to the center of the room, drops her book bag, and perches on the corner of the bed. "Do you care about me at all?"

I pull my head out of my hands and look up at her on the bed. I know what I should say, and my mouth opens to form the word "no." But instead, what I hear escape very softly from my lips is, "Yes." And hearing myself say it shocks me out of my stupor. I spring to my feet and channel all the ice from my dying brimstone heart into my words. "I mean *no*. I was just doing my job."

"I don't believe you," she says, fiery incredulity in her words and her face.

She should be screaming. Running. Anything but this. I spin around and throw a general growl out at the world—and catch my reflection in the mirror on the bathroom door.

What the Hell?

I walk to the mirror and stare at myself as I work harder to push off my human form. When nothing changes, I turn back to her.

"Frannie. Look at me and tell me *exactly* what you see. What's different?"

"Well . . . the horns are kinda new, and your eyes are glowing a little more than usual. And I hate to say it, but you stink." She scrunches her face and pinches her nose. "Can you turn off the rotten eggs? I like cinnamon better."

"That's all?"

"Is there supposed to be more?"

Tail . . . hooves . . . fangs. "Well . . . yeah."

"Like?"

"Nothing." I grab my T-shirt off the floor and yank it on. "We're going for a ride."

17

✝

For Heaven's Sake

FRANNIE

We run through the rain, my hand in Luc's, and slide into his car. I'm afraid to ask, but I do anyway. "Where are we going?"

"There's only one person—and I use that term loosely—that might know what the hell is going on," he says as he starts the car.

As Luc drives the storm picks up, and by the time we pull up to Gabe's house it's a full-on deluge, fat drops of rain sheeting the windshield and pounding on the roof like a thousand tiny hammers. And the whole way, all I can think about is that I told him I love him.

What was I thinking?

He's a demon. I still can't get my mind around what that even means. He had *horns*.

And I told him I love him.

Oh God! Where did that even come from?

I don't love him, do I?

No. Love doesn't exist.

But neither do demons.

I glance at Luc as he cuts the engine and turns to look at me. I'm terrified of him, but as stupid as I know it is, my terror has nothing to do with him not being human.

Oh God. *Do I love him?*

He pulls me out of the car and up the walk onto the porch to ring the bell. All the windows are dark.

"Maybe he's not home," I say, hoping. 'Cause I'm not ready to do this with the two of them.

"He's here," Luc answers just before the door opens and the sight of Gabe takes my breath away.

I can't be here with both of them. Not when I'm this confused. 'Cause three days ago I was just as terrified at the realization that I might love Gabe.

I turn to Luc. "Is this a good idea?"

"He might know what's happening."

"Happening to who?" Gabe asks, reaching for my hand and pulling me through the door.

"Me," Luc says, following behind.

Gabe turns on the light, and stares Luc down. "So . . . ?" he asks, closing the door behind us.

"I can't change," Luc says, his voice heavy and low.

Gabe looks shocked, like he actually knows what Luc is talking about and it means something. "Show me."

Luc steps back from me, closes his eyes, takes a deep breath, and sprouts small, black horns. I stare, fascinated, and resist the urge to reach up and touch them.

"Try harder."

"That's it. That's all I got."

"And he's not as hot as before," I add. Luc looks at me, and there's something in his eyes—hope, maybe.

Understanding dawns on Gabe's face. "I was wondering . . ."

Luc's horns are gone. "Wondering what?"

"Do you remember telling me that you didn't want Frannie to get hurt?"

Luc's eyes shift to mine. "Yes."

"And I told you I believed you."

"Yes."

"It was starting then. Your thoughts were hanging right out there for any old angel to hear. I can't hear a demon's thoughts."

Luc's eyes narrow. "You've been in my head?" he growls.

Gabe snorts. "Yeah. And I have to tell you, your plan sucked. You loved her, whether you knew it or not—a fact that shot the rest of your sad plan to Hell, so to speak."

My eyes snap to Luc.

He loves me too?

Luc glares at Gabe and turns to stare out the window.

My mind is reeling, thoughts, images, and emotions all flying around at random. I'm hearing and thinking things I know are impossible—but I also know they're true. And there's a tiny piece of my core that feels relieved, like it knew this was coming.

Luc—Lucifer—hot—horns—demon. It somehow seems more real now, with Gabe standing here, than it did in Luc's apartment.

Gabe.

I hear my breath catch in some distant place as the pieces of the puzzle click together in my head. Gabe—Gabriel—his glowing smile—and all his warnings. And, what he just said . . . *for any old angel to hear.*

No.

I look at Gabe, unable to clear the stunned expression from my face. *Angel?*

He looks at me, eyes cautious, and answers my unspoken question aloud. "Yes."

"*No!*"

Why is that so much harder to accept than Luc being a demon?

Because there are no angels—no Heaven—no God.

The room spins, and I bend over, bracing my hands on my knees, trying to pull air into my collapsing lungs. But my throat tightens more as I think about Matt, completely cutting off my airway.

If there's a God, why did he take my brother?

My legs go out, and the last thing I feel before I black out is Gabe swinging me into his arms.

✝

When I open my eyes, Luc's worried face is the first thing I see. He's sitting on the edge of the couch, holding my hand. Gabe is pacing behind him. I pull a shuddering breath and try to sit, but Luc lowers me gently back down on the couch, adjusting the throw pillow behind my head.

"I don't understand any of this." My voice is little more than a rasping whisper.

Luc gazes down at me, promising everything with his eyes. "Ask me anything."

My thoughts are a hopeless, twisted jumble and what comes out is a ramble. "You're here . . . both of you . . . what . . . why?" I finally manage through a dry mouth with a shaking voice.

His voice is soft, like he's talking to a frightened child—which, I guess, he is. "Because that's where *you* are."

"Me . . . you're here for *me* . . . ?" I feel the blood drain from my head again, and stars dance in front of my eyes.

"Yes."

"Why?" I whisper.

A sardonic smile quirks Gabe's lips as he sits on the arm of the couch at my feet. "I'm here to protect you from him." He nods toward Luc.

My whole body shakes and I feel like I could puke. "Protect me from . . . Luc?"

Gabe turns to Luc, the disdain clear on his face. "You didn't tell her? You're a real piece of work, you know that?"

Luc looks tormented as he stands abruptly and moves to the window. His hand grips the window frame so hard I'm surprised the wood doesn't splinter, and his gaze drops to the floor.

Gabe eases in next to me on the couch. He folds me into his arms and I sink into him. "He's here to tag your soul for Hell."

"Tag my soul . . ." I feel my head start to swim again as stars flash brighter in my eyes. Then my throat starts to close off when I think about why I belong in Hell. "Because of . . . what happened?"

Gabe pulls me tighter to him. "No. It has nothing to do with that."

Luc turns back from the window and looks at Gabe and me with the question in his eyes.

I pull my gaze away from him and settle deeper into Gabe. "Then, why me?"

Gabe pierces Luc with a steel gaze, and Luc looks suddenly unsure. "I never knew for sure," he finally says. "All I knew is that I needed to tag her."

"Hmm, so Beherit must have a lot of faith in you, then," Gabe says, sarcasm overflowing.

Luc stares death at Gabe. "Shut the hell up. It's not my place to know." But then he looks at me in Gabe's arms, and his gaze drops to his hands.

"Touchy, aren't we." Gabe's expression softens. "You have a good guess, though."

Luc nods but doesn't say anything.

Gabe pulls me closer. "You're special, Frannie. You have special . . . skills. Certain gifts that both sides would kill—literally—to get their hands on."

"Both sides . . . like, Heaven and Hell?"

He nods.

"I don't have any gifts."

"But you do." He looks at Luc. "Doesn't she?"

Luc's eyes shift tentatively from the floor to mine. "You see things, Frannie."

"I don't know what you're talking about."

"You have Sight . . . visions. Ghalib, Taylor's dad. You knew."

My throat tightens as I think about my nightmares—things

245

I saw before they happened. The faces that follow the lightning in my head: Matt, Grandma, Ghalib, Mr. Stevens, and so many others.

Gabe pulls back and looks into my eyes. "But there's more. Something even bigger."

I look back at Luc and his face goes white. He shakes his head slowly. Gabe looks up at him and nods.

"Sway . . ." Luc whispers, his brow creasing as if he had a sudden headache. He drops his head and pinches the bridge of his nose. "Unholy Hell . . ."

"What?" I say. A shudder runs down my spine and Gabe pulls me close again.

"Hitler, Moses . . . what do they have in common?"

I'm in no frame of mind to work out a riddle. "Just tell me what's going on." I hate that my voice sounds so small and weak.

"You know the story of Moses. He had the ability to make people listen: to sway their opinions, their thoughts. There had never been anyone like that before. When Lucifer saw what he could do, how God worked through him, he realized he'd screwed up. The next time someone showed up with that same degree of Sway, Lucifer wasn't going to get beat out. He fought—dirty, I might add," he says, glaring at Luc, "and he won. We all know what happened in Nazi Germany. There hasn't been another with that same power until now." He shares a meaningful glance with Luc and then looks back at me. "You."

I look at Luc, who's standing wide-eyed and slack-jawed, horrified.

"Listen, here's the deal. If *they* get to you," Gabe juts his chin toward Luc, "influence you, you're Hitler—but worse. If you

246

stay with us, you're Moses. Your power is only going to get stronger." His jaw clenches and he shakes his head. "And you're not naïve for believing people are innately good, Frannie."

I feel so small, my whole body collapsing down on itself as everything real, everything I've ever known, vanishes. Pieces of a hundred questions tease me, but I can't put them together in a way that makes sense—except one.

"Why now?" I hear myself whisper.

"You're coming into your own now. When you were young, we were able to Shield you, to keep you off their radar." He shoots a glance at Luc. "But not anymore."

My voice is still a harsh whisper. It's all I can manage. "What do you want from me?"

He traces a finger along the collar of my shirt to my chest and taps it there, over my heart. "Just for you to follow your heart. Do what's right."

I bark out a mirthless laugh that doesn't even sound like mine. "I'm no saint."

"I never said you were. But, like it or not, this is what you are. *Who* you are. And my job is to be here for you—in any way you need me."

LUC

And as he says it, I know Gabriel is right. This is what I felt in her soul. It's why Beherit sent me out looking for her and why King Lucifer wants her so badly that he's willing to chance breaking a rule or two.

She looks stunned—eyes wide like a deer in the headlights. "You guys got the wrong sister. You must be mixing me up with Grace."

Gabriel nestles his face into her hair. "You're already swinging the balance. You, Frannie. Not Mary or Kate or Grace or Maggie. You. If you have the power to transform Shit-for-Brains over there," he glowers at me, "just imagine the difference you can make in the mortal realm. The difference you've probably *already* made without even knowing it."

My back hits the wall as if someone pushed me, and my legs won't hold me anymore. I slide down the wall and sit on the floor.

Sway.

Frannie's got Sway. And if what Gabriel just implied is true, her power has never been rivaled in a mortal. He's saying her power is what changed me—a creature of Hell. And not just my mind, but my physical being. *How is that possible?* Even Moses had no influence over the celestial or infernal. And if that's true, it's not just the masses she can sway. She has power beyond that of even King Lucifer. She could change the shape of Heaven and Hell.

My king's words echo in my head. *It's my turn. This is my chance. I will be out from under Him—finally.* King Lucifer thinks He can manipulate Heaven—maybe even the Almighty—through Frannie.

"*Be careful what you wish for,*" she whispers, as lost in her own thoughts as I am in mine.

There's torment in Gabriel's eyes as he looks into Frannie's.

"Your power is getting stronger every day. You need to see that you have pull on people's thoughts and emotions and therefore their actions." He glances toward me and his eyes drop to her hand, where he twines his fingers with hers. "And it's not just *people* you have that effect on. You'll always get what you want if it's in your control."

Frannie pulls away from him and suddenly there's rage. Black pepper floods the room. "I want my brother back. I don't have *that*," she spits.

He looks at her with sad eyes. "The only one with control over that is God."

All I can do is watch as her expression shifts from rage through shock into panic. "This is wrong. I'm not a saint or an angel. I'm not even a good person. I'm going to Hell. I already know that."

Why would she think that? I look at Gabriel. His expression is pained and sickeningly sympathetic. He pulls her to his shoulder and she melts into him. When the scent of Frannie's warm chocolate seeps through his celestial stench, I feel something cold and black wrap around my heart and squeeze. I'd kill him if I didn't think Frannie needed him.

"What happened—the reason you think you're going to Hell—it wasn't your fault," he says into her hair.

"You're so full of shit," she spits, pulling away. "I killed my brother."

The bottom drops out of my stomach. The boy in the picture—that explains the haunted look in her eye when I asked about him. So much pain—the same pain that was buried so deep that first day we met, when I asked what she'd like to undo.

Gabriel is still looking at her, shaking his head. "You didn't kill him, Frannie. It was his time. That's all."

It's like watching a volcano erupt. The words spill out of her mouth like burning lava. "Yeah. Just keep telling yourself that if it makes you feel better about stealing children from their families."

Gabriel slides a little closer to her on the couch, but she moves away. "He *is* with his family. God called him home."

"Well, then, your God *sucks*."

I move across the room and sit next to her. I take her hand, wanting—no, *needing*—to do something to ease her pain.

"I think what Gabriel said is true, Frannie. If you killed him you'd already be tagged for Hell, and you're not."

"Well, I should be," she says, pulling herself away from my touch.

I lift her chin with my finger, staring down into her deep sapphire eyes. "No, you shouldn't," I say and lean in to kiss her. For only the third time, I push my power on Frannie, to draw out all her pain and her misdirected anger. It's not nearly enough, but it's all I know how to do.

FRANNIE

I hesitate, but then I look into those black eyes that can see my soul. And when his lips touch mine, I feel everything shift, and all my anger melts away. When his eyes finally release me I feel calm, the acid in my core and the ache in my heart gone.

Gabe pulls a deep sigh and looks at me with wounded eyes, and my guilt crushes me. I need them both in ways I can't even understand. Gabe moves across the room and sits in the chair under the window.

I drop my head and stare into my lap.

Luc squeezes me. "So, back to my original question. What the hell is happening to me? What exactly is it that I'm transforming into?" He glowers at Gabe. "*Not* one of you. Please, for the love of all things unholy, tell me I'm not going to become some goody-two-shoes angel. I couldn't take it."

Gabe glowers back. "Don't know. Anything's possible. Let me know if you start sprouting wings."

I look up at Gabe. "Could he become like me? Human?"

Luc looks at me with that same hopeful expression I saw on his face earlier. Gabe answers, resigned. "It's possible. This is unprecedented as far as I know. I have no clue what's happening, except it's clearly happening and it's just as clearly significant. And you're the key. You're going to change the world, Frannie. This is big."

"Big . . ." I say, trying to figure out what that means. "So, are we talking, like, 'bringing him to Jesus' big," I say, waving my hand in Luc's direction, "or 'virgin birth' big?"

Luc scowls and a smile just touches the corners of Gabe's mouth. "Based on what you're capable of, I'd be thinking more along the lines of 'virgin birth' big. Although, if you could bring *him* to Jesus, that'd be pretty huge too."

Luc bolts off the couch and is across the room like a shot, eyes storming. "You can't be serious."

"Don't be such a doofus. If it wasn't big, would He have sent me? Her name is Mary, after all. Could anyone without Sway convince the masses of a virgin birth? The second coming of Christ?" A grin far too mischievous to ever be considered angelic flits across Gabe's face. "What's wrong, Lucifer? You don't want to be Joseph?"

Luc wheels around and braces his hands on the wall, sending up a growl that curls my hair. "Unholy Hell! This can't be happening." Then he spins back and stares at me, eyes wide.

I pull myself out of the couch and stand there, not sure what I'm feeling. I think about Gabe's kiss. If that was Heaven, I want more. I remember thinking I could just live there, in that peace and love. But that's not what he's saying—not what he's offering. I'm supposed to have some power, to do something with it that's supposed to save people. And as I think about that, panic takes over, making it a little hard to breathe.

Gabe tucks me into his side and wraps his arms around me. This time I let him, 'cause I need him. I melt into him as his summer snow buries me in calm and my breathing starts to ease.

When I can get enough air, I look up at him. "What's going to happen to me?"

His eyes are miles deep. I want to dive right into them. "Well, first off, this." He leans in and kisses my cheek, too close to my mouth, and my heart speeds up despite his calm. "You know I'll always be here for you. If you ever need anything," he glares at Luc, "you know where to come." Distress creeps into his eyes. "But after that, I'm not sure."

I press deeper into Gabe as Luc glares at us from the window. "You're playing a little fast and loose with those wings, don't you think?" he spits at Gabe.

In response, Gabe pulls me tighter into his body and smirks at Luc, but I see the uncertainty in his eyes. I sink into him and let his summer snow bury me so I don't have to think.

18

✝

Angels and Demons

FRANNIE

It's almost comical to watch these guys. They're so busy trying to hate each other that they don't see how alike they are. Well . . . alike except for one being all dark and dangerous and the other blinding me with his radiance. But other than that . . .

I'm starting to get my mind around some of this. In the week since Luc and Gabe filled me in, they've both backed off to give me room to think. And Gabe's backed off in other ways. We're almost never alone together, and he's hardly touched me. Which I'm not sure I'm happy about. I haven't asked him why, but I'm pretty sure Luc's comment about losing his wings might have something to do with it.

All the white in Gabe's kitchen creates a glare, and I'm not sure Gabe's not adding to it. He glowers at Luc, and Luc stares him down, challenging him.

"It's beyond my comprehension how, after everything you've seen, you can still have that attitude. The only reason the Almighty doesn't send another flood is that the first one was useless."

Gabe shakes his head. "People do stuff every day to prove you wrong. Completely selfless acts of kindness."

"I disagree. Nothing is selfless. At the bottom of every good deed, there's a self-serving motive."

"Dude, you need to lighten up."

I roll my eyes. "Give it up, Gabe. He's hopeless." I open my calculus book on the kitchen table and push my empty ice cream bowl aside. "I know you guys are geniuses and all, but finals start tomorrow, and I've got to study or UCLA is gonna change their mind about me."

Luc looks at me and smiles. "What's the deal with UCLA anyway?"

"What do you mean?"

"Just curious why you feel compelled to go three thousand miles away for college."

"Well . . . partly 'cause it's three thousand miles away. But really, they have the top international relations program in the country, and I'm thinking I can double major in political science or maybe Middle Eastern studies."

Luc raises an eyebrow. "And do what?"

I feel warmth creep into my cheeks. "I think that most of the crap that happens in the world is 'cause people don't know how to talk to each other. You know, 'cause of differences in culture or religion. Stuff like that. That's why I started that whole pen pal thing. I wanted to try to understand. So . . . I guess I'm thinking I'd like to do something bigger. Not quite sure what or how . . ."

Gabe smiles. His glow is blinding me again. "Lofty goals."

"Shut up," I say, embarrassed. I know how stupid it sounds, what I want to do, but I've always wanted it. I've always been good at talking to people, helping them find common ground. Like now, with Luc and Gabe—although I think their only common ground might be me, so I guess that doesn't really count.

"And you think you're going to make a difference." Luc's expression is serious now.

"Probably not. But it can't hurt to try," I say, watching my fingers twirl the pencil on my calculus book.

"You *will* make a difference, Frannie." Gabe is suddenly as serious as Luc.

"Will I? I'm not sure I'll get the chance."

Luc and Gabe share a wary glance. They know I'm right. Then Luc looks hard at Gabe, and, behind his eyes, there's anguish. "Tag her."

"You're even dumber than you look," Gabe says with a sardonic smile and a shake of his head.

"What's stopping you?"

Gabe's expression darkens as his eyes shift to mine. "Frannie's stopping me."

My stomach's in my throat. "Hold up. How am I going to have a life if I'm tagged for Heaven? How is that better than being tagged for Hell?"

I watch as Luc struggles with the answer. "The Almighty . . ." He hesitates and glances at Gabe for confirmation. Gabe nods and Luc continues. "He won't use you as . . . poorly."

"But He'll still use me. It won't be my life anymore." Resentment and anger are threatening to take control of me. I stuff them into the black pit. "I don't want to be Moses or Hitler. I want to be Frannie."

Gabe finally speaks. "If you're tagged for Heaven, I can protect you. It would be extraordinarily difficult to reverse your tag, and eventually they'll stop trying. If you remain untagged, they'll keep coming for you."

"And so will you." My heart sinks. There's no way out of this. Suddenly I feel claustrophobic—trapped and terrified. I slide my calculus book in front of me with a shaking hand. "So, do you guys get this stuff?" I say, needing to change the subject.

Luc's worried gaze lingers a moment longer, but he takes my cue. He pulls my book toward him. "Which one are you working on?"

I slip my paper out from under his fingers, and he jerks his hand.

"Ow!"

Gabe cracks a smile. "Ow? You're kidding, right?"

When Luc lifts his hand and turns it over, a tiny bead of crimson blood is sprouting on the tip of his middle finger. A paper cut.

"Well, that answers that," Gabe says.

Luc just stares, openmouthed, at the growing bead of blood. Then he turns to me with a tentative smile on his lips just before he loops his other hand behind my neck and pulls me into a kiss.

When he finally lets me go, I look into his smiling eyes. "What did I miss?" I ask, a little breathless and totally confused.

He grins. "Demons don't bleed."

Gabe's eyes are storming as Luc lets me go and I try not to feel guilty. "And neither do angels," he says.

LUC

I try to wrap my mind around what this means on the way home, but I'm having a hard time. Am I mortal? Am I turning human? I think about what that would mean for Frannie and me as she sits next to me in the Shelby with her head on my shoulder. My pulse pounds in my ears—something new—as I think about all the possibilities. Can we be together? *Really* together?

But a downside of turning human is that the thread that binds me to the nefarious is thinning. Good and bad. Good because I've decided that they're a bunch of shitbags and I really don't want to be in their heads anymore. Bad because I can't tell when they're here. If I can't tell when they're here, I can't protect Frannie from them.

I take my right hand off the wheel to pull a small box out of the console between the seats and wrap my arm around her shoulders, holding it in front of her face. "I have something for you."

"What is it?"

"Well, how it works is you take the box out of my hand and open it," I say with a grin.

"Jerk," she mumbles, grabbing the box and yanking it open. She pulls the crucifix out by the chain and watches it dangling there for a long minute.

"Put it on. The cross is iron with gold edging, and the Jesus is silver and platinum."

She looks at me, a cynical expression almost masking the mischievous gleam in her eye. "I can see that. If you're trying to lure me into bed with gifts, this was the wrong choice."

I can't help chuckling. "That really wasn't my intention, but I'll tuck that tidbit away for future reference."

"So . . . is this a joke?" she says eyeing me warily.

"No. It's a weapon."

"I thought it was vampires that have a problem with crosses."

"They do. But in this case, the other side keeps saying 'Jesus saves' and I'm hoping they're right."

"What the hell are you talking about?"

"Every demon has a weakness—something programmed into us by King Lucifer at the time of our creation to keep us from becoming too powerful." A product of His paranoia, no doubt. "Mine is gold. I don't know what Belias's is, or Avaira's, but this crucifix hits on the most common weaknesses. I want you to wear this, and if either of them comes near you, gouge it into them or scratch them with it. It will at least slow them down a little."

"You really think I need this?"

I turn away from the road and look her dead in the eye. "We need all the help we can get." I watch as her eyes widen. She loops the chain around her neck and fingers the crucifix.

"Why is this happening?" she asks, her voice deceptively calm.

My grip on the steering wheel tightens. "I don't know."

She looks up at me with big, wounded eyes. "Whatever Gabe thinks I'm supposed to do . . . I don't want it."

"I don't think it's a choice. Your Sway is something you're born with, like blue eyes or blond hair."

"But I can change those things—wear contacts or dye my hair."

"That's not really changing them, it's just disguising the truth. Your Sway is going to be difficult to hide."

She sinks into the seat, dejected. "How can I make them all just leave me alone?"

"I don't think you can. Hell won't stop coming for you until you're tagged, one way or the other."

She groans and buries her face in her hands. "I just want to be me. I want to have my life."

I reach for her and she drops a hand into mine. I squeeze it. "We're *both* going to find a way out, Frannie. I promise." I just have no clue what it is yet. I stare out the windshield, because the only way out I can see for her is to let Gabriel tag her. "Frannie?"

"Yeah."

I hesitate. "Will you tell me about your brother?"

She lifts her head and looks at me warily. "Why?"

"Because I can see how much you're hurting."

Her face darkens and her eyes look haunted. "What do you want me to say? I killed him. End of story."

"I know that's not true."

She pulls her hand away from mine and folds her arms tightly across her chest. "Yes it is."

"Tell me what happened."

She turns to face the window. "No."

"Please, Frannie."

I reach for her hand again, but she yanks it away. She turns back to me and her expression is feral, a pinched snarl. The bitter scent of garlic rolls off of her, filling the car. "Get out of my face, Luc."

I pull a deep breath. "It might help to talk about it."

My sympathetic tone only serves to aggravate her more. "Nothing's going to help. He's dead!" she spits.

I pull over to the shoulder and she reaches for the door handle. I reach across and grasp her arm before she can get it open.

She squirms out of my grasp. Garlic and black pepper sting my nose. "Leave me alone, you bastard!" Angry tears flow freely down her face as she glares up at me.

"Let me help. Please . . ."

With surprising strength she pushes me hard into the door.

"I . . . hate you," she says. But there's no conviction. She sounds defeated, spent. Her face drops into her hands again as all her anger dissolves into tears. When her sobs slow, I brush the tangled locks off her damp face. She stares silently back at me as the last of her tears roll down her cheeks.

"We were in a tree." Her voice breaks with every word. "He loved to climb trees . . . and . . ." Her body hitches as she tries to stifle another sob. "He was climbing so fast. I couldn't keep up." She turns her head away from me and leans on the door. She makes a sound like a wounded animal, somewhere between a whimper and a moan, and then she's still for a long time.

"He fell?" I finally prompt.

She heaves a sigh. "I was so mad . . ." Before she can finish the thought her voice chokes off and silent tears start again.

I slip my arm cautiously around her and pull her to me. She

leans into me and I hold her and say nothing until she's ready to talk. When she does, her words are barely audible. "I hated that he could climb faster, so I . . . grabbed his leg . . ." She pauses and I pull her tight to me. "I ran for Mom, but . . ." Her voice is a raw wound, catching in her throat with every word. "He was my . . . twin . . . the other half of me. And I killed him."

And there goes my brimstone heart, shattering into a million pieces. "I'm so sorry," I whisper into her hair. "But you were only seven, Frannie. It wasn't your fault." I pull her closer and wish there was some way I could fix this for her. But even my magic can't banish her personal demons. She's got to face those down on her own. All I can do is hold her while she cries.

As I sit here with my face buried in her hair, feeling the sobs rack her body, I wonder if love truly does conquer all, because otherwise, despite what I promised her, I think we're screwed.

FRANNIE

When we get back to Luc's, Taylor and Riley are sitting on the hood of Riley's car in the parking lot, and I'm trying to remember when I told them where he lives. "What the hell are they doing here?"

"Gearing up to kick my ass, no doubt," Luc says.

"Well, you deserve it."

He looks at me from under an arched eyebrow, making me tingle all over.

We pull into a parking spot near Luc's building, and I work to get myself together as they bounce over to us. I'm happy to see Taylor looking almost herself again. Today was her first day back at school after her dad, and she's been pretty down.

"We came to kidnap you," Riley says, wrapping her arms around me from behind.

"You're coming with us. Girls' night," Taylor says.

"It's not 'night' and it's not Wednesday. What's the deal?"

"Just shut up and do as you're told," she smirks.

I step forward and hug her. "How you holding out?"

She looks a little confused for a second then says, "Fine."

"Did your dad come home today?"

She glances quickly at Riley and back. "Yeah."

"He's doing okay?"

"Yeah."

I wait for her to elaborate, but then decide she must not want to talk about it. "So, what's going on?"

"You're coming with us."

"Sorry. Luc and I are kinda busy," I say.

He looks at me, and I see his eyes drop to the crucifix under my shirt. "No, it's okay . . . I think you should go."

I glower at him. "I thought we had plans." At least I did. Plans involving cool sheets and warm bodies . . .

"Go ahead, Frannie." He steps away from us, scanning the lot and buildings with growing concern on his face.

"Are you all right?"

"Yeah," he almost growls. "Just go."

Something's not right. I force my eyes away from Luc and scan the parking lot then shift them to Taylor. "Where are we going?"

"It's a surprise," she says with a sparkle in her eye.

When I turn to kiss Luc good-bye his eyes are still darting.

"What's up?" I whisper in his ear as he leans down.

"Nothing. I'll see you later." He kisses me, and I force myself to let him go.

I slide into the back of Riley's car. As we pull out of the parking lot, Riley keeps looking at me in her rearview mirror.

"So, really. What are we doing?" I ask.

"You'll see," she says into the mirror.

"How did you guys find me? I never told you where Luc lives."

Riley glances at me in the mirror again. "Yeah, you did. Remember that time at school?"

"Actually, no. So . . ." I look back at Luc's complex, fading into the distance, "this is all a little weird, don't you think?"

Taylor turns and looks at me. "You've been blowing us off for Lucifer. You left us no choice."

Lucifer? Suddenly alarms are ringing in my head. I work to stay calm. Panicking isn't going to help anything. I feel the weight of the crucifix against my chest and breathe into it. "Yeah, I guess. Sorry. But what about Riley and Trevor? They're just as bad." I watch for Taylor's reaction.

They share a quick glance, then Taylor turns back to me with a grin and says, "Yeah . . . I had to kidnap her too."

Wrong reaction. *Shit!* And as I look at her, I notice for the first time that her eyes are glowing red. Just a little behind her gray irises, but enough that it's just noticeable in the shadows of the car.

I don't know what's going on, except I'm pretty sure I'm screwed.

I look for a spot to bail, but by now we're out of town and there are no more stop signs. We're heading out into the middle of nowhere. Riley's driving much faster than usual, or I'd open the door and jump. I'm trying not to freak as I look out at our surroundings . . . and then I get it. We're heading up to the quarry.

We park near the trail into the swimming pit, and I open the door and start to move away from the car.

Taylor—or whoever this is—swings behind me in a flash. "Hey, where you going?"

That's a really good question. Where *am* I going? I look up the dirt road. The main road is at least half a mile away and the dense woods are quiet. Too early for the groups of summer swimmers. There's nowhere to run. "Nowhere. So, what are we doing here?"

"Just hanging out. Maybe skinny-dipping. Sound good?"

Yeah, sounds great. "Not really up for skinny-dipping. Water's freezing."

Taylor shoots a glance at Riley, and her eyes flash red. "We'll have to huddle up for body heat," she says with a lascivious grin.

This is bad. I watch Riley slide her keys into the pocket of her cutoff shorts as she heads up the path. Taylor is hanging back, waiting for me to go first. I follow Riley, trying to figure out how to get those keys.

We wind our way down the wooded path, and when we get to the quarry, Taylor saunters over to the edge and sits on a rock. Her eyes flash, and an evil smile turns up the corners of her mouth. "I say we get naked. The water looks great."

"Mmm . . . sounds good." Riley says, eyeing me with that same gleam. "But I gotta take a piss. I'll be right back." She slinks off into the woods. *Crap*—there went the keys.

Taylor gets up and comes over to where I'm standing. "You look so uptight. Chill," she says, grabbing my hand and pulling me to the rocks. She's as hot as Luc ever was. She sits me down and stands behind me, rubbing my shoulders, then starts pulling my shirt over my head.

I yank it down. "It's way too cold for that. I'm serious," I say. I don't turn to look when I hear her growl. I need to think, but my heart is thundering in my ears, making it hard to concentrate. Then I hear the faintest rustling in the woods. I look up and exhale the breath I'd been holding as he walks out of the trees, silky black hair glistening in the sun. *Thank God.* "Luc," I say, shaking Taylor off and standing up. I take a step forward, but then he lifts his head.

"Hi Frannie," he says with a wicked gleam in his glowing red eyes. "I'm Belias."

I look at him and know I should run, but my feet seem rooted to the ground, and I'm feeling a little dizzy all of a sudden. Out of the corner of my eye, I see Taylor slink off up the path.

"I haven't been able to stop thinking about you since the night we met in front of your house." His voice is velvet, and I feel my legs go soft. He steps slowly forward till he's right in front of me. He touches my face and traces a burning path across my cheekbone. "Everything is fine, Frannie. It's going to be great." His hot hands slide around my waist, pulling me to his burning body.

The black fog permeates my brain as I melt into him. He

feels like Luc, and I can't help but lose myself in his touch. When his lips touch mine I can barely breathe. My hands slide around him and I press into the curve of his body, but then some little corner of my mind screams, "*No.*" I pull a deep breath and try to think. Almost instinctively, my hand gravitates to the cross dangling from my neck as I fight to hold on to my remaining shred of conscious thought. With my last scrap of free will, I pull back from his kiss, look up at him, and smile.

Then I yank the cross from my neck and jam it into his eye.

A bestial roar shakes the woods as he drops to his knees, clawing at his bubbling face. He shimmers for a second, almost like a mirage, as something terrifying peeks out from under his skin.

The smell of rotten eggs instantly clears my head. I turn and run full speed up the path without looking back. I don't know what the hell I'm gonna do when I get to the car. Is there a car? Were Riley and Taylor ever really here? I don't know what's real.

I'm trying not to cry, a useless effort, since I'm pretty much crying anyway, and everything is a green blur as I stumble up the path, so I don't see Taylor lying there till I trip over her and launch face first into the dirt. As I scramble to my feet, I hear something moving through the woods toward us. Belias. *Damn!*

I grab Taylor under the arms and drag her, but we're moving too slowly and he catches us. I prop her against a tree and step in front of her, crouching into judo stance, as he bursts out of the woods and onto the path.

"Frannie! Thank God!" Luc grabs Taylor and throws her over his shoulder. "Let's go!" He pushes me in front of him as we run up the path, and when we get to the road he throws

Taylor into the backseat of the Shelby with Riley, who's lying there unconscious.

We climb into the car and slam the doors.

"Jesus, Luc! What . . ." But then I remember.

Belias! He was in a Black '68 Shelby Cobra that night. This isn't Luc.

My heart stops. "Oh, shit!"

"What is it, Frannie? Are you okay?" The Shelby fishtails as he guns the engine, sending gravel flying up behind us.

I look in the backseat at Taylor and Riley, then back at Belias. What do I do? I breathe and try to think. And when I look back at the road there's a tall, raven-haired girl standing in the middle of it. The girl from Luc's bed. "Oh, shit!" I say again.

I expect Belias to slow down, but instead he stares out the windshield, determined, and speeds up. I bring my arms up, expecting her to come crashing through the windshield, but instead she evaporates. Poof—gone.

When we get near the main road, I grab the steering wheel and yank. The car swerves to the right, nearly swiping a tree before Belias yanks the wheel back and brings the car up onto the dirt road.

"What the hell are you doing?!"

"Go to Hell!" I yell and try to grab the wheel again, but he pushes me back.

"Frannie, please! Stop trying to kill us, will you?"

I look in his eyes. God, he looks just like Luc. And then it hits me . . . what he said when he found us on the path. He said, "Thank God." Would Belias say that? Would Luc?

"Luc?"

"Who were you expecting?" The rasp from the backseat makes me jump, and the smell of rotten eggs chokes me.

I turn to see the real Belias—I think. But he doesn't look like Luc anymore. There's no mistaking what he is: steaming, crimson skin, flat, pinched face, and horns, with one clawed hand around each of my best friends' necks. But what gives him away as Belias is the black ooze dripping from where his left eye once was.

Luc slams on the breaks and I nearly slide onto the floor. Then he turns and points a glowing fist at Belias.

"Do you really want to do that?" Belias says, shaking Riley and Taylor's unconscious bodies. "Course, Frannie didn't come out all that worse for wear, did she?" A grimace pulls at his leathery lips, exposing a mouthful of fangs. "Go ahead. Give it a shot."

LUC

"Luc?" Frannie says, urging me with her eyes.

"I can't," I say, dropping my fist. "He's right. If he doesn't shield them it would kill them."

"Good boy," Belias smirks.

"What do you want?" I say.

He coughs out a rasping chuckle. "You have to ask? I thought you were smarter than that, being a First Level and all."

Unholy Hell.

I look back at Riley and Taylor. Can I sacrifice them for Frannie? My head says yes, but my annoying new conscience tells me it's wrong. Plus, if we survive this, Frannie would never forgive me.

"So how is this supposed to work?" I ask past the lump in my throat.

"Frannie gets out of the car," Belias says, gesturing to the side of the car, where Avaira is now standing, a scowl gracing her flawless face, "and she and I have a little party in the woods," he finishes with a heinous grin.

I look at Frannie as she reaches for the door handle, the tangy citrus scent of her terror replaced with the spicy-sweet of clove and currant—her soul, ready for the taking. My hand shoots out involuntarily and grabs her wrist. She tries to pull away, but I shake my head, pleading with my eyes.

"There's no choice, Luc," she says, her expression calm, resigned.

She tugs her arm away and I let her, my mind racing. Pushing open the door, she looks back at me one last time before climbing out and standing next to Avaira. With a burst of brimstone, Belias is standing next to her, slamming Frannie's door.

I pull slowly forward and watch in the rearview mirror as Belias takes Frannie's wrist and starts to drag her across the road, toward the woods. As he moves, I can see he's weak. The crucifix did more damage than he let on. He shouldn't need Avaira, but she's following behind for backup, her glowing fist targeting the back of the Shelby.

And then I drop the Shelby into reverse and floor it, sending Riley and Taylor to the floor in the backseat. I duck as Avaira's blast takes out the back window. Belias drops Frannie's wrist and lifts his fist just as I slam into him at full speed. He goes careening over the car and onto the dirt road in front of me, but I don't wait to see if he stays down. I throw it into first and push open the passenger door, slowing as I reach Frannie. She throws herself into the seat, and I floor it, door still open, running over Belias on our way to the main road.

She pulls herself the rest of the way into the car, slams the door, and looks out the shattered back window at the lump in the dirt—Belias. Avaira is nowhere in sight. "Is he . . . dead?"

"Unfortunately, it'd take a lot more than a 1968 Shelby Cobra to kill him, but he'll feel it for a while." I can hear the shake in my voice. "Truth is, your crucifix to his eye probably did more long-term damage. That's going to set him back a bit." I grab her hand. "Are you okay?"

"I think so," she says, checking herself over as we pull out onto the main road.

I feel her shake as I wrap my arm around her shoulders and pull her close. This is as far from me as she's ever going to get.

19

✝

Dance with the Devil

LUC

Frannie straightens Riley's legs and sits next to her friends on my bed. "Are they gonna be okay?"

"Yeah. It'll take a little while for them to come around. Demon possession can knock the Hell out of you."

"You can just jump into other people's bodies whenever you want?"

I nearly gag thinking about it, but then I remember being in Frannie—how incredible it was. "If they're tagged for Heaven they're off limits, but otherwise, yeah. It's usually pretty uncomfortable. It's cramped . . . and sort of sticky and slimy."

"How does it work? Are you, like, both in there at the same time?"

"Pretty much. It takes a very strong mortal to hold his own

against a demon who is trying to control him, so it's usually like the mortal's not even there, aside from taking up space. But it's not always like that." I think about dancing with Frannie again and feel a tingle work through me, making me shudder.

She looks at Taylor and Riley on the bed. "Will they remember anything about Belias and Avaira?"

"Probably not. When a mortal is possessed it's almost like they go dormant. They won't remember, and it's probably best if they don't know what happened."

She stands up, meanders over, and wraps her arms around me. "How did you know?"

And that's the problem. I didn't until it was almost too late. I shake my head. "My sixth sense was buzzing when we got out of the car. It never occurred to me that Belias and Avaira would resort to possession. I figured when you left with Taylor and Riley, Belias would make a move to follow and I could take him down. But as soon as you pulled out of the parking lot, the buzz stopped. I'm embarrassed to say it took me a few minutes to figure it out, and, when I did, it was almost too late. I knew which direction you went . . . and then I remembered the quarry. Belias was there that night."

"What does he want with me?"

"The same thing I did." My heart aches. I know how hard this is for her to hear. But she needs to understand that they won't give up until she's tagged—one way or the other. "They'll keep coming for you."

She stiffens. "I hate this. Why is this happening to me?"

I hold her tighter. "I don't know," I say, wishing I did.

She sighs and presses her face into my chest. "So it's always going to be like this." A tear slips over her lashes, and I wipe it away. "I just want a normal life."

I want to hold her and tell her it's all going to be okay, but I'm not going to lie to Frannie anymore. "I think you gave up normal when you fell for a demon." *And maybe an angel.* The thought sits like a stone in my core, weighing me down. I kiss the top of her head and sigh, "But I don't see them stopping until they have you."

"There's nothing we can do?"

"We can try running, but I'm not sure there's anywhere we could go that they wouldn't find us."

Her expression is suddenly determined. "I'm *going* to live my life. Otherwise what's the point of fighting? I may as well just let them tag me now."

I pull her closer, wishing it could be that easy. "There's your Sway, Frannie."

"What do you mean?"

"Your Sway. If it's strong enough to change me, you should at least be able to use it to defend yourself."

"How does it work?"

"That's something you'll have to figure out for yourself, but once you learn to control it, it should be some protection."

She looks up at me, and I see the fear and trepidation in her eyes. "What was Belias gonna do?"

"Belias is a creature of lust, an incubus, so his technique usually involves seduction and soul sucking. But that's only with mortals who are already tagged—I think." I remember my conversation with Belias under Frannie's tree. "He *did* say the rules were changing . . ." I feel her shudder in my arms.

"This sucks," she says, looking back at Riley and Taylor on the bed.

And just then, Taylor's eyes snap open. Taylor gasps and sits up. "What the hell . . . ?"

"Hey, Tay," Frannie says, walking over and sitting next to her. Riley groans and opens her eyes, still looking groggy.

"What's going on?" Taylor checks her clothes and looks around suspiciously.

"Just hanging out," I say with a little push.

Riley sits up, still dazed.

"Hey, Ry. How you feeling?" Frannie says.

"Like shit," she answers.

Taylor swings around and stares at me. "Where the hell are we?"

"Welcome to my humble abode," I say through a smile with another push. "Don't you remember coming up?"

Her eyes glaze over a little. "Maybe . . ."

"You want another beer?" I head for the fridge.

"No!" Riley practically shouts, rubbing her forehead.

✣

We get Taylor and Riley loaded into Riley's car, which Frannie and I circled back to retrieve, and watch as they pull out. I look around and sigh in relief, thinking about how close that was— for all of us. I loop my arm protectively around Frannie as I steer her back up the stairs to my apartment. Once inside, she latches all the deadbolts and locks while I throw up a field, my own infernal deterrent. Then she drapes herself over me, and I feel my heart speed up. She's still shaking a little . . . or is that me? I'm not sure. "You okay?" I whisper in her ear.

She presses into me. "I am now," she says. Then she's looking up at me with curious eyes. "So, what you said earlier . . . about being able to be in other people's bodies . . ."

"Yeah . . ."

"I was kind of wondering . . . could you . . . you know, do that with me?"

I look at the floor, feeling more than a little guilty, and watch the toe of my boot scuff at one of the filthy linoleum daisies. "I have."

I'm surprised when I look up and find her smiling. "When?"

"Just before I first kissed you."

"You mean before *I* first kissed *you*."

I crack a wide smile. "Actually, I kissed you first. You just slept through it."

She laughs. "Could you do it again? I mean the thing where you're inside me. I promise I'll stay awake."

My heart takes off. But as I fantasize about slipping through Frannie's lips, being in there with her again, I realize that I might not be able to do it anymore. Things are changing fast. "I'm not sure."

She stretches up onto her tiptoes and kisses me, then gazes into my depths and whispers, "Try."

I kiss her again, pulling her to me as tightly as I can, and as her lips part, I let my essence flow through them. I'm surprised again at how effortless it feels—because she's inviting me in, I'm sure. I feel that same overwhelming rush of sensations I felt the first time, many of which I now have names for. Love, for sure, but also joy, hope, and pure awe for her sheer beauty. She's more beautiful on the inside, and that's saying something. We dance—and I'm in Heaven.

I leave just enough of myself behind to control my body, and as I hold her on the outside, I caress her on the inside, drinking in her gasps and moans as I explore her, inside and out. I feel her body's physical reaction—not to mention my own. Before I know it, we're on the bed, shirts on the floor, and it takes everything I have to stop. My heart aches as I reluctantly pull my essence back, and I'm left with that same feeling of being empty and alone in my human shell.

She sits up on the bed and huffs. "Why'd you stop?"

"A knowing act of lust with a demon will earn you a one-way ticket straight to the Abyss. I'm sure of it. We can't do this until I know it's safe for you."

"They . . . you . . . you're taking everything. My life . . . everything. This is all I want. Just this one thing. Please? You're almost human."

"I don't know that. It seems to be the direction I'm headed . . . and I really want to . . . obviously." God, how I want to. "But just the fact that I can still do . . . that," I shudder, "means it's not safe yet."

She flings herself back into the pillows and blows her unruly tresses out of her face. "This bites."

I shift up onto my elbow and kiss her. "You're the only one who's ever known who I am, who I'm not, and who I want to be. And somehow you love me anyway. I'm not taking any chances with you, Frannie."

She rolls on her side and gazes into my eyes. A wicked little smile just curls the corners of her pouting lips. "That was amazing," she says, tracing the lines of my cheekbone with the tip of her index finger and making me shudder. Then her smile widens. "Probably better than sex anyway."

I smile back, dying to prove her wrong. It was amazing. Mind-blowing, actually. But I can't imagine sex with Frannie would be anything less. "How much do you remember?"

Her smile widens and she trails a finger down my chest to the button of my jeans. "All of it."

I can't stop my own smile. "Interesting."

Her finger trails along my stomach at the waistband of my jeans, driving me insane, and I'm right on the edge of diving back into her when she says, "Where is Hell, anyway?"

I almost laugh. "At the core."

She looks into my face, surprised. "Of the Earth?"

"Yep."

"So all those kids digging to China are in for one hell of a surprise."

"Literally," I chuckle.

"How did you get there? Did someone like you come after you?"

"No. I'm a creature of Hell." I shoot a sideways glance at her, not sure how she'll take that, but she just looks thoughtful.

"What do you mean?"

"Demons are created in Hell. We were never human."

"I don't get how that works."

"We're born from sin. My sin is pride, just like the original—King Lucifer. My name is a dead giveaway. Only creatures of pride are arrogant enough to take His name."

Her eyes shift to her hand on my chest. "Would it be really weird if I said I think I kinda knew all along?"

I smile. "Yes."

Her eyes flit to mine and away. She opens her mouth to say something then closes it again.

My smile widens. I lift her chin with a finger and fix her in my gaze. "What?"

She blushes and her face pulls into an embarrassed grimace. "Nothing," she says, lowering her lashes.

"It's obviously something."

"I want to feel your horns," she blurts without looking at me.

I grimace. "Why?"

She rolls with her back to me. "Forget it. It's stupid."

I roll her back and shift onto my elbows above her. "You're not going to run screaming from the room?"

She lifts her eyes to mine, then lifts her head and kisses me. "After what you just did? What do *you* think?"

I close my eyes and push off my human shell and shudder when I feel Frannie's fingers running slowly through my hair. There's a tremble in her touch as she traces one finger around the base of my left horn, then up to the tip and back. I feel both of her hands wrap around them as she pulls me down into a kiss, and they vanish as I sink back into her.

When I pull back, I stare down into those sapphire eyes looking for any sign of fear or disgust, but all I see is love. I still can't believe that look is directed at me.

"Will they try that again . . . with Taylor and Riley, I mean?"

I sigh and trail my finger down her nose, over her lips, down her chin and along her neck, stopping short of that insanely hot red bra. "Probably not. They know we'll be looking for it."

"What are we gonna do?"

I roll off her and shake my head. "I don't know. My sixth sense is slipping. This is dangerous, Frannie. I can't see them coming like I used to. I'm not sure I can protect you anymore."

She smiles. "I need another cross, and I think you need a talisman. Something to ward off evil spirits."

"And just where am I going to get this talisman?"

If I didn't know better, I'd swear *her* eyes were glowing. She sits up and turns her back to me, undoing the clasp of her bra and sliding it off. As I watch, I feel things . . . stirring . . . and it's taking every ounce of restraint I can muster not to jump her right this second. She pulls a pillow in front of her and turns back, her hair spilling across one side of her face. She tosses her bra to me with a sinful grin that would put any demon to shame.

"Your talisman," she says.

"If you think this is going to ward off evil spirits," I say, holding it up, "then you don't know much about evil spirits." I look at her and work to control my breathing. "You have no idea what you're doing to me." Truth is, *I* have no idea what she's doing to me either. This is completely uncharted territory. But, whatever it is, I think I like it.

Still grinning wickedly, she says, "I'm not sorry."

But then I see it. The answer. I hesitate for just a second, letting my eyes eat Frannie alive, before hanging her bra on my headboard and tossing her shirt to her. "As much as it pains me to say it, you have to get dressed. Gabriel has something we need."

FRANNIE

"I'm not going to let him tag me," I say on the way to Gabriel's house.

"I wish you would. That'd be the surest way. But there are other things that might be almost as good."

"Like what?"

"Being a Dominion, he's privy to information I'm not. He's also got power I can only dream of."

I think about our kiss—how it made me feel—and raise my hand to my lips and sigh.

"What's going on with you two?" Luc's voice is soft, but with an edge.

"Nothing." I think.

"You're a terrible liar."

"I'm not—" lying, I start to say. But I am. 'Cause there *is* something going on. I just have no idea what it is. "I kissed him."

Luc slams on the brakes, skidding to the side of the road. "You *what*?"

"I kissed him."

He just stares at me, rage storming in his eyes. "When?"

"Before us—mostly," I say.

"*Mostly?* What's mostly?"

And his rage triggers my own. "You know what? It's none of

your business. At least he wasn't nearly naked in my goddamn bed! And I'm still not convinced you weren't doing Avaira!"

His jaw clenches and his eyes narrow. "Did he kiss you back?"

I slide down in the seat and cross my arms tight across my chest to keep from hitting him. "I told you, it's none of your business."

"Well this is just rich," he says, his voice acid, "not only are you bringing down demons, but Dominions too." He pulls back up onto the road and stares blindly out the windshield. "So, do you want him? Because whatever you want, you can pretty much have, what with the whole Sway thing."

I glare at him. "Just take me home."

I keep my arms wrapped tightly around me. The ache in my chest threatens to dissolve into angry tears, but I force myself not to cry. I won't give him the satisfaction.

He pulls over on the side of the road again and just sits there, staring straight ahead—forever.

"I can walk from here," I finally say, reaching for the door handle.

"Stop." His hand darts out and grasps my wrist.

I jerk my arm away. "Let go!" But when I turn to look at him, his face is soft and his eyes are deep.

"Frannie, please try to remember that I'm new at this. I've still got feelings—emotions—raging through me that I can't even begin to identify. I don't know what I'm supposed to do with them. I didn't mean what I said. I'm sorry."

I fight against the tears again. I really want to be mad at him. I want to hate him, 'cause it feels safer than loving him.

I tug on the door handle. "Too late." I step out of the car, but before I get ten feet, he's there, wrapping his arms around me from behind.

"Let go of me!"

A passing car slows and pulls onto the shoulder just as I pull Luc's arm off me and throw him over my shoulder onto the ground. A tall, skinny man about my dad's age gets out and looks at me with wide eyes. "Do you need help, miss?"

I look down at Luc, and, for a second, I'm madder, 'cause he's laughing.

"You think it's funny?" I sneer. But then I realize how ridiculous we must look, and there's no stopping the stupid smile that pulls at my lips.

"Miss?" the guy says, taking a cautious step toward us.

Luc pulls himself off the ground as I break into an uncontrollable giggle. He looks at the guy. "We're fine . . ." his gaze shifts back to me, "I think."

I can't stop laughing, but I nod.

The guy doesn't look sure, so I work really hard to stop giggling. "Thank you, but I'm okay."

He eyes Luc warily. "If you're sure."

I clear my throat and try to look serious. "I'm sure."

As he climbs back in his car and pulls away, I feel Luc's arms snake around my waist and pull my body into his. "Are you done beating me up?" Luc says into my hair, and I can hear the smile in his voice.

"Maybe." I spin in his arms and wipe a smudge of dirt off his cheek. "Are you done pissing me off?"

He grins. "Maybe."

He grabs my hand and tows me back to the car. But as we pull away, something he said hits me hard, like a fist to the gut, and I feel suddenly sick.

"Do you think I cheated?"

He loops his arm over my shoulders. "What?"

"You just said I could pretty much have whatever I wanted. Did I make you love me?"

He turns and looks into my eyes, a bemused smile on his perfect lips. "You did."

"No, I mean did I *make* you love me. Like, you didn't really want to but my . . . influence—this Sway thing or whatever it is that Gabe thinks I can do—like, *made* you."

"That's irrelevant."

"Not to me."

"Frannie, what matters is that what I feel is real and genuine. I wouldn't want to go back to what I was. How I got here doesn't matter, just that I'm here."

"That's just stupid. That's like saying I beat you in poker 'cause I stacked the deck, but you're glad I have all your money."

"If you took my money and bought me paradise with it, I *would* be glad you had it. And that's what you've done." He reaches for me and draws me to his shoulder. I shove him away and look out the window as he pulls back out into the road. I feel his eyes on me, but I can't look at him, knowing what I've done. I've given a whole new meaning to the term "mind games." But more, in some selfish little corner of my mind, I hate that he didn't *fall* in love with me. He was pushed. He doesn't love me for me. He loves me 'cause he had no choice.

LUC

Frannie's sitting on the arm of a chair, staring out the window, and Gabriel is sitting on his couch looking at me like I'm nuts. "The Shield only works for angels and some mortals. Last I looked, dude, you're no angel."

"What do you mean, 'some mortals'?"

"Well, Adam and Lilith were the first we tried it on, and you know how well *that* went. But there have been others where it's worked." He shrugs. "Go figure."

"You mean Eve—Adam and *Eve*," Frannie says to the window.

Gabriel cocks half a smile. "You're right, it didn't work on Eve either, but Lilith was Adam's first wife."

She turns and looks at him, then at me, as if hoping I'll confirm that Gabriel has lost his mind. I shake my head. "Long story." Then I turn back to Gabriel. "Why didn't the Shield work on Frannie?"

Gabriel glares at me. "It did. Until you showed up."

"Oh."

"What didn't work on me? What's this Shield?"

Gabriel answers. "It's essentially a shield against detection by evil. It hides you from all things infernal."

Hope sparks in her eyes. "Could it hide me from angels too?"

A sad smile flits across Gabriel's lips. "No."

She looks dejected again as she asks, "Why didn't it work on me?"

"I don't know. Sometimes it partially works. It only takes one demon who's particularly sensitive to you, for any reason . . ." He shoots a glance at me.

She looks at me, uncertainty in her eyes. "So you're saying, even with this Shield, Luc found me anyway."

"Looks that way," Gabriel says, but her eyes stay locked on mine.

I nod reassuringly at her and smile. She's so afraid she manipulated me into loving her. It hurts that she can't see how much more it is now. How *big* it is. It may have been her Sway that started the ball rolling, but the way she makes me feel . . . that's not her Sway. It's just her.

Her gaze shifts to Gabriel. "Try it on me again."

"You're still under the protection of the Shield. I think that's why Lucifer is the only one who's found you so far."

I frown. "And Belias and Avaira."

Gabriel's eyes shoot to me. "What are you talking about?"

"Your radar sucks. They've been here for a few weeks."

His surprise turns to antipathy. "You should have told me, but I'm sure Belias found *you*, loser. You're like an infernal lightning rod. You're still bound to them, and that psychic thread will be hard to sever."

I can think of one way to sever it right now. "Which brings me back to my original request."

Gabriel eyes me warily. "I've never heard of anyone trying it on a demon. I'm thinking this isn't such a great idea."

"But I'm not a demon anymore, remember?"

"In body, you may be becoming mortal, but in essence you're still theirs—a creature of the Underworld."

I know he's right, because I couldn't have done what I did

with Frannie earlier otherwise. "If no one's tried it on a demon, how can you be sure it won't work on me? What's the risk?"

"The risk . . . well, let's see. There's the risk of *death*. Forces of light—especially forces this powerful—tend to kill forces of evil. Even if it didn't kill you, it could alter you in ways I can't even guess at."

Frannie stands and steps toward me, her eyes full of concern. "Is somebody gonna tell me what's going on?"

Gabriel looks at her with a sardonic smile. "Lucifer is asking for a miracle."

She rolls her eyes. "Aren't we all? But, really . . ."

I can't help the smile. "He's serious. That's exactly what I'm asking for."

"A miracle," she says, as if waiting for the punch line.

"Yep."

That obviously wasn't the answer she was hoping for. "Great."

Gabriel laces his fingers in hers and stares into her palm. "The Shield of Light makes angels invisible to detection by forces of evil. Angels can protect a mortal under their Shield when it doesn't work directly on the mortal. That's part of the reason I'm here—to shield you." He looks up at her and she holds his eyes with hers.

Chocolate.

Jealousy bubbles up and I choke it back—for her sake. "Your radar sucks and your Shield must be defective too. I smelled you coming a mile away," I smirk.

Gabriel's eyes stay locked on Frannie's. "I let you detect me. Hoping to scare you off."

A bark of a laugh escapes my chest. "As if!"

"So, what is this Shield? What would Luc have to do?" Frannie asks.

Gabriel pulls his eyes away from Frannie and shoots a cynical look at me. "Grow a halo."

She rolls her eyes again. "Be serious."

We both look at her, dead serious.

"Great," she says again.

Gabriel eyes me skeptically. "It will only work on a pure heart with the purest intentions."

Frannie cracks a smile. "I could have told you that wouldn't work on me."

Gabriel is still staring at me. "It would be dangerous to try on a mortal tagged for Hell, and I think you're a few steps beyond that."

"So . . . it could kill him?" she says, her smile gone.

"Yes."

"Then he's not doing it."

I look at Frannie, who now is looking at me with wide eyes, a little shell-shocked. My intentions are pure, I know that. My only intention is to save her from a fate she doesn't deserve. But my heart? I'm not so sure. If it's pure, Frannie made it that way. "What do I have to do? How does it work?" I ask, knowing I have to try. If I can't protect Frannie, I'm useless. Worse than useless. I'm a liability—a beacon for the Underworld.

Gabriel eyes Frannie, probably weighing how she would react if something happened to me at his hands. Fury, vengeance . . . all sins.

"Gabriel, this is my decision. Not hers," I say, drawing his attention back to me.

His eyes pull away from her and focus on me as he nods.

"Hold up," Frannie says, fiery incredulity all across her face, but fear in her eyes. "You're serious that he could die?"

Concern passes briefly over Gabriel's features. He can't lie . . .

"That's a risk, because he's still tethered to Hell."

"What do you mean?"

"He's a creature of the Underworld, no matter what he's becoming. His life force is spawned from Hell, and he'll always be connected."

I feel my insides boil as my disgust for what I am starts to feed on me. I can't look at her. I can't handle seeing that same disgust for me mirrored in her eyes.

But when she doesn't respond, I glance in her direction. She looks me in the eye and her expression turns cold. "I don't think you should do this, Luc. Not for me. Because I don't love you. I don't want you anymore."

And even though I know she's lying, the crushing pain in my chest is almost incapacitating. "You don't mean that."

"I do. I don't want someone who loves me 'cause he has to. I want someone who loves me for me." I feel my heart go dead in my chest as she turns to Gabriel. "What needs to happen for you to tag me?"

"You need to forgive yourself."

For the briefest of instants, pain twists her face, but, just as quickly, she smoothes it away. "Forgive myself . . . for Matt, you mean."

"Yes," Gabriel replies with a sad smile.

Everything in me wants her to be safe—wants Gabriel to protect her. But what I'd never tell her is that, once she's tagged for Heaven, I'm certain things between us will change. Gabriel said it: no matter what I'm becoming, I'm a creature of Hell. Frannie's life, and her priorities, will change once she's tagged for Heaven. She won't want me or need me for long. But she'll be safe.

"Do it, Frannie," I say and turn away. Because, despite my best intention, the pain in my words rang clear.

It's silent for a long moment, and when I turn back, Frannie looks unsure. Lost.

Finally, Gabriel speaks. "As much as I hate to say it, this is the wrong reason. You *will* forgive yourself eventually, and when that happens, you'll be tagged for Heaven. It's not something you can force, even for him." He spits the last word, and his face twists into something less than angelic.

She looks at me and a tear slips down her cheek. She flings herself into my arms and nearly squeezes the life out of me. "Luc, don't do this. We'll figure something else out." I can feel her heart thrumming against my chest.

I pull back, kiss her, and look at Gabriel. "Let's do it."

"Stop! *No!*" she yells, squeezing tighter and burying her face in my chest.

"Frannie," Gabriel says in a sweet, soft melody, "Lucifer is right. If you insist on being together we have to try this."

Frannie pulls her face out of my chest and looks up at him. He's glowing again—what a show-off. But it seems to work, because her grip on me loosens. But then I feel her hands on my face, and I can't resist as she pulls me into a kiss.

Gabriel steps in front of me. "Take off your shirt."

I pull it over my head and Frannie takes it from me, hugging it to her face. He lifts his hand to my forehead, and I notice it's wet. Then I'm burning hotter than the Lake of Fire.

Holy water.

Of course this damned Shield of Light would involve holy water. These holier-than-thou types can't seem to accomplish anything without it. I hold my breath—more difficult now than it used to be—and screw my eyes shut against the pain. I feel the skin on my forehead blister and peel where Gabriel marks the circle there. When his hand moves to my chest and leaves a bubbling red handprint over my heart, I hear the groan escape my throat, and it's all I can do to keep from pulling away from his touch and doubling over. I grimace, because I know Gabriel's enjoying this.

Stop being such a goddamn baby and suck it up. This is what you wanted.

I grit my teeth and am acutely aware of Frannie sobbing, piercing my heart, as she holds my hand in a death grip. Gabriel says some words in an ancient language, but I don't hear them. I don't hear anything but Frannie. She's all that matters.

And then she's in my arms, kissing the raw skin on my chest. I open my eyes and she looks up, tears streaming down her face.

"I'm so sorry," she whispers through her tears.

My pain is lost in her face. I wrap my arms around her and smile. "Why would you say something stupid like that?"

I feel her exhale sharply, the last of her sobs, as she reaches up to touch my blistered forehead. "You're okay?"

"Never better."

I take my shirt from her hand and shudder as her finger

trails over the welts on my chest. I slide it on and take her hand, pulling her to the door. "We've got one more stop."

FRANNIE

Grandpa sits across his coffee table from us, in the loveseat, his elbows on his knees, his pipe forgotten in his hand. He looks a little pale, and, for a second, I'm afraid we gave him a heart attack. He glares at Luc, sitting next to me on the couch. "A demon," he repeats for the sixth time. At first he laughed and told us to stop pulling his leg. He's not laughing now.

Luc holds Grandpa's gaze without wavering. "I was. I'm not totally sure what I am now."

"Human," I say. "You're turning human."

Luc shoots me a wary smile.

"How does that work?" Grandpa's voice doesn't boom. He sounds uncharacteristically weak.

"Frannie's . . . special," Luc says.

Now Grandpa's voice does boom. "I know that! That doesn't explain anything. Why are ya here?"

"I beg your pardon, sir, but it explains everything. Frannie has special talents. Power that is invaluable to the Underworld. I came to claim her soul for Hell, but her power is changing me."

Grandpa jumps off of the couch. "Get away from her! Frannie, get over here." He lunges toward us and grabs my arm, pulling me off the couch and around the coffee table. He tucks me under his arm protectively.

"Grandpa, please. Just listen to us."

"I'm hearin' ya loud and clear," he says, glaring at Luc. "Get the hell back to where ya came from. Ya can't have Frannie."

"He doesn't want me!" I blurt and then blush and smile at Luc. "Well, not like *that*, anyway."

Luc smiles back, but then his expression becomes grave. "Sir, I really need your help."

There's venom I've never heard in Grandpa's voice. "You want me to help you drag my granddaughter to Hell?"

"No, I want you to help me tag her soul for Heaven."

I hear my breath catch, and I squirm out from under Grandpa's arm. "You shit! You said you wanted Grandpa to help hide us."

"You need to figure out how to forgive yourself Frannie. I think your grandfather's the best person to help you do that. This Shield might work, but if it doesn't, Gabriel's the only one who can keep you safe. He loves you, Frannie, and he's got some pull with the Big Guy. He may be able to keep things reasonable for you."

"I want my life, goddamit!"

"What are ya all talking about?" Grandpa looks a mix of frightened confusion.

"Frannie's soul can't be tagged for Hell if it's already tagged for Heaven. But Frannie can't be tagged for Heaven unless she forgives herself for M—"

"Stop!" I scream. "Just stop! This isn't what I want!"

"But it's what you need," Luc says, gazing deep into my eyes.

"Go to Hell!"

"I will, but I'm not taking you with me."

I'm a huge ball of frustrated anger. I want to kill him for stabbing me in the back. "Get out!"

"Frannie?" In my rage, I'd forgotten Grandpa was here. "Talk to me."

I look at him, and everything is lost in a flood of tears. I hug him and hold on for dear life. He sits on the loveseat, bringing me with him, and I lay my head on his shoulder and cry for what feels like forever. When I lift my head and look around, Luc is gone.

"What did he mean, Frannie? About forgiving yourself?"

The tears well up again, and my throat chokes off. I can't say it, can I? Not to Grandpa. 'Cause if he hates me, it would kill me. But when I look in his eyes and see all his wisdom . . . "I killed Matt, Grandpa."

He doesn't say anything, but as the tears start to fall again, he pulls me to his chest in a bear hug and I feel safer than I have in ten years. I sink into him, exhausted. When I wake up, he's still holding me. And then we talk . . . and I tell him everything.

He doesn't say anything for a really long time, and I'm sure I've ruined everything. Now that he knows what a terrible person I am, things will never be the same. But then he looks me hard in the eye. "Sounds like you've been luggin' this load of horse manure around for a long time."

He hates me. I knew it. I feel my chest cave in, like my heart just collapsed.

"Listen, Frannie. I wasn't there and I don't know what happened, but I do know this heart," he pats my back, "and it's a good one. If what ya say is true, it was just a terrible accident."

I shake my head hard, like maybe I can throw off the guilt. "But I was so mad. I . . . hated him."

"I'm pretty sure ya couldn't hate anything if ya tried, Frannie.

Ya don't have it in ya. Sounds to me like what happened just happened. Nobody's fault."

But he's wrong. It was my fault.

"Everybody's got their own crap they carry around with them. I know that firsthand. After your grandma died . . ." He trails off, shaking his head. He squeezes my shoulders a little tighter. "It's human nature to blame ourselves when bad stuff happens—to think about what we coulda done so things woulda turned out different."

I see the guilt on his face and it kills me. "What happened to Grandma wasn't your fault, Grandpa." It was mine. I should have tried harder to make Mom come over.

"But that doesn't mean it ain't gonna feel that way." He pulls his arm from around my shoulders and grasps my hand. "You and Matt were closer than most. I don't know what happened in that tree, but no matter what it was, *you* weren't gonna come out of it okay. But there comes a time when ya gotta see it for what it was: an accident."

I feel the hard ball of cold terror I've carried in my chest for the last ten years soften a little around the edges. Part of what he's saying is true. I didn't *mean* to kill Matt. So maybe I'm not a monster.

But that doesn't make it any less my fault.

I tuck into his side and sit there for hours more.

20

✠

Speak of the Devil

LUC

For three days I sat on a tree branch outside Frannie's window before she would speak to me again. She had a rough time with finals, but it helps to have friends in high places. With some divine intervention she finished okay.

I wasn't planning on going to graduation. I mean, how many high school diplomas does a guy really need? But then it occurred to me that I may need this one if I'm truly turning mortal.

I'm hiding in the shadows of the scoreboard waiting for Frannie when there's a tap on my shoulder. I turn and find Gabriel, leaning on the goalpost, smirking at me, and it hits me how blind I am without my sixth sense, which is mostly gone.

He flicks the ridiculous maroon graduation gown fluttering around me. "Nice dress."

"Go to Hell."

"Not likely," he says, shrugging away from the post.

I look over at the grandstand as Frannie shows up with her family.

"Why did you . . ." I glance back at Frannie.

"Back off?" he finishes for me. "Because she made her choice."

"How do you know?"

He smirks at me. "You're joking, right? Look at yourself."

And it hits me. I'm on my way to becoming human—and *she* did that to me. That's how much she wanted me. What's left of my power surges, and I feel the crackle of hot electricity dance over my skin. "And I suppose you came out unscathed? Still have your wings?"

He smiles. "It was touch and go there for a while."

"If she . . . if it had gone the other way, would you have given them up?"

His eyes flick to Frannie and back as his smile pulls to one side and his eyebrow quirks. "Would I have had a choice?"

What I see in his eyes—what he's trying to hide behind that amused expression, maybe even from himself—is that he'd willingly give up his wings for her.

He steps behind the scoreboard. "Just because you're no longer a threat to her soul, don't think I won't be watching. Give me an excuse, and I'll smote you on the spot." And then he disappears—gone, as if he was never there.

I watch from the football field as Frannie's mom fusses with her hair and cap. Only Frannie could make these ridiculous caps and gowns look so hot. I'm imagining what she's got on underneath—and underneath that. Hopefully I'll have a chance to find out later. I already know it's not her red bra. Maybe something black . . . and lacy . . .

She comes out onto the field with Riley and Taylor as her family makes their way onto the bleachers, and I laugh out loud at the look on her dad's face when she walks over and kisses me. And then I see Grandpa staring at me, his expression stern. But just as I'm about to look away, he smiles and nods in my direction.

Frannie looks up into the stands at her father. "We're gonna have to do something about that."

"I think it's a lost cause," I say, hoping I'm wrong. I pull her close and kiss her again.

"You guys make me sick. Get a room," Taylor sneers.

Riley grabs Taylor's hand and starts pulling her toward the gym. "They're lining up. Let's go."

I loop my arm around Frannie, shooting a glance at her father, and we wind our way through the sea of maroon caps and gowns to the line forming behind the gym.

The music starts and all the good little lemmings walk in double file. They told us to stay two feet apart, but Frannie wraps her arm around me and pulls her body to mine as we start up the football field to our seats. I can't wipe the grin off my face.

We sit, and I look around at all the sweaty bodies baking in the sun as Principal Grayson drones on about new beginnings and other such nonsense. About thirty minutes in, I realize why I've always avoided these graduation ceremonies like a plague of rats.

Just when I'm convinced that after seven millennia I'm going to die right here of boredom, they start calling names and our row stands. I walk across the platform, and Principal Grayson hands me my diploma with a grin and a sage nod. I wait at the bottom of the stairs for Frannie, and as she walks toward me, her gown blowing back in the breeze, outlining those curves, I can't help but fantasize about later. She's supposed to be staying at Taylor's tonight. I wonder if she could be talked into a change of venue. She gets to the bottom of the stairs, and I lift her off the ground and kiss her.

As I lower her back to her feet she says, "Mmm, nice. That's gonna score you some points with the parents."

I look into the stands and see her parents standing there, slack-jawed, Dad with a camera perched, forgotten, in his hand. And Grandpa is laughing. "So what's the plan?"

"I'm working on it. But I'm pretty sure it doesn't include molesting me in front of them."

✝

Frannie's family comes down to the field after the ceremony, her dad still glaring.

"So," her mom says, "you're going to the party with Taylor and Riley?" She's trying to be cheerful, but her smile is as fake as cubic zirconia.

Frannie rolls her eyes. "Yes, Mom."

Frannie's grandpa meanders over and pats me on the back. "Luc will take good care of her. We have an agreement. Don't we, son."

I smile, relieved. "Yes, sir."

"I think Frannie's in good hands," he says, winking at me.

Frannie's mom's fake smile can't hold, and she glowers at Grandpa. "Dad, really. This isn't your affair."

"No, you're right. It's Frannie's," he says and winks at Frannie this time.

Frannie speaks up. "I told you. I'm going to the party with Taylor and Riley, Mom. You know our deal. And don't forget, Riley and I are staying at Taylor's tonight."

She eyes me suspiciously, and I can see Frannie's dad ready to protest, just as Taylor and Riley appear and grab Frannie.

"Hey Mrs. Cavanaugh," Taylor says. "So, I'm kidnapping Frannie, 'kay?"

Frannie's dad's eyes soften a little, and her mom says, "All right. But I want you girls to stay together." Her eyes flick to me and back to Frannie. "All night."

Then Taylor looks at Frannie's dad. Her whole face softens, and it almost looks like she's going to cry. "Thanks, Mr. Cavanaugh. Dad's pretty excited about starting his new job. He really appreciates your help finding it."

"You're welcome. It's the least I could do. I'm glad he's feeling better."

"The counselor is really helping all of us," she says. She hesitates, then steps forward and wraps Mr. Cavanaugh in a hug. Once his surprise clears, he lifts his hand and pats her back.

"I'm happy that I could help," he says.

She pulls away and for the first time ever, I notice color in her cheeks. Then the Tayloresque gleam returns to her eye. She hooks her arms around Frannie and Riley. "Let's go, girls. We have some serious partying to do."

Frannie hugs her family, and I hold out my hand to Frannie's grandpa. He shakes it and then I shift it to Mr. Cavanaugh. He hesitates but then reaches for my hand. As he shakes it he gives it a very firm squeeze—a warning.

"Have a good evening," I say to all of them with my most reassuring smile and a tip of my head. I turn to walk with Frannie, Taylor, and Riley to the parking lot.

And my heart stops.

Avaira.

She's standing with her back to us, her long, straight, raven hair glistening in the bright June sun. I pull Frannie behind me and feel my diminishing power crackle over the surface of my balled right fist. Avaira turns slowly and I raise my fist, then I release the breath I'd been holding as my heart resumes a rhythm.

It's not her.

I'm paranoid, seeing Belias and Avaira everywhere. Because I'm sure they're still here—and desperate. They have to know that time is running out.

I wrap my arm around Frannie, who looks startled, and my heart rate settles back to normal as we make our way to Riley's car. Frannie curls herself around me. She peers over her shoulder at her friends, who are busy pulling off each other's caps and bobby pins, and whispers, "What was that all about?"

I just shake my head.

Her eyes narrow, but she lets it go as her friends approach. "So, I'll see you there?"

"Wouldn't miss it. How long are you guys going to need?"

She, Riley, and Taylor share a shrug. "We're just going to Taylor's to change, and we'll head right up to Gallaghers'. So, like, a half hour maybe?"

I kiss her again. "See you there," I say, knowing—as usual—that I'm not going to let her out of my sight. I never do, but she doesn't need to know that. No sense stressing her out more than she already is. I'll do anything to help her feel like her life is normal—at times, anyway.

FRANNIE

He thinks I don't know he's following me all the time. He knows I want my life, and he's trying so hard to let me have it. I don't want to burst his bubble, so I don't say anything, but, really, I like knowing that he's there. When I can't sleep at night, I stare out my window through the trees at the glint of the moonlight off the hood of the Shelby, and wish I was out there with him.

I look around Gallaghers' backyard through beer-blurry eyes and see him leaning against a tree looking hotter than hell. Just as I start stumbling toward him, Riley and Trevor come sneaking out of the woods. I change my direction, staggering up to her, and brush the bramble out of her hair with my fingers as Trevor makes his way back up the stairs to his crew on the porch. I crack a smile. "Hey, Ry. You guys spending some quality time in Gallaghers' shed?"

Even in the bit of moonlight filtering through the trees, I

can tell her blush is flaming. And I recognize the look in her eye, 'cause I've been seeing it in the mirror recently. "He's unbelievable, Fee. The stuff he does with his—"

I hold up my hand. "Too much information, Ry." But then I can't stop the grin from spreading across my face. It's great to see her so happy. "When you guys gonna tell Taylor?"

"Trevor's going to talk to her tomorrow—I think. He said that yesterday too, though . . . and last week."

I crack up. "She's gonna beat the shit out of him, and he knows it. I think you're gonna have to do it."

She groans as Taylor blasts into us, screaming, nearly knocking me to the ground. Taylor wobbles nearly to the point of falling, and Riley catches her and steadies her on her feet. "Come party with me, losers." Taylor giggles and loops an arm around each of our shoulders.

"Hey Trev!" I yell. "C'mere!"

He looks over warily, then slowly, and with much trepidation, starts making his way down the stairs. When he finally reaches us, I loop my free hand over his shoulder.

"So, Tay, Riley and Trevor have something they're dying to share with you," I say, slipping out from under Taylor's and Trevor's arms and linking them together.

If Taylor didn't need the support, she would have pushed her brother's arm off, but instead she leans on him. "What?"

I watch as Riley and Trevor share a glance then link their free arms around each other, closing the circle.

I turn my back on the happy little circle and look around again.

Roadkill is set up behind the house, and Delanie is blasting out a perfect Paramore. It's pretty amazing how much better they sound with someone who can actually sing. Reefer looks up at me and smiles. I wave and smile back. I laugh when I think about what Taylor called him: a geek of the Guitar Hero variety. He is, and it's cool.

And suddenly I feel all emotional. It must be the beer, 'cause my eyes well up when I realize how much I'm gonna miss all this. But I hope I'm not gonna miss Luc. I've been afraid to ask what's gonna happen after graduation.

I stumble toward him and stop to look back at my friends when I hear Taylor screech, "You stupid shit!" She shoves Riley, but only succeeds in knocking herself on her butt in the mud.

I turn back, smiling, and make my way to Luc. When I get to him, I hook my hands over his shoulders and lean in to steady myself. I rest my head on his chest, and he wraps his arm around my waist and pulls me close.

"Hey," I say into his shirt.

"You having fun?"

"Yeah, but you're not."

"Why would you think that?"

"Dunno. You're just standing here."

"Enjoying the view," he says squeezing me a little tighter.

"Fee! You suck!" Taylor shouts at me.

In answer, I push back from Luc and flip her the bird. Then I reach up and twist my hand in his hair, pulling his face to mine. He grins and lets me, and when he kisses me I seriously want to climb right into him.

"C'mere," I whisper in his ear, sliding my hand under his

T-shirt and running my finger along the skin at his waistband. I want him alone—now.

"Where are we going?" I feel his body stiffen as I hook my fingers around the button of his jeans.

"Just for a little stroll." I turn and start to tug him by the waist of his pants toward his car.

He smiles. "What about your friends? This may be your last bash with them."

"To hell with my friends."

I tow him past a line of cars on the side of the road to the Shelby parked near the woods. When we get to it, I push him into the side and lean in, pressing myself into him. Roadkill must be on a break, 'cause I can hear Led Zeppelin wailing from the boom box about a stairway to Heaven, but all I care about is Luc.

"What did you have in mind?" he asks, searching my face as if looking for something he lost.

"Finding our own stairway to Heaven. Your backseat looks comfortable. I haven't had a chance to check it out yet," I slur, pushing away from him to open the door.

So, I'm feeling pretty dizzy, but the potent smell of rotten eggs cuts through my drunken haze instantly. I start to turn, but a pair of hot arms grab me from behind. Reflexively, I drop into a crouch and grab one of the arms from my waist. I lose my balance as I flip the person it's attached to over my shoulder onto the ground in front of me. I see his face just before I fall backward into the mud.

Belias's one good eye stares red death at me. His other is covered with a black eye patch.

The next second, I'm being scooped off the ground and thrown into Luc's car.

LUC

I scoop Frannie off the ground and throw her in the car as Belias picks himself up and dives at us. I summon what's left of my power and hit him in the chest with a blast so pathetic it would have embarrassed me a few weeks ago. Now, I'm pretty proud of it. It knocks him back to the ground, slowing him down enough that we're in the car before he picks himself back up. Remembering last time, I throw up a field around the car—probably not enough to keep him out, but it's all I've got—and gun the engine.

But when I look in the rearview mirror, there's a bright flash of white light and someone is standing over Belias. Gabriel? It has to be. But he looks different—smaller, somehow.

I breathe deep to slow my pounding heart. "Are you okay, Frannie?"

"Yup," she says, and when I glance at her, she doesn't even look scared.

"You're sure?"

She actually smiles. "Yup." Then her head lolls back on the seat and she closes her eyes.

"Frannie?" I nudge her.

Nothing.

"Oh, for the sin of Satan," I mumble to myself.

Now what? I can't take her home like this—drunk and covered in mud. There's my apartment . . . but it's not safe. I need backup. So there's really only one option. Hopefully he'll beat us home.

When Gabriel opens his door and looks at Frannie, wrapped in a blanket in my arms, his eyes widen and his mouth drops open. "She's not . . ."

"She's fine, don't freak. She just doesn't hold her beer very well."

"I think you're way past having to get her drunk."

"Out of the way, smart-ass," I push past him into the family room.

"Watch the white . . . everything," he says. "What did she do, mud wrestle?"

I lay her on the couch. "Close. Can't you just throw some holy water on her and clean her up?"

He smirks at me. "Some things *do* require a miracle. This, however, only requires Tide with bleach. Take off her clothes, and I'll throw them in the machine."

"I'm thinking the miracle is the better option. I'm finding these teenage hormones a force to be reckoned with." I look at Frannie and shake my head. "Truth is, they're kicking my ass."

His mouth curves into a smile far from angelic and his brows shoot up. "I'll do it." He bends over her and pulls off her muddy sneakers. I shove him out of the way. "Wait in the kitchen."

He shrugs and saunters off in that direction, wicked smile still in place. When he's gone, I tug her shirt over her head and groan.

Damn! I was right—black lace. What a waste.

Once her jeans are off, I tuck the blanket around her and toss her clothes at Gabe. I drop into the chair next to the couch and close my eyes, letting my head loll back. When he comes back, he sits in the chair across from me.

"Thanks for the help," I say looking at Frannie. "I couldn't take her home like this. Her parents already know I'm the devil, and, now that I'm not anymore, I'm hoping to prove them wrong." I wave in her direction. "This won't help my cause."

"Is she supposed to go home tonight?" he asks.

"No. She's supposed to stay at Taylor's."

"We can let her sleep it off here, then."

I swallow my pride. "Also . . . thanks for the help at the party tonight. I'm not the demon I used to be. There's not much left in the old spark plugs."

"What are you talking about?"

"You know, Belias . . . at the party."

"Wasn't me, dude."

"Whatever you say. But thanks."

He shakes his head and smiles.

I gaze at Frannie's sleeping form, so petite, on the couch. "Gabriel?"

"Yeah."

"Her soul is still clean, isn't it? I haven't . . . you know . . . tainted her or anything? I can't tell for sure anymore."

Concern passes briefly over his features before it clears and he answers, "They have no claim to her, if that's what you're asking. But I'm not sure how long that will last if she keeps hanging with you. You're a bad influence."

"I'm sure I am. So, should I expect to be smote anytime soon? You know, the wrath of God and all that?"

A smile plays at his lips. "Unfortunately, no, but it'd help if you backed off."

I know he's right. I've always known it, but . . . "I don't seem to have any choice in the matter anymore. I can't stay away from her."

He smirks. "Yeah. I got that when you let me burn you alive with holy water."

"Does this mean the Shield didn't work on me?"

"Hard to say. If Belias and Avaira have been hanging around for a few weeks, like you say, I'm sure they're following you."

I look back at Frannie, asleep on the couch. There has to be some way I can protect her.

"So maybe if we just disappeared—went somewhere else—she'd be safe?"

"Maybe. We won't know unless you try. But you know as well as I do the real solution."

"Tagging her soul for Heaven," I say, resigned. "Why is it so important that she forgives herself?"

His face suddenly goes all angelic. "Forgiveness is the key to everything, Lucifer."

"You celestials make everything so hard." I shift in my chair, sitting upright. "What would happen if Belias just . . . killed her?" I feel something black and heavy tighten around my heart thinking about how close he's already come.

"She'd go to Limbo with all the other untagged souls, and you know Michael would fast-track her to Heaven. Frannie's essence—her soul—is the key. As far as we're concerned, she's no less valuable in Heaven as on Earth."

"That's pretty much what I figured." I've seen that essence, and I know he's right. Dancing with it, blending it in mine . . . it was unlike anything I've ever experienced. "I won't let anything happen to her."

"I know. That's what I'm counting on." The threat is clear in his voice.

I look at her, asleep on the couch. "I won't let them have her," I say, knowing them is me. But just for now, I slide onto the couch and lie next to her, wrapping my arms around her and holding on as if my life depends on it—because I'm pretty sure it does.

21

✠

Fire and Brimstone

FRANNIE

"You know I was just yanking Lucifer's chain about that whole virgin birth thing, right?"

I pull my head off the car door and look up at Gabe through the haze of my hangover. "What?"

"You know . . . that night you came over. After he told you about . . . what he is . . ."

"Oh, yeah. So, I'm not Mary?"

"No."

"Thank God. I'd make a shitty mother," I say, rubbing my forehead. "Plus, I'm hoping not to be a virgin too much longer." I drop my forehead back onto the car window with a thump that sends a shock wave through my head, turning my brains to tapioca. "Awww . . ." I groan.

Gabe laughs. "Serves you right."

"Shut up."

We pull up to my house, and Mom comes out onto the porch. Gabe opens my door and props me on my feet. I try to keep my legs under me as we move up the walk, but Gabe has to mostly drag me along. When we get to the stairs, he gives up and scoops me into his arms.

"Did you kids have a nice time?" Mom chirps.

What I want to know is, how many seventeen-year-old girls could show up hungover at nine o'clock in the morning draped in some guy's arms (even if that guy is a real honest-to-God angel, which my parents couldn't possibly know) and get a "did you have a nice time?" It's disgusting. Course, if I were lying here in Luc's arms, things would be different.

"Did we, Frannie?" Gabe is trying not to laugh and, if I had the strength, I'd punch him in the face.

But instead, I mumble, "Shut up," into his shoulder.

Mom follows us as he carries me up the stairs, and they tuck me into bed. I can hear sisters giggling, but I don't open my eyes to see which ones.

Gabe sits on the edge of my bed. He runs a finger along the line of my jaw and even though I feel like death, I shudder. "You gonna be okay?"

"I will if you shoot me," I beg.

He leans down and his lips glide across my cheek to my ear, where he whispers, "No can do." He chuckles and I'm wondering if *I* can shoot *him*.

"Then get the hell out," I say, rolling on my side and pulling the covers over my head.

I hear Mom shuffle out of the room chattering about chicken soup. But Gabe's still here—I can feel him.

"What do you want?" I mumble into the sheets.

"The same thing I've always wanted. I want to tag your soul. You need to forgive yourself."

"No."

"Why? Why do you need to hold on to this?"

I'm not going to let myself cry. "Because." I breathe against the tears. "I need to."

"Need to what?"

He's making my head throb. "Can we do this some other time?"

"Let's do it now. What did you mean, 'I need to'?"

I groan as a sharp pain shoots through my brain. I pull the sheets off my head for some air. "I can't do this. You know everything I'm thinking anyway. Can't you just pick what you're looking for out of my head and leave me alone?"

"If you were thinking it, I could. That's where I'm trying to get you—to where you know why you can't let it go."

"Because I can't."

"Why?"

"Oh, God! Just go away."

The bed creaks as he slides closer and I feel his cool breath in my ear. "I'm not going anywhere, Frannie. I'll always be here for you—no matter what." His lips slide over my cheek and my headache's suddenly gone, replaced with a deep ache somewhere else. Somewhere I definitely shouldn't be aching. I roll and twist my hand into his hair. His lips brush mine—just as

Mom pops back into the room with two steaming mugs in her hands.

"Oh! Oh dear . . ." she says.

Gabe's eyes smile into mine for a second longer before he shifts off the bed and stands. "I've really got to get going."

"Oh, don't go," Mom says with an awkward smile, holding out a mug. "Have some soup."

He smiles at her. "Thank you, Mrs. Cavanaugh, but Frannie's in good hands." He turns back to me. "I'll check on you later," he says, backing toward the door.

"'Kay." It's all I can manage.

He leaves and I roll on my side toward the wall, ignoring Mom and her soup and trying to figure out what just happened. And I think about Luc. He's supposed to come over tonight, and I'm gonna try out this Sway thing with my parents, if I can figure out what it is—maybe change their minds about him.

But maybe my mind needs some work first.

I think of his Shelby parked across the street right now and feel my heart pound. I love him. I know that now. So why the hell do I still want to kiss Gabe?

LUC

I follow Gabriel and Frannie back to her house and sit out front most of the day. I watch her window, wondering what to say to impress her parents, or at least convince them I'm not the devil incarnate anymore. But as I sit here, staring at her window, I feel a sharp pain in my gut, and there are noises coming from down there. As time passes, the pain gets sharper and the noises get louder until it's impossible to ignore.

Unholy Hell, is that my stomach? Am I hungry? As I lift my arm to rub my stomach, I catch a whiff of myself and groan. Brimstone's got nothing on the way I smell right now. That's some serious stink. Not likely to impress Frannie's parents. Being human is turning out to be extremely inconvenient—and a little gross.

Before dusk, once I've confirmed that Gabriel is here, I take off and swing by the McDonald's drive-thru on my way back to my apartment for a shower. Turns out Big Macs aren't all that bad. Who knew?

It also turns out that there are more downsides to being human than I'd hoped. The list of stuff I'm going to need, just in the personal hygiene department, is staggering. I'm thinking about everything I need to take care of before my magic's completely gone—lots of big bank accounts and investments, lots of alternative identities for both Frannie and me in case we need to run, maybe an academic scholarship to UCLA—when I step through the door to my apartment and the pungent smell of brimstone hits me like a baseball bat to the face. I feel my face involuntarily pinch against the stench. So, okay, maybe I really don't smell that bad after all. How did I ever think the smell of brimstone was pleasant?

I look up through watering eyes at Beherit—my boss. Even though I can't sense the presence of demon or deity anymore, I should have expected this. He's here in all his Hellish glory: steaming, leathery, black-flecked crimson skin; short, twisted black horns that nearly scrape the ceiling; and his tail wrapped around his pelted satyr's waist. Though he'll never admit which sin he's born of, the fact that he's always draped in a short red robe and wearing his golden crown makes it obvious. He belongs to pride. His back is to me, admiring the Doré print near the kitchen. I think about backing out and closing the door—I was never here—but a twitch of his pointed ear lets me know it's too late for that.

I step through the door and close it behind me. "Is this a social call, Beherit, or is there something you need?"

He turns slowly, his hoof scraping across the linoleum, leaving a smoldering black gash through the daises there. There's no humor in his flaming red eyes, and his fangs flash as a grimace contorts his flat, pinched face.

His voice is a low raspish hiss as he says, "What I needed was for you to do your job, Lucifer. Do it without stabbing me in the back. Did you really think you were worthy of my position? Well, now we all know better, don't we? You've demonstrated your ineptitude quite spectacularly, especially to King Lucifer."

The smell of dog breath and rotting meat permeates the brimstone. I smell it before I hear the snarls. Hellhounds. Perfect.

"This apartment complex doesn't allow pets, Beherit. I'm sorry, but you'll have to take your pooch ..." I look toward the bathroom door as three immense black dogs, one with three heads and all with the glowing red eyes that demark all infernal creatures, come slinking out, "oh ... excuse me, pooch*es*, and leave."

"A shame. I thought you'd enjoy the company. You've been here for so long I figured you may be feeling a bit homesick."

"No. I'm really doing just fine, thanks."

In a smoking red flash he's across the room, and I'm choking as his burning fist clamps around my throat, nearly lifting me off the ground. And for the first time, I realize I truly am human, because my lungs are screaming for air as he holds me here, suspended and oxygen deprived.

"You're doing far from fine!" he rages and throws me across the room. I thud hard into the wall, face-first, and drop to the floor at the paws of the hounds, struggling to catch my breath. Turning human is really working to my disadvantage at the moment, and the blood trickling down my forehead and into my eye is definitely not going to help with the hound situation.

I sit up, brushing the back of my arm casually across my forehead, ignoring the throb in my head and the growl of the hounds. "Was that really necessary?"

Beherit's red eyes flare, and his face stretches into a heinous grin. "Blood? Oh, this is getting better by the minute," he says, stepping over and drawing a talon quickly across my chest, slicing through my T-shirt and the flesh under it like warm butter. As more blood seeps from the wound on my chest, he raises his head, sniffs the air, and scrunches his face. "I knew you didn't smell right. Thought I might be coming down with a cold." His bloody eyes shoot to the hounds. "This will save me having to drag you back to the Fiery Pit. So much easier than Belias and Avaira." He shakes his head slowly, a forlorn frown on his leathery lips. "Three of my best—what a waste . . ." Then his eyes flash. "Though, that's what happens to traitors. King Lucifer will see the error in his judgment when it's *me* who tags the child's soul. You and Belias were never worthy."

317

Belias and Avaira, thrown into the Fiery Pit. I should be ecstatic, but instead my stomach turns. No second chances in the Underworld.

He sighs and his frown pulls into a grin. "They say if you want a job done right you have to do it yourself. But I don't understand, Lucifer. This should have been an easy one. She's such a tiny, helpless thing."

Frannie's face, so kissable, floats in front of my eyes. Tiny, yes—but far from helpless.

He looks to the hounds. "Cerberus, Barghest, Gwyllgi, I'll leave you to your job. I have mine," his eyes shift to me, "or, more accurately, *yours*, to do." And then he transforms into *my* human form.

No!

I swallow back my fear with the lump in my throat. "Really, I don't think we're going to be able to pull off the twins thing, Beherit. After all, we're trying to be inconspicuous. Twins draw too much attention," I say, pulling myself off the floor.

I watch as my face snarls back at me. "No worries. There won't be two of us for long," he says, and my face grins at me. He snaps his fingers, and the hounds are on me as he walks out the door.

What I wouldn't give for a box of Milk-Bones right now.

FRANNIE

When the lightning hits my brain, it shocks me awake. I roll to the side and dry heave into the trash can next to my bed as the image of Luc, laying in a heap on the floor and covered in blood, floats behind my eyelids.

"*NO!*"

The next thing I know, my mom is at the side of the bed, panicked. "Frannie, are you sick? What's wrong?"

Through my stupor, "No . . ." is all I can say . . . over and over. It's like every brain cell has short-circuited. I can't function—or think.

She starts to lift me to sitting. "Come on, honey. We're going to the doctor."

I find my voice. "No! I need Luc." My heart is beating impossibly fast, and I'm inching toward hyperventilation as stars dance in front of my eyes. "I need to find him."

And just then, there's a honk from the driveway. I spring from the bed and fly to the window. Luc is parked there in the Shelby. He smiles up at me and sticks his arm out the window, waving me down.

"Oh God!" I feel my blood start to flow again. He's not dead. "I have to go, Mom," I say, tugging my jeans on under my baggy T-shirt and running for the door on shaky legs.

"Frannie! What's this about?" she says as she chases me down the stairs.

"Nothing. Just give me a minute." I step through the door and slam it behind me. I run to his car and jump in, throwing myself around him.

"I'm happy to see you too," he says, a wicked gleam in his eye.

I pull back and look at him. He's alive—for now. "Something's going to happen. I saw you . . ."

"What, Frannie? What did you see?" He doesn't look frightened or concerned. If he looks anything, it would be eager—hungry.

"There was blood . . . you were . . ."

"Dead?" he finishes for me with a grin.

I just nod.

"Do I look dead, Frannie?"

"Not now. But it's going to happen."

"What? What's going to happen?"

"I don't know . . . maybe Belias . . ."

He interrupts me, shaking his head. "I've taken care of Belias. No need to worry about him anymore."

"What do you mean? Is he gone?"

"Very."

"So, something else, then . . . I know you're in danger."

"I'll be fine, don't worry."

But I am worrying. He reaches for me, and, as he pulls me into a kiss, I begin to calm down. My breathing slows and my heart ticks back down to a nearly normal pace.

I look up at him. "It was really creepy, Luc. Promise me you'll be careful."

"I was born careful. Nothing's going to happen."

I wish I could believe him. I look up, and my mom is staring out the front window at us. I'm sure she thinks I've lost it, which isn't going to help our cause at all. Especially after the Gabe thing earlier. I sigh. "So . . . you ready?"

"For what?"

"You know. The whole impressing the parents thing?"

"Oh. Yeah. About that . . ."

"Come on, Luc. I thought you were good with this. I really want you to be able to hang here this summer." More so now. I want him close.

"I'm really not up for it right now. I'd rather be alone with you," he says, and his eyes are on fire, making me tingle all over.

"What are you thinking about?"

"All the really outrageous things I could do to you—how I could make you feel if you'd let me."

I swallow thickly and take a deep breath as he pulls me to him. "Where's this coming from all of a sudden? You're the one who said we couldn't . . . you know." But the thing is, I'm starting to think about some of those "outrageous things" too.

"I've changed my mind. I want you," he says, his lips hot on my neck.

I tip my head back, giving him easier access. "So the whole lust thing is . . . what? No big deal now?"

"Nope. No big deal," he repeats as he reaches under my shirt. "We could just slide into the backseat . . ."

"Jesus, Luc! My mother's looking out the window at us right now," I say, pushing him away and tugging at my shirt. "Why are you acting so weird?"

He smiles wickedly. "You're driving me crazy."

"Fine, then let's go to your apartment."

"It's sort of a mess right now. Someone let some dogs in and they got into the trash. Tore it to shreds."

"What? Who would do that?"

"Just an old friend. Nothing to worry about," he says with a wildly wicked grin, and, just for a second, I'm sure I smell rotten eggs. "Let's go somewhere else. I want you where I can make you crazy." He kisses me, hard and deep, then slides over in the seat and starts the ignition. He lays his hand on my thigh as he pulls out of my driveway.

We pull over on the corner of First and Amistad, near the park at the edge of my neighborhood. Almost before the car has stopped, he's all over me again. I look around and see the park is nearly empty. The play structure is abandoned, and the last of the moms is just pushing her stroller across the street in the pink dusk.

I lean into Luc's burning kiss as his touch, hot on my skin, raises goose bumps all over. After a long, deep kiss, I pull back gasping for air, my heart hammering, and hear his honey sweet whisper in my ear, "I want you so bad." I shudder as he eases his hands under my shirt and unhooks the clasp of my bra. My hand skims across his chest and under his T-shirt. "You won't ever forget this. I promise," he says, and I feel his fingertips burn a track across my belly toward the button of my jeans.

And it's then that I notice he's on fire. Hotter than he's been in a long time. My breath catches. "Hold up," I say, grabbing his hand just before it reaches its target. "I don't know where this is coming from. You've been telling me for weeks that we can't go there. I need to think." But it's really hard to think when he's offering me what I want more than anything.

For just an instant I swear I see rage darken his face before it smoothes into a perfect calm. "What's there to think about? I'm tired of waiting, Frannie. I want you so much I can't stand it anymore. I promise I'll make it amazing for you. The things I'll do to you . . ." The rest is lost as his hot tongue slips into my ear.

I can't focus, thinking about the things I want him to do to me, but what he said before still echoes in my head. *We can't do this until I know it's safe for you.* I take a deep breath and work to connect my last rational brain cell to my mouth. "What's changed, Luc?"

"Me. It's safe, I know it is. I'm human now. They can't get to us."

I want so badly to believe him, but that brain cell is fighting to be heard. I push his hand away from where it's working the button of my jeans. "That doesn't make any sense. You said we were in more danger now 'cause you couldn't see them coming." And all of a sudden I smell it again, rotten eggs. *Oh God— brimstone. Belias?*

Luc's eyes flare red, lighting up the dark car. "Come on, baby. You're killing me," he says. I feel like gravity just doubled and all the oxygen has been sucked off planet Earth. Luc would *never* call me baby.

Holy shit! *Belias. Think!*

I hear Gabe's voice in my head: *If you ever need anything, you know where to come.* And even though I know it's probably a bad sign that I have so many voices in my head that aren't mine, for the moment, I'm okay with it.

"I know where we can go," I say, hooking my bra and trying not to panic. "We're house-sitting for a friend, just around the corner. The house is empty. We'll be all alone." My voice shakes, and my heart's trying to commit suicide by throwing itself relentlessly against my rib cage.

"Now we're talking. Where to?" he asks, starting up the Shelby.

"Take a left here."

I take him on a loop around the neighborhood, past Taylor's and back past my house, pretending to be lost, before I make up my mind what to do. Then, as we drive by the house with the huge potted Christmas cactus and porch swing I say, "Here," pointing to Gabe's house.

"Finally. I was starting to think you were just being a tease."

This guy is majorly pissing me off. "Just pull into the driveway."

He pulls in and I'm wondering if I did the right thing. Am I putting Gabe in danger? Will he know this isn't really Luc? And my biggest question, the one that's been eating me alive— if this is Belias, where *is* Luc? The vision of his bloody body crumpled on the floor taunts me, and I swallow back my terror along with the bile rising in the back of my throat.

As I step out of the car, my panic slips into despair. The house is dark. What if Gabe's not here?

Luc-a-like is around the car, grabbing me, and we start heading for the front door. It's only then that I realize I don't have a key, and I can't exactly knock, since the house is supposed to be empty . . .

"I think the front door might be unlocked," I say, hoping I'm right.

When we get to the door, I see I'm more than right. The door is actually swinging open, exposing the darkness within.

"Remind me never to have you house-sit," Luc-a-like snorts.

"Yeah . . . well . . ." My mind is racing. Maybe Gabe has something gold or silver that I can use.

He pushes me through the door and closes it behind us. It's

pitch black, and he's all over me—hands everywhere. As I look desperately around in the dark, I don't need to see it to remember that everything is white. No gold, no silver. No nothing.

"Let's find a bed," Luc-a-like rasps in my ear.

"Um . . . maybe upstairs," I say loud enough that if anyone is here they'll hear me.

He pulls me toward the stairs, lit only by a thin silver slant of moonlight crossing the family room from the window and trailing up the lower few. But as we reach the banister Luc-a-like freezes in his tracks and looks around warily.

"Whose house did you say this was?"

"Just a friend's."

He looks at me with a grimace, and, as I watch in the pale moonlight, he morphs into—something. In just a few seconds, he's towering over me, the heat burning my scalp where he's grabbed a handful of my hair. The stench of singeing hair and rotten eggs is unbearable, making my eyes water.

Reflexively, I drop into a crouch and swing a leg high into his chest, but he's suspending me by my hair, so my balance is off and I don't get any leverage behind the kick. Still, the crunch of his bones under my foot is unmistakable.

I think the thing is chuckling—not the reaction I was hoping for—except it sounds choked and dry, almost like coughing.

"Oooh . . . fire!" he rasps. "I like that." Then he drags me a step back from the stairs. "Very clever, mortal. But, see, we demons have a sixth sense." He turns and hisses loudly, "You're too late, Gabriel."

I regroup and take another swing, this time at the arm holding me suspended. But I barely connect. He leers down at me, shaking me by the hair. "This was charming before, but now it's becoming annoying. Stop."

Just as my heart sinks, Gabe's symphonic voice comes from everywhere all at once—surround sound deluxe, "You'll want to let her go, Beherit."

And then he's there, at the top of the stairs, except I can't see him. All I see is a vague shape from which intense white light is emanating. His glow illuminates the whole room, including the monster holding me captive. I look up at its hideous face and hear myself groan as all the blood in my body runs instantly cold. It's not Belias. This one is bigger and nastier-looking, if that's possible, and smells much worse—as if breathing wasn't already hard enough through my panicked gasps.

"Gabriel, you've always had a wonderfully droll sense of humor. Why would I let my prize go?"

"Because she's not your prize. You don't have any claim to her. Her soul is clean."

"Hmm . . . yes, Lucifer didn't give me much to work with, did he? He found this assignment . . . challenging." He scowls down at me and chuckle-coughs again. "Falling in love. *Love!*" He lets out a sharp bark of a laugh. "How quaint is that!"

"Yes, it was a completely transforming, life-altering event. You've heard the saying, love conquers all?"

"Well, in the end, it hasn't conquered anything, has it? He's dead and I'm holding the prize."

"Dead is all relative, don't you think?"

My heart soars at the sound of Luc's voice. But as I pivot toward the kitchen, like a Christmas tree ornament dangling from a string, my heart sinks. Luc is covered in blood, his T-shirt in tatters and several deep gashes across his chest, shoulders, and right cheek.

"Oh my God," I gasp.

"Your God can't save either of you," the monster rasps and chuckles. He lifts me up to his eye level by my hair and it feels like my head is ripping off my body. "You belong to the other team now."

"You seriously want to rethink that, Beherit," Luc says, stepping through the kitchen door into the family room.

Beherit laughs—a thunderous bellow that shakes the entire house. "You're making threats? You—a half-dead mortal with no leverage?" he snarls, lowering my feet back to the floor, where I continue to dangle like a marionette. "I'll deal with you when I'm finished with your little pet." He shakes me by my hair.

"Oh, I've got leverage. And it's ironic that you should mention pets . . ." Luc's smile makes my heart sputter, and I feel my arm reach out to him. His eyes bore through mine, and in the door behind him, I see five pairs of huge, glowing red eyes staring back at me from the dark of the kitchen. Luc steps sideways at the same instant he snaps his fingers, and three ginormous black dogs, one with three heads, explode from the kitchen door, teeth bared, and are on me in a heartbeat.

Except, they're not on *me*, they're on *him*—the thing holding me. And Luc is there too. He has my hand and he's yelling something at me. With the noise of the dogs and my confusion, I don't get it right away, but then I understand. He's saying, "Use it, Frannie!"

My Sway. What do I do? I don't even know what it is or how it works.

"Let me go." It comes out as a strangled croak and nothing happens. I try again. "You don't want me! Let me go!" I say louder.

I feel his grip loosen on my hair as he bats at the snapping dogs with his other hand. Luc is pulling my arm. Dogs are everywhere, snapping and snarling.

"You don't want me!" I scream. I yank myself away from Beherit, leaving behind a large handful of singed hair, and Luc pulls me across the room. One of the dogs follows me, and I crouch, ready to unleash a kick, but Luc pulls me back just before my foot connects with its shoulder.

"You really don't want to piss Barghest off. Especially after he's just saved our sorry asses."

"Barghest?"

"An old friend of mine. I was on what you might call canine patrol for a long time—guarding the Gates of Hell. Barghest and I were pretty tight for nearly a millennium, though it took him a little longer than I would have hoped to recognize me in all my humanity," he gestures to the bleeding claw marks across his chest.

Barghest tips his head to the side as he whimpers, then he turns and sits, his back to us, and growls at the foray at the bottom of the stairs. I can't watch as the dogs rip at Beherit, so I turn back to Luc and try to find a spot I can touch him.

"Why didn't they attack me too?" I ask, nestling into his right side.

"I told them not to." He grins again. "And my talisman—your red bra—came in handy for scent. Now it's Barghest's job to protect you."

I let go of Luc and turn to look at the dog sitting in front of me, his shoulders at the same height as mine. "Protect me from what?"

Luc's face darkens for just a moment. "Hell," he says, "and everything in it."

I start to tuck back into his side when I feel something brush through my wild hair. Luc suddenly pulls back and doubles over. "*Ahhh*."

"Luc? What's wrong?"

He groans and looks up at Beherit, his face contorted in pain and his eyes glowing red. Then I see the glint of the handle of a dagger sticking out of his shoulder. As Luc pulls it out, I understand. Gold. Luc's weakness.

Heart pounding out of my chest, adrenaline on overload, I turn to Beherit and see Gabe advancing down the stairs, enveloping him in white light. It's almost like looking into a cloud during an electrical storm. Little flickers of lightning flash in the white light. The hair on my body stands on end, and the smell of ozone is thick in the air. And when the lightning bolt shoots out of Gabe's palm and hits Beherit, I scream.

Beherit's face twists in agony, and his groans roll through the house as the dogs continue to attack. But his focus is on Luc and me, and, under the pain, there's a triumphant sneer.

As I stare, frozen with fear and rage, another golden dagger materializes in Beherit's hand. That shocks me out of my stupor.

"Stop!" I yell. "Leave him alone. He doesn't matter to you anymore." I step forward, between him and Luc. "I'll come with you if you leave him alone."

As Beherit roars in victory, Luc grabs my hand, still doubled over. He's shaking his head, his eyes wide and bulging as he bites back an agonized moan. Curls of black smoke issue from the bleeding knife wound in his left shoulder. "No. Use your Sway."

I can't think. I choke back a sob and turn to Beherit. "Stop!" I yell again, and Barghest growls as I pull loose from Luc and take another step forward. "Leave Luc alone! I'll come with you. Just leave Luc alone! Please!"

My heart's throbbing as I move slowly across the floor toward the stairs. My shirt rips where Barghest tries to get a mouthful of it, but I keep walking. Gabe's white light flashes brighter in a warning that I ignore as I step within reach of Beherit.

Beherit raises his head and roars again. At the same instant I feel talons pierce the flesh of my shoulder, I crouch and lunge for his other clawed hand, where he's still holding the golden dagger. I grab the dagger, swing around, still in a crouch, and leap up, pushing it hard into his chest. "Go to Hell!" I scream.

But it's drowned out by his scream, high and long, a sound I can't imagine doesn't rupture my eardrums. As I hit the ground, I close my eyes and hold my breath, not knowing what the sensation will be when he kills me.

As Beherit's scream dies away, intense heat sears through me. But instead of agony I feel serenity settle over me. Maybe death, even at the hand of the devil, isn't so bad after all.

But then I realize the heat is coming from behind me, and I

open my eyes to find Barghest between me and Beherit, tearing at Beherit's arm. When I turn, Luc's there, and it's not just his eyes—his whole body is glowing red. It's *his* heat I feel coursing through me as he wraps me in a protective field.

Gabe's light flashes again, nearly blinding me. Beherit shrieks, and, through the glare, I see thick black ichor oozing from where the dagger pierced his chest as tendrils of thick, oily smoke enfold his upper body in a cloud. What feels like a sonic boom knocks me back a step, and when Gabe's light fades, all that remains where Beherit was is a bellow of hissing black smoke and the stench of burnt meat and brimstone. He and the dogs are gone.

Gabe rushes down the stairs, his glow fading as he comes, and now I can see the expression on his face. Anguish.

"Gabe?" He runs past me, and I feel black dread squeeze my heart just as I hear a thud behind me. I turn back to see the image that I've been unable to shake since I awoke with it in my head: Luc lying crumpled on the floor, corpse-white under smeared crimson blood.

22

✠

Redemption

FRANNIE

The hospital is too cold and too bright and it smells and I hate it. But I can't leave, even though they already told us Luc isn't going to make it. I can't leave him here.

The only thing getting me through this is Gabe. His arms are around me like a cocoon, and he hasn't let me go, even when they stitched my shoulder.

"I don't get it," I say through my tears. "He was human, so why would it matter that Beherit took all things Hell with him? That wasn't Luc anymore."

There's pain in Gabe's eyes and sympathy on his face. "You changed him physically, but his life force was tethered to Hell. It's what he was for over seven millennia. There can't really be a separation. And, in the end, he embraced that side of himself. He called on that infernal power to save you."

I think about Luc—his heat and how he glowed as he used the last of his power to wrap me in a field—and my heart shrivels into a hard ball. He should have saved himself, not me.

People walk through the hospital waiting room like it's any other day. Like the world didn't just end. How can that be? The world should be crashing down all around us.

My shoulder stings where the anesthesia is wearing off, and I can feel the tug of the bandages and stitches, but I wish it was worse. I wish Beherit *had* killed me. Then maybe Luc and I would be together. I bury my face in my hands and I feel Gabe's arms around me, pulling me to his shoulder. "This can't be happening. It's all my fault."

"I'm so sorry, Frannie."

"This is *so* not fair. He was good—I know it. He doesn't belong in Hell."

"He wasn't tagged for Hell. There's no guarantee that's where he went."

"But you said Beherit took him back to Hell."

"No, Frannie. I don't know that."

My breath catches. "You mean he could be in Heaven?"

He strokes my hair. "It's possible. His mortal soul was clean."

LUC

It's quiet and white and . . . empty. A void. Just like my mind. I'm aware of a body—mine, I guess, but I can't see or feel it. I can't see anything. I'm peaceful and I let myself drift. But then I'm being pulled through time and space in a dizzying rush.

King Lucifer.

When I stop and the vertigo settles, I open my eyes, sure I'll find myself in Pandemonium. But instead I'm at the end of a long white corridor that fades into the distance. In front of me is a pair of swinging wooden doors with a peeling plastic sign taped to it reading LIMBO.

Limbo. Where untagged souls go after death to be sorted.

So, guess that means I'm dead.

The sudden realization that I won't see Frannie again—touch her—kiss her—hits me hard, rocking me back on my heels. I fight to get air into my lungs, but then I remember that I don't need to breathe anymore. I'm dead.

But Frannie's not. She's safe.

It's that knowledge that helps clear my head. Frannie's safe. Without me in the way, she'll let Gabriel tag her and she'll be fine. He'll protect her. This is good. The only way I could ever leave her. She'll be better off now.

I gather myself and push through the swinging doors into an endless room. The ceiling is low, with humming florescent fixtures, but the walls stretch away into oblivion. In front of me there's an old wooden desk with various magazines scattered over its dark, nicked surface and a handwritten sign taped to the front. The writing is a sloppy cursive scrawl in heavy black marker and reads, TAKE A NUMBER AND HAVE A SEAT. Next to the sign is a plastic red number dispenser. I step up to the dispenser and look beyond the desk. As far as I can see, stretching into infinity, there are rows of black plastic chairs, most of which are occupied by the countless souls waiting to hear their fate. Others mill around aimlessly, wailing and crying about being dead. All are in shades of gray or beige, some shot through with black, vermillion, or ochre—the middle ground. These are the souls that weren't tagged before death because they didn't clearly fall on one side or the other.

I look down at myself for the first time, expecting obsidian black, but instead I find bright white with swirls of sapphire blue and dusk rose. *White?* I gaze in awe for more than a few minutes then collect myself and draw a number from the dispenser. The paper tab tears off, and I look to see a large ONE stamped on the green paper in gold leaf. I look up at the lit monitor over the desk. "Now serving number 64,893,394,563,172,289,516," it declares. I look back at my number.

One.

"Number one, please report to office number one." I hear the androgynous, monotone voice clearly in my head, but the monitor doesn't change. And as I stand here wondering where I'm supposed to find office number 1, a carved wooden door materializes in front of me with a large golden 1 painted on it. I turn the knob and push the door slowly open.

Gathering myself and stepping through it, I find myself in a large, brightly lit room with an immense mahogany desk and a high-backed chair in the middle. The room looks deceptively inviting. The comforting scent of hickory wafts from a cheerful fire burning on the hearth of a large fireplace in the back of the room. Beige leather couches and chairs are scattered between numerous bookshelves. Among the titles strewn across a low mahogany coffee table near me, I see Dante's *Purgatorio* and can't help smiling. Michael has done his homework.

His back is turned to me as he hovers just off the ground to one side of the fireplace, white robes blowing gently in a non-existent breeze.

Very theatrical.

He turns slowly and smiles, but there's no warmth in that smile. He tugs on his black goatee and studies me. His dark hair and skin contrast with his pale blue eyes, making them appear to glow and giving him an ominous look—meant to intimidate, no doubt. Michael is known for that.

"Welcome, Lucifer. Apparently the Almighty has put you on the fast track. I would have made you wait." He gestures to a comfortable-looking leather chair in front of his desk. "Have a seat."

"No thanks. I prefer to stand." I've been around too long to let my guard down around an archangel. Especially this one. An eternity of passing judgment has given him a God complex.

The whole innocent-until-proven-guilty concept applies to Heaven and Hell as well, and Limbo is under Heaven's control. *Michael's*, specifically. You'd think that would work in their favor, but Michael believes in strict quality control, so actually the numbers usually come out to Hell's advantage.

I take one more step forward. "What's the deal? Why am I not in Hell?"

"If you're that eager to burn in the Inferno for all eternity, so be it. I mistakenly thought you might want to discuss alternatives." He waves his hand dismissively and turns to glide behind his desk.

I swallow my pride, along with the thick lump in the back of my throat. "Wait." I follow him to the desk and slide into the leather chair. "What alternatives?"

His eyes soften and his expression hints at amusement. "It appears there's someone in the mortal realm who wants you back. Quite desperately, actually. It's really quite touching. It also happens that this *someone* has a fair amount of Sway, which apparently extends to the celestial, because Gabriel is having a difficult time saying no."

My head spins. *Is it possible?* Could Frannie have enough Sway to will me back to life? I've never heard of such a thing happening. But I've also never heard of a demon becoming human . . .

"From the look on your face, I take it this would be an acceptable alternative?"

I snap out of my musings to find a smile on my face and a tear coursing down my cheek. I wipe both away and look hard at Michael. "Is it possible?"

"It is. But there are conditions. This isn't a free pass."

My heart sinks. *A catch.* There's always a catch. "What conditions?"

"What we know is that Frannie changed you. Her Sway is powerful." What he doesn't say, but I read in his eyes, is that by powerful he means dangerous. A mortal with Sway over mortals is one thing. But a mortal with Sway over the infernal and celestial is quite another. He's scared of her.

As if he read my thoughts, because I'm sure he did, his temper flares. "She wants you now, and she got you by making you mortal." He spits out the last word as if it tastes bad. "What none of us knows is what will happen when she doesn't want you anymore. Humans, after all, can be quite fickle." A self-satisfied smirk settles across his features as he listens in while I ponder that.

I know it was Frannie's Sway—her love—that changed me, but I'd never stopped to consider what would happen if her feelings changed. If she didn't want me anymore, would I stay human? Die? Change back into a demon?

"What conditions?" I ask again with a heavy heart. There's no use putting up a front when he's in my head.

"Convince her to forgive herself so Gabriel can tag her for Heaven."

It sounds simple enough, and it's what I've wanted her to do all along, but I don't miss the look in his eye as he says it. Something vacillating between greed and lust.

"What will happen to her once she's tagged?"

"That's not your concern," he says dismissively with a wave of his hand.

I spring out of the chair. "Like hell it's not." My hands on his desk, I lean across it, toward him. "She wants a life. If she's tagged for Hell, she won't have one. She'll be King Lucifer's puppet. Tell me that won't happen if she's tagged for Heaven."

"I can't say what will happen. It's not my call."

My voice shakes as I fight to keep my rage in check. "I don't believe you."

He stares at me and shakes his head. "You poor, pathetic boy. Acting like you have any pull here. You *will* do this, or you'll burn in the Inferno."

I look back at myself. *White.* I can't see how it's possible, but I'm clean. No black. No gray. No red. White. "What sin sends me to the Inferno?"

His smile is amused, but there's frustration hidden behind the façade. "You're joking."

I can't read his thoughts, but I can read his eyes. He's bluffing. I keep my voice soft—calm—as I call him on the lie. "You don't have to send me back to Frannie, but you can't send me to the Abyss."

His eyes flare red for just a second before he pounds his fist through the top of the desk. To my ears his voice sounds as indistinct as a thunderclap, but in my head I hear the words within the roar clearly. "Maybe not, but I can make you wish I had!"

Can Heaven be a living Hell? If there's anyone who could make it that, it would be Michael. But it's better that it's *my* living Hell—not Frannie's. Before looking into Michael's eyes, I would have thought Frannie being tagged for Heaven was a good option. They generally don't use their own too roughly, and with Gabriel looking out for her . . .

Now I'm not sure. Frannie's only chance at a life may be if she stays untagged. Gabriel wouldn't betray her . . . would he? "Fine. The Abyss it is."

Shock stretches his eyes wide. Apparently that's not the answer he expected. In his misplaced confidence, he forgot to spy on my thoughts. "I don't think you understood me. You're doing this. I'm giving you a second chance. You should be grateful."

"I don't believe in second chances." I turn and walk out the door. As I slam through it, Michael's growl trails off, and everything goes quiet and white. I'm drifting again. If this nothingness is Heaven, I may have made the wrong choice. I'm not sure I can just drift for all of eternity.

But then I picture Frannie's sapphire eyes, and I'm no longer drifting, I'm soaring. I hear Frannie laughing, smell the clove and currant of her soul, feel her touch as surely as if she were here with me. And then my essence is swirling and blending with hers.

This is Heaven.

FRANNIE

In my dream, Luc and I are dancing under the stars—spinning and laughing like we're one person, sharing one body. I feel him everywhere, inside and out. His touch feels like Heaven, and I hear myself moan. I want to be this close to him forever—to die right here in his arms.

"Frannie?" Gabe's voice is soft in my ear. As I open my eyes and they adjust to the harsh lighting, it takes me a second to get my bearings. We're still in the waiting room at the hospital, and I'm cradled against Gabe's chest. "Hey, Frannie, wake up," he says, smoothing a hand over my burned and snarled hair.

It's the sting in my shoulder and the telltale smell of singed hair that confirms that it wasn't all just a really bad dream.

"Frannie?" he says again.

"Yeah, I'm awake. Can we just go home? Please?" I say into his chest as I feel tears sting my swollen eyes.

"Hey," Gabe says, and I feel his finger under my chin, lifting my face to look at him. When I look at his face, he's smiling, and the pain is gone from his sparkling blue eyes.

"What?" I ask. "What happened?" I look up at a smiling doctor in green hospital scrubs.

"Your friend is out of surgery," the doctor says. "I truly can't explain it, short of a miracle. They resuscitated him in the ambulance, but he was in bad shape when he got here. We lost him for a long time on the operating table, but we were able to get him back. He really shouldn't have survived . . ."

"So . . . what are you saying?" The desperation in my voice rings clear.

"It looks like he's going to be fine. We'll know for sure in the next few hours. Just keep praying."

My heart explodes into a million pieces and I start to hyperventilate. Tears course down my cheeks as I struggle to breathe, and I bury my face in my hands. "Oh my God. Luc."

23

✠

On a Wing and a Prayer

FRANNIE

They finally let me in to see Luc this morning, but I can't bring myself to even look at him. Because, after everything, I know what needs to happen, and I've spent the last two days agonizing over it. I stare blindly out the window at the mist falling outside, making everything look filmy and ghostlike. I know I should say something, but I don't trust my voice. I pull a deep breath and try to concentrate on what I have to do.

I lean my forehead into the glass. "The doctor didn't say he found anything . . . weird in there when he was digging around?"

"No."

"So, I guess that means you're human now?"

"Guess so."

I can't breathe. I need to get out of here. I move toward the door without turning around. "I should probably go."

"Frannie, talk to me." His voice, the desperation in it, stops me in my tracks.

I raise my hand to my face, trying to erase the evidence of my tears. I turn slowly to face him, and his expression almost kills me. How can I do this? I'm not strong enough. I drop my eyes to the floor.

He holds out his hand to me, and I can't help myself. I walk to the bed and sit on the edge of it. At his touch, my heart races, but I still don't look at him.

"Tell me what you're thinking," he says, and I feel tears well up in my eyes again.

"I'm thinking we shouldn't be together. I'm bad for you."

He heaves a huge sigh. When he speaks, he doesn't even try to hide the laughter in his voice. "You? *You're* bad for *me?*"

I can't believe he's making fun of me—making light of this whole thing. Anger flares deep inside me, and I hear it in my voice. I pull my eyes from the blankets and glare at him. "I almost got you killed. You were immortal and I took that from you. You'd have lived forever if it wasn't for me."

"Living forever isn't all it's cracked up to be. The piece of forever I've lived is plenty."

"You're just saying that." I turn my head away, trying to clear it and get myself together.

He reaches up for my cheek and turns me to face him. "Frannie, look at me." My eyes reluctantly slide to his. "For this feeling," he taps his free hand on his chest, "I'd have given up anything. I'd say my immortality was a small price to pay, but I don't feel like I've paid anything. I feel like I've *been* paid with the most valuable thing anyone could ever want." A tear slips over my lashes, and he wipes it away. "You love me. What else could I ever ask for?"

I feel hot tears on my cheek as I lean down to kiss him.

"Don't mind me or anything." And out of the blue—literally—Gabe is sitting in the chair under the window, looking all angelic.

Luc glares over my shoulder at him. "You really need to stop doing that. Didn't your mother ever tell you it's rude not to knock?"

But then it hits me. I know what needs to happen. I hop up, feeling a thousand times lighter, and walk over to Gabe. I grab his hand and pull him out of the chair. "We need to talk."

I drag him out the door as Luc watches with concerned amusement on his face, and we find a bench in the hall. I sit with my elbows on my knees, resting my forehead in my hands.

The din of the hospital is white noise—generic—and I focus on that to slow the whir of my spinning head. I wind my fingers into my hair and stare at the floor between my feet. "You want to tag me for Heaven."

"Yes," Gabe says.

"And they'll stop coming for me if you do."

"Eventually."

"But I have to forgive myself."

"Yes."

I pull my head from my hands, surprised at how light it feels. "I'll cut you a deal," I say, the anchor lifting from my heart.

✝

Gabe leans back on the bench and smiles up at me as I walk back into Luc's room. I slide onto the edge of his bed, and his eyes narrow as he laces his fingers in mine. "What was that all about?" He can't hide the jealousy in his voice.

"Nothing," I say.

He drops my hand and his eyes search mine.

I run a finger over his cheek, outlining the bandage on his face, and he shudders. He pulls a sigh and reaches for my face. "You know, when I told you to use your Sway with Beherit, I meant to save yourself, not me."

I press my cheek into his hand. "I couldn't think. I just ... knew what I wanted."

He pulls me into a kiss, but just as our lips touch, there's a knock at the door. He holds me around the neck when I try to back away, and we finish our kiss. Then he smiles and yells, "Come in!"

The door swings open. Gabe smiles, all proud of himself for knocking. "Heads up!" he says, and, with a flick of his wrist, a shiny silver object on a chain sails across the room.

Luc grabs it out of the air before it slams into his face. "Thanks," he says to Gabe.

Gabe props himself on the doorframe. "I'm not your errand boy. Next time you need something, get it yourself."

I look at the object in Luc's hand. It's a crucifix; larger than the last one and with a pointed end.

"I had this for you ... that night." He smiles wanly. "But I got a little sidetracked before I could give it to you." He folds the crucifix into my hand.

Gabe meanders into the room. "You're going home tomorrow."

I pull away from Luc and look at Gabe. "How do you know?"

He shoots me a sardonic glance and slouches back into the chair under the window.

"Gabriel . . ." Luc's face shifts through frustration into anger and finally seems to settle on confused. "How . . . ?" he asks.

"The decision was already made. It was never up to Michael." His glance shoots to me and his eyes sparkle. "She wanted it, and you earned it." Then he looks back at Luc, his expression serious. "Plus, we need your help."

Luc nods at him. "Thanks."

He quirks half a smile. "It wasn't my decision either. You've impressed Him." His eyes shift to the ceiling.

I look from Luc to Gabe and back, confused. "What are you guys talking about?"

Luc smiles at me. "You've got archangels quaking in their boots."

That was a very unhelpful reply.

Gabe slides out of his chair and moves to the side of the bed, placing his hand on my shoulder. "Let's just say there was some dissension in the ranks, but we've got it sorted now." He looks back at Luc. "How are you feeling?"

Luc flashes his winning smile and squeezes my hand. "Invincible."

"Well, just remember that you're not anymore, so if you want to be around to look after Frannie, reckless abandon isn't your best strategy."

Luc rolls his eyes.

Gabe grins, blinding me. "Yeah, that's what I thought you'd

say, so I recruited you some help. He's fresh out of training—just yesterday, as a matter of fact—but there's no one better for the job."

"Hey Frannie." The voice is musical, like Gabe's but different. It's lighter somehow. I turn and, on the other side of the room, there's a boy, maybe seventeen, medium height, with sandy-blond curls, sky-blue eyes, and the face of . . . well . . . an angel. He's leaning against the wall, hands in his jeans pockets, smiling at me.

All the air is knocked out of me and my legs suddenly go weak. "Matt?" I can barely get the word out. He looks just like the image from my head—the way I pictured he'd look if he was still alive.

He smiles and the glare burns my retinas. "In the flesh—sort of."

I turn to Gabe. "I don't . . ." but I can't form the rest of the thought.

Matt laughs—a sound like wind chimes. "I'm your guardian angel." He laughs again. "Would you ever have thunk it when I was sticking gum in your hair and stealing your bike?"

My shaky legs start moving, carrying me across the room. I feel the tears start to slip down my cheeks, but there's not a thing I can do about it. I can't even begin to reconcile the emotions whirring through me. But as I reach him, it's guilt that finds a voice. I can't look him in the eye. "Oh my God . . . Matt, I'm sorry."

He wraps an arm around me and pulls me to his shoulder. "There's nothing to be sorry for, Frannie. You need to let it go."

347

"I can't." I look up at Gabe, whose eyes bore a hole through me. I can almost feel him rummaging around in my head, looking for the answers.

"You have to, or there's no point in my being here." He shoots a glance at Luc.

All my insides are Jell-O and my head feels full of cotton. I can't think. But then a thought peeks through the fog. "Mom and Dad. Oh my God! They're going to die when they see you!" My breath catches when I realize what I just said. "I mean . . ."

Matt pulls me to his shoulder again. "No, Frannie. They can't know. Nobody can."

"Why?"

"It's just how it is. It's strictly forbidden for us to show ourselves to anyone who knew us. Especially family."

I pull my face out of his shoulder. "I knew you."

He glances at Gabe. "An exception was made due to extenuating circumstances," he says in this low, official-sounding voice.

I look up and Gabe is shaking his head.

I smile, but then I'm crying again. "So I killed you, but I'm the only one who gets you back? How is that fair?"

"I have no clue what to say to get you to see it wasn't your fault."

"But it was my fault." I sob into his T-shirt, getting snot all over him. "I was there, remember? The one yanking on your leg and pulling you out of the tree?"

"You know I can't lie now, right? It wasn't your fault. You have to believe that."

I start to feel really dizzy as my throat closes. I let go of him and drop my hands to my knees, trying to suck air into my collapsing lungs.

"Get a nurse!" Luc says, and I hear him struggling with the IV stand.

But then I smell summer snow and feel Gabe's arms around me. "Frannie, breathe," he says, his breath cool in my ear.

I shudder and pull tighter into him.

"Slow and easy," he whispers.

And I find he's right. If I breathe slowly, I can get some air in. The stars dancing in front of my eyes start to fade.

I straighten up and Gabe lets me go. I stare at Matt, wiping my nose on my sleeve. I can't believe this. I've wanted him back so much, and here he is. I dive into his chest again and wrap my arms around him, determined to never let him go. "Oh my God."

He smiles. "It's going to be okay, Frannie. Really."

His smile is contagious. I sniffle and smile back through my tears. "Why do you look seventeen—or how I thought you'd look at seventeen? How come you don't still look seven?"

His smile widens. "Camouflage. There'll be times I need to be visible, and a seven-year-old following you around would look pretty stupid, don't you think?"

"I guess."

Luc clears his throat loudly. A goofy grin stretches my face as I pull Matt over to his bed. "So, Matt, this is Luc. Luc, Matt."

Luc's brow creases, then his eyes spring wide. "It was you . . . at the graduation party, with Belias."

He looks at Luc without smiling. "That was my field test."

"I assume you passed?"

Matt glares at him. "Of course." He turns to me. "So, I won't be around all the time," his eyes narrow and shift to Luc briefly, "because there's stuff you guys do that I really don't want to see. But if you need me, I'll be there."

Luc holds out a hand to Matt. "We're happy for the backup."

He just looks at Luc's hand, his expression bordering on repulsion.

All of a sudden, the joy I felt is gone. I look between them, trying to understand what just happened, as Luc drops his hand.

"Don't try to be a hero, Lucifer," Gabe says to break the awkward silence. He fixes Luc in a hard gaze. "If you need help, call for it."

Luc glowers at him. "Yes, mother."

He smiles. "Speaking of mothers, you have some visitors."

And just then, there's a knock at the door. Matt vanishes as it swings open, and it's a good thing, because Mom and Dad are standing there, McDonald's bag in hand.

"A godsend," Luc mutters, then grimaces. "Hospital food is an acquired taste."

✝

I managed to weasel out of the church retreat that my family is at 'cause I'm still recovering from the "dog attack."

Instead, I browse through my closet, deciding what I'm gonna need in LA, and glance at Luc, who is standing near my dresser. He's been out of the hospital for a week and most of the bandages are off. A bloodred scar twists down his face from just below the outside corner of his right eye to the middle of his cheek. Dark and dangerous is now scarred and sexy. Mmm ... yummy.

"Are you taking this?" he asks with a raised eyebrow, the strap of my black lace bra looped over his finger.

"Probably. I need something to get those UCLA guys all hot and bothered."

His face darkens as he tucks it back into my drawer.

"Course, if you come with me, I won't have time for any of those lightweights." I try to seem casual as I saunter over and wrap myself around him, but I'm all kinds of tense.

His expression clears as he ties my hair back in a knot. "Where else would I be?"

I blow out a nervous sigh. "So, you'll come to LA?"

"I'd like to see you try and stop me," he says with his wicked grin.

I look around at my papered walls, and it hits me for the first time how much I'm gonna miss home. But what I also realize in this instant is that anyplace with Luc is home. "What are you gonna do when we get there?"

"Maybe take a class or two ... get a job." He shrugs. "Whatever."

"With seven thousand years of job experience, you should be able to find something."

He cracks a smile. "I don't think there are too many openings in damning souls to Hell."

I smile back. "It's LA. You might be surprised."

He laughs but then gets all serious and pulls me tighter. "I'm really not sure this is a great idea. It's not over, you know. If King Lucifer let him live, Beherit will send someone else—or come back himself now that it's personal." He rubs his chin with his thumb. "You actually may have killed him, Frannie. From his reaction it looked like gold was his weakness. That dagger to his brimstone heart . . . hard to say."

I'm not sure how I feel about that. I pull away and look up at Luc, trying to shake off the sudden wave of guilt. "So if that's true, according to you, I'm tagged for Hell now for sure."

His eyes flash, and he goes instantly pale. "What are you talking about?"

"If I killed him, I'm just like Tom. You said no extenuating circumstances. Straight to Hell for me. Do not pass Go, do not collect two hundred dollars."

Uncertainty clouds his eyes. "It was self-defense. And killing a demon is different," he says, like he's trying it out to see if it sounds right.

"Now you're making exceptions? You're such a hypocrite."

His face hardens into a determined scowl. As if he can make it so through sheer force of will, he says, "You're *not* tagged for Hell."

When I don't say anything, he turns toward the window, his face dark and brooding. He stares out at nothing and says, "This is my fault. I never should have come here."

"They would have sent someone else—someone like Belias."

He shakes his head slowly and turns back to look me in the eye. "He never would have found you."

But Luc did. We've been connected from the beginning. I press into him and he folds me into his arms.

"I just want to keep you safe," he whispers into my hair. "Gabriel and Matt can do that better than I can."

"I feel safe right here," I say, still burrowed into him.

"We can't do this on our own, Frannie. We're going to need Gabriel's and Matt's help. Especially if you insist on going to LA."

I pull back and look at him. "Okay, so if going to LA isn't a good idea, what do you suggest we do?"

"We should just take off. Find somewhere to hide." That wicked sparkle is back in his eyes, and a hint of a smile curls his lips. "Maybe buy some deserted tropical island somewhere . . . just us, clothing optional."

I laugh, kinda liking the sound of that. "I could live with that, but you're the one who said they can find us anywhere."

He looks hopeful. "That was before. Did you notice? Beherit didn't know I was at Gabriel's that night. I shouldn't have been able to surprise him—and I had the hounds with me, so my Shield hid them too. With some help from Matt, this might just work." He thinks for a second, then smiles. "And I suppose LA's as good a place to get lost as any."

I hope he's right, but right now all I want to do is lose myself in him. I press tight into his body and bury my face in his chest. "I love you."

"I know. That's the only thing that saved me. You're my redemption." He leans down and kisses me.

I gaze into his perfect eyes and trace my finger lightly down the scar on his cheek. He closes his eyes and shudders, then sighs. I press closer into him, knowing what I want. "Do that thing again."

He smiles and opens his eyes, but his brow creases. "I don't think I can."

I stretch up on my tiptoes, loop my arms around his neck, and pull him into a kiss. "Try," I whisper into his lips, wanting to feel that close to him again.

He closes his eyes, takes a deep breath and leans into me, kissing me deeply. After a minute he pulls back. "I can't. My essence is human now—a soul. It can't leave my body while I'm alive." But he doesn't look disappointed. He's smiling.

My pulse quickens and I feel an electric tingle course through my body, waking every cell. "So . . . does this mean we can . . ."

His eyes are deep, black pools as he stares down into mine, and I swear I can see *his* soul. Then they flash and he nods. He leans down to kiss me, and, as we sink into the sheets, into each other, I know this can't be wrong.

LUC

I didn't know it was possible to feel like this. I kiss her and feel my new flesh-and-blood heart expanding right out of my chest, filling me with indescribable bliss.

We can be together—really together.

Her hands start on the button of my jeans, and I wish for the ability to just magic our clothes away.

But that was my old life. No . . . not a *life* at all. Just an existence. I wrap my arms around Frannie and pull her closer. This is living.

I pull back and look at her, sure I've never seen anything so beautiful. She closes her eyes as I trace a finger along her eyebrow and down her nose, but just as my finger reaches her lips, her eyes snap open and her features twist in pain. "NO!" she gasps, bolting upright. I feel her terror just as if it was my own.

Her face is ashen as she rolls and vomits into the trash can next to the bed. She sits and hugs her knees to her chest. "Me . . ." Her whisper is barely audible.

I pull myself up and sit next to her. "What is it? What did you see?"

"He's coming," she says, her voice strangled. Then she's off the bed like a shot, pulling on her shirt.

"Who?" I say, struggling to keep up. I slide my feet onto the floor and button my jeans. "Who's coming, Frannie?"

The room starts swirling, and then Gabriel is there, all human pretense gone. He hovers just off the floor in his flowing white robes, and I see Frannie's terror mirrored in his eyes.

Matt appears next to him. "He's coming."

And then, like a wrecking ball, some unseen force hits Frannie, lifting her off the ground and throwing her hard into the wall. Matt dives for her, but he's too late. She slides into a heap on the floor.

"Frannie!" My legs have me across the room and over her crumpled form in a flash, and when I pull her into my arms, I see the steam start to rise off her skin. She's a thousand degrees. "Frannie!" I say again, shaking her. Then she opens her eyes and I understand.

They're glowing red.

"Lucifer," she says in a voice that's hers but not, "who's got the prize now?"

"No!" I hear my voice as if from a great distance as rage nearly rips me in half.

"Beherit!" Gabriel's voice vibrates through me. "You can't do this. You have no claim."

"Oh, but I can . . . *am*, actually." Frannie's lips pull into a sinister grin. "I've got special orders from the king Himself. Anything goes."

I hold Frannie and, as I look into those glowing eyes, I know the game is over. If King Lucifer wants her so much he's willing to throw all the rules to the wind, I'm not sure even the Almighty could save her.

I can't give up.

I look at the crucifix dangling from the chain around her neck. Gold. I yank it from her neck and raise it above her.

But Matt grabs my wrist. He glares at me and rips the crucifix out of my grasp. And he's right. I can use it to drive Beherit out, but at what cost?

She starts to pull free of me, and I let her. But then, by instinct, I reach for her hand, holding it in a death grip. Frannie is still in there, and a desperate piece of me needs to stay connected. She pulls herself to her feet, seeming taller, and turns to look me in the eye.

"How quaint, Lucifer. But you two are well past the hand-holding stage, don't you think?" She grabs my face and pulls me into a hard kiss. But it's not Frannie, it's Beherit, and I feel tendrils of his essence start to work their way through my lips.

As I pull back, she gasps loudly and her face screws tight as a strangled "no" works its way up from her depths. Gabriel sweeps her out of my arms and into his. He cradles her in one arm and draws a circle on her forehead with the index finger of the other as he whispers something I can't make out.

Her eyes snap open, still glowing red, and her face pulls into a grimace. "Good luck with that, Gabriel."

As asinine as it is, I find myself jealous that Gabriel can actually do something other than just stand here staring, and I have to fight the urge to rip her out of his arms.

"A fighter, this one," she says in a strained voice distinctly *not* hers.

"Fight him, Frannie," I say, reaching for her hand.

Her face twists with effort. "I want you out." Her voice is little more than a whisper, but it's hers. Her body writhes in Gabriel's arms. He lowers her to the bed, and I pull her into my arms, sending her all my strength.

"That's it, Frannie," Gabriel says. "You have the power. Use it."

The flood of hope overwhelms me. *Sway*. Frannie has Sway. If she fights—if she wants it enough . . .

"You don't want to be in here." Her voice is stronger, and when her eyes open, there's only a glowing ring around the irises. "You don't . . . want me," she growls.

She continues to writhe with the internal struggle for control then suddenly goes still, as if one of them has given up the fight. I gaze into her eyes, panicked nearly to the point of insanity. "Frannie?"

Her eyes roll back for a moment, and a moan starts from deep inside her, growing in intensity. Her face becomes red and her eyes bulge. There's a flash of red energy, and she jerks then goes limp.

Breathing back the panic, I cradle her to my chest. "Frannie?

Can you hear me?" She finally looks up at me with clear blue eyes—still scared, but lucid.

"He's gone," she says with a weary smile. I take a few deep breaths to slow my hammering heart then lean down and kiss her.

FRANNIE

I squeeze Luc's hand where he sits next to me as I lie on the bed.

"You did good. Your Sway is getting stronger," he says.

I'm still shivering and my teeth chatter. "Why can I only remember a little of what happened?"

"You may only remember the parts when you were in control."

"I feel like someone ran over me with a bus. Why didn't it feel like this with you?"

"Well, I didn't pick you up and throw you into the wall, for starters," Luc says. He and Gabe exchange a look, and Luc shoots him a vindictive smile. "But I guess it's different when you've invited the demon in."

Matt drops into the desk chair and glares at Luc.

Gabe looks at me with a rueful smile. I shrug, not sure what to say, but then a shiver racks me again and I feel nauseous. Out of the blue the tears start, and I'm helpless to stop them. "I'm not going to have a life, am I?" I say between the sobs.

Luc pulls me tightly to him, but he doesn't answer.

Gabe stands in my door and just stares at me. "Nobody

knows the future, Frannie. Everything that happens changes everything else. But the deal is, you're valuable to both sides. The chance that you'll be able to get through this untagged is pretty much none. And once you're tagged—either way—you can be manipulated. I'm obviously not all that objective, but if someone was going to be jerking me around, I'd rather it wasn't Hell."

My heart is so heavy. I know what needs to happen, what I need to do, but . . . "How do I forgive myself for the worst thing I've ever done? The worst thing *anyone's* ever done?"

"Start by remembering what really happened." Matt glides to the foot of the bed and sits. Luc untangles himself from me and moves to the door with Gabe, giving Matt and me some space. "I fell because I was trying to climb too fast. It was my fault."

My throat tightens as I remember it. "No. I grabbed your ankle. I was mad, and I pulled you out of the tree."

"Stop it. You've been beating yourself up for so long. It wasn't your fault. You need to let it go." He wraps me in his arms, and I sit like that for what feels like forever.

"I just wanted you back," I finally say.

He smiles. "You have me."

My heart feels so heavy. "Not really. You're still dead."

"You're right. I don't have the life I would have had if I hadn't fallen out of the tree, but that doesn't make why I'm here any less important to me. And it doesn't make my dying any more your fault."

He looks at me for a long time, and I don't know what to say. Finally he says, "Gabriel says you need to forgive yourself, or we

359

can't protect you." A smile turns the corners of his lips. "You gotta do it, Frannie. I can't blow my first gig because of an un-cooperative client. It wouldn't bode well for the rest of eternity."

"I can't—"

His smile is gone as he cuts me off. "He says you have to fig-ure out why you can't let go of the guilt."

"Because . . ." I fight tears as I pull his journal from under the mattress. I think of all my conversations with Matt in this book. All the things I told him so that he could have a little piece of me—my life. How I needed to keep him alive in my heart. "I needed it to keep from forgetting. I needed to hate myself 'cause the pain kept it fresh. It kept part of you alive."

All of a sudden I'm sure I'm going to throw up. There's something inside of me that my body needs to get rid of. "How do I do this? Let it go?"

"It's okay to feel sad about it, but you have to let go of the guilt. It has to come from inside. You need to remember what really happened."

I rest my forehead on my knees and close my eyes, waiting for the nausea to stop, but it only gets stronger as I relive the scene in my head. Matt climbing, his foot slipping. I screw my eyes tighter and groan as he falls. In my mind, I see my hand grab for him, but all I catch is his sneaker, and it comes off in my hand. I hear my scream as he hits the ground.

My eyes snap open, and I roll and dry heave over the trash can. Matt's arms are around me, and he pulls me to his shoul-der, where I sit and shake.

Finally, I lift my head and look at him, tears streaking my cheeks. "Why'd you have to fall?"

He shrugs.

I'm not surprised by how mad I feel, but I *am* surprised when I realize I'm mad at him. I push away. "You should have slowed down—been more careful."

He nods. "But there was nothing you could do. It was an accident."

I drop my face into my hands and breathe back the anger. When my shaking slows, I pick the journal up off the bed and press it to my forehead, then hold it out to him. "I did this for you . . . or more for me, I guess. All along, you've been the only person I could really talk to."

He takes it from my hand and smiles. "I've been talking back. Did you hear me? Told you to stay away from him," he says, glancing toward Luc.

My heart sinks. "Why do you hate Luc so much?"

"*Why?* You're kidding, right? He almost got you killed, Frannie. He's one of *them.*"

"He's one of *me,*" I correct, my voice raised.

Luc and Gabe stop whispering and look at us. Luc steps forward, concern on his face. "He's entitled to his opinion, and he's got good reason to think the way he does. I *did* almost get you killed . . . more than once."

"No. That would be *me* that almost got *you* killed," I remind him.

Matt looks at Luc, his expression still sour. "I hate the thought of you anywhere near her, and if you hurt her—in any way—I'll kill you myself."

Luc nods, holding Matt's eyes with his. "Duly noted."

Luc turns and looks hard at Gabe, and I know he's thinking

the same thing as I am. Gabe said Matt was the best angel for this job, but I'm starting to wonder.

Matt softens his posture and leans his forehead into mine. His voice is low, meant just for me. "Frannie, I'm having a really hard time with this. Are you sure? About Luc, I mean? I just can't make myself trust a demon, no matter what Gabriel says."

"I'm sure, Matt. He loves me. Can't you just read his mind? Then you'd see."

"Sorry, I'm not high enough up the food chain for that particular skill. Dominions or higher."

"Please, just give him a chance."

His eyes harden again as he glances toward Luc, but then he pulls me into a hug, and I hear the smile in his voice. "You're not gonna pull that Sway crap on me, are you?"

I smile into his shoulder. "That depends entirely on you."

LUC

I watch Frannie with Matt as I stand in the door with Gabriel, and I know this is it. *Talk to me outside*, I think, and he nods and slips through the door with me into the hall.

"She's ready," I say.

"Yep."

"Tell me you'll take care of her. The look in Michael's eyes . . ." I shudder.

Gabriel leans into the wall. "We've got her backside, which is pretty nice." He quirks a smile.

"Can you be serious for like two minutes?"

He scowls at me. "Fine. Stop stressing. The Almighty knows she's special. And remember, Moses's life didn't suck. She'll be fine. She's not going anywhere."

"But she's not staying with me either. I just need to know she'll be okay before I let her go."

His eyes hold mine, and his jaw clenches as he contemplates that. "I'm not going to pretend that nothing's going to change, but what happens from here is up to Frannie. You're not a demon anymore. You're human, with a clean soul and a completely clean slate. If Frannie still wants you," he almost seems to choke on the words, "then there's no reason you can't be together."

And that's the key: if she still wants me. She'll belong to Heaven. *To Gabriel.* Will she still want me after? Her life will outgrow me—the tagalong, used-to-be demon. It won't be long before she doesn't need me or want me. I crack open the door and gaze at her. She looks so tired, but she also looks at peace, and I know it's time.

Gabriel pushes through the door, and I walk behind him, stopping just inside. But then Frannie holds her hand out to me, and I stride to her side, needing to feel her touch.

"You're ready," I tell her, and she nods her affirmation. "Good," I say to myself. "This is good," I repeat a little louder—for her. Then I kiss her quickly and stand.

I turn to Gabriel. "Okay," I say, giving him the signal.

He smirks. "Okay, what?"

"Tag her. She's ready."

"It was done before we walked back into the room. What'd you think, we have some big "Pomp and Circumstance" thing?"

I glower at him. "You're such an asshole. I thought maybe you'd give her a heads-up, that's all."

"If she's ready, why does she need a heads-up?"

"Stop talking about me like I'm not here," she says, glowering up at us.

"Should I have given you a heads-up, Frannie?" Gabriel teases.

Frannie grins. "No, but maybe Luc would have liked one."

I start and stare down at her. "What are you talking about?"

Frannie's eyes are brighter than I've ever seen them. "Tag—you're it!"

I look at Gabriel, stunned. "You're joking."

He smiles and shrugs. "It was one of Frannie's conditions. Plus, you've impressed the right deity, though Michael was less than thrilled."

I try to digest what Gabriel is saying. "I'm tagged . . . for Heaven . . ." I say, trying it on.

"Could you at least pretend to be happy about it? Otherwise, I may have to take it back."

I feel the grin spread across my face as Frannie reaches up for my hand. I grab it and sit down hard in the desk chair next to the bed. "Holy shit."

Matt cracks a dubious smile. "You can say that again. A demon tagged for Heaven. . . ." He shakes his head.

"So, what's going to happen?" Frannie asks. "I mean with my life . . . college and all . . ." her gaze shifts for an instant to me then back to Gabe, ". . . you guys."

Gabriel sits next to her on the bed and grasps her other

hand, visibly struggling with what to say. But his eyes say what he can't. I see it, clear as day, even if she doesn't. He'd give up his wings for her. All she'd have to do is ask.

His eyes drop from hers, but his hand grasps tighter. "What happens from here is up to you."

ACKNOWLEDGMENTS

My most heartfelt thanks to my extremely patient husband, Steven, for providing basic life necessities and keeping us all sustained during my obsession with my imaginary friends. To my girls, Michelle and Nicole, for being a source of inspiration for everything that I do. To my parents, who, from the beginning, taught me to believe in myself. To my omnipotent über-agent, Suzie Townsend, for taking that initial leap of faith, which, at the time, must have felt more like cliff diving. To my seriously cool editor, Melissa Frain, for taking something I loved and helping me make it into something other people might love too. To Eric Elfman and my Big Sur group for making me believe I don't suck at this and giving me the confidence to put what was in my head on paper. To my fellow ladies of lit, Andrea Cremer and Stephanie Howard, for keeping me on track.

And, because my Muse is a wannabe rock star, a special thanks to Chad Kroeger and Nickelback for "Savin' Me," the incredible song that inspired the character Luc, and to Isaac Slade and The Fray for writing the intense and deeply thought-provoking "You Found Me," the inspiration for Frannie.